Tesla | THE MODERN SORCERER

Tesla | THE MODERN SORCERER

Daniel Blair Stewart

Frog, Ltd., Berkeley, California

Published by Frog, Ltd.
Frog, Ltd.books are distributed by
North Atlantic Books
P.O. Box 12327
Berkeley, California 94712
Cover art by Daniel Blair Stewart
Cover design by A/M Studios
Book design by Nancy Koerner
Printed in the United States of America

Library of Congress Cataloging-in-Publication Data
Stewart, Daniel Blair.
     Tesla : the modern sorcerer / by Daniel Blair Stewart.
          p.   cm.
     ISBN 1-883319-91-9 (alk. paper)
     1. Tesla, Nikola, 1856–1943. 2. Electric engineers--United
States--Biography.   3. Inventors--United States--Biography.
I. Title.
TK140.T4S67   1999
621.3'092--dc21
     [B]   99-11911
                                                                CIP

1 2 3 4 5 6 7 8 9 / 05 04 03 02 01 99

Dedicated to my parents,
Robert and Elaine Stewart

Table of Contents

PART FOUR: MORGAN

PART FIVE: TESLA

Tesla | THE MODERN SORCERER

PART ONE

Nikola

CHAPTER ONE

Daniel

The horse bucked and reared. The boy sailed into space. The horse bolted and ran.

"Daniel!"

A woman in a long black dress ran from the house to the spot where the boy had fallen, and knelt beside the boy. She cradled him in her arms and wailed.

"Daniel. Daniel. Daniel...!"

Four children stopped playing in the stony field and walked hesitantly toward the woman holding the fallen boy, who looked up suddenly and called out:

"Milka! Angelina! Come here! Marica, you stay with Niko. You two, stay there."

A man dressed in a black suit and collar hurried toward them from the chapel across the field.

"Daniel! Djouka—what happened to Daniel?"

"It was—the horse, Milutin! The stallion threw Daniel. He struck his head!"

"Pray—let me see!"

He reached the spot where his wife clutched their son in her arms.

She gently extended Daniel to his father, the priest.

"He's still breathing. Come with me! I must carry him to shelter."

He strode to the house, holding the boy in his arms. His wife opened the door, and he walked quickly to the great padded couch under the windows. They stretched the boy out and propped his head up on pillows. The priest solemnly took his son's pulse while his wife knelt beside him. The three girls, then Niko, the little boy, cautiously, silently, entered the room.

"Stand back," Djouka told her children. "Give your father room."

"Send for the doctor," the Reverend Milutin said gravely.

Daniel was put quietly to bed. The doctor diagnosed that he had suffered from a concussion.

Outside, the sun set behind the forested mountains and night crept slowly out of the shadows and into the sky. The Arabian stallion wandered back to the house and barn shortly after nightfall. Milutin took the reins and sadly led the horse to a stall in the barn. He locked the doors behind him and returned to the house.

Upstairs, little Niko whispered to his sister:"I know Daniel will be alright."

"Sssssssshhhh!"

Niko felt guilty: he had been thinking bad thoughts about his brother. The children eventually slept. Their mother and father did not. Even when twelve-year-old Daniel finally drifted from a state of shock into fitful sleep, his parents maintained their vigil. When dawn pushed gray light through the overcast sky, they maintained their vigil. Daniel woke up an hour after sunrise and complained of a headache. Reverend Milutin praised God and gave thanks for a wonderful recovery.

Daniel was still weak and had a great lump on his head. Djouka assigned the task of taking care of him to her eldest daughters, Milka and Angelina. She instructed her two youngest children, Niko and Marica, to take care of each other.Then she went upstairs and took a nap.Milka and Angelina gave Daniel tea and bread, then they cleared Marica and Niko away from the bedroom doorway.

Young Niko protested: "But—Milka!—I just wanted to know!"

"We all want to know," Milka responded.

"I'm all right," Daniel called out, sitting up in bed.

"Daniel, you lie back down," Milka called back to him.

"I'm fine. I just want to wash up. Is there any hot water?"

"There is warm water on the stove."

"Good." Daniel stood up and put on a nightshirt.

"You take care, Daniel," Milka said. "You'll wake Mother if you're too loud."

"She needn't have stayed awake all night for me."

"She did. She and Father both did."

"Well, they needn't have. Where is Father?"

"At the chapel. He's meeting with someone, a schoolmaster or someone."

"Someone important, Daniel," Angelina said.

"Someone who works with the academy," Milka said. "I think uncle Petar will be there, too."

Daniel journeyed from the wood stove to the bathing room, carrying a steaming kettle. He staggered briefly against the doorway, steadied himself, swayed dizzily, steadied himself again.

Angelina: "Daniel!"

He slammed the door shut behind him.

"Milka—I'm worried—he's not recovered yet!"

"Don't worry. That big bump will subside...but—I *do* know what you mean, Angelina. He looks pale."

Niko crept away, to the front door of the house, to the porch, to the tall, slender trees that stood in a row. He sat beside the porch, behind a fragrant juniper bush, dreaming and silently fretting, worrying about his older brother. Daniel was the shining star of his family. He was better than clever, he was brilliant. He was more than smart—he was *intelligent*. He was *special*. Niko closed his eyes and pictured Daniel: he was tall and slender, perfectly handsome. He had blue eyes, like Niko's, but darker and deeper. Daniel had the ability to remember *everything*. He had learned half a dozen languages in just as many years of schooling. He could solve intricate mathematical problems in his head. Rarely did he write out equations. His father had taught his children how to visualize images with perfect clarity. Of course, Milutin had taught these things to Niko, too: at five years of age, Niko was also regarded by his family as a very clever child. But Daniel was— almost—better than human.... Niko sometimes thought such things: *better* than human. Daniel never seemed to think such things. Daniel's great virtue was that he was superior to other people but did not think of himself that way. He generated a great sense of embrace, a great, all-encompassing personal affection that made his inferiors feel elevated to the status of his equals. Niko suppressed that thought, but he knew it was true: Daniel *was* superior to other human beings, and it *was* his virtue to regard other people as his equals. Niko contemplated a moral paradox: virtue is knowing of your innate superiority while remaining unaware of it in the presence of inferior people.Moral paradoxes are quickly submerged in rational minds. Moral, rational consciousness cannot tolerate any slight tendency toward hypocrisy. Mental and moral superiority must be kept out of conflict in the mind of the thinker. So, Niko submerged his dilemma.Another moral dilemma surfaced briefly: he resented Daniel's superiority while at the same time not really believing in it. Niko, too, was clever beyond anyone's expectations, but at the age of five he stood in the shadow of his older brother. He would show them. He would show his family, some day....

He heard angry shouts coming from inside the house. He ran up the steps to the porch, to the front door—

"Daniel! Get away from there!" Milka was struggling with her brother in the doorway that led down to the cellar.

"There's nothing wrong with me. There's nothing wrong with me!"

"Daniel, you've had one dizzy spell since you've been awake—"

"I must ride him. That horse can't get away with throwing me. I must ride him again!" He was wearing his riding boots. His saddle was hung on a peg in the cellar. He was obviously on his way downstairs to fetch it when his two sisters had tried to detain him, but he was determined to prove himself and tame the horse.

Angelina cried, "Go after him, Niko! Help him!"

Niko rushed to the top step. Confused, faltering, Daniel reached for the banister. Niko lunged to grasp him, but Daniel tumbled over backward, and his limp body plunged to the bottom of the stairs.

"Daniel!"

Milka and Angelina called out in unison. "Oh—no!"

Niko wailed as he rushed down the stairs to where his older brother had fallen. He reached Daniel first. He held his brother's head in his tiny arms. Djouka awoke from her nap and joined her three daughters in a chorus of agony. Daniel was carried up the stairs and back to bed by his mother and sisters. His father was summoned from the church. With the entire family present, Daniel regained consciousness just long enough to raise his arm toward his little brother and ask, "Niko...? Why...?"

"Daniel, I meant to catch you! I reached out to hold you!"

The Reverend Milutin looked at his wife and scowled. "What is Daniel saying?"

"Niko—" Angelina gasped, "You didn't push him, did you?"

"No! No, Angelina! I wouldn't push—I would never push—"

"Oh, Niko, how can you *live* with that?"

"Hush, Angelina!" Djouka commanded.

"Niko.... How could you...?"

Daniel sighed, then died.

Nikola's entire world exploded. At that instant, his joy of life also died.

CHAPTER TWO

Nightmares

After his brother's death, Niko's nights were filled with terror-dreams. He would begin to drift off to sleep and experience the sensation of falling. He would wake up suddenly, his heart pounding, sweat bristling from his forehead, only to drift to sleep again, dreaming of falling into the void—or down the cellar stairs.

He dreamed of reaching up to the figure at the top of the stairs. "Daniel…"
Daniel would turn and scowl.

Niko dreamed of falling down the stairs in weightless terror, never touching the walls or the banister or the jagged steps… He would wake up in abject horror.

Sometimes he would dream about being crowded at Daniel's bedside, with his mother and sisters crying, and Daniel would awaken briefly from death, point at Niko, and say, "Niko…how could you…?" And little Niko would wake up, sit upright, and listen to his heartbeat.

His parents became aware of his nightmares and pacified him the only way they knew—they tried not to mention the circumstances surrounding Daniel's death, and his father distracted him during the day by teaching young Niko the same mental exercises he had taught his firstborn magical child. Niko cherished these memories.

He remembered how he had sat with his father on a log in the forest one afternoon, the first summer after Daniel's death, and learned how to create and maintain clear, vivid mental images. "Think of a ball," said the Reverend Milutin Tesla, gesturing with his hands. "Think of a globe, a big blue ball, if you like. Close your eyes, if you need to. There, there. Can you picture it, Niko?"

Niko held his breath. He clamped his eyelids rigidly shut. He wrinkled his brow in intense concentration. He had been practicing making mental pictures in his mind for years—his older brother had originally taught him how, after Milutin had instructed him. Niko craved attention. Milutin knew this, and now he was teaching the younger boy what he had taught Daniel.

Niko scrunched up his whole face and created an image. A ball…. A huge, blue ball, suspended in space, without gravity. Hanging in the midst of a starless, black void…. He was falling toward the ball.

He jolted upright. "Ah!"

"What? Niko—be calm!"

"I'm sorry, Father…."

"That's alright! Apparently, the blue ball you envisioned frightened you."

"Y-y-yes! I was falling toward it, Father! I was very far away, and I fell toward it. It was horrible, father, it was really frightening!"

"So I see! Is there anything you would rather picture in your mind than a ball?"

"Clocks. I think about the insides of clocks a lot, Father."

The Reverend Milutin laughed. "Clocks! Has your mother been teaching you about clocks, Nikola?"

"Yes, sir."

"Excellent. Your mother is a good, creative mechanic, Nikola. She is very clever with machines. You should listen to her: she will teach you how to fix anything and how to invent much, much more. Now, do you ever imagine all of the parts of a clock moving together, Niko?"

"Oh, yes, Father, I certainly do!"

"Very good. That's half of it."

"What is the other half of it, then?"

"To see in your mind what you have never seen as clearly as what you remember."

"I understand, Father."

That summer, little Niko invented his first machine: he had overheard his father talking to his mother about something called a "perpetual motion machine," and when he asked what it was, his mother told him simply that it was a fabulous machine that never stops moving.

Not knowing that this was scientifically impossible, Niko applied his already considerable talent for visualization to the task of solving the problem of building such a machine.

He sat on a stone overlooking the stream behind the churchyard. Suddenly, he experienced a flash of light that imparted a clear picture of a machine. Niko knew instantly how to build it. He ran all the way back to his father's barn and fetched tools—a hammer, nails, a saw, boards, and two barrel tops. He found a round piece of wood with a hole in the middle, and with the hammer he widened the hole.

Within hours he had built his perpetual motion machine. It was a waterwheel fed by an aqueduct: a trough made of boards, supported by sticks, and fed by the rushing stream.

The wooden trough spilled over the waterwheel, supported through the center by a stick held up by the mossy boulders jutting from the bank beside the stream. When his mother and father arrived to see the spinning contraption, they were astonished. They laughed and had to agree with Niko when he said, "As long as this stream shall run in this spot, my perpetual motion machine shall continue to spin!" The waterwheel had no paddles. It spun swiftly under the rushing, spilling current. Niko was radiant with pride.

Later that night, he dreamed of a funeral.

The next day, in the afternoon, Niko watched the horses in a field. He remembered the Arabian stallion—the horse that had killed Daniel. The same horse, the winter before, had thrown Reverend Milutin and galloped away one night, leaving him alone in the woods, which were prowled by wolves. Milutin had trudged many miles through deep snow, returning just before dawn. Nikola saw a funeral again in his mind; this time he saw a bleak and ragged sky. Weeping women, dressed in black, surrounded a carriage piled high with garlands and wreaths. Niko tried to push the image away with his hands, but he saw it too clearly.

He sat up with a start, not knowing if he had been awake or asleep. His heart was pounding furiously. A gray mare grazed peacefully, nearby.

He forced himself to envision something—anything—*anything* but the funeral…the vision of the weeping women, veiled in black, and the flowers in bouquets piled on the old wooden cart under the tattered sky returned to his senses again and again. The image overpowered his mind. It dominated his sight, flooded his ears, and chilled his skin. He could even clearly smell the flowers. Over and over…. He screamed and ran, arms flailing, back to the safety of his father's house.

He entered school at an early age and sprinted through books and mathematical problems like an intellectual Olympian. His mother taught him memory exercises, which he practiced on his studies—and he memorized entire languages in months.

He learned several Slavic dialects, then added French and German to his acquired tongues. Soon he would learn English. Then he might memorize Latin and Greek. But he kept his real accomplishments internal. He had been applauded for his waterwheel, yet no one seemed to notice why it spun so much faster than other waterwheels: it had been fashioned from barrel tops and a big disc cut from a log. It had no paddles. Paddles, as Nico envisioned them, dipped into the water at the bottom of every turn of the wheel, so the water slowed the wheel down.

Secretly, Niko prided himself on having outshone his older brother.

His family moved from the Serbian town of Smiljan to Gospic, in Croatia, the year Nikola started school. He was six years old then, and he already fancied himself to be an accomplished scholar. His studies presented little problem to anyone but his teachers, who could not feed his monumental hunger for knowledge fast enough. His Uncle Petar frequently came to visit his father. He was High Priest of the Serbian Orthodox Church in Bosnia. When he visited, he gave Nikola instruction in mathematics. The boy instantly took to geometry. He soon *thought* in geometric patterns, with and without accompanying equations. His algebra was very advanced, but geometry opened new horizons of visualization. Niko explored this mathematical science with his internal eyes. By the time he was seven, he had read nearly every book in the school library.

He had also been excluded from a fishing trip by a gang of older boys.

Questioning them about fishing, having heard of the sport but not knowing how it was done, he envisioned himself holding a pole and dangling a hook from a string. While the other boys fished upriver, Nikola fashioned himself a pole and a line and a hook. He took sticks and wire from a tumbled-down fence and connected them with a length of twine. The experiment might have worked if the boys had told him about bait, but even so he did catch a frog.

He remembered the time he fell into a vat of milk that was being scalded for sterilization. He had been inspecting the process for his own education, trying to understand the relationship between unseen germs in the milk and disease, which he understood had to be prevented by cooking, by heat. He remembered the night he spent in an abandoned church he had tried to explore. His family feared he had been eaten by wolves. A local farmer found him the next morning, calling out from the stony walls. He remembered seeing the flying machines.

Often he would experience a brilliant flash of light in his brain and he would see pictures in his mind—perfect pictures of flying machines. Some were big and round, some were slender and adorned with propellers. They had finlike, stiff wings, mounted with spinning windmills. He became obsessed with flight. He concentrated on using these images of flying machines to fight off the nightmares.

He had long ago forgotten the emotions surrounding his brother's death—or his life before that—he knew only how to visualize perfect mental images of machines that could fly, soar, and carry people into the sky.

Nikola experimented. He clutched an umbrella and leaped off the peak of the roof of his house; only a miracle saved his legs from being broken. He was so shaken he spent six weeks in bed recovering.

The creation of imaginary flying machines continued to act as a bastion against the nightmares: Nikola found it necessary, again, to experiment with mechanical flight. He would not be so foolish as to leap from the two-story house again, but he would recruit other subjects for experimentation.

Insects. Mayflies. Alive and flying. Using their wings to do what the propellers on his imaginary flying machines did.

One night he glued slender sticks together to form a crosspiece. He attached a spindle by means of a pulley and thread. He had spent the whole day collecting mayflies, putting them into a jar, and now he glued sixteen of them to the crosspiece. He had intended to demonstrate this contraption to a friend who had stopped by for the evening, but the young man's attention turned immediately to the jar filled with the bugs. He promptly opened it, tossed a bug into his mouth, crunched loudly, and gulped it down.

Nikola's eyes bulged with horror. His friend was feasting on May bugs.

Nikola threw up, then forced that memory out of his mind. Immediately, he saw the funeral procession on the gravel road, and he heard the sobbing of the women.... He concentrated harder. He remembered facts: the names of the planets, the fact that Jupiter had six moons and Saturn had four moons, the Earth only one.... He remembered Galileo and the telescope, and the year of the Inquisition, and how somebody named Lamarck was teaching that animals and plants inherited acquired traits, like calluses, and that such traits passed on could account for the changes living things had gone through since prehistoric times.

He remembered much. He remembered all of his knowledge. He tried to envision everything he knew, all of it at the same time. Even Daniel would be proud.

He contemplated his brother, then banished the thought of him from his mind. Finally, he banished the image of the funeral from his mind.

He remembered how his handmade fishing pole had caught only a frog. He remembered the leap of the bullfrog for the dangling hook. He remembered how all the boys in the neighborhood made similar fishing poles and soon managed to snag multitudes of frogs from the fishing banks.

As always, he kept his real accomplishments internal and secret.

His sisters grew up, got married, left home. He grew older and forced himself to become more intelligent. He read the books of Jules Verne. He was intrigued, obsessed by the endless possibilities of science.

He remembered when Gospic acquired a town fire department. It was to be equipped with a water pump for the hoses, replacing the old bucket brigades of the volunteer firefighters. At the opening ceremony, little Nikola ignored the speeches and studied the gleaming metal pump, taking it apart in his mind and trying to visualize how it worked.

When the time arrived for the demonstration, the hose gurgled but no water came out. Nikola was standing around with a gang of boys as the firemen disconnected the hose from the pump to the river, straightened it out, inspected it, and reconnected it. A frustrated official bellowed for the boys to get away just as the pump started up again—but still no water issued forth.

Nikola experienced a burst of light inside his head.

"I can fix it!" he shouted back. "Let me fix it, Mister! I can fix it!" Nikola stripped off his jacket and ran for the river. "You keep pumping!"

He leaped into the water.

He swam into the dense, murky green, blinked his eyes against the sediment, and found the suction hose. It had been kinked. The sides were squashed together by the pressure, sealing it. Nikola wrestled with the hose and straightened out the kink. Water immediately rushed through, swelling the line as it poured up to the pump.

Nikola's head broke the surface. He gasped for breath. Water burst from the fire hose. It thrashed madly about, gushing with foam and spraying the frantic men who leaped to subdue it.

Later, the Lord Mayor of Gospic took Reverend Milutin Tesla aside and said, "You have a most amazing son, Reverend Tesla."

The priest nodded silently. A tear swelled, stinging his eye. He was trying not to think of Daniel.

CHAPTER THREE

Nikola

Niko thought about his past accomplishments. The real triumph of his waterwheel was that it had no paddles and could turn faster than other waterwheels. The triumph of his fishing pole and hook was that it caught frogs.

He boasted about these accomplishments; he knew he was different, that he did not think like other people. Sometimes flashes of light filled his eyes and brain with pictures of functioning machines. He was filled with ideas and had a perfect memory. Unlike other kids his age, he knew mathematics, other languages, and practiced eidetic visualization.

In his mind was the image of a superman. He was determined to live up to that image.

He forced himself to learn more and more, to study everything from mathematics to philosophy to science. He forced himself to envision pure geometric images. His father, over the years, had taught him to create imaginary landscapes. Now, he created mental visions of a world transformed by machines like none that existed in the world around him but which he could understand perfectly. Comprehension accompanied visualization. He would build these wonders himself.

His mother taught him mechanical skills. She had been the eldest of seven children and had forfeited her education when her own mother went blind. Though she could not read or write, she could quote entire volumes of poetry from memory and recite works of literature en rote, even if she had only heard them read aloud once. She had invented new tools for the processing of milk, as well as useful devices to make farm work easier. Her dexterity was astounding: many times, Nikola had seen her tie two or three perfect knots in a single plucked eyelash.

Nikola revered his mother.

His father, however, was growing noticeably concerned over his son's preoccupation with mechanics and science. The Tesla family tradition had been for the men to enter the clergy and the women to marry military officers. This new science of invention—there had been nothing like it until now, and it was a burgeoning new field, but what of its future? How did it fit with God and all of his principles?

There was a dangerous heretic named Lamarck who said that all life was evolving; animals and plants were changing slowly over the ages so there was no need for a creator. Reverend Milutin Tesla did not trust this new science. He wondered if heretics and unbelievers should even be given a chance to change the world.

"That is what it all might come down to," he told Nikola in his study one night, after his son approached him with news that he had chosen his life's work—to become an electrical engineer and inventor.

"But, Father, aren't the scientists and inventors just learning about the principles of nature created by God?"

"That is a subtle illusion, Nikola," Milutin said. "Where, in all their works, do they mention God?"

"Well, Father, Galileo fought against the Inquisition—"

"There might have been reasons why he had to fight the Inquisition, Nikola."

"But, I don't see—"

"That's enough of this discussion. You are to go to Seminary at the end of your term at Real Gymnasium."

"Yes, Father."

But his father could not ward off storms and prevent lightning: when the air bristled with electricity, Nikola responded with tingles of life and awareness bristling through his body, clarifying and expanding his senses. When the sky darkened with clouds and the sun went black and the wind howled and moaned through the webs of bare branches, Nikola became alert: he saw blue flashes of electricity when dark figures trudged through the snow, he saw a haze of purple light surrounding the rugs and carpets, and he saw the fur of the house cats sparkle in the dim lantern light of his home.

When he thought about all this, he could scarcely breathe. During a lightning storm, cold purple fire sparkled all over the world. The night intensified the ultraviolet glow. The shimmering light would gather in streaks just as a spark discharged from the rug or a gloved hand touching a doorknob. He noticed that purple flames flickered from everything except wood.

His mother had once demonstrated how to generate such a spark by rubbing a key against a bearskin rug—the purple flames, to Nikola's delight, massed together around the key, then vanished when the key discharged a tiny spark against a metal lamp stand. A gas lamp.

Nikola pondered the problem of how to make these purple flames turn into real, white light—enough to read by—that could replace the yellow glare of the gas lamps. He knew electricity was the key: if only he could penetrate its mysteries and learn to understand it, he could make it do what he wanted it to do. When lightning struck and lit distant horizons, Nikola shuddered with awe. He felt privileged to see a brief, flickering window to a mystery. He intended to use his flashes of insight to perceive that mystery and control its hidden forces. He also used the visions that the lightning imparted to him to vanquish the nightmares he had suffered since the death of his brother. To these visions he added the flashes of light that filled his mind with pictures of machines, marvelous machines. To these inspirations he added his own exercises in mental concentration. In combination, these were his mental tools against the nightmares. He was no longer forced to dream of the funeral procession, nor did he see Daniel's frightened face as he tipped backward, at the top of the long flight of stairs, over and over again. Instead, he dreamed—and saw—fantastic and awesome machines. With his powers of concentration, he molded himself, in his own mind, into the image of the disciplined superman he wanted himself to become, to atone for the death of his brother and to become the living superman Daniel had truly been. His family had long ago stopped mentioning the name Daniel Tesla, as if he had never existed. The family had a new champion: little Nikola was the family genius. Not even his father could deny that.

Djouka begged her husband to let Nikola attend technical school after his graduation from Gymnasium. "He would be wasting his talent in the Seminary," she argued. "Let him go on to the Polytechnic college."

"That is too expensive," Milutin protested. "I can get him into the Seminary easily, cheaply. We can afford that. Where, in all of Gospic, can I get the money to send him to the Polytechnic?"

"We will have to start saving now," she said. "Oh, Milutin, when will we have another chance to educate one of our own for such a promising future?"

Milutin considered those words for a long time. A stab of pain pierced his heart: he was trying—forcibly—not to remember Daniel. "We can afford what we can afford," he said finally, "And no more."

He strode out of the house and across the field to the churchyard. Djouka Tesla glanced up to see Nikola peering down from the top of the stairs. Before she could utter a sound, he fled back to his room and loudly closed the door.

He awoke one night with a start. The house was on fire. The flames were purple.

He sat upright in his bed and blinked his eyes in horror. As his heart grew tight and his pulse exploded in his chest and beat against his temples, he realized the flames were cold. The fire tingled, but he was not burned.

He moved his hand before his eyes and saw that the flames followed the motion like strands. His skin glowed with purple light, and purple fog hung like smoke in the dense air. He felt dizzy, but he calmed his breathing and stared into the purple fire.

An irresistible force of curiosity drew him out of bed and made him crawl to the window. He crept onto a trunk covered with a wide lace doily. He drew back the curtains to peer out over the snow-covered landscape. He gasped with awe and wonder as a vast, luminous rectangle descended through the clouds. It loomed overhead and hovered over the snow just outside the window.

The great cube of light contained a shape—a machine, with a propeller and a carriage. The carriage supported stiff wings and a motor. Suspended from the center of the carriage by a superstructure of metal beams was a man in a metal chair operating a control panel.

Nikola was overwhelmed. The flying machine in the square of light rotated slowly: the man in the center of the carriage manipulated a knob and the wings snapped from a vertical alignment to horizontal, and the propeller descended from above the pilot to directly in front of him.

When the image rotated again, Nikola comprehended what he saw. The flying machine could rise vertically or soar horizontally. He stared at the magnificent machine for many hours and memorized every detail of what he saw. Then the fabulous vision faded and the purple fire dissipated and Nikola felt sleepy again. He crept to bed. The sky lightened before sleep claimed him.

Years later, he drew diagrams of the machine and even patented it. He worked out complex mathematical descriptions of its flight.

He would disobey his father at night, to stay up and read books, secretly, by the light of tiny torches of his own design. This caused the Reverend Tesla much chagrin. Nikola also took advantage of the heaviness imparted by sleep so long delayed: when he could read no longer, he blew out the little torches and pulled the blankets up to his chin and closed his eyes....

He would see a vast field of blue light. He would gaze into the blue for an eternity. Flashes of green flickered. Glimmered. Sparkled. Fleeting flecks of green light advanced toward him, layer upon layer, like fragments of green glass falling in overlapping rows, until all light everywhere was broken into shards of flashing green.

Colored lights streaked out in fine lines from some unseen point hidden by the glare in the center of his vision. The streaming colors enveloped him. He felt his body race forward—into a bleak zone of formless, dense gray....

Nikola saw clouds in the void that billowed out of nowhere. He floated in empty space, suspended before these turbulent nebulas. He conquered the clouds: he inflicted great mental power onto them, and molded them with his imagination into the familiar shapes of people and animals. Then the cloud-forms gave away to real, remembered landscapes, and the faces of his family and friends. Then he saw machines. Strange, wonderful *machines*!

Finally he slept.

To satisfy his obsession with machines, he took apart every clock or watch he could get his hands on. His uncle Petar laughingly called him "dangerous." His mother reprimanded him out of exasperation; he often failed to reassemble these devices after dissecting them. Sometimes when he tried to rebuild them, they failed to work again.

He was fourteen years old when he had his first brush with death.

He and his friends were swimming in a lake when an idea hit him: he would dive off the floating platform in the middle of the lake and swim under it, reappearing on the other side. He swam out to the platform and climbed onto it. When he had made his friends aware of his presence on the wooden structure, he dove off the edge, doubled back, and swam into the shadow under the platform. He swam endlessly, until his arms and legs and lungs ached, until he knew he had passed beyond the far edge of the platform.

He swam to the surface—and struck his head.

He was still under the structure. Somewhere in the middle of it. He groped above his head and felt the slimy, hard wood of the beams where he expected— and needed—to find air. He pushed forward painfully, pumping water with his arms and legs, randomly now, desperately seeking air, air, air. Bumping painfully against the wooden planks again and again, he choked, gulping water reflexive-ly. His arms and legs wearied, and he started to sink. He clawed the cold water above his head.

A flash of light burst through his terror. In his mind erupted a picture of the bot-tom of the platform: there were gaps between the wooden beams, and there was air between the beams and the top of the platform. The air was accessible through the gaps between the boards. He struggled back up to the shadowy underside of the platform and gripped the tiny gaps between the planks. He pulled his body against the cold, slippery wood. He pressed his lips against a narrow gap and inhaled.

He choked and sputtered, coughing snot and saliva. Air and a little foam filled his mouth, his lungs. Fighting the urge to choke, he sucked in a little more air, just a shallow breath. He clutched the beams under the platform, crawling meticulously along the treacherous edge, sipping air through the gaps, until his hands felt the side and he rocketed up, burst through the water, and gulped precious air.

Electricity, water, flashes of light, pictures imparted to his brain—

Water was both a pleasure and a peril to him. He had nearly drowned not once but twice, and both times flashes of light and information in his brain saved him.

He enjoyed swimming out to a dam across a pond from an old abandoned flour mill. The rains of spring were carrying off a generous snowmelt, and Niko was alone; his friends did not want to brave the cold water so early in the season. He leaped into the pond and started swimming toward the dam—and was snatched by the racing current. The water was pouring over the lip of the dam in an unseen cataract. It slammed Niko against the stone masonry and pinned him with his head barely above the surface.

He was caught in a cold, liquid death-grip. He struggled until the scraping of his body against the stones wore slashes and sores into his skin. Yielding to the torrent would sweep him over the edge of the dam in the grip of the cascade. He would be flung to the rocks far below. When he gripped the rough, stony wall, the force of the water crushed his chest and made it impossible to breathe.

He lifted himself slightly but the roaring surge nearly flipped him over the edge. He crouched down against the rocks, and the crushing force of the current clenched his ribs.

A flash lit his mind with strange logic.

He understood that the force of water is only proportional to the area of the sur-face it is flowing against—so he turned to his left side and the water seemed to flow around him instead of directly against his chest. He was suddenly stabilized.

He tilted his head back and drew in a deep breath of air. He inched along the jagged stone masonry while adjusting every movement of his arms and legs and torso to match hydrodynamic principles.

He came to a gap in the side of the dam, a spillway. Infinite caution guided Nikola's aching arms and sore body as he pulled in a final lungful of air, then dipped under the surge and crawled sideways, under the edge of the overflow, toward the other side of the spillway. He reemerged within reach of an over-hanging tree branch. He hauled himself out of the water onto the grassy shore. He breathed in huge, moaning gasps, coughing out gurgling water and gulping gasp after gasp of air. He remembered, eerily, how flashes of light, imparting pic-tures, information, had saved his life under the floating platform two summers before.

He caught a fever from the prolonged exposure to the cold, cold water. His wounds became infected and he suffered for weeks, bedridden.

During those teenage years, Nikola attempted to built a model of one of his vividly imagined flying machines—"a flying machine with nothing more than a rotating shaft, flapping wings, and…a vacuum of unlimited power!"

The Real Gymnasium in Gospic had a good physics department, and Nikola found everything he needed to construct his device in the campus machine shop. The curious machine consisted of a rotating cylinder divided into two compart-ments, fitted with a rectangular wooden "trough." The cylinder fitted into the trough by rotating bearings. Air was evacuated from on side of the cylinder by a hand pump.

When it was ready for demonstration, Nikola announced, "Behold, my flying machine! With this device, I intend to demonstrate that flight can be accomplished with a device that is heavier than air. To this end, I have utilized a vacuum, one of nature's most powerful forces." When he activated the hand pump—pushing down repeatedly on the steel handle—the shaft rotated slightly with a flat hissing sound. That was all.

The slight motion had been induced by a leak in the box. The unattainability of a perfect vacuum caused the tiny movement of the shaft. The laughter of his class-mates spurred him on: he was determined to overcome all human limitations and transform the world through the science of electrical invention. His father alone stood in his way.

Winters were intensely hard on young Nikola: he fell ill every year, just after the onset of the cold stormy weather, and during his last year at the Real Gymnasium he became desperately sick with pneumonia—and "complications," as the doctor put it. His mother feared he had malaria.

Deathly illness was in danger of taking its toll on the Tesla family again. Nikola begged his father to let him read. Anything. Books. Poetry. Literature. Science....

"Nonsense," his father replied, time after time. "You're too weak, Niko. You would perish if you tried to read!"

"Please, Father!"

"Milutin, please let him read!"

"Djouka, it would be unhealthy for him. He is very, very sick."

"Then all the more reason to let him read! He longs to, so much."

Every day Niko and his mother pleaded, and every day Milutin refused. After the winter snows had fallen and remained for six weeks under eternally gray skies, Milutin gave silent consent with a nod. Nikola would be allowed to read again.

His mother rushed to the Gospic Library. Although she could not read, she found a fat volume with a pleasant cover: the engraving showed two boys, one white and the other black, fishing from the side of a wooden raft on wide, flat water. She selected an armful of volumes, then returned to her son.

Nikola lifted off the top book. He read the title, *The Adventures of Huckleberry Finn*. Nikola fell into the story, in English, of a runaway slave and a farm boy—and he fell into the world of America, a world unlike anything he had ever known. He was amazed by the language he read in those pages. This was not Classical prose, it was colloquial. Spicy with jargon and explosive with hyperbole, the adverbs and adjectives bounced across the pages.

By the time he had read the volumes his mother had acquired for him, he had recovered enough to go to work at the Gospic Library, cataloguing the books. He uncovered and read the early works of Mark Twain there, and he read much, much more.

He memorized most of what he read. If he could not recall a passage perfectly after the first reading, he gave it a second glance.

Although he had managed to banish his boyhood nightmares years ago, he acquired a new fear: illness. Deep in the back of his mind, he pondered how microbes caused illness—and he knew that he was especially susceptible to such microbes. He avoided touching people. He deftly avoided handshakes. In fact, he resolved to wear gloves whenever possible. And he never, never, *never* touched hair.

Still deeper in the back of his mind, he feared that microbes came from outer space, beyond the limit of the air, in clouds of dust that he reasoned must almost certainly be out there.

He remembered the mental exercises his father taught him as a boy—especially trying to guess each other's thoughts, which he got very good at, and the first time he created the mental image of a vast, blue ball....

Sometimes, when reclining, he experienced the hallucination of falling toward a featureless, blue sphere. Sometimes, when he saw round shapes, he felt possessed by this feeling, so he came to fear round shapes.

He felt uneasy the first time he saw billiard balls.

Once, a woman wearing a pearl necklace greeted him at the door of his father's church, and the sight of pink pearls jolted him with fright.

He preferred to eat from oval plates and oval bowls. In short, he had developed phobias—and obsessions.

He learned of a mighty and powerful waterfall somewhere in North America called Niagara. It was said to be the mightiest waterfall on earth. Nikola believed—no, he *knew*—that he, Nikola Tesla, would someday utilize the power of this titanic cataract and use it to power a world of machines of his own design.

This obsession reached a peak during Nikola's final year at Real Gymnasium: this was also a climax in the inevitable conflict with his father over his future—either the Serbian Orthodox Church or electrical engineering. Cholera struck the populace of Gospic that winter, and Nikola came down with terrible gut cramps and diarrhea. Within days, he was extremely weak. He had purged his system of everything. Meals were passed undigested. He could not eat.

The doctor was convinced he was approaching death again. Days lingered into weeks, and Nikola was losing his will to live.

He pleaded—again and again—with his father to be allowed to go to engineering school.

"Preposterous!" his father exclaimed.

His son was nearly too feeble to argue.

Milutin left the room.

Nikola's father had abandoned him.

Nikola knew that a cure was at hand but his father withheld it from him.

Days later, his father bellowed, "Electrical school is too expensive! I can get you into Seminary when you finish Real Gymnasium in the spring! That will cost me nothing. A family fund can support that. But this fund will not cover expenses incurred by mechanical training! So go to sleep, and do not dream of things that cannot be!"

That was his father's final word on the subject—until, days later, the doctor told Milutin his son was slipping in and out of consciousness and that he was going to die. He remembered how, the year before, he had allowed Nikola to read, which had led to his speedy recovery.

Milutin recanted, and remained by his son's bedside, waiting for him to return to consciousness. When Nikola's eyes fluttered for an instant, Milutin exclaimed, "Nikola! How can I help you get better?"

Nikola gathered all his strength to answer:

"Perhaps...I will...get well...if you let me study...engineering..."

Milutin seized the boy and held him. He stared desperately into the half-lidded blue eyes. "Nikola, Nikola, do not go! I command you—do not go! Stay with me, stay with all of us. Stay here, with us. You can go to engineering school. You will go to the best engineering school in the world and you will come back a great engineer. You will return to us a great mechanic, a great engineer."

Faintly, unmistakably, Nikola smiled.

"You heard me! You heard and understand. Thank God. Yes, Nikola, you will go to engineering school, and you will return to us one day a great engineer."

Nikola smiled dreamily. His body relaxed in his father's arms.

Milutin could sense the difference between sleep and a coma. He was immeasurably relieved: Nikola was sleeping, and color flushed through his cheeks.

He was already recovering.

CHAPTER FOUR

Reality

Nikola never knew if he had *not* killed his brother Daniel. His memory of the event contained a blank spot: all he really knew was that Daniel had died believing Nikola pushed him. After all, his last words were, "… Niko…how could you…?"

After Niko had run from the porch to the top of the cellar stairs, the blank spot interrupted his memory. The next thing Niko remembered was grasping at thin air with his tiny arms, looking into Daniel's face as he fell over backward. His eyes met Daniel's, and he glimpsed the horror that filled them. But Nikola could not remember the exact moment of the accident. He did not want to remember that he had been thinking envious thoughts about Daniel moments before.

He was agonized by the thought that Daniel had gone to his death thinking Nikola had pushed him from the top of the stairs. Young Nikola tried to redeem himself of the sin he had unknowingly committed against his brother by attempting to embody his brother. That was his moral obligation: to be the living embodiment of Daniel Tesla. Then—to surpass even the embodiment of Daniel, to reemerge as Nikola, Nikola reborn, Nikola the superman.

Of course, he did not consciously think these thoughts.

The guilt he felt surrounding Daniel's death was too painful to bear. Nikola resolved it with suppression. Banished to the subconscious, Nikola's memory of the instant of Daniel's fall down the stairs was kept hidden from conscious scrutiny, and this crucial mental block became a potent source of powerful mental energy and discipline.

In reality it did not matter whether or not Nikola had pushed Daniel down the stairs, or if he had lunged forward to save him. All that mattered was that Nikola now had a source of mental energy—a constant drive to overcome subconscious guilt—as well as a tool to help him accomplish the task, that of perfect mental discipline. His father's mental exercises helped accomplish this task.

He and his father had become very good at the game of Guess My Thoughts, but Milutin sadly realized these visualizations were getting out of hand: Nikola's ideas and experiments were dangerous not because his inventions were designed to harm people, but because they would improve life for people. Perhaps these new inventions would make unbelievers out of the faithful. Milutin shuddered at the thought. Yet he could not guess what raging storms of doubts and emotions fought within Nikola's mind and memory.

His mother suspected what depth and intensity the inner turmoil had reached and she tried to nurture her son back to happiness and wholeness, but by trying she loomed larger in his life than even his brother Daniel. She arranged for Nikola to attend Higher Real Gymnasium in Karlovac. He was to stay with his father's cousin and her husband, a retired military officer whom Nikola addressed formally as Colonel Brankovic.

Colonel Brankovic was a tough, heavy-handed man, and Nikola was taken aback by his manners and attitudes.

His wife was a lovely woman. She reminded Nikola of his mother.

Soon after his arrival in Karlovac, Nikola was stricken with malaria. The surrounding lowlands were soggy with swamps and marshes. Mosquitoes thrived. Nikola fought fevers that passed suddenly: he would rise from bed and return to school to catch up on his studies. He took his textbooks home at night—and memorized them. Even when he was bedridden, he managed to stay awake long enough to master his assignments, well in advance of the school deadlines: despite bouts with fevers and much time away from class, he was due to graduate with honors from Higher Real Gymnasium in Karlovac one year early. He was seventeen years old.

His father had become reluctant—again—to send Nikola to technical school. His father reminded him of Colonel Brankovic.

Something existed in marriages that repulsed Nikola. He wondered if *all* marriages were merely arrangements between a stern, domineering husband and a nurturing, lovely woman.

Puberty had been hard on him: he had not expected it, was not prepared for it, and he resented the powerful new urges that it brought. He responded to his sexuality by letting it drive him deeper into his mental life.

After returning to Gospic after graduating from Higher Real Gymnasium, Nikola fell ill again with cholera. An epidemic had struck the town, and Nikola immediately came down with the disease.

Even after Milutin had agreed to let Nikola attend technical college, lack of finances blocked the decision. Milutin had sent many applications to many schools—and all requested too much money for tuitions. By the end of 1872, Nikola was summoned to spend three years in the military. College was clearly beyond his grasp.

Although Serbia and Croatia were not at war, borders were being patrolled constantly and "incidents" occurred frequently, in which undeclared skirmishes led to "accidental" deaths. Nikola knew his time was too vastly important to be wasted three years at a time in military duty. Milutin knew this too—and he knew he had to act, to reconcile his unfulfilled promise to his son.

They faced the arrival of winter with trepidation. Plans were made for Nikola's immediate future. Father and son agreed that Nikola must be spared military plans at all cost. He had lost one son. He dared not lose another.

"How is your health, my boy?"

"Just fine, Father."

"Good."

"Will it be a cold winter?"

"There is no way to know that."

"I see."

"We must get you out of here. Soldiers will be coming for you any day now."

"I understand, Father. Where should I go?"

"Nikola, remember the best parts of your boyhood. What were they?"

"When I was in nature."

"Yes. I have seen in you a powerful love of nature, Nikola. You must go into the woods to escape the armies of men. You know about shelter, Nikola, and you know about finding direction in the mountains, do you not?"

"Yes, Father. These are things I appreciate. You and Uncle Petar taught me many gifts of knowledge."

"I am glad you appreciate what we have taught you. Here's what I will do: I will work for these next months, however long it takes, to establish connections in the military. Maybe the Colonel can help me. I want you to take off from here. If you need food, let me know. I will keep a brief appointment one day every week at the abandoned churchyard on the site of the old township. I will also help you find shelter across the border if you need it. You still have sympathetic relatives in Serbia. Remember that."

"Thank you, Father."

"Together, we can get you out of the army and into technical college, like I promised. Especially now that you have finished with honors ahead of your classmates at Higher Real Gymnasium. Let's get inside. We have preparations to make...."

They spent the night preparing a hiking pack with fishing gear, camping utensils, survival equipment, and books. Nikola would have to continue his studies, even on an adventure into the wild untamed mountains.

They hiked through the old township, past the abandoned churchyard, and into the rugged mountains. They feared wolves but encountered none.

The thought of storms intrigued Nikola: he yearned to see the dense overcast break loose from its mountaintop moorings and spill over the peaks, blazing of fierce wind, snow, pelting rain—

Lightning. Give me lightning.

He shared a campsite with his father during their second night in the mountains. They ate fish and smoked venison in silence. Nikola thought, Give me lightning!

"This is a wonderful campsite, is it not, Nikola?"

"A wonderful site. A world of a view."

"What were you thinking, Nikola?"

"Guess."

"Perhaps—let me see...."

Nikola held the thought frozen in the focus of his attention: Give me lightning! His father asked slowly, "Storms?"

"Lightning."

"I see. I wondered: I sensed you were looking forward to storms. You love the lightning, don't you, Nikola?"

"Yes, Father. It...fascinates me."

"You want to harness and control the lightning, is that right?"

"Yes, but most of all, I want to understand it, Father."

"I see. I am glad. Son, the mysteries of nature have led me to a deeper understanding of God."

"If that awaits me, then let it be so."

"Remain open to the presence of God all around you."

"Thank you, Father. I place myself in the hands of God now, tonight."

"Yes. I will go in the morning. I must, Nikola. The soldiers will be looking for you. I will tell them you got a job on a merchant ship. You will be back in a year. I will tell them just that."

Nikola set up a permanent camp under an overhang, a great cleft in the rock that sheltered him from rain and snow. It was almost a shallow cave. A fire warmed it up nicely.

He discovered during his wanderings an abandoned farmhouse, so overgrown with berry vines that it retained warmth and shed the stormy rains.

He ate salmon and trout and the venison his father smuggled to him whenever they secretly met at the abandoned churchyard on the outskirts of old Gospic. Nikola foraged through the forest for the delicacies he had learned to enjoy since his early childhood. Although the winter snows had come, he was enjoying his time alone in nature and—miraculously—his health did not fail. Here, the air was clean. Life was what it was meant to be.

As winter dissolved into spring, legions of birds returned to the forest. In summer, Nikola studied salamanders in a pool.

As autumn billowed down from the north, it brought—finally!—lightning. He braced himself for the first storm of the changing season. He sought a vantage point: a massive conifer stabbed at the clouds from atop a granite pinnacle. He climbed the rocky cliff, then he climbed the towering tree.

Sticky spicy pitch soaked his leather gloves. Resin glued bits of debris to his hair. He sweated, even though the wind lashed him with cruel cold. He clung to the trunk, two-thirds up, and the vicious wind pushed until the tree swayed with brittle, crackling sounds.

The belly of the sky blackened with clouds. Suddenly, the lightning exploded. A splinter of blinding light, stolen from the gods, shattered the cloud shadow and seared the air. A brilliant flash, staccato flashes, a moment of silence as even the wind held its breath in anticipation, then—thunder boomed down from the mountaintops.

Another spear of divine fire stabbed the sky with light, and the cliffs battered echoes of thunder down the canyons.

Night pressed down against the mountains. The blackness was illuminated by the stabbing, slashing bolts of electricity.

The storm lasted through the night. Lightning, thunder, and wind pounded the peaks and crevices. No rain fell. By morning, the storm had abated. Dawn lifted the blackness, filtering blue light through veils of gray.

Nikola climbed down from the tree. He made his way to the campsite he had made for himself, beneath the overhang in the cliff. He pulled dry wood out from a cleft in the rock, mixed it with kindling, and struck steel against flint to spark a flame.

His year alone in the Velebit Mountains had come to an end. When he met his father several nights later in the churchyard of the abandoned chapel, he was greeted with good news:

"I have managed to put aside enough money to pay for a year at a very good technical school, Nikola. You will be going to college soon."

"That is wonderful news, Father."

"I am vastly pleased that you have not been afflicted by any winter maladies this past year."

"I have never felt better, Father."

"I can tell, Nikola."

He met his father twice after that, at the abandoned churchyard, and he returned to Gospic at night. The "great technical college" turned out to be the Polytechnic Institute in Gratz, Austria.

He was nineteen years old when he emerged from the mountains to the campus of the Polytechnic Institute. For the first time in fourteen years, with the blessings of his father and healed by the power of nature, Nikola Tesla stepped out from the shadow of his brother, reborn.

CHAPTER FIVE

Truth

Professor Poeschl was a strange and hairy man. Nikola both adored and despised him. He had huge hands and feet—traits that disgusted Nikola. Yet, the small, huge, horrible, hairy man could not change how he had been born— such huge hands and feet. Such hairy hands!

He was (thank God!) not bearded, but he had massive, wiry, and thick eyebrows. His titanic mane of black hair had probably never been combed. Yet, he was a genius. Nikola admired him beyond measure, even though his appearance evoked revulsion. He delivered brilliant lectures on the subject of electricity; he *lived* electricity. He animated his lectures with sweeping, dramatic gestures. He spun his huge, hairy hands in wide arcs while explaining principles that made even the achievements of Newton, from his laws of motion to the triumph of calculus, seem simplistic by comparison. He taught. He demonstrated. He experimented.

He explained how certain principles of physics could be predicted by mathematics. Nikola sat spellbound. He stared at the squat, barrel-chested man, so opposite of himself. Professor Poeschl was German. His accent was thick and guttural. He was a living wonder of a man. He often wandered between the rows of students as he lectured. They would lean out of the way of his wild gestures.

Once, he glimpsed strange drawings on Nikola's desk. He paused and studied them—they were partially buried under pages of notes and diagrams. Nikola rarely took notes—he memorized the contents of books and lectures—but

Professor Poeschl's vivid dissertations contained precious bits of knowledge, equations and proofs, that Tesla wanted to record.

Among them were drawings of things Professor Poeschl had never shown. Nikola stared up at the hairy man with fear in his eyes.

Professor Poeschl said, "Interesting. Interesting. See me after class." Then—mercifully—he was gone.

Nikola sweated with discomfort and anxiety until the class was over. He tried to listen to Professor Poeschl's lecture, but was distracted by his uneasiness. After the rest of the class had been dismissed, Tesla approached Poeschl's desk reluctantly. "Interesting drawings, Nikola. Do you mind if I see them?"

"N-no, sir. Not at all." He extended the pages. Poeschl studied the drawings, then shrugged.

"I did not draw them during class time, sir."

"I wouldn't mind if you had. Can you stay a while? Where were you rushing off to?"

"The library, sir. This is my last class of the day. Higher mathematics has been postponed until next week."

"Good. Very good. Interesting drawings. Tell me—this sketch is not the ring around the planet Saturn. Yet, it looks mechanical. Explain what it is."

Nikola chuckled. "No, no, sir, it's not Saturn. I will admit there's a resemblance—"

"What is it? A tube or something? A tunnel or something?"

"It's—a fancy of mine…"

"Explain it, then."

"Well, imagine this, Professor, a giant ring around the Earth's equator, built of immensely hard substances, sir, and pressurized from within, for it would have to be built in space, above the atmosphere, and, if my calculations are right, it would assume instantly, upon completion, an orbital motion to match the rotation of the Earth. At that point, tensions and pressures would be evenly exerted throughout. The scaffolding used to build it could be taken down."

Professor Poeschl stared, blinked, and finally uttered, "Very clever…" He flipped immediately to the second drawing. "What's this?"

"A tube. Across the bottom of the Atlantic Ocean."

"Ah. What does it do? These look like railroad cars inside of it. Yet, there are no tracks. A transportation tube, for cars without tracks. You have a few equations for calculating air pressure, stress patterns—it's all very complete, if I already know the idea behind it, but, tell me, Nikola—how do you get these cars to travel through this tube without a track?"

"Pneumatics, sir."

"Ah, that makes sense."

"We prepare the car for transportation—actually a string of cars, joined by couplings—and we seal the cars airtight against the walls of the tube. Then, we evacuate the air at the far end of the tube, which moves the cars, pushed from behind by the pressure on the other side."

"Interesting. It would be efficient, if you could perfect a powerful enough vacuum. Interesting. Very interesting.

Nikola grinned proudly.

Poeschl turned back to the drawing of the orbiting ring, then looked up. "This idea is flawed. The ring itself would have to be so perfectly circular, and built at such an exact constant distance away from the land and sea below, that if it were even a centimeter off, a mere centimeter, Nikola, the whole thing would collapse.

"Now, this pneumatic tube idea—that's a much more practical idea! A magnificent idea. Work out the calculations on that. That would be worth your while. Have you any other ideas, Nikola? Surely, your imagination has produced much, much more than just these!"

"Yes, Professor. Many ideas."

"Ah, indeed. You are a very bright student, Nikola."

"Thank you, sir."

"I think you can benefit from what I have to teach you. You are smart, Nikola, very smart, but you need pragmatics. Fortunately, you are very advanced in mathematics. That is very good. And you have vision! Never let go of that. You just need to know how things work. Do you understand? Pragmatics, the rules and limitations of what you want to deal with, this is the real, material world of nature, is it not?"

"Yes, sir," said Tesla, remembering the lightning storms.

"Very well, then." Poeschl handed back the drawings. "Tomorrow we will see a demonstration of motion, hard, hard work, delivered by electricity."

Tesla was excited. "I look forward to that, sir."

The next day, Professor Poeschl unveiled the Gramme machine. It consisted of a wire-wound armature surrounded by a casing of electromagnets. When the commutator fed currents to the electromagnets, the armature spun and the Gramme machine became a motor. When the armature was turned by hand, it generated a weak but measurable current. The machine was connected to the vat of a high-voltage battery, and the armature spun. The commutator connecting the battery and the electromagnets sparked loudly and violently.

One by one, Nikola's classmates stood and filed past the roaring, crackling motor.

Nikola studied the Gramme machine. He eyed the commutator suspiciously and glanced up at Professor Poeschl.

"Take your time, Nikola."

Tesla winced at the staccato snapping of the spark. "Is there anything that can be done with that…annoying discharge?"

"Nothing! We can reduce it, but we cannot eliminate it."

"Then take the commutator off!"

"Nonsense! The action of the motor depends on the quick reversal of polarity of the current to the electromagnets. If we feed the electromagnets current directly, the armature would freeze up as soon as the opposite poles line up and magnetize together."

"Then feed constantly reversing current through the magnets instead of direct current."

"Many electricians want to abandon direct current, Nikola. It is hard to move direct current through wires over long distances. Additional generators are placed along the lines, to boost the power from city to city, especially through telegraph lines.

"There is evidence that alternating current, in which the polarity is reversed at the rate of many cycles per second, can overcome this distance obstacle and does not require secondary stations along the power lines. It is just impossible to generate high voltages of alternating current. May it not ever be so!

"But for now, Nikola, we use a commutator to reverse the current from the electrodes coming from the battery, or we use direct current to an alternating current transformer. And they are very expensive and only practical for low to moderate voltages."

"So, what can be done about that?"

"Nothing, in our lifetimes."

"I disagree. Much could be dispensed with if direct current was dispensed with, and alternating current could be sent—anywhere."

"Utterly impractical."

"You could dispense with this nasty commutator."

Professor Poeschl laughed. "It is inherent in the nature of the machine. It may be reduced to a great extent, but, as long as we use commutators, the sparking will always be present to some degree.

"And as long as electricity flows in one direction, as long as a magnet has two poles that have opposite effects on the current, we will have to use a commutator to change, at the right instant, the direction of the current flow in the rotating armature."

"That is obvious. The machine is limited by the current used. That is why I am suggesting getting rid of the commutator entirely by using alternating current."

The professor became impatient. He motioned for Tesla to return to his desk. "Mr. Tesla will accomplish many great things, I am sure, but he will never do this. It would be the equivalent of converting a steady, pulling force like gravity into a rotary effort. It is a perpetual motion scheme, an impossible idea."

After class, Tesla went to the library. He was memorizing the works of Voltair for amusement. All were several hundred pages long and printed in microscopic print. But Voltair was worth it—especially the satire.

His first year had started with promise: the dean of the technical facility had written to his father: "Your son is a star of the first rank!" At the end of Tesla's second year, his nephew, Nikola Trbojevich, also attending the Polytechnic, reported to Milutin Tesla that the "star of the first rank" had been "fired from the college" and had even been reprimanded by the police for "playing cards and leading an irregular life." There was truth to this statement.

Nikola had discovered the mathematics of a poker game and the Newtonian physics of billiards—once his aversion to round objects calmed enough for him to concentrate on hitting a cue ball. He had squandered the last of his college money and was forced to move back home with his parents, in Gospic.

His father was especially displeased.

"This is not enough!" he bellowed one night, after Nikola offered to share with him a generous portion of the fruits of his lucky streak. "This is only a fraction of what your tuition cost me!"

"I can get more. Tomorrow night. I can recover it all—and get enough to go back next year."

"That is not the way to do it. Gambling is only a trick of the devil."

"Father, there is no devil and you know it. That scientist Lamarck says—"

"I know all about those scientists! I know of their heresies. Is that what they taught you at the Polytechnic Institute? That there is no God, just electricity? Take away God from the world, Nikola, and you leave the world with only the devil."

"I have studied the mathematics of cards, Father. I calculate the odds of any given hand. I can remember all the cards any player has taken from the stack, and I can figure out what hands the other players probably hold. That's how I made this money tonight, and tomorrow night I can make much more."

"You have spent all your earnings on who knows what, Nikola! You don't visit the young women in town, do you? No drinking—although I detect the aroma of wine on your breath now. What do you do with the money? Win back your losses?"

Nikola winced, then turned toward the stairs. "Take heed, Nikola. You can only calculate the odds of an honest game."

Nikola froze. He turned to face his father.

"Have you noticed cards with bent corners, Nikola?"

"That isn't funny."

"I did not intend to be funny. Have you?"

"What are you trying to tell me?"

"The cards are marked."

"I've spoken to the dealers. They're always on the lookout for players who cheat."

"I'm sure they are! You are gullible, Nikola. You are easily misled. If you believe what card dealers tell you, then you are as silly as the mice and frogs those scientists you revere dissect."

"I'll show you!"

"I'm sure you will, Nikola."

The next night at poker, Tesla approached the card dealer with a scowl. "I would like to see the cards," he demanded.

"Got a reason?"

"I want to inspect them, that is all."

"You don't trust me?"

"Let us say, I want to insure the honesty of the game."

"Get out of here!"

Tesla was escorted from the room by two huge men with bulldog faces. He walked the streets for an hour, considering how to insure the honesty of a game. Finally, he purchased a deck from the bar in a tavern, ordered a glass of Chablis, and waited for a familiar face to appear from the back. He was led through a dark hallway to a room in the back, where cigars burned in the pale yellow gaslight. Nikola strode past the big man to the dealer.

"Substitution?"

"Please."

"That's permissible. Give me your cards."

Tesla handed him the unopened deck.

"Brand new," the dealer commented.

The paper wrapping crackled.

"Got money?"

"Yes, sir. Of course."

"Sit down. Deal you in."

Tesla glanced around, found an empty chair, and drew it up to the table.

The dealer switched decks with sleight-of-hand.

Tesla sat. He traded half of his small fortune for a stack of chips. The dealer shuffled the cards, and the other players were silent as the hand was dealt. Nikola was disappointed with the cards he had been dealt. He placed a small bet to keep his place open, but had no luck and folded after a few hands were played. The next round was worse. Whatever he did, he could not establish any winnings. His pile of chips dwindled.

He cashed in the remaining chips and journeyed into the night, searching for another game. Billiards caught his eye. He turned a corner around a familiar tavern, and found himself pushing his way through a crowd toward a green table and the clacking, rolling balls. Soon it was his turn to challenge the current winner. Tesla placed a large bet, enough to sustain interest in the game. He broke the balls with the first shot, but none went in.

His opponent sank three colored balls during the first round.

Tesla called, and made, six shots. The other player cleared the table, but failed to place the eight ball. Tesla caught up with him, but also failed to pocket the eight ball.

The black ball dropped into a side pocket on the very next shot. Tesla lost money. The evening was utterly miserable; the events had confirmed his father's most dire warnings.

He returned to his father's house. Milutin was seated in his study, reading the Bible under the yellow glare of the gas lamp. They ignored each other as Nikola went upstairs to bed. All the next day, his father ignored him.

Niko went to the library and read books until sunset. By night, he was visiting the taverns and cafes, stealing into the back rooms and sitting morosely at the card tables. He lost more money.

His days were excruciating. His father had all but disowned him.

Nikola was obsessed not so much with making money but with perfecting the mathematical probabilities of receiving certain cards, or Newton's laws of motion applied to the physics of billiard tables. But he was successful at neither task. When the very last of his money from occasional winnings had dwindled away, Nikola begged his mother to give him any money she could spare. She did not argue, as he expected. Instead, she smiled gently.

"Here. I have borrowed some money for just this occasion."

Nikola was horrified. "I cannot do this."

"Why not?"

"I-I can't take this money!"

"Why not, Nikola?"

"Because if I...if I fail to win this amount twice over, I will have...I will have..."

"What will you have, Nikola?"

"Never mind. Put it away. Please—get it out of here."

"I will put this money back. But you must take a little money, some of my own that I have saved."

Nikola stared at her. His expression fell. He looked tired, impossibly tired, and much older.

"You did well your first year at the Polytechnic Institute, Nikola. Perhaps they will take you back if you demonstrate some ability to live a stable life."

Nikola's face was dark, glum.

She went upstairs. He could hear her moving about in the attic, then she returned down the stairs a few moments later.

"Here, Nikola. Take this money instead."

"What is this for?"

"If you take this, do one thing with it. Promise me one thing, and it's yours."

"Yes?"

"Take this money and go to Prague. Go to the University there. I can arrange for you to attend. If your father sees that you are serious about returning, he might help you for another year."

Tesla was silent. He looked deeply into his mother's eyes for a long time. Finally, he scooped the money out of her hands and into his pockets. Within a few days he was on a train headed for Prague. He had been thoroughly sobered by the confrontation with his mother.

During his second year at the Polytechnic Institute, the science of telegraphy had undergone a revolution in the United States. Two upstarts, a man named Gray and a man named Bell, were contending for preeminence in acoustic telegraphy in court battles, while another man named Edison was establishing telephone companies throughout the United States and Europe. Edison had even demonstrated some kind of a voice-recording machine. This man Edison was someone to keep an eye on.

Tesla renewed his determination to finish engineering school and contribute great inventions to his astounding age. He remembered the words of Professor Poeschl:

"Impossible!" The very word defied Nikola.

He stayed in Prague only long enough to take a job in Maribor. A friend of the Tesla family informed him of employment opportunities at the Bell Company. Maribor was near Gratz; Nikola planned to return there after acquiring new funds. The job paid sixty florins a month. Tesla kept the job as an unskilled electrician for twelve months, during which time he lived "very modestly" and saved a considerable sum.

He waived the Institute at Gratz in favor of the less expensive college in Prague; it was a very good university, and he had saved enough to last two years. Added to his two years at the Polytechnic Institute, this would complete the four years necessary for him to acquire a master's degree.

His father died during his first year in Prague. Nikola felt a hollow gap open up inside of him when he received the news. He had yet to accomplish the things he wanted his father to see. Again, he tried not to think of Daniel. He applied his mind exclusively to the task of learning the practical applications of electricity.

In 1879, the clever American inventor Thomas Edison announced the debut of the light globe.

Tesla was twenty-four when he left the University at Prague for a job with the newly created Bell Company in Budapest. The prospects looked promising— except there was no job opening. No such company.

There had been a company proposal a few months before. Money had even been promised by the government. Perhaps, someday, a telephonic system would be developed, extending all the way to Paris. Someday.

Nikola was stunned, then despondent. The clerk suggested he should apply for work with the government. Tesla fled from the room.

The next day, he was employed as a draftsman for the Hungarian Government Central Telegraph Office. His talent sparked attention, and the Inspector-in-Chief placed him in a key position in the engineering department. His duties expanded, including everything from drawing diagrams to calculating costs of proposed projects—and redesigning telephone equipment.

Tesla found the diaphragms in the microphones inefficient: he instantly designed an extra-sensitive sound adjuster. It reproduced human voices with almost perfect clarity. He went on to improve circuitry, transmission lines, and components. If only he could liberate electricians from reliance on direct current!

He created a superior sound-repeater. The idea came to him in a flash as he went to bed one night.

He had been transferred to the Telephone Exchange. It had opened in the early part of 1881, and Tesla, at the age of twenty-five, had been placed in charge of the facility. He had virtually redesigned the telephone.

After seven to eight months, he had recreated the microphone, improved components utilizing ceramic materials instead of tubes and wires, and turned sound-repeaters into loudspeakers, amplifiers. He had worked himself into a state of jubilant exhaustion while fueling his body on a scant diet. One night in the late summer, he crawled to bed after a particularly demanding day but could not fall asleep. He needed sleep. His head ached. His eyes burned. His heart pounded. The ticking of the clock increased in volume until it jarred him, and when the dawn crept through the window, it glared so brightly Tesla buried his face in the pillow.

He tried not to breathe. The gushing roar of his lungs deafened him.

Something dreadful pounded down the hallway. The walls seemed to vibrate with booming thunder.

The doorknob had clattered and clanged like a loud bell, then the maid stepped into the room.

The maid leaned over Nikola and yelled, "Is everything alright, mister Tesla?"

He wrapped pillows around his head and started to moan, but his own voice stung his ears.

The maid shouted, "Oh, my god, mister Tesla is ill!" She hurried out of the room, the sound of her feet on the floor like thunder.

Lying in bed, feverish, flushed with heat, then racked by cold chills, Tesla felt his strength spill out of his body. His consciousness drained with his strength until his brain was merely haunted by the ghost of a mind.

CHAPTER SIX

Breakthrough

For weeks Nikola languished, bedridden, while his acute sensitivity to light and sound intensified. The slow passage of time became the most agonizing sensation of all.

He summoned his feeble will to write notes to the doctor, the nurse, or the housekeeper. Such tasks as sipping a tepid bowl of soup, swallowing the doctor's potassium pills, or struggling to the washroom and toilet in the morning were impossible ordeals for him.

He shivered. His skin trembled and quivered. He convulsed spasmodically at times. A nurse had been stationed at his bedside, and the strangeness of Tesla's condition horrified her; neither she nor the doctor had ever seen anything like this. They stared uneasily at the pale body.

His heart palpitated violently. The doctor recorded heartbeats at the rate of 160 per minute, and even up to a frightening 260 beats per minute. Sometimes his heartbeat would fail, and long moments would pass while the physician checked desperately for a pulse.

His diminished consciousness *became* his amplified senses. He could still hear the clock ticking, though it had been removed from his room. The ticking echoed from three doors down the hall.

The physician in attendance confided to the hospital staff that he had never seen or read or heard about anything resembling Tesla's condition. He requested consultations with other doctors, and within weeks medical circles throughout Budapest were enthralled by this mysterious ailment—"unique and incurable."

"Doctor, does the potassium seem to help?"

"Potassium is for the nervous system. Of course it is helping."

"Doctor, do you suppose he can hear us now, even down a flight of stairs?"

"Good God, I hope not."

Tesla's bed had been placed on blocks of hard rubber to deaden the vibrations of the street traffic pounding through the floor into the frame.

After weeks of insomnia, Tesla was finally able to drift to sleep one night when the sounds from the city streets were especially quiet. He awoke at noon the following day. As mysteriously as the affliction struck, it suddenly abated.

The nurse was astounded. She dared not speak, fearing he had not overcome the malady. When Tesla motioned for her to draw near, she gasped and leaned forward unsteadily.

"Where...have...I...been?"

She fled from the room and down the stairs, returning with the doctor. Tesla was sitting up in bed. They froze. Faking composure, the doctor asked, "How are you feeling, young man?"

Tesla blinked. "I'm confused."

After a thorough examination, the doctor determined that the patient had recovered from his mysterious ailment.

His first nonmedical visitor was his friend Anital.

Anital Szigety was a mechanic who worked at the Telephone Exchange. He was also an athlete. He was a happy, smiling chap with long brown hair, broad shoulders, and a wide mustache. He had also known Tesla from the University in Gratz, which they both had attended, and both had graduated with high honors. Now, he was helping to implement Tesla's innovations.

Szigety visited Nikola upon first hearing of his recovery. They talked about the mysterious illness, they talked about good weather in February (a miracle)—everything except Tesla's future with the Telephone Exchange. His "breakdown" had thrown his future with the company into doubt, despite the many miracles he had performed for them. His reliability, not his productivity, were in question.

Anital Szigety cheered the young electrician up: he visited Tesla every afternoon to play chess and entice him into accompanying him on long walks. He convinced Tesla to pursue physical training to guard against ill health; when Nikola's strength had returned, he and his friend were off to the city park in Budapest to run in wide circles under the trees.

Then they returned to Tesla's hotel room to discuss engineering problems.

"Something is troubling you, Nikola," Szigety said as they sat down.

"It is a blankness that I have been left with, Szigety, after this illness."

"Tell me about it, Nikola."

"It is—it—"

"Perhaps not now...."

"No! I must. It is the problem of alternating current. We have discussed it before, Szigety, almost endlessly."

"I don't see what can be done about it—"

"I was thinking about it every minute, even as I worked, until..."

"You never lost touch with your job, Nikola, although we could tell you were preoccupied."

"I can't remember a thing! I thought about the problems and the complexities, and now I can't remember anything. None of it."

"I'm sure it will come back. Perhaps now is not the time to solve engineering problems."

"It is a blank spot in my mind, Szigety. It is not there. But if I can get a magnetic field to rotate! That's all it would take: inducing rotation in a magnetic field."

"Just make a magnet that changes polarity very fast!"

They laughed, and Nikola finally felt liberated, set free.

"Perhaps, Nikola, you will invent a battery that changes the polarity of its terminals over and over again!"

"That's the problem Szigety—reliance on batteries."

"Then we must build a better generator, Nikola."

"We need a new type of generator."

They joked about the problem until Tesla resigned himself to the futile notion that, unless some wild breakthrough occurred, he would have to begin his research on alternating current all over again.

Szigety stayed for dinner and left when his host grew tired. Tesla went to bed shortly after sunset.

He experienced those familiar visions that accompanied the onset of slumber: he dangled in the midst of a void of lucid blue, then shifting flecks of green advanced, sparkling, overtaking his senses. Twirling prisms of light were all he could see. Then—a gray void, filled with billowing clouds, which he molded into familiar shapes with the power of his imagination. He awoke the next morning refreshed.

He needed to apply for reinstatement at the telephone exchange but was unable to face this task. Not when he felt so refreshed. Instead, he read books and articles. This year, 1882, was a grand year for science: Thomas Edison was busy showing off incandescent lighting in the Americas, and the noisy debate stirred up by Darwin was still raging in the halls of European natural science. Tesla championed Darwin's theory: it did away with the need for a creator, and it justified Tesla's belief that human beings, like all other animals, were "meat machines." After death followed oblivion. Naturally.

Szigety and Nikola walked to the city park, where they took off trotting up the hills, along the winding paths between the wooded areas. Nikola broke from his run at the edge of a glade that sloped into a gentle hillside.

"Come up the hill, Anital, and see the sunset!"

"Slow down, Nikola! Let me catch up with you!"

Tesla had reached a point between two trees and was reveling in the colors of the sunset. Prismatic rays gleamed through layers of wispy golden clouds. He called out,

"The glow retreats, done in the day of toil;

It yonder hastes, new fields of life exploring!

Ah, no wing can lift me from the soil,

Upon its track to follow, follow soaring!"

He completed the stanza from Goethe's *Faust*, then snapped into a rigid stance. He pressed his arms against his sides. His back stiffened. He threw his head back, unnaturally.

"Nikola—what is wrong?"

"Look! Look, Szigety. Look at the sun!"

"I see nothing!"

"Look at it! Look at the sun!"

"Let us rest, Nikola…"

"Watch me!"

"What? What is this?"

"Watch me! Watch me reverse it!"

Szigety looked from the sunset to Tesla, bewildered.

"What!?"

"Watch me! Watch me reverse it!"

"Let us sit and rest for a while!"

"Don't you see it?"

Szigety glanced at the sun, then looked back at Tesla, then spied a park bench farther down the slope.

"The sun is reversing! See it, Szigety!"

"But Nikola, I see nothing!"

"And what is that sound? That humming? Can you hear that?"

"A sound? I hear nothing—"

"It is coming from over there! Follow me, Szigety!"

Before Anital could protest, Nikola hurried toward the sunset, around the branches of the trees. Szigety, frustrated and concerned, followed.

"Do you hear it? That wonderful sound!"

"Nikola, come back with me! We will both rest—"

"There it is!"

"There is what, Nikola?"

"Look! There! There it is—my machine!"

"What? I see no machine—"

"There it is, Szigety! Hear how smooth it runs? See how smoothly it is running? There is no sparking, there is no commutator. There is only smooth motion and a steady hum. That is all!"

Szigety blinked and stared in mute amazement.

"See! See how easy it is. I reversed it. Now watch me: I will reverse it again. See? See how easy it is?"

"Nikola, are you ill?"

"Szigety! It is right here before me, my alternating current motor. I have solved the problem! Can't you see it right here in front of me?"

"Nikola, you are frightening me! There is nothing there!"

"It is the rotating magnetic field that does it, Szigety. It rotates and drags the armature around with it. Isn't it beautiful? Isn't it sublime? Isn't it simple? I have solved the problem. Now, I can die happy. But for now, I must live, I must return to work. I must build this motor, this generator, so I can give it to the world.

"No longer will men do hard tasks. No longer will men be slaves to labor. My motor will set them free, it will do the work of the world."

Tesla traced a smooth line in space with his hand, felt around invisible angles and contours, caressing the smooth casing of a machine only he could see. Finally, he stood upright again, walked back a few paces, and studied his perfect mental image. Szigety could only guess what his friend was seeing, visualizing. He studied Tesla, frowning.

"Like any motor, it can also be used as a generator." Tesla spoke in monotone and seemed to be speaking entirely for his own benefit. "I can turn the armature...." He quickly drew a diagram of the machine in the dirt with a stick he found nearby. Szigety stared at the simple lines, bewildered.

For Tesla, the barrier between vision and reality had dissolved for a time, and the result was a glimpse of the future, a future he would create with his own hands. He was about to embark on the greatest quest of his life—the creation of the polyphase induction motor and generator, and the advent of a new technology of alternating current.

CHAPTER SEVEN

Current

Not only was Nikola's future with the Telephone Exchange uncertain, the future of the company itself was uncertain. The Puskas brothers, owners of the company and friends of the Tesla family, responded to Nikola's sudden loss of employment by sending him to Paris with a letter of recommendation for a position with the Continental Edison Company.

He was received by Charles Batchelor, a tall stately Englishman with a fine black mustache.

"This is quite a letter of recommendation," Batchelor commented. "'There is not an electrical problem that this young man cannot solve'—that is mercifully high praise, Mr. Tesla."

Nikola gazed out the window. Autumn colors, bathed in the yellow glow of afternoon, splashed the city streets below. "Thank you, Mr. Batchelor. I can accomplish whatever I apply my mind to."

"That's extraordinary—if it's true. The Puskas credit you with having improved voice diaphragms and repeaters for telephones. Is that true?"

"Yes, that is true."

"Very interesting. And—compensation?"

"My contribution to my company! The Puskas brothers have been friends of the Tesla family for a long time."

"I see. Fine. Now—the plant foreman will assign an assistant to you, and you will be in charge of maintenance and repairs. Among other things, you will be in charge of modifications whenever we implement new machines and new systems. Do you understand?"

"Perfectly, sir."

His office was established in a small room with a desk and a filing cabinet. Two walls were glass: he could view the assembly lines in the manufacturing facility and even look into the engineering department on the far side of the factory. Tesla soon found out that his job consisted of gathering teams of workers and taking brief, exhausting trips to France and Germany.

The autumn chilled into an unpleasant winter. He was busy solving the problems of others and had no time for his own projects. His spontaneous ideas continued to take form in his mind and find their way to drawing tables, then to modifications and improvements of existing systems, innovations even Mr. Edison might appreciate—or envy. Years later, he wrote, "When natural inclination develops into a passionate desire, one advances toward his goal in seven-league boots. In less than two months I evolved virtually all the types of motors and modifications of the system."

Tesla soon found Edison Continental unresponsive to his plans for alternating current. He became insistent, but his insistence was met with indifference, then intolerance.

Finally, Batchelor took him aside in the corridor and delivered a staunch warning: "Mr. Tesla, you have contributed some excellent improvements to our dynamo system. The company appreciates that, as well as your uncanny problem-solving ability. But you are violating company policy by even discussing alternating current, much less a full-scale conversion to it. In this enterprise, mere mention of alternating current is an infraction. Do I make myself clear?"

Tesla scowled. He leaned forward and stared into Batchelor's eyes. "On whose authority is this company policy dictated?"

"Word of Thomas Edison himself, sir."

"I see."

"I hope so, Mr. Tesla: the future of electricity is in his hands at this moment."

"... I see."

"Very good, sir. Now, can you have the plans ready for our improved dynamos? When can we begin implementing them?"

Tesla shook his head. "I have the plans ready. The blueprints are being drawn up now, according to my specifications."

"Very good. But you have no idea when they will be ready?"

"By-evening." Tesla continued to scowl darkly, but Batchelor was dutifully, even jovially, ignoring it.

"In the meantime, Nikola, you have a job to prepare for in Strasbourg."

The Edison Continental Company had received word the day before that the lighting plant in a German railroad station in Strasbourg had just been rejected by its principle customer—the German government.

During the opening ceremony of the lighting factory, while German royalty sat before a speaker from the electrical company, the demonstration lights had been switched on—and the short-circuit that resulted blasted a hole through the wall. The explosion prompted Emperor William I to cancel the plant as a subsidiary of the government. He had been one of the spectators of the debacle.

Batchelor promised Tesla a bonus if he could repair the electrical malfunction and save their alliance with the Germans. Tesla spoke fluent German, which was another advantage of sending him to Strasbourg.

He was met at the station by Mr. Bauzin, the mayor of Strasbourg. He had been escorted by a team of workers who were ordered to gather some crates he had shipped from Paris aboard the same train. The boxes were taken to a local machine shop. Arrangements had already been made with the machinists to assemble the contents of the boxes. Mr. Bauzin escorted Tesla to his hotel room, where his baggage was duly checked, then on to the Strasbourg railway station to inspect the malfunction at the lighting plant.

Instead of going right to work, Tesla was asked to fill out a series of forms.

The next day, he was also instructed to fill out a few brief forms.

Tesla spent day after day hunched over stacks of complicated forms, answering detailed questions and writing "No Answer" to the endless succession of unanswerable questions.

Paperwork assailed Tesla for several weeks. Red tape included a full inventory of the lighting plant and manufacturing facility, plus related installations. He was also required to write updated reports on the status of the defective generator. He finished this with an estimate of the time and necessary materials to complete the repairs. His nights were spent at the machine shop, fashioning a working model of the very motor he had seen a year ago, in the park, with Szigety. He had not seen Anital in almost a year.

At last, the motor had been built—just as the repairs on the generator had been completed.

The improved generator was successfully demonstrated, and Tesla was hailed. M. Bauzin had taken an interest in Tesla's completed polyphase motor. It also performed flawlessly. Tesla's assistant and Mr. Bauzin were the only ones present during this second demonstration. As the machine spun, whirring quietly, Tesla explained the advantages of alternating current over direct current. Mr. Bauzin listened, patiently at first, then with a sense of awe and wonder. Tesla switched the polarity of the current: the armature froze, then, with a snap, spun instantly in the opposite direction.

"The motor can be used as a generator, the generator can be used as a motor. The electromagnets spin the armature, producing power. Electrify the armature and rotate it, and you generate current."

"I see. This is exciting news! Mr. Tesla, I believe I can contact investors for you. I know many prominent citizens of Strasbourg who would like to have a chance to develop such a system."

Tesla was ecstatic. At last—he had a chance to demonstrate his polyphase system, first to the business community of Strasbourg, and soon to the world.

The businessmen were summoned to the plaza in the town square the next day. They mulled about the platform on which the strange new machine was mounted, and commented in Tesla's presence, "This had better be good!" "What does it do?" "What is the potential here?"

Tesla leaned over the machine and flipped a switch. The machine growled, then hummed. The armature spun smoothly, rapidly. The businessmen studied the machine, then one of them asked, "Is this all?" The small crowd muttered with discontent. Frowns fell like shadows across their faces. They stepped back and wandered away from the machine. They clustered on the grass and began talking privately.

"Don't you see?" Tesla cried. "Don't you see? Don't you understand?"

The men moved away from the platform and the machine.

Tesla was calling them back, waving his arms. "This machine can liberate the world! It can liberate men—save us from drudgery, spare us from toil! Don't you see? Don't you understand?"

The men dispersed, but they did not stop grumbling.

"Apparently, they did not see. Apparently, they did not understand."

"Perhaps it wasn't dramatic enough...."

"Perhaps you shouldn't have spoken of liberating the common men from toil."

"What do you mean?"

"Look at them! They aren't interested in the common citizens and their toil. They're concerned with making profits on their investments."

"Is that all?"

"Yes, that is all, I'm afraid."

"But—this could be the biggest—"

"Yes, indeed, it could! But until you make it something that those men will want to buy and sell, it looks like it will remain the mechanical curiosity that could, incidentally, liberate the hardworking masses. Yes, it could—I do not dispute that. But what profit do businessmen see in the liberation of the men who work for them?"

"I don't understand..."

"I'm afraid you want to liberate the workforce that supports these gentlemen, Nikola. What profit is there for a businessman who lets his labor force be liberated from him?"

Tesla shook his head, then turned the machine off.

"Come with me, Nikola. You—and you—put the machine away and take it back to the station at once. Nikola, come with me."

Nikola trudged silently after the mayor, whose carriage took them to his manor. There he consoled Tesla in his study with several carefully preserved bottles of St. Estephe 1801.

"These bottles were left after the invasion of Alsace."

"I am grateful, Mr. Bauzin."

"Drink, Nikola. This was still a very valuable day."

"In what way, Mr. Bauzin?"

"It was not a performance, sir. It was a rehearsal."

"What do you mean?"

"Think of it this way: you have experience at preparing such a demonstration! You will know what to do better the next time."

Tesla tipped his glass and tasted the tart, aromatic wine.

He was off the next day, aboard a train returning to Paris. He was relieved. At last he could claim his bonus and get on with the task of improving the Edison dynamos—they needed it. They were so badly designed. Tesla arrived at his office the next morning with complete plans in his mind to overhaul, retool, and mass-produce an improved system of motors and dynamos, as well as a new type of regulator for the dynamos.

His enthusiasm died when he learned that no bonus was forthcoming and that his modifications and improvements of the Edison dynamos had been noted, accepted, and would be implemented when deemed profitable. By afternoon he resigned.

Batchelor took Tesla aside and promised him a new position with much more authority and access to more resources, as well as a letter of recommendation. "Go to the states, Nikola," Batchelor advised. "There are opportunities there that just do not exist here. Oh, Europe is where the money is, but it's old wealth, Nikola. These people have been sitting on family fortunes for so long they don't know how to stand up anymore, if you know what I mean."

"I think I understand, sir."

"I'll send you with a letter to Thomas, written to him directly. Take it to him yourself. I'll be bound for the states tomorrow, noon, myself—but don't wait for me to arrive. Mr. Edison frequently sends me to the New Jersey laboratory while he stays in New York City, conducting business."

"So, I am to take your letter—"

"I have already mentioned you to him in my correspondences. With a letter of recommendation from me to him, I could open doors for you in the states no one else could qualify for. Use this opportunity I give you, and you will go far."

Tesla listened intently. Before he left Batchelor's office, he pocketed an envelope containing a very simple message:

> I KNOW TWO GREAT MEN, AND YOU ARE ONE OF THEM.
> THE OTHER IS THIS YOUNG MAN.
>
> SINCERELY,
> CHARLES BATCHELOR

CHAPTER EIGHT

Voyage

The train pulled away from the station. Nikola snatched his boarding pass off the counter and pushed his way through the crowd on the loading platform. The train chugged, pushing skirts of steam into the morning air, slowly pushing down the track.

"Aaaaaaalllllll—aboard!"

He caught up with the train and launched himself onto the railing beside the rear door of a passenger car. The conductor made way for him, and he was inside at once.

"Ticket, sir."

His boarding pass was gone. His hands flashed from pocket to pocket, and he discovered that his wallet was gone. His boarding pass must have fluttered out of his pocket as he ran. His wallet was with his baggage, which was—

"Sir, has the baggage been loaded on board?"

"We finished loading the baggage on board a long time ago."

"I'm sorry I was late—my carriage was misdirected—"

"Fare, sir?"

"Oh, I have that, let me assure you.... " He searched his pockets for coins. He gathered all the loose change he was carrying and paid the fare exactly. Now he had no money left over.

He strode to the baggage compartment to see if his bags had been loaded aboard and found, to his dismay, they had not. He trudged back sullenly and found himself an empty seat. He stared out of the train window at the passing scenery, the farms and vineyards of France.

At the harbor, he desperately explained his predicament to the steamship officials. They listened to his pleads. The officials agreed that if no one showed up to claim his berth, he could board at the last minute.

When the steamer's horn sounded its two low notes and the steamship engines roared and made the dark water churn, when the giant ship was flanked by tugboats, Tesla was granted permission to go aboard and claim his berth.

Amid little fanfare, the *Saturnia* departed. Tesla stood on deck, watching the harbor skyline slide away, replaced by the restless blue sea. Hollow winds of emotion blew through him. He would be arriving in America without a penny.

However, he still had the letter from Batchelor. He could feel it in his shirt pocket. Soon he would be meeting with Thomas Edison. He would have a superior job, then he would have money. Then he would deliver his miracles to the world.... The steamship pushed through the restless water in the direction of New York Harbor.

Tesla dined in silence in the captain's quarters. The captain was a bearded man who was not given to idle conversation. This suited Tesla. The ship's steward and first mate were also silent men, as were the preferred passengers, all of whom were European businessmen.

Once, Tesla mentioned his polyphase system to them. He was not disappointed at another failure to arouse interest. He finished his dinner in silence.

Day after day, the steamship *Saturnia* surged forward through the Atlantic without incident.

Nikola was in his quarters one night when he heard a disturbance on the deck. He left his cabin to investigate and stepped onto the upper deck in time to see a small, frantic melee erupt in the midst of a crowd of officers and crew members. The crew had been voicing grievances with the stern captain. Tesla had befriended some of the crew members and was sympathetic to their claims of unjust treatment. When the fight broke out on the lower deck, Tesla leaped over the railing and landed on his feet in the middle of the mutiny.

An officer swung a belaying pin—Tesla blocked it and struck the officer in the face. A fist struck him harmlessly in the cheek. Tesla deflected blow after blow, then delivered a few lucky punches of his own. When a surge of officers and a handful of loyal crewmates subdued the riot, they found Tesla in the middle of the frenzy, still swinging his fists defiantly. They arrested him but quickly let him go; he was reprimanded for being a "possible troublemaker" and was barred from the captain's dining quarters for the rest of the voyage.

Tesla was standing on the prow of the ship, looking out at the horizon, when the *Saturnia* reached the eastern seaboard. The New York City skyline loomed over the water, and soon the harbor materialized. He had eagerly awaited his arrival in America for so long. Charles Batchelor had assured him it was a land of promise!

He sailed past the Statue of Liberty, nearly completed. It had been designed by the great sculptor Bartholdi as a show of solidarity between the United States and the people and government of France. It was to be unveiled in October. Perhaps there was hope for peace between nations after all.

Tesla had been told that the president, Chester Alan Arthur, was a statesman.

Americans thought of a statesman as a politician who did not scandalize his office irreparably by the end of his term. No one knew for certain if President Arthur was even a United States citizen. Some said he was Canadian.

Perhaps the alliance between Canada and the United States was further proof that peace between the nations was possible. Tesla was excited by unlimited possibilities as the *Saturnia* pulled into port.

America.

PART TWO

Edison

CHAPTER NINE

Fire

The boy dangled the burning match over the pile of straw.

He had tossed the straw down from the hayloft and piled it against the beam that supported the hayloft. A red rooster strutted on the railing, high overhead. A few white hens scratched and clucked in the corners of the barn, between the sacks of feed and bales of hay. The mare and the cow were in their stalls. The shadows smelled musty and the air was quiet.

The flame burned his fingertips. He let the match fall. It tumbled, end over end, nearly dying before it vanished between the yellow strands. A puff of smoke appeared. Hungry yellow flames ate the blades of straw.

The boy stared at the fire.

Flames leaped and crackled and whitened. Smoke flew upward, changing from white to black, billowing above the hayloft. The smoke frightened the animals: The rooster cackled nervously. The mare whinnied. The cow lowed.

The fire brightened and roared. Heat smacked him in the face. He remembered his mother's favorite saying: "Hotter than the hinges of Hades!" He knew that hinges—and latches—always got burning hot on a summer day. He turned and ran. He reached the back door of the barn. The latch didn't burn his fingers, and he escaped into the sunlight, shutting the door after him.

He dashed to the top of a nearby hill and sat under an oak tree, contemplating death. Black smoke billowed from the cracks in the roof of the barn. The animals wailed their piercing, wild death-screams.

Orange fire burst from the roof and walls—just as the animals fell silent. His mother burst from the farmhouse and ran across the field. She waved her arms and screamed. She caught sight of her tiny son sitting peacefully under the oak tree.

"Oh, Al, what have you *done?*"

He stiffened.

She strode up to him and yanked him by the armpit and dragged him to the farmhouse. "Wait until your father gets home, young man!"

She threw him into his bedroom and slammed the door shut. The boy feared his father would beat him.

He feared the man more when he didn't. His father came home around sunset. He stormed into the room, bellowing with rage, saying nothing coherent, drunk again and violent with words.

The boy spent the night sitting upright in bed, fearing what his father would do to him in the morning and remembering, over and over again, how the animals had perished in the flames.

CHAPTER TEN

Water

"Hurry!"

"Where we goin'?"

"Hurry! Follow me!"

Two boys ran down the rocky slope. A red-wine-colored sunset sailed across the sky. They reached an embankment and the older boy climbed down steep boulders toward the deep, dark water.

"C'mon! C'mon for a swim!"

"Is it—is it alright, Al?"

"Whaddya mean is it alright?"

"It's just—"

"Sissy! Sissy, sissy, sissy!"

The older boy slipped out of his clothes, left them hanging on a branch, then plunged in. He swam underwater to the middle of the canal, then his head bobbed up and he cried out, "Sissy! Sissy! Sissy!"

"I'm coming! I'm coming!"

The younger boy undressed awkwardly and threw himself into the frigid water.

The older boy circled him like a shark. He splashed water into the younger boy's face, which made him gulp and choke—then his head went under. Fingertips danced just above the ripples.

His head appeared briefly, then slipped under again. The older boy circled silently.

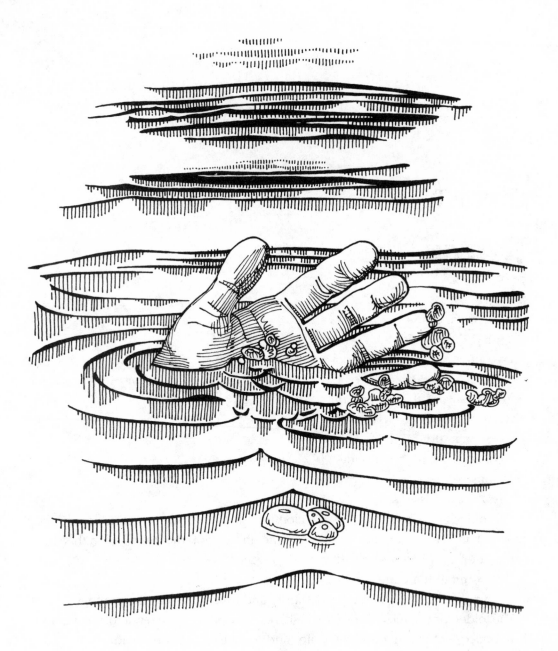

The fingertips danced, then went under.

Slowly, reluctantly, Al swam to the shore. He climbed, shivering, onto the boulders.

He dried himself off with his shirt, pulled on his pants, then climbed to the top of the embankment to sit under the darkening sky and watch the obsidian water.

He sat until the stars crystallized out of the darkness.

When the night blackened the world, he trudged home, barefoot.

His mother was waiting for him at the dinner table. She was a large, plain woman with a great jaw and hanging double chin. She looked up from her soup bowl. "Dinner's ready, young 'un."

"No thanky, Ma. I'm not feelin' right."

"What's wrong? You're all wet—have you been swimmin'?"

"Yes, ma'am, an' I think I got a chill."

"Sit down an' warm up on some stew."

"No thanky!"

"Al, you'll catch your death of cold, you will! You'll join Carlisle and Samuel and Eliza, you will! You don't know what it's like to be a mother, boy. You just don't know."

He stared at the stew pot in the middle of the table. Then he turned abruptly and went to the stairs.

"Alva?"

"Yes, ma'am?"

"You alright?"

"Yes, ma'am. Just a chill. That's all."

"There's somethin' peculiar goin' on, Alva. You're not tellin' me somethin'."

He was silent.

She tried to pry him open with questions and hard looks, but he did not respond. He departed up the stairs to his bedroom. Hours passed.

He sat upright, propped against the pillows, remembering the canal, the splashing of water, the head submerging, the water turning calm and the night descending....

His father returned home from the saloon in town. The voices of his parents blended as they spoke excitedly in hushed tones that meant mistrust. Someone pounded on the front door of the house. The boy shivered.

A man's deep voice was talking excitedly just outside the house—Al could tell where the voices were coming from. There were many people outside the house.

Al's mother added her voice to theirs, and the sounds of all the voices were stretched tight with alarm. Then the crowd departed. Al's father went with them. His mother returned inside. Her rocking chair creaked quietly. Ages passed. The front door boomed open again.

"Nancy!"

"Sam—ssssshhhh! Little Al is asleep upstairs, He wasn't feeling good...."

"Nancy, I've got to talk to Alva."

"Sam—you don't think he had anything to do—"

"I don't know. I aim t'find out!"

Footsteps thundered up the stairs. The bedroom door burst open. A tall man with wild, long hair and a tangled black beard burst inside.

"Thomas Alva, Mister Lockwood says his boy's been missin' since this afternoon. Says you a'been with him. You got anything t'say about that?"

Silence.

"I know you're awake, Al. Don't try to fool me."

Al slowly rolled over and moaned. "Pa?"

"Yes, boy?"

"Pa, promise y'won't...y'won't git mad 'r nothin'?"

"Boy, y'c'n keep yer promises!"

Footsteps clattered, flooded up the stairs. His mother burst into the room. She pushed herself between father and son.

"Sam! Get these men away!"

"I'm not sendin' anybody away until I find out what's goin' on. Now, Nancy—"

"Don't hurt him!"

"I wasn't goin' to—"

"Don't hurt him! Can't you see he's frightened out of his wits?"

"Nancy, I—"

She looked deeply into her child's eyes and quietly asked, "Were you with him?"

"Yes, ma'am."

"What happened?"

"We—we went for a swim...in the canal."

"The canal! Haven't I told you never to go there?"

"Yes, ma'am."

"Nancy? You hear that?"

"Sam, don't let them come in here!"

"Lemme talk to him!"

"Sam—"

"Lemme talk to him myself!"

"Sam, he's only a child—"

"Ma! Pa! He—he just didn't come back is all!"

Mr. Lockwood stood in the doorway.

Al repeated, whimpering, "He—he just didn't come back is all!"

Mr. Lockwood wailed in anguish. He staggered out of the doorway and into the hall with his hands clutching his head. Nancy pushed Sam out the door and into the hallway.

"Git! Y'all—git! Git out o' here! All of you!"

"Can't you see yer boy is in trouble again?"

"Yeah, Sam, he's your child—"

"Sam, I wouldn't take this lightly—"

Above the other voices, Nancy commanded the mob to leave.

Alva sat on his bed looking out the window until morning, remembering the fingertips stirring the water before they vanished—and the fire in the barn, just four years ago....

Chapter Eleven

Al

He had been beaten many times in the name of the Lord. His mother often beat him in the name of Our Lord Jesus Christ. His pa just plain beat him. His were really fierce beatings. After a while, they didn't hurt anymore. They even felt dreamy and strange after the pain went away. The schoolmaster, Reverend Engle, also beat Al in the name of the Lord, but even he didn't beat anywhere nearly as mean as his pa did. His pa was the meanest beater he knew.

Funny thing that the faithful beat less harshly than those of little faith, as his ma called his pa.

He was a sickly boy, tall and thin and frail. His head was too big, his forehead too wide. His mother thought he had the look of a genius.

He ran away from school often. He played hooky and got caught. That always led to a beating. He took time off from school because he got sick frequently. Instead of going back in the spring, when the weather and his health cleared up, young Al plotted to run away again and this time not get caught.

His mother explained everything with the Bible. She had read the Bible to him throughout childhood. At first, it filled him with wonder. Then the Bible stories sounded funnier than tales about elves and talking bunnies.

Experimenting—that was how to understand the secrets of nature. He learned that when he read *Parker's Natural and Experimental Philosophy*. The Reverend Engle had disapproved of that book, too.

Thomas Alva was his mother's last bastion of hope. Whenever he fell ill, every winter, she would wail at his bedside and remind him that she had already lost three of her dearly beloved children before he was even an infant: Carlisle died at the age of six, in the winter of '42, five years before Al was born. Four years before his birth, his brother Samuel died at three. Eliza also died at three, the same year he was born, in 1847. Little Al had all the ages and dates right because his mother reminded him often.

His sister Marion was eighteen years older than he; she was married and living far away. His brother, William Pitt, was also a lot older than he, but his mother did-n't like him much. That left Harriet Ann, and she was a lot older—and also a girl.

He remembered the voyage he had taken on the steamboat when he was five years old, the year he burned the barn down. His family had crossed Lake Erie to meet his grandpa, Sam. He was terrified of the old man.

He looked like his pa, only older and uglier. He had long white and black hair and a beard. He reeked of whiskey and cigar smoke, and coughed with the most terrifying sounds young Al had ever heard.

Al's father was always quick with a joke or funny story—anything to lighten the moment. But the old man knew no fun. He sat on his porch and scowled at the weather.

They spent the summer in the town of Vienna, right on Lake Erie, where Al learned to fish and swim. He also met his uncles. He liked his uncles.

Now he was back at home, in Port Huron. He was twelve. He had just read his father's favorite book, Thomas Paine's *The Age of Reason*. Now he understood his father better, why he was such a doubter. His father was a Freethinker.

His father had been profiting from real estate over the past few years, and sel-dom beat him anymore. With a little money in the bank and a few fulfilled ambi-tions behind him—like the tower—he seemed happier now.

The tower had been his dream. It had taken him weeks to build. Two years ago, as Al recalled.

His father had bought an old farm, foreclosed on, and he hired some men to build the tower after he resold the farm.

It had been a hundred feet tall. Al was appointed gatekeeper. He charged visi-tors twenty-five cents to climb to the top and an additional ten cents to look through the beat-up old telescope at the horizon. Once, he had taken six hun-dred people in the course of a day to the top of what the neighborhood called "Edison's Tower of Babel."

The local papers proclaimed it to be "The Highest Tower in America." Young Al would stand on the observatory platform with his telescope and "sweep the skyline like a Columbus discovering a new world."

That was a long time ago. For the past year, the tower was mostly abandoned. It had become rickety, weather-beaten. Fainthearted visitors never made it to the top. Even the courageous bolted for the stairs when strong winds made it sway. It had been dismantled last winter.

At twelve, Al decided to say good-bye to his childhood self. He started by dismissing his nickname, Al.

He insisted his friends and family call him Tom or Thomas. Anything but Al.

CHAPTER TWELVE

Science

At thirteen, Tom decided to be a great scientist. To be a great scientist, he needed to have an assistant. Along came happy, willing Michael Oates—"Dutch Boy," as Tom nicknamed him.

Taller, thin, gawky, Michael Oates helped with dissections, gathering and classifying minerals and conducting many, many chemistry experiments.

Tom built a lab in the basement. On a stained workbench was an elaborate assortment of glassware, mostly culled from junk pits and abandoned houses. Some of it Tom picked up on his excursions, by train, to Detroit. There was a chemical factory there, and it was easy to purchase marvelous compounds from them. He once terrified a servant so mightily that the man nearly died. Tom explained it was an "experiment" to see if "excessive fright" would turn a black man "white with fear." Neither perpetrator nor victim ever said what the experiment had been that had induced so much fear.

Michael Oates did not appreciate the direction some of his mentor's experiments were taking.

Tom's arithmetic was terrible—even though he had a knack for making money. He had a fun side, too, and could charm anyone at times. Michael Oates appreciated that quality about him.

Tom had tested self-built flying machines: he nearly broke his legs more than once. He recruited a volunteer for a much loftier approach to the problem of flight. Selected to volunteer was Michael Oates.

Tom explained what sounded like a good idea several times to Michael Oates—inflating the human body with gas. Gas was lighter than air. The inflated person would float to the ceiling—or to the sky.

"Let me explain again: the body makes its own gas. I just want to speed up the process."

"That's the part I don't understand, Tom...."

"I've been studying the effects of Seidlitz powders and I'm convinced they will do it, Michael. Seidlitz powders. They're the key to flight."

"Huh?"

"Seidlitz powders. Yes, Seidlitz powders."

"I *still* don't understand...."

Tom was indignant. "Well, Seidlitz powders give off gas when they get dissolved in acid. And—dummy—do you know what yer stomach has in it? Acid! Real strong acid, too. Hydrochloric acid."

"Oh! I see. I didn't know that."

"Let me prepare the solution...."

He dissolved the powders in a flask nearly full of water and sternly commanded Michael Oates to drink it. Reluctantly, the young assistant gulped down the milky solution. He grimaced—then doubled up in agony, dropping the flask to the floor.

"Don't worry. That's just the beginning of the gas reaction."

Oates gagged, choked, sputtered. His eyes bulged and his face went from purple to white.

"Oh, Michael, you sissy, you're not sick—"

Oates retched. His lips were frothy. He trembled violently.

Tom stopped trying to explain to his friend that he wasn't really sick and backed away in horror. "Now—now—it's alright! Yes, yes! I have a solution! I have an *antidote!*"

Michael Oates writhed on the floor, moaning, farting boisterously, and shaking spasmodically.

"Here! Take this!"

Oates struggled to gulp down another mixture. Then he screamed.

"Here! Drink *this!* I *know* it's the antidote!"

"Here! I'm *sure* this is the antidote!"

"Michael—drink *this!* I *know* it'll work!"

The cellar door burst open. Tom's mother screamed, "Thomas Alva—what have you done?"

"I—I—I—I—I—"

"Tell me rightly, young 'un!"

Tom broke down and uttered a string of incoherent syllables.

"Seidlitz powders!" His mother heard what she needed to hear.

Michael Oates recovered miraculously—but not his basement laboratory. His mother smashed all the glassware and locked every bottle labeled Poison in a heavy box.

He reestablished a makeshift laboratory in the baggage car of the Grand Trunk Railway. He worked as a newsboy and candy butcher on the line from Port Huron to Detroit. The baggage car was also the publishing office and editor's desk of Tom's newspaper, the *Weekly Herald*.

There was much news in those days: a beleaguered nation, beset by turbulent economic and political forces, was sliding toward a civil war. Young Tom cared about politics only to the extent that range wars, riots, "Injun wars," political debates (Stephen Douglas accusing Lincoln of wanting to: "Vote, eat, sleep, and marry with Negroes!"), and railroad wars all became opportunities to make money. Then—*everything* became an opportunity to make money!

Tom had been working for Wilbur Storey at the time. Storey was a scowl-faced man with a handlebar mustache, always wearing a bill-cap that left his bald head exposed. He was of the opinion that "niggers," Jews, "Eye-talians," and various "people of color," should be treated like "Injuns" and put away on very small reservations without food or water.

Storey hated Lincoln's election to the presidency.

When the Battle of Fort Sumter broke out, Thomas thought it was the most exciting thing since the election of Lincoln, while Storey shouted that it constituted the downfall of the Union.

Thomas arrived extra early at Storey's office the morning after the Battle of Shiloh: after much begging and pleading, Tom bought 300 papers and Storey reluctantly advanced him 700 more.

"You'll be glad!" Tom called from the office doorway as he vanished into the street.

After the papers were loaded aboard the train, Tom leaped to the telegraph office and halted at the telegrapher's desk. "Have you seen the newspaper, sir?"

"Why? Should I have?"

"Battle o' Shiloh! Read alla boutit." He shoved a newspaper under the telegrapher's nose.

"Well?"

"I want you to announce it, sir."

The telegraph operator laughed.

"I'll pay you money, sir."

The telegrapher laughed again. "Lemme get this straight—yer offerin' t'pay me t'announce a story over the wires I haven't even received yet?"

"Yes, sir."

"That sounds like a bribe."

"Yes, sir."

"How much money?"

"Here."

The telegrapher took Tom's envelope and looked Tom over. His face was innocent—too innocent. He had just nonchalantly offered a bribe. "Where'd you git this?"

"Been savin' it, sir."

"I can tell! You really want to sell papers, don't you?"

"Yes, sir."

"Well, there's no harm in that. I just wonder why it hasn't come over the wires yet...."

"It's in print, sir."

"You'll sell your papers! Now—git outa here!"

Tom vanished out of the telegraph office and flew to the train, boarding the baggage car to hawk his papers. A crowd gathered instantly. "Battle o' Shiloh! Read alla boutit! Battle o' Shiloh—!"

The newspapers sold in a flurry.

At seven, the train pulled out. Tom stowed the rest of the papers and waited for his first stop, which was Utica. The telegrapher must have sent the message: a crowd was already eager to assimilate the "special edition." Tom raised the price from three cents to ten and sold out the allotment in minutes.

When the train reached Mount Clemens, he was selling them for thirty five cents. By the time the train reached Detroit, Tom had sold out.

To Tom, the words "Sixty thousand feared dead—maybe thousands more!" meant an opportunity to pull heaps of coins from the pockets of businessmen. He returned, gave Wilbur Storey his due, and left swiftly for the long walk home. This success made Mr. Storey trust Tom with his "message to Garcia."

One night, after Tom checked in with his earnings, he was told that Eber Brock

Ward, the famous millionaire, needed to send a message to his friend Captain Garcia. The message had to be delivered before dawn.

Captain Garcia's cabin was only fourteen miles away, but a storm had interfered with telegraph communications. Western Union couldn't get a messenger to the captain's house before morning. For fifteen dollars, Tom was hired—conditionally.

The condition was that Tom would hire another boy. "We'll surely need two lanterns," Tom explained.

"Eh? Why?" ·

"One will surely blow out along the way, especially on a night like this, sir."

"Hmmmm...lemme think...." Storey consented to let Thomas hire another boy and both would make the journey for thirty-five dollars. Of course, Tom hired the boy for ten. Nobody knew the difference.

Tom and his companion marched along the dirt road to Captain Garcia's cabin during a brief pause in the rain. Shadows fell away from the lantern light. The shadows contained bears.

"I don't like this!" the younger boy complained.

"Ssshhhh!" Tom thrust the lantern ahead as he strode down the dark and muddy road. The wind shrieked suddenly and brought rain and bitter cold. Tom could see bears in the depths of every haunted shadow.

"I don't like this, Tom!"

"Ssshhhhh! Shut up, will you?"

The journey continued without end into the long and perilous night. Unseen dangers were hidden within every shifting slab of black the lanterns could not illuminate. After an hour, the wind roared, hurled rain, and one of the lanterns went out. Both boys were hysterical. They ran until the younger boy fell and the second lantern almost went out. Gathering themselves up, steadying each other with false bravado, they plunged into the howling storm, the moonless night, toward the cabin of Captain Garcia.

In his terror, Tom became philosophical.

He decided that he really didn't like nature. In fact, he hated nature. Cold, stormy nature. Nature with bears and wolves in it. He hated it because it terrified him. After many hours, the second lantern went out.

"T-Tom! We're doomed!"

"Ssshhh! Don't say that!"

"Q-quick! Let's climb a tree!"

"Stupid! Bears can climb trees!"

By the time the foggy dawn replaced the moonless night, they caught sight of Captain Garcia's cabin. Blue smoke was streaming from the chimney. They delivered the message and were dismissed.

Tom never forgot the ordeal. He vowed to conquer nature.

The baggage conductor was a grizzled old Scot named Alexander Stevenson. He tolerated Tom's laboratory on wheels, and the rolling office for his scandal sheet. Of course, the "news" in it was mostly drivel: that rascal mostly made it up! The news in Storey's *Detroit Free Press* wasn't much more reliable, Stevenson noted. Some of it was intended as humor—"'Let me collect myself,' as the man said when he was blown up by a powder mill."

Only Tom Edison thought that was funny.

He had nearly blown his friend Michael Oates into the afterlife. Edison, Oates, and Jim Clancey had gotten ahold of some gunpowder and blew up a stump near an old icehouse by a church. Tom told Michael Oates to cover the fuse with his hat when it burned down. Michael Oates obeyed, and the stump exploded. Michael Oates flew, for the first time.

The icehouse collapsed. The cap sailed onto the top of the light tower overlooking the church.

The world's first baggage car laboratory came to an end when Alexander Stevenson detected a fire in the baggage car. Flinging the door open, he found Tom batting at eerie white flames sizzling through a pool of foul chemicals on the floor. Stevenson jumped in and stomped on the flames—not knowing that blazing phosphorus eats away anything it touches.

Stevenson screamed and fell against the baggage counter. He gripped his feet, burning his hands. Flinging overcoats and luggage off the racks and onto the pyre, he finally put it out, then screamed a torrent of invective at Tom while boxing him about the ears.

He felt his eardrums pop at each blow.

When the train stopped, Stevenson hurled out the remnants of the glassware, the bottles of chemicals, and the old printing press that cranked out the Weekly Herald, phony news stories and all. Then, Stevenson pitched onto the platform the young scientist who wanted to conquer nature.

Tom continued to work for Wilbur Storey.

A continuing news saga caught Tom's attention not long after the loss of his laboratory and printing press. It concerned one Mr. Morgan.

In May of 1861, Mr. Morgan, son of a prominent banker, was approached by two men, Simon Stevens and Arthur M. Eastman, who extended a wonderful opportunity to invest in the purchase and resale of five thousand U. S. Cavalry carbines. The profit was to be made in the steep resale value of the rifles—to be purchased for three dollars, fifty cents apiece and sold back to General Fremont, who was commanding Union forces in St. Louis. The rifles would be purchased there for twenty-two dollars each.

The rifles were defective—rotten stocks, rusted barrels—but they had been jury-rigged to fire a few shots on the battlefield before inevitably jamming.

Young Thomas was impressed by the sheer audacity of the scheme. In the reports and articles that followed, he learned that, although Fremont refused to authorize the transaction and 109,912 dollars remained unpaid, Stevens, Eastman, and Morgan sued the government in a federal court of claims and won fifty-eight thousand dollars. Young Thomas eagerly awaited every story that broke.

When Morgan was determined to have been the one who had signed the voucher for the first twenty-five hundred carbines, Edison applauded him. When he, Mr. Eastman, and Mr. Stevens received their full amount from the government, Edison revered him. When news of other "Deadhorse" claims came over the wires, whenever greedy entrepreneurs won court cases over fraudulent claims, Tom Edison and Wilbur Storey cheered.

Wilbur Storey openly supported the president of the Confederacy, Jefferson Davis. He attacked the Emancipation Proclamation. These attitudes impressed Thomas Edison.

Tom acquired a second printing press and started rolling out copies of another tabloid, *Paul Pry.* He enjoyed fabricating lies about famous people—and publishing them. His talent for fabrication flourished when he got a job as a telegraph operator. He had learned Morse code one winter, bedridden with bronchitis. He soon became fluent, and another of the things he and Michael Oates had experimented with was telegraphy.

Noticing that the fur of cats emitted sparks during lightning storms, Tom and Oates captured cats and rubbed them against wires and strips of metal. The results were negative. Infuriated tabbies left stinging scratches.

Tom was beginning to lose his hearing.

He had tried desperately to climb aboard a rolling train while carrying a double armload of newspapers out of Smith Creek Station. As he ran, the edge of the platform came dangerously close. The baggage conductor reached down and grabbed

Tom by the ears, lifting him into the baggage car. Tom screamed. Everything in his head loudly crunched and burst.

His hearing diminished rapidly.

He saved the life of little Jimmy MacKenzie in the summer of '62 by leaping off the Mount Clemens Station platform, dashing in front of a rolling boxcar and snatching the little boy off the track. His father, Mr. James MacKenzie, stood a few yards away, unaware.

Tommy Southerland, baggage man and witness, stood in MacKenzie's office boasting of Tom's heroism, telling how Tom's foot had nearly been crushed off.

A year later, at sixteen, Tom applied for a job as a telegrapher.

Mac taught him the trade by day and at night, in spite of his deafness, how to play guitar. Two weeks after he commenced training, Tom had built himself a telegraph. Then, he and several other boys were involved in a violent accident in Thomas Walker's jewelry store. Something about battery acids and "volatile compounds." The result was that he had "blown himself out of a job."

Mac rescued Tom again, and found him a new job at the Stratford Station in Ontario, along the Grand Trunk Railroad line.

He worked at night. He slept in the battery room. Sulfuric acid soaked his clothes from the puddles on the floor.

Telegraph operators were a crude, notorious bunch. They were nomads. Tom found himself in Adrian, Michigan, then Toledo, Ohio. Exotic, faraway places beckoned him: Cincinnati, Memphis, Louisville, New Orleans. It was idyllic, getting hired and fired, hopping trains and getting hired and fired again....

He'd lost a job because he invented a signal timer to do his "sixing" for him. "Sixing" was the custom of sending a "six" over the wire, once an hour after dark, so the other telegraph operators knew you were alright. When Tom wouldn't respond to their incoming messages but still sent his "six," a railroad investigator burst into the room unannounced and found Tom sleeping at his desk.

He was fired and nearly arrested in Canada when he failed to change a signal semaphore from "Danger" to "Caution."

Among the telegraph tramps Tom encountered during his wanderings as a plug operator, he encountered two mentors. One, Milt Adams, was the epitome of the gentleman telegrapher, dapper and dignified. Milt trained Tom at high-speed telegraphy.

His other source of inspiration was Hank Bogardus—"Bogie." He was a tramp telegrapher who was always borrowing money. He encountered Tom one night and

hustled him for five dollars, then vanished for several days. He cornered Tom again as he left the office at the end of his shift. Bogardus begged for ten more dollars.

"Bogie—you look so damned horrible I barely recognized you!" Then he caught a whiff of Bogie. "Ten dollars! You want ten dollars? Ha! Bogie, you only get five. That breath alone should *cost* you five dollars!"

Bogie had been a first-class man, but drinking and gambling claimed all of his earnings. He eventually died in a boxcar, frozen in the snow on the way to another job somewhere.

Tom applied his inventiveness to the task of electrocuting vermin in the various offices he worked in: his favorite trick was to electrify strips of metal stuck to the floor so that rats, touching parallel strips, would die.

Milt's training in high-speed telegraphy paid off twice. Tom became a first-class man.

He had failed to impress the Memphis telegraphers—they had been pretty fast, those boys. They resented the Northerner. The St. Louis operator was nicknamed "Chain Lightning." Tom's supervisor put him on the wire to "blow the kid up." Chain Lightning was fast, but so was Tom. The St. Louis operator tried every trick in the book, from slurring words together to shortening the longer words, dropping vowels and making contractions. Tom's accuracy became evident to anyone with practiced ears: he was sending the copy on at top speed and straightening it out at the same time. He had started fifty words behind, caught up, then sent his own message:

"—St. Louis—get—a—hustle—on!"

The Memphis operators cheered. Chain Lightning had been "rawhiding" Memphis for too long. One of the men called out, "Here's to the Yankee who can rawhide St. Louie's Electric Cyclone!"

He left Memphis for Cincinnati after the Southerners had "failed t'git th' look of th' slick operator into him."

He was in Cincinnati the night Lincoln was shot. He had been in the telegraph office of Western Union. Outside the front doors of the office, on the street below, a crowd of people had gathered, anxiously discussing something. Something important.

A messenger boy was sent outside to learn what was taking place.

The boy reappeared with a look of anguish. "The president's been shot!"

All eyes swept from the boy to the master-telegrapher. He looked up, puzzled at first, then shocked and horrified: he had been taking copy and sending it on so fast he ignored everything but his finger clicking against the telegraph key.

Tom lost that job too and wandered for two years between Boston and Montreal. There, he contacted Milt Adams during the Great Blizzard of '68. Milt cleaned Edison up and walked him to the office of Western Union manager George F. Millikan.

Millikan, a personable chap, had only one question: "When are you ready to work?"

Tom shouted: "Now!"

While Milt set up Edison on the line, Millikan secretly conspired with old-hat operators to "Put up a job on the jay from the Wolly West!" Someone wired ahead to New York City to put their fastest sender on the line "to salt the new man."

The New York sender was nicknamed Speed King. He nearly lived up to his name, until Tom Edison caught up with his rapid-fire word stream and fired off the message, "Say—young man—change off—and send with your other foot!" The Boston operators hooted and howled with laughter. Speed King had met his match.

All telegraphy then was "duplex" telegraphy: two messages sent over one wire in opposite directions. Many skilled operators said "quadruplex" telegraphy was impossible.

Milt Adams and Thomas Edison parted company in Boston. Milt headed for San Francisco, Edison for New York. Edison was obsessed with the problem of multiple-message telegraphy.

He carried his skills to the Gold Indicator Company, where he traded "services" for permission to sleep in the battery room.

The newly invented "electrical indicator" supplied and recorded gold quotations from the Gold Exchange on Wall Street. When the machine mysteriously malfunctioned, young Thomas repaired it as one of his duties.

On his own, Tom tried to create an improved electrical indicator. The device consisted of a spare Morse register he found on a shelf, rigged via clockwork to another embossing register. Tom controlled the speed at which the tape from one embossing register fed the telegraph tape into the second embossing register.

Sam Wallick, the office manager, ordered the "automatic repeater" to be disassembled.

Tom disconnected but did not dismantle the device. He and Ed Parmalee took it down to the Union Station, where Tom explained to the executives that his "automatic repeater" successfully automated the retransmission of messages, sending the embossing strip directly from one machine to the other. When Tom and Ed Parmalee tried to demonstrate their prototype, it failed. Tom was seized by a fit of rage. He hurled the machine violently onto the pavement, again and again in front of the office building.

His "automatic voting machine" failed too, although it worked in another sense: Congress had no need to record votes without taking advantage of the long-winded political custom of "fillibusterin'."

When the office of the Gold Exchange Company burst into "panic and pandemonium" one afternoon, Tom volunteered to repair the electrical indicator—at the exact moment that Dr. S. S. Laws stepped into the room He was not only Vice President of the company, but inventor of the machine.

"Fix it! Fix it, boy, and be quick!"

A broken contact spring had fallen between two gears. Tom removed it and reset the contact wheels at zero. The entire work force of the company was dispatched to the three hundred offices throughout the city for the purpose of resetting three hundred machines back to zero. Two hours later, gold quotes were sent, uninterrupted, throughout the city.

"What's that boy's name?"

"Tom Edison, sir."

"Very good. Tell him I'll put him on salary for three hundred a month."

Edison was working at the central office, 18 New Street, on Black Friday, the morning of September 24, 1869.

For months, a ruthless and corrupt businessman named Jay Gould had been using his connections with the equally corrupt Grant Administration to buy up and hoard the entire gold market. He intended to drive up the price of gold and the price of wheat as well. Secretary of the Treasury George S. Boutwell disrupted this "heartless and cynical" scheme to monopolize U. S. gold reserves and drive up the price of other commodities.

Boutwell was getting accustomed to Grant's drunken, vicious, scandalous behavior. When the price of gold plummeted from 162 to 135, the gold indicators could not keep up with the stock indicators.

Tom Edison sat at the desk in the telegraph office. By one in the afternoon, he had caught up with the signal and released the results of the final gold quotes to the multitude of brokers, bankers, and businessmen crowded inside the office.

A fellow operator called out: "Shake, Edison! We're okay! We haven't got a cent!" The crowd in the office burst into laughter.

Edison reflected upon his new direction: he would become the greatest inventor the world had ever known. He also had a secret goal in the back of his mind: to meet and hopefully secure funding from that prominent young financier, Mr. Morgan.

CHAPTER THIRTEEN

Voltage

Edison's infatuation with electricity combined well with his fascination with pain. Other people's pain.

Once, he and an accomplice wired a series of high-voltage batteries to a high-voltage transformer that was, in turn, connected to a metal urinal in the men's washroom in a train station at the edge of a small town. Edison and his fellow practical joker peered through a crack in the roof-boards of the station to watch the victims take turns standing on the wet floor and grounding the current through their urine streams.

One after the other, the men staggered out of the station, wetting themselves and reeling onto the street, where they collapsed and writhed in agony. Edison and his friend rolled about on the rooftop, laughing hysterically.

He had been thrown out of his mother's Christmas party for the severity of his humor. Upon arriving in Port Huron he greeted the guests at the party with a handshake—boosted by the discharge of a series of batteries strung on his belt, hidden by his overcoat, wired to a Ruhmkorff coil under his sleeve. A sheet of metal glued to the palm of his leather glove sent a jolt of high-voltage electricity into the ungloved hand of the guest.

Women fainted. Men buckled to their knees in pain. Edison laughed hysterically.

Nancy Edison threw Tom into the cold, black blizzard.

He wandered around Port Huron for several days, waiting for the snowstorm to subside. Then he caught the first train back to New York City.

After the gold panic of Black Friday, the office of a new company appeared: Pope, Edison, and Company, Electrical Engineers and General Telegraph Agency, Office, Exchange Buildings Nos. 78 and 80, Room 48.

Edison had been pondering the problems of multiple telegraphy for several years at that time; he was convinced it was a possibility.

George Bartlett Prescott was chief electrician at the Edison workroom. He had a multiple system in his mind, but no money for development of a prototype. He approached Edison cautiously about his design.

Edison later stated, "At that time I was very short of money and needed it more than glory. This electrician appeared to want glory more than money, so it was an easy trade." Prescott once confided to a friend, "I have never seen a man more hell-bent on glory than Tom Edison."

Edison and Franklin Pope, formerly of the Laws Reporting Telegraph Company, and their clandestine financial backer, J. N. Ashley, publisher of the *Telegrapher*, presented an improved "gold printer" to Marshall Lefferts, President of Western Union. The next day, Lefferts summoned Edison to his office.

"Well, Edison, what do you want for your 'universal printer?'"

Confidently, Edison remarked, "Well, General, make me an offer!"

Lefferts chewed on the eraser end of his pencil. "How would forty thousand dollars strike you?"

Edison nearly buckled from dizziness. When his heart stopped pounding against his ribs, he took a deep breath, steadied himself, and said, "I think that is fair."

"Alright. I will have a contract drawn. Go about your duties and return in three days and collect your money."

Three days later, Edison signed the paper without even reading it and rushed to the bank with a check.

He returned to General Marshall Lefferts' office. "The man at the bank refused to cash it!"

Lefferts looked at the check and laughed. "All that's the matter is that the check must be endorsed!"

The men in the office laughed.

"The clerk probably told you that and you did not hear him because of your hearing. I will send my secretary over to identify you."

Once more at the bank, Thomas Edison endorsed the check and the bank clerk counted out a huge pile of small bills. The teller was mistrustful of this shabbily dressed man whom the secretary introduced as "one of the coming inventors."

Stuffing his pockets, Edison shot for the door. Bills trailed out of the tattered pockets and onto the street, where the "coming inventor" danced back repeatedly to snatch them up.

Later, Edison wondered what had happened to the forty thousand dollars—it had helped him create quite a workshop, but it was dwindling.

The sounds in the workroom dissolved into stillness. The men were going home. Deep blue light leaned on the windows. The gas lamps in the office held back the evening hue.

Edison was worrying about money. He was pondering the problems of multiplex telegraphy. He was trying to ignore the night. The door opened.

"Mr. Edison, sir?"

"Prescott! What can I do for you?"

"Well, sir, it's come to my attention that you are a bit preoccupied with the problem of quadruplex telegraphy."

"Well, yes, I have been."

"Well, sir, Mr. Edison, I have been working on that problem, too, and I think I have come up with a working set of principles that can be applied, sir."

"Glad to hear it, George. I'm glad because I—" Edison stopped and smiled. Then, he resumed: "So, tell me, Prescott, what has your fancy brain come up with?"

"Well, it has to do with the principle of diplexing, sir."

"Oh, yeah! I made some advances in that. I was just getting to know the field. Go on."

"Well, in 'duplex telegraphy' you have differential relays at the end of each line. Two wires, wound around each other in a coil, one right to left, the other left to right. Am I correct so far, sir?"

"Go on."

"These, together, form an electromagnet. One end goes into the earth, the other goes to some other station. Thus, the current is divided."

"Yes, yes, yes, we know all that. Hurry on, man, what's your point?"

"We know in principle that when the telegraph key at the distant station is open, the current in the wire sets up opposing forces that neutralize the signal. But—when the key is closed, the current activates the instrument at the receiving station. Thus, the relays at both ends of the line allow the other telegraphers to control each other's machines."

"Why, yes, yes, yes, Prescott, this is all elementary. Go on."

"Well, Mr. Edison, sir, the breakthrough I have come up with is to vary the *direction* of the flow of current."

"Uh, yes, man, go on—tell it!"

"Well, what I've thought of, sir, is to introduce a polarized relay at the end of the line. This can be an electromagnet with a single wind, and between the terminals we can mount a permanent magnet that swings free. The end of the permanent magnet that we place between the two terminals should be the north pole of the magnet, sir.

"We make the magnet swing back and forth by reversing the direction of the battery current with a pole-changer. Then, we install *two* sets of equipment at the stations, two sets hooked up to one wire, and, theoretically, we should be able to send *four* messages over the same wire at the same time."

"Let me get this straight," Edison said, "we set up two sets of machines—four machines in all, at every telegraph station, at both ends of every telegraph wire, and we vary both the direction and the flow of the current, is that it?"

"Yes. We could make one set of instruments respond to the voltage, the other set could respond to the polarity, positive or negative."

"Very clever, Bartlett! You're a good man. When do you want to start work on it?"

"Start, sir?"

"Yes. When?"

"I hadn't thought about that—"

"How about tonight?"

"Tonight? Why, I don't...see why not...."

"Very good. Tonight."

Edison had formed a valuable alliance with telegrapher Ezra Gilliland. His father, Robert Gilliland, had developed the mimeograph pen.

After Marshall Lefferts resigned as head of Western Union and William Orton took his place, Lefferts received a secret communiqué to the effect that Orton had heard about Edison and Prescott's work in duplex and quadruplex telegraphy and wished to support that work.

Edison's partnership with Pope and Ashley had been conveniently absorbed by Western Union. He now had a new partnership with Marshall Lefferts, who was now head of the Gold and Stock Company. Edison furnished him with telegraph printers.

Edison's financial future was guaranteed. He had only one problem: a man his age should consider marriage.

He was terrified of women. His problem was not mere bashfulness, it was fear.

Edison set up a shop in nearby Newark. He commuted by train to his office in New York City. By the end of 1870, Edison had signed an agreement with George Harrington and Daniel Craig to form the American Telegraph Works. They supplied auxiliary equipment for the Automatic Telegraph Works.

Edison hired a Swiss machinist to be his model maker. The man's name was John Kruesi. He signed an Englishman to be his technical draftsman. He was Charles Batchelor. Together, they became drinking buddies. They called themselves the "creatures of the night." They haunted the late-night taverns and vaudeville shows on their nocturnal excursions to New York City.

Edison's work for George Harrington at Automatic Telegraph had gotten far behind by the end of his first year under contract with the firm. Although he had acquired a reputation among his laborers for chiseling their wages to pay his bills, even though it was claimed he owed "hundreds of dollars" in back pay, he never seemed to have any money.

Harrington barged into the Edison office during the first week in April. The matter of acquired debts had been shunted off to him—and he refused to deal with someone else's financial problems. The Edison machine works were not turning out printers fast enough. They were running in the red, Harrington reminded Edison repeatedly.

"Now, George, you have a full third of all my inventions already, relating to telegraphy."

"What good is it to own your patents, when you can't keep up production, delivering the operating systems?"

"I need to get out from under the machine shop, George. It's a burden, anyway. I can't do my work when I'm always down there untangling things for those damned foreigners! Think of it—this automatic telegraphy didn't come of its own. It had to have me to invent it, right?"

"Perhaps, I guess...."

"There you go! I have the best technicians, the best trained machinists, I just have to leave production to Pope or Kruesi, although I'd like to have John free to develop prototypes for me. So, you see, telegraphy is no mere trade, George; it's a science."

"I see. But I have to support myself too, Thomas. I have my own men to answer to—Palmer, Reiff, Painter—you know them, at least you've met Reiff and Painter, right?"

"Yes, yes, fine men, fine fellows."

"Well, what am I to tell them, Mr. Edison? Have you any ideas?"

"Tell them what I told you. Appoint somebody to take over telegraphic printers, if you have to, and let me go on to further experimentation."

"I can't tell them that! I need returns, man, returns!"

"You'll get them! Just have a machine shop manager manage the machine shop, not me!"

"How can we do that?"

"Help me get out from under Pope and Ashley and I'll sign over to you future patents. How's that?"

Harrington's eyes narrowed, then widened. "You'd do that?"

"Sure. Just let me work with Prescott a while longer—he and I both know how you feel about Western Union."

"Is it Western Union—or is it Orton?"

"Western Union isn't too popular with the railroads. Why is that?"

"I haven't noticed any particular animosity, sir."

"Yeah? You sure?"

"But there is between certain of my associates and, yes, I will admit, Mr. Orton."

"Associates—Josiah Reiff and Uriah Painter, is that right?"

"I cannot say, sir."

"That's alright. Tell them, if you have to, that you have an opening—and it won't last forever—on all future Edison patents. Do you understand?"

"You would do that, sir?"

"What, sell out to the highest bidder? Ha! That's what the game's all about, George."

"I see. It is tempting to me, personally, but I can't say about the other men."

"Of course not, But too many cooks spoil the broth, so to speak. Why bring the others in on it? I know how much you hate Western Union!"

Harrington smiled. "There's rumor that Jay Gould has plans for Western Union."

"Gould should stick to railroads and phony stocks, if you ask me. Have you been watching the career of this man, Morgan?"

Harrington stiffened. "I'd rather not speak of Mister Morgan, sir."

"He sure as hell beat Gould a few years ago. Ha!"

"Listen, Edison—I know this sounds impulsive, but I think I can arrange to draw up a new contract, an exclusive, something that will, shall we say, liberate you."

"George, now you're talking!"

The contract negotiations started immediately.

In truth, Edison had been courting Western Union executives all along. He had formed solid friendships with the general manager, Thomas T. Eckert, and company president William Orton. He had made their acquaintance through Franklin Pope. Back in 1871, the first test of the Edison and Prescott duplex and diplex systems had been viewed by president Orton and no less than William H. Vanderbilt.

The test signal had been sent to Albany and returned to New York City. Operators reported a successful transmission. Orton and certain other "directors of the company" gave Edison five thousand dollars on account, then Orton vanished on what his secretary explained was an "extended tour." Things had changed a great deal since '71.

Thomas T. Eckert, the general superintendent of Western Union, had said, "Not another cent!" when Edison approached him for cash, insisting Eckert pick up the funding where Orton left off.

This helped him solidify his friendship with Western Union rivals, beginning with George Harrington himself, and—hopefully—Josiah Reiff, Uriah Painter, and maybe General William Palmer, builder of the Kansas-Pacific Railroad Company. Word had reached Edison by that time that Palmer was interested in acquiring Edison's future developments in automatic telegraphy. Surely, George Harrington must have known that, being an associate of Palmer's. But then, Thomas Edison wasn't thirty thousand dollars in debt to General William Palmer, either. The new contract would be, at the very least, a good way of absolving debts. But that's all it would turn out to be.

CHAPTER FOURTEEN

Mary

Edison was haunted. Demon memories came for him at night.

By day, he was the man of the workplace. At night, around town, he was a regular at all the night spots. Alone, much, much later, he became a terrified animal.

His work crew or his executive staff sometimes discovered him either asleep or huddled wide-eyed under a desk, beneath a stairwell, inside a broom closet—any obscure corner or cubbyhole. He was frequently found snoring, oblivious until prodded, but occasionally a startled employee would come upon Edison staring fiercely out of some black shadow in some particularly uninviting part of the workshop or machine shop.

Charles Batchelor knew that Thomas Edison was not a happy man. Driven— yes. Happiness mattered not. What was important was that Edison's driving force be controlled. Edison had learned to control this force well—for the most part. Yet, he had certain disturbing...ideosyncrasies.

The frightmares he suffered while hiding in some corner were the least of his eccentricities. He never changed his clothes. He almost never bathed. He shaved every two or ten days. Fortunately, whenever the "creatures of the night" got together to drink at some late-night pub or take in a vaudeville burlesque, the reek of lab chemicals overtook Edison's more intimately exuded odors. Such places were always dense with cigar smoke. Other patrons always identified Edison and his cohorts as "scientists." That went far in explaining the stench of chemicals as well as their eccentric behavior.

His outbursts of temper were more than many—most—workers could tolerate. Batchelor thought it was inevitable that Edison and that pit-viper Zenas Fisk Wilbur had hit it off as well as they did. Edison *did* have an unerring sense about people's vices....

Zenas Fisk Wilbur reeked of vice the way Edison reeked of perspiration and battery acid. He was head patent examiner for the Department of Philosophical, Mathematical, and Mechanical Patents. He was the very man Edison routinely greeted on his trips to the patent office.

Although Edison refused to imbibe spirits, he sometimes departed from his office in the evenings, bought a bottle of red wine or whiskey, and journeyed to the back door of the patent office. Hours later, he would hurry back to his office in the darkness of night with an armful of crude sketches of machines, which Batchelor would render as technical drawings worthy of submission to machinist John Kruesi. In this way, Edison's future as an inventor was guaranteed, as was Wilbur's access to free liquor after closing time at the patent office.

Edison, Batchelor, and Kruesi prowled anonymous taverns in the yellow gas light. They caroused from The Dew Drop Inn to the House of Lords, or the Bunch of Grapes. Tucked away in Printing House square was Oliver's, a late-night saloon that catered primarily to telegraphers.

The "creatures" had converged on Oliver's one night when Kruesi and Batchelor once again brought up to Edison the matter of marriage. Even Batchelor had wedding plans.

Kruesi let loose with a joke: "Hey, Charles—I was in this very pub the other night, when y'know what happened to me? I'll tell ya! There was this lovely young lady, just sittin' there across the bar, and d'ya know what she did?"

"I say, Johnny, what's she do?"

"Well, she turned around real slow and she rolled her eyes at me. Then, d'ya know what I did?"

"S'pose you tell me, John."

"Well, I picked 'em up 'n' rolled 'em back! Ha! H-h-ha-a-a!"

Kruesi and Batchelor roared with laughter. Edison looked perplexed, then wounded, then composed.

"Very funny joke, John, very funny." Batchelor said.

"Did I ever tellya the time Sommers and I hooked a Ruhmkorff coil—"

"Endlessly, Thomas, endlessly." Batchelor turned back to Kruesi. "Thomas, what are you going to do about that sweet little tart who has eyes for you in the workroom?"

"Charles, I have no idea what you're talking about."

"Tell him, Charles."

"Tell me what? Confound you—tell me what?"

"Oh, nothing." Batchelor turned away nonchalantly. "The great Thomas Edison doesn't have time for involvements, anyway…."

"Charles, come on. Someone in the workroom? Who?"

"A woman, Thomas, a woman."

Kruesi snickered. "A very pretty woman, too. A girl, really. A girl."

"What would I want with a girl?"

"What, indeed, Thomas? She's of marriageable age. Well, what, indeed?"

"Come off it, Batchelor. Be serious."

"I am, Thomas. How long is it going to be?"

"Mary," Kruesi said. "Her name is Mary."

"I see," Edison said sullenly.

"You know her?" Batchelor feigned surprise.

"I know of her. She runs a printer. Will Unger helped her get the job, I know that, and John Ott helped Unger get his job. So I'd say it was destiny, Charles."

Batchelor laughed. "She is pretty, isn't she? And—I know Thomas is drawn to dark-haired ladies…."

"Here, here, Batchelor!"

"So it seems to me to be a match made in Heaven."

The next day, Edison slipped out of his office and strode directly to the machine shop, where he met William Unger supervising two workers at a lathe. "What can I do for you, Mr. Edison?"

Edison smiled broadly. "It has come to my attention, Mr. Unger, that I have a young woman in my employ who is an acquaintance of yours."

"You probably have several, sir, if you don't mind me saying."

"Tell me, Batchelor brought up last night that…that…that there's a certain dark-haired girl who—who has, as he put it, has eyes for—ahem!—has eyes for…."

"Has eyes for you, sir? Yes, you must mean Mary Stilwell. Yes, I'll say she has eyes for you! Thomas Edison—you're all she ever talks about!"

"Ahem! I see…."

"Well, sir, if you want to know, she's Mary Stilwell, her father is Charles Stilwell, and he's friends with my cousin, John Ott. You know John, of course."

"Of course."

"Well, jobs are tough—you know how it is—so we hired her to run the printer and her father's been grateful ever since. She comes from a good family."

"I see."

"So, she tells John and me all the time how…infatuated she is with you, sir, and me and the rest of the guys, we think highly of her."

"Tell me—how would you go about approaching her, you being a ladies' man and all…?"

"Oh, who, me, sir? Why, I'd just go up and tell her Hello!"

"I couldn't do that!"

"Excuse me, sir, but—why not?"

"Well, the impropriety of it!"

"Impropriety, sir?"

"Well, would it be appropriate?"

"Why not, sir?"

"Well...I...don't see...why not...."

Later that same afternoon, Thomas walked up to her work table, introduced himself, commended her for her work, and told her he would be happy to see her around the workplace. Her response to this flurry of attention was sudden breathlessness, a blush, a steady gaze into his eyes, and a perfect smile. She would never forget that moment, although the memory of it would change meaning as time passed.

Their courtship was awkward and uncertain. Although she knew he was attracted to her, she realized he was deeply, deeply intimidated by her as well. Their courtship proceeded in this precarious state of imbalance.

She lived ten blocks from Edison's shop in Newark, and they rode the ferry together. Frequently they took in shows and concerts at Taylor and Sylvester's Music Hall. Finally, Edison approached Charles Stilwell on "a matter of great, personal importance," and Thomas Edison and Mary Stilwell were married on Christmas Day.

After a brief, slightly delayed honeymoon, Edison went back to work. She noticed a change in her "Popsy Wopsy." He was suddenly distant. Too distant, in fact, to be anything but heartbreakingly impersonal when she discovered herself to be pregnant.

She also discovered a visitor in her home: Sam Edison had come to meet his daughter-in-law. She found him to be crude, foolish, drunk.

By April, Sam Edison was gone and Mary's sister Alice had moved in. Mary feared staying in her own room at night. She did not explain why to anyone except Alice, and Alice told no one.

Edison left on a business trip to meet Josiah Reiff, secretary of the Automatic Telegraph Company and treasurer of the Kansas-Pacific Railroad, and returned from the journey with another valuable business connection, a man whose friendship—and riches—he had carefully courted. In the spring, business and personalities exploded. Edison and Harrington feuded, then severed business connections. Edison also quit his partnership with William Unger in the manufacture of automatic printing machines—"No profit in 'em anymore!"

Mary greeted her husband's return with dread. Only her sister's presence gave her any comfort. She realized he did not love her at all.

The marriage bed was her greatest nightmare: He slept with his clothes on. Unwashed. He never bathed, never undressed, smelled harsh and acrid from chemicals, snored loudly, and—worst—he sometimes roughly, sometimes violently mounted her, then collapsed on the bed indifferently. She dreaded and loathed those few nights she was forced to endure with her "Popsy Wopsy."

He spent most of his nights in the lab or in the machine shop. That was fine with her. He caroused late into the night with John Kruesi, now that Batchelor was married, and Mary was relieved whenever he failed to come home. Sometimes she would discover him in the morning, sleeping in the broom closet underneath the stairwell or huddled under the desk in his study, staring wild-eyed, like a trapped rodent....

They had plucked their nicknames out of an Ada Alexander song that had been popular during their courtship. She had been so innocent then....

During his many nights away from home, Mary discussed in hushed tones the ordeal that living with Thomas Edison had become for her.

"At least he's not a drunk!" Alice said to her one night as they sat in the lamplight that glowed over the kitchen table.

"If only he was a drunk! If only he showed *some* emotion!"

"Mary! Don't say that."

"His whole family is...disturbing to me, Alice. His brother William gives me the willies. His father was drunk nearly every day that he was here! Oh, Alice, what am I to do?"

"There, there, dear sister, let me comfort you..."

The embrace of her sister was the only comfort Mary Edison knew.

CHAPTER FIFTEEN

Business

Edison quietly invaded the office of Zenas Fisk Wilbur. Wilbur was at his desk. Blue cigar smoke was illuminated by a hazy halo of lamplight.

"Hey, Wilbur, y'got any goodies for me?"

Zenas Wilbur leaned close and grunted, "Hey, Thomas, y'got any goodies for me?"

"Ha ha! Zenas, I've got the *good* stuff for you!"

Wilbur brought two glasses out of a tall cabinet behind his desk. Edison filled one glass only. "You know I don't imbibe."

"Just thought—"

"You always offer and I always decline, Zenas. More for you. Drink up. Now— whatchya got for me?"

"Here. Take a look at this. A guy named Sawyer just filed a caveat on what he calls 'electric illumination.'"

"It'll never work. This idea's been kickin' around for a while. Lemme tellya somethin' Zenas, these ideas come and go and if those boys can't make something like this practical, I'm damned if I'm going to waste any time on it."

"I wouldn't be so quick to—"

"Electrical illumination, indeed!"

"He's building up some capital, Tom. He's got some attention. Swan made it work. Now, Sawyer's got a better lamp, and he's gonna market it with a vengeance."

"Let him. Swan didn't make it work, either. That's why he went outa business."

"Swan went outa business because the change from gas to electricity was too expensive in London, even for the rich. No market for his lamps."

"No market here, either."

"That's where you're wrong, Tom! Out west—the mining camps, the cow—towns springing up. They don't have to convert—just build for electricity from the ground up. Best for something as temporary as a mining camp, anyway. West—there's expansion out there, Tom, expansion."

"Ha! No money out west. All the money's here!"

"Not so. Mining, cattle ranching, farms springing up—gold. There's gold out west, Tom—gold. And...opportunities."

"Well, let Mister William Sawyer exploit those opportunities! Thanks, anyway, Wilbur. I'll tellya—keep an eye on those Sawyer patents. Get me anything you can find on or by or about Joseph W. Swan, and let me know if there are any new developments, any new caveats filed...."

"I think you're wise, Tom."

"Yeah, yeah, yeah, lemme see...anything in telegraphy? Anything like the Stearns system?"

"I gave you the Stearns system, Tom. You owe me one for that."

"I thank you, indeed! Yes, the Stearns system. That really helped us a lot. Prescott and I really made a breakthrough in quadruplex telegraphy when you handed the Stearns patents to me!" Edison laughed and Wilbur drank, and they spent several hours enjoying each other's favorite forms of bliss. A man named Alexander Bain, circumventing a Morse patent, discovered that electrolysis could separate hydrogen from oxygen in water, and the resulting hydrogen instantly corroded the tip of an electrified metal stylus.

Batchelor learned of Bain's experiments through a company spy. Examining the drawings and descriptions at his desk, with Edison peering over his shoulder, Batchelor exclaimed, "Little's solution is a failure. I can make as much of a mark with my fingernail."

Edison rejoiced. "If we get the edge on Bain, we can market an electric reproducing stylus right around the corner from now!"

"We've got to keep an eye on Bain."

"That's what I keep Wilbur around for."

Batchelor frowned. "He's being investigated again. For corruption."

"He's always being investigated for corruption!"

"Doesn't that concern you?"

"Hell, he's first cousin to Rutherford B. Hayes! I bet Hayes will even be President someday!"

"Perhaps. Let's hope so, for Wilbur's sake—and yours."

Edison had just been rehired by Western Union. He had successfully played the foes of Western Union against each other, sold his time and services to the highest bidder, and kept his business dealings confidential.

Edison had invented the words "diplex telegraphy" to circumvent use of the word "duplex" by Stearns. As scientists, Edison and Batchelor relied on guesswork and serendipity.

"Batchelor! Add a teaspoonful of nitrate of ammonia. See what happens."

"Very good. That's it."

"What happened?"

"I don't know! It's not mentioned in the chemistry book...."

"Damn the chemistry book. Throw in a pinch of aurichloride of sodium and see what happens."

"How shall we enter this in the notebook?"

"Uh, how much aurichloride of sodium did you add?"

"Just—a pinch..."

Even after endless—and aimless—experimentation, they failed to circumvent the Bain patent.

Edison entered the office of Western Union President William Orton on February 6. He showered Orton with diagrams, drawings, and schematics for a "combinational system" that would combine "automatic plus diplex telegraphy, perforated transfer paper, plus chemical receiving paper." Orton was both bewildered and impressed. He was not certain what questions to ask, but commended Edison and told him to report any new advances.

Edison was enthusiastic. "I can make you a basketfull of devices!"

Orton was beginning to feel uncomfortable. "Very well. I'll take all you can make. A dozen or so a bushel."

"You're doing the right thing! Now, about the duplex system...."

"Not so fast. You and Batchelor have failed to bolster my confidence in automatic telegraphy."

"Then how 'bout a diplex system?"

"Explain the difference."

"Well, since you don't think we can send two messages opposite ways down the line, how about two messages, same line, same direction?"

"Can you do it?"

"We think we can."

"How does Batchelor feel?"

"He's assertive. Lemme askya, William, do you think a diplex system would be more valuable than this here contraplex system?"

"I agree, Thomas, it would."

"Well, there you have it. I'll tell that to Batchelor when I see him tonight in the lab."

"Good luck."

Edison was with Batchelor every night for weeks—including the night of February 19, the night his daughter Marion was born. Mary's sister Alice and a doctor were present at the birth; tradition, plus the father's aversion to matters human, forbade his presence. Mary's mother also attended the birth. She sensed all was not right with her daughter, but Mary refused to confide in her. All she would say was, "He *is* a good man! He *is* a good man!"

One afternoon she enticed her daughter, Alice, to whisper things that were not wrong with the Edison marriage. "He *never* drinks. He has never beaten her. He brings in much money. He leaves her alone a lot and she always has a *lot* of privacy...."

After twenty-two nights of experiments, Thomas Edison and Charles Batchelor tested twenty-three duplexes. Nine failed. Edison sailed for England the third week in April, accompanied by an assistant, Jack Wright.

Edison rented a hotel suite at Covent Garden, then set up shop at the post office on Telegraph Street. Wright went to Liverpool. Their first tests of duplex telegraphy failed.

Edison hated London. He hated the diet of boiled beef and flounder. He complained that his "imagination got sick." When he switched to pastries, his "imagination got all right."

He was clearly not being taken seriously by the British, even when an occasional experiment succeeded.

After six weeks in England, Edison wrote to Murray to sell the system for the equivalent of five hundred thousand dollars.

Murray cabled:

> HERE'S MY HAND, OLD BOY. EXTRAORDINARY WORK YOU
> HAVE ACCOMPLISHED AMONG EM BRITISHERS. NO OTHER
> MAN LIVING COULD HAVE BROUGHT SUCCESS FROM OUT OF
> SUCH LABYRINTHINE *COMPLEXITY*.

Edison's confidence in Murray had been strained past the breaking point. He had been receiving wildly contradictory reports from Murray as to the state of the shop back in New York. One letter said, "Running smoothly!" Another read: "Don't feel uneasy." What did he mean? Then: "I've had a hard time since you left." Finally: "Automatic is dead here only when you are present to give it life business is dull money is worse than ever. I will meet all notes without selling machinery but I shall be left poor because it takes all the profits."

Murray's communiqués were becoming incoherent.

Edison learned that two of his patents had been rejected because other inventors had already patented such devices, and his technical descriptions were inadequate to establish priority. Edison felt his empire slip away.

He cabled Murray the next day, sent Jack Wright to Liverpool again to conduct more experiments, sent Mary and his baby two hundred dollars, and left London on the first steamship he could book passage on.

CHAPTER SIXTEEN

Sound

"Hello, Zenas. Look what I brought ya."

"Come in. Quick."

"Is everybody outa the office?"

"They've all gone home."

"Good."

"Tom—did anybody see you? See you come in?"

"What if they had, Zenas? What's t'stop an old friend from seein' his buddy after work? Come 'round, Zenas. These're modern times."

"I see...gimme that bottle!"

"Now, now, Mr. Wilbur, just look, look here, willya? Kentucky's best, your favorite."

"Tom, Tom, Tom—thank you."

"*Thomas* to you, Mister Wilbur."

"I'm sorry, Thomas...Mister Edison."

"That's better. Here, Zenas, drink to your health. And mine!"

"Ssssshhhh! Keep your voice down—"

"Don't be so goldamned nervous, Zenas. No one can hear us."

"Let me—let me have another, Thomas—"

"There. Not too much, now."

"Thanks, Thomas."

"There, now, Zenas. That's enough. Now—let's get down to business, shall we?"

"Yes, yes, Mr. Edison. Anything you say."

"Hey, by the way, Zenas, I want to congratulate you for a job well done."

"Sir?"

"You followed our advice, Batchelor's and mine. Thank you." Edison was referring to the decision to drop George Bartlett Prescott's name from the quadruplex telegraphy patents. "What have you got for me, Mr. Wilbur?"

"Thomas, there are some things you don't know...."

"Yeah? Such as?"

"Well, a guy named Maxim, Hiram Maxim, just filed another caveat on electrical illumination. There's a field you oughta catch up on. Another is acoustic telegraphy."

"Yeah? Whaddya got on that?"

"Nothing, yet. Word has it a man named Gray—Elisha Gray—is working on an acoustic telegraph—a sender of sound through wires instead of Morse signals."

"Ha! It'll never work. Same with illumination. Has this Gray got anything patented yet?"

"Not yet. I'll let you know."

Edison stooped over the desk in the yellow glare of the kerosene lantern, shuffled through the papers Zenas gave him, and grunted.

"I can't use any of these. Thanks a lot, Wilbur. Thanks for—nothing."

"But—Tom—I did what I could!"

"That's '*Mister* Edison' to you, Zenas, you reprobate." Thomas Edison stormed out of the office and into the night.

He returned to his office and was received by Charles Batchelor. "Anything?"

"Of course not. What good is he?"

"Well, for one thing, he *is* the cousin of Rutherford Hayes. And he *does* know Grant rather well...."

"Grant's debauched. You know that. And that Hayes character—well, a fine president he'll make—provided he gets in, that is."

"Oh, he'll get in. The people are getting disgusted with Grant."

"Maybe, maybe. Maybe that reprobate Wilbur can be of some use to us, after all."

"He has been already. It was easy enough to persuade him to drop Prescott's name from the quadruplex system."

"Yeah? Well, what did he do on it?"

"He worked on it by night and day while you worked on automatic printers, that's what he did!"

"Kruesi couldn't get the shops to manufacture a good one. The damned things took up all my time."

"Exactly."

"I can't help it if Wilbur's been lax in getting the goods to me."

"Of course, Thomas, a certain amount depends on what's being done out there."

"I know what's being done! There're two Brits out there who're working on some kind of sound recorder—but I can't get word on how the damned thing works because they haven't filed anything in the States yet.

"I keep hearin' a rumor that somebody's progressed electric illumination beyond Swan. First I heard it was Sawyer, now there's somebody out there named Maxim, Hiram Maxim. Oh, sure, I tell Wilbur I don't believe it—but I do.

"Then he tells me tonight I oughta be on the lookout for something called 'sonic telegraphy' or 'acoustic telegraphy'—that's it: acoustic telegraphy. Somebody named Gray is at the top of that...whaddya think, Batchelor?"

"I think that we ought to get some specs out of Wilbur. If we can't, our work here in New York is finished."

Much had happened during the three years since Edison's voyage to England. The Panic of 1873 left millions homeless. Starvation knotted the stomachs of multitudes of people.

Edison spent money lavishly. He sent Mary and his daughter money. He sent his brother, William Pitt, money. He bought chemicals, new equipment, hired more workers, and sent his father some "drinkin' money."

In the wake of the Panic of 1873, the Vanderbilts pressured William Orton at Western Union to drive down the wages of the labor force to raise higher profits.

Orton began to fear Edison. He wondered, late at night, what kind of man he was....

The English post office tested the London-Dublin line. It failed. A communiqué was fired across the ocean:

"Get Edison over here!"

The British would pay no more money.

Harrington and Gouraud agreed: Thomas Edison would return to England. The memories of seasickness, poor diet, miserable working conditions, and a lukewarm reception by the British combined to make Thomas Edison ill. Physically ill.

Bronchitis struck him one night while he slept in the battery room of his laboratory, breathing the sulfuric acid fumes and lying on the cold wet floor.

Orton went to Europe in Edison's place. During his two months abroad, he received no help from Edison, whose recovery depended on privacy and a complete withdrawal from all matters. Because of his dual alliance with Western Union, the Automatic Telegraph Company lost investors overnight.

Reiff wanted to hurt Orton with the sale of Automatic Telegraph. On September 11, he gleefully announced he had "found someone." This "someone" was the very man Edison had derided as "a sneaky weasel." The man was none other than Jay Gould.

Opportunist, monopolist, entrepreneur, Gould had been the target of caustic derision. His detractors even claimed that he cheated at poker. Gould claimed he never played poker.

He had contributed mightily to the Panic of '73. He had corrupted the Secretary of the Treasury and Grant's own son-in-law, attempting to corner the gold market. His aim had been to drive up the price of wheat. His plan failed— but not before he claimed eleven million dollars on the eve of the stock market crash.

Reiff met with Gould and returned optimistic. He shot a brief note to Harrington: "We shall shake the foundation of things. Batchelor the faithful and Murray the persistent will be duly cared for. The old wheelhorse Thomas Alva Edison and I will pull together."

On December 10, after a successful test of the quadruplex system, Edison saw Orton.

He begged for an advance on his prospective profits.

"How much?"

"'Oh, ten, nine, eight, seven six, five, four, three...or two thousand dollars or so....'"

"Sorry. I don't negotiate that way."

Edison slumped. Defeated.

Orton struck up a deal, ordering twenty sets of quadruplex systems. Edison was to be given an advance of five thousand dollars on account. Negotiations regarding cost of repairs and maintenance led to conflicts and the negotiations eventually broke down.

Reiff had mentioned a "mysterious angel" in a letter to Harrington sent in September, and Edison was informed that it was now time to meet him. The "mysterious angel" was none other than Jay Gould.

Gould took pleasure in confronting his enemies, the Vanderbilts. He called this practice "spiking the Commodore."

Edison had a secret reason for meeting Jay Gould: through him, he wanted to meet John Pierpont Morgan. Sometimes, Edison reasoned, the best way to call someone to you is to court their most hated enemy.

He empowered Tom Eckert to arrange for a meeting with Gould. On December 20, Eckert visited Edison's shop—accompanied by the small, slightly stooped figure of Jay Gould.

Gould's long beard had once been red. His gray hair had also been red—and there had once been much more of it. He was quiet. Intense. Serious.

The Great Thomas Edison demonstrated quadruplex telegraphy.

Gould departed from the demonstration overwhelmed. His silent demeanor vanished. As his carriage drew him back to his mansion, he chatted about what a great inventor Thomas Edison was—and how he hated "the Commodore." Negotiations between "the plotters" (as they called themselves) commenced on the twenty-seventh of the month.

Reiff negotiated the sale of the Automatic Telegraph Company and all Edison patents to Gould. When Edison's connection to Prescott was brought up, Reiff explained that it had been rendered invalid.

"Harrington owns the rights to *all* automatic telegraphy inventions."

Gould turned to Edison.

"I confess…I've been signing so much, so fast, sir, that I don't quite know what I own the rights to anymore…."

Gould drew in a deep breath. "I see…."

Eckert cried out, "Damn it! *Forget* about Prescott!"

On January 4, 1875, Eckert escorted Edison to the Gould mansion on 5th Avenue, New York City, to pay a "mere social call." Instead of the expected butler, the wiry millionaire greeted them at the door. He explained to them that he enjoyed living almost entirely alone.

He led them to his study. He sat behind a wide, mahogany desk, lit by a gas lamp. "Shall we get down to business, gentlemen?"

"Certainly," Edison spoke up.

"Well, then." Gould leaned forward. "Who owns quadruplex telegraphy?"

Edison looked at Eckert. Eckert looked at Edison. Finally, Edison confessed, "I don't know, sir."

Gould faced Eckert squarely.

"That hasn't been decided, sir. Nothing—none of this—has been decided."

"I see."

Silence.

"Here's what I'm willing to offer: I give Edison the position of electrician at the Atlantic and Pacific Telegraph Company, plus one hundred thousand dollars. That will be in the form of three thousand shares of Atlantic and Pacific stock plus twenty five thousand in cash."

Edison stood abruptly. "That's too small, the cash figure."

Gould nodded. "Then I will give you thirty thousand."

"All right."

"Do you want it now?"

Eagerly: "Part of it."

Gould stood suddenly. "Come downstairs."

Gould may have preferred living alone, but he had not been alone at that moment. They met a man with tangled black hair and a huge mustache. He was Giovanni Morosini, secretary-bodyguard for Mr. Gould.

Edison agreed to give power of attorney to Gould over the quadruplex rights, receiving ten thousand dollars immediately from Morosini. The contract was drawn up and signed three nights later. After the celebrated signing, Edison returned at night to the Gould mansion.

He departed with 10,670 dollars, plus 16,500 dollars in Union Pacific bonds, worth more than ten thousand dollars on the open market. Money flew from Edison's hands. He left for Port Huron to visit his father.

On January 11, Thomas Eckert resigned from Western Union. When Orton heard the news, his face whitened.

The messenger boy cringed in the doorway of the office, terrified. Suddenly, Orton snatched up the wastebasket and vomited. Five days later came "the great unraveling."

An executive committee from Western Union prepared a lawsuit.

A messenger greeted Edison in his office, immediately after his return from Port Huron. Edison exploded with rage. The terrified messenger fled. Just outside the office, Batchelor overheard:

"Orton's not being fair!" "He doesn't own quadruplex telegraphy!" "He can't use my system!" "Trouble!" "I'll attack them, that's what I'll do! I'll *attack* them!"

Batchelor laughed.

"They'll learn what it's like to fight men who sleep with their boots on!"

Batchelor laughed harder.

Lawsuits were filed. Countersuits were filed. By March 20, the Commissioner of Patents ruled that the Edison/Prescott contract was valid and the 1871 contract with Harrington was invalid. Rights to quadruplex telegraphy would not go to Gould.

Reiff filed a lawsuit in August. Party to the suit was Thomas Edison. Reiff had come to hate Edison, to "hate him blind."

While Edison considered his victory over Prescott's idea of quadruplex telegraphy, a man named Elisha Gray read a paper entitled "The Transmission of Musical Tones" at his March 17 lecture before the American Electrical Society. The news exploded like a bomb in the Edison office.

"Where's Wilbur on this one?"

Batchelor shrugged. "You've fallen out of touch with old Zenas, Tom. It's time you renewed your old acquaintance."

Edison promptly did. That evening, Zenas Fisk Wilbur received an unannounced visitor just before closing hours at the patent office.

"Please wait in the reception room," the secretary told Edison.

When the clerks had all gone home, and only the janitor prowled the building, Edison and Wilbur "got down to business." Edison had brought no bottle. Wilbur was confused.

"You don't wanta uncork one in fronta the cleanup man, do you?"

The "mangy reprobate," as Edison called him behind his back, wagged his head, suppressing his temper.

"Besides, Zenas, I have a matter to discuss with you."

"Yeah? What is it, Edison?"

"That's *Thomas* Edison to you, *Mister* Wilbur!"

"So? *Thomas* Edison. What do you want, *Thomas* Edison?"

"Just a minute of your time, Wilbur. We can go somewhere—the drinks're on me. Just—what is it, Wilbur? You let one get away from me."

"What's that?"

"'Acoustic telegraphy,' as one Mister Gray puts it."

"I see. You certainly don't beat around the bush, do you, sir?"

"Oh, yes I do, Zenas. I beat around a lot of bushes. That's how I get what I want. I beat around bushes. I beat them with sticks. And—d'ya know what I get, Zenas? I get telegraphy inventions, that's what I get. Telegraphy inventions. And you, why you, Zenas, are one of the bushes I beat around!"

"… I see."

"Yes. No word from you, Zenas, while this man Gray gives a lecture on something I'm supposed to know a lot about. Already."

Gathering himself up, rising out of his chair, Wilbur shouted, "I told you about sonic telegraphy almost two years ago, Edison so don't threaten me."

"Oh, did it sound like I was threatening you, Wilbur? Don't take me seriously enough to call anything I say a threat. Let's just talk about a golden opportunity I seem to have missed. Well, yes, I do seem to recall that you have been talking about something called sonic telegraphy or acoustic telegraphy, whatever…."

"So—has this man Gray filed anything yet?"

"He hasn't filed anything, sir."

"Nothing? That's impossible. He lectured just two days ago, on the seventeenth."

"He lectured, but he filed no patents."

"None that you know of?"

"They'd go through me, sir. I would know."

"Then we still have an indeterminate amount of time."

"Before what, sir?"

"You're joking, Wilbur. Before he files for a caveat, of course."

"I want a drink, sir…."

"We can go in a minute or so, Zenas. Just cooperate. Now tell me—we still might have an advantage. What does Mr. Gray intend to do with his acoustic telegraph?"

"He wants to send voices over the wire directly, not just musical tones. He's having trouble with the mouthpiece is all."

"What principle does it work on?"

"Well, from what I can tell, Thomas, he's working from some early patents by Page and Reis, both working separately about thirty or forty years ago, I guess. Page was an American, a physicist. Reis was German. I don't know what he did for a living.

"Anyway, around 1835 or 1837 or so, Page discovered when he electrified and de-electrified a metal bar—"

"An electromagnet, Zenas."

"I know that! Damn you. Anyway, he turned it on and off rapidly, over and over again, until it produced what he, Page, called 'musical sounds.' Well, not long ago this guy Reis picked up on that research—"

"When was that?"

"About 1860 or so," Wilbur snapped. "Now—d'ya want me to go on, or not?"

"Go on, Wilbur. Just include the details."

"*All* the details?"

"All the important ones."

"I see. Well, anyway, in 1860 or in '61 or so, this German guy Reis sends sounds over an electrified wire."

"I see. And this guy Gray has picked up on the German's work."

"That's what it looks like."

"Thanks for a job not too well done, Zenas. I should have had all this by now."

"I told ya all about Gray's work a long time ago, Edison. You coulda looked into the matter by yourself. You don't need me."

"How about patents by this Page or the German? Why haven't I received them?"

"I tried to call it to your attention—"

"Give me everything you can on both those men. D'ya hear me?"

"Right! Charles G. Page and Philip Reis. By tomorrow. Now, Thomas, about that dri—"

"One more thing: he's having trouble with the mouthpiece."

Wilbur nodded.

"Describe the trouble."

"I can't."

"Why not?"

"He hasn't filed anything yet. Not a thing. I don't even know what his system is like."

"Get me anything he has as soon as he files it. With luck, all I have to work on will be a mouthpiece, a transmitter. Thank you. Good night, *Mister* Wilbur!"

"Edison—you owe me one!"

"So I do. Here. Take a few dollars. Go to the House of Lords. Have a few on me."

They departed without saying good-bye.

CHAPTER SEVENTEEN

Competition

"That bastard. He's selling out on me."

"Sir?"

"Charles, he's got somebody else on his payroll."

"How can you be certain?"

"I asked him to give me a peek at the patents!"

"You tell me he says Gray hasn't filed anything yet."

"Yeah, but I found out tonight Gray's not the only one who's been working on it. Gray's just the latest."

"You say that chap Gray's been having a bit of trouble with the mouthpiece?"

"Yeah, the mouthpiece, as he calls it."

"I see. We may have time to rectify the situation. If we can construct a workable transmitter using whatever principles Gray is utilizing, then we may get the jump on him yet."

Edison laughed. "That'd be another feather in the old cap, wouldn't it?"

"Yes, Thomas. A big step away from simple telegraphy inventions."

"I just wonder who else we're competing against...."

"Sir?"

"Listen, Batchelor, I *know* that old reprobate, Wilbur. He's playing me against someone else in this, I know." Edison could not discard the unsettling feeling that he had an unseen rival after hours at the patent office.

Wilbur turned over to him the patents by Charles G. Page and Philip Reis, spanning the years 1837 to 1861. The principles were still poorly understood, and all available diagrams and technical descriptions were sketchy. In frustration, Edison and Batchelor experimented blindly to build a mouthpiece for a sonic telegraphy transmitter.

"It must be a diaphragm," Batchelor announced one day in June.

They were experimenting with magnetically attractive, moveable diaphragms.

"At least that's my impression of the most workable design, Thomas."

"Well, Batchelor, go to work on it."

"Do you still feel we've got a competitor?"

"Yeah. More than ever. I do."

On July 27, in 1875, Edison and Batchelor found, to their dismay, that Elisha Gray had been issued two patents for what he called "electroharmonic telegraphs." Both devices used the same principle: by splitting signals into harmonics, the current could be transmitted at different frequencies. Thus, many signals could be transmitted over one wire. Including voices.

Less than two weeks after the patents were issued, on a hot day in early August, Orton summoned Edison to his office.

"Let me remind you, Mr. Edison, that electroharmonic telegraphy will render your quadruplex system obsolete."

Edison's temper boiled but he said nothing.

"Perhaps you should take this book home with you, Edison." He picked up a volume from the middle of his desk pad.

" *The Wonders of Electricity,* " Edison read. "That's Braille's book. I used to have that book."

"Reread it. It has the original Reis experiment in it."

"I see."

"No hard feelings, I hope."

Edison turned to depart. "Nope. None at all."

Edison left the office and swiftly sought the company of Batchelor. He found him in his office, reading a newspaper.

"Yes, Thomas?"

"Batchelor, we gotta talk. This guy Gray got two patents issued to him and I didn't even know he filed caveats on 'em. Where's Wilbur at this time? Now— Orton calls me into his office, says I gotta get the jump on Gray, 'cause if I don't, then his so-called harmonic telegraphy will make the quad system obsolete overnight. Damn it, Batchelor, who is this other guy?"

"What other guy, Thomas?"

"The one we're competing against, Batchelor."

"How do you even know there is such a man?"

"Just a hunch and a damned strong one. You know my reasons, Batchelor."

"I admit they're good, knowing Wilbur as well as I do." All we can do is hold our breath together, Orton, you and I."

Grays' harmonic telegraphs were tested on the eleventh of September at the main office of Western Union in New York City. Edison and Batchelor attended the demonstration incognito. They were there to survey the crowd.

The test successfully transmitted signals from New York to Boston. Confirmation from Boston was almost immediate.

From a corridor, Edison and Batchelor took turns surveying the crowd. They saw no familiar faces. People passed, peered at the machines, none too eager to get close.—Except a swarthy man with a long gray beard and fierce black eyebrows. He drew a quick sketch of the instruments, then vanished furtively.

"Did you see that?" Edison whispered to Batchelor.

"I most certainly did."

"What should we do?"

"Follow him, Edison."

They hurried to the spot where the man had been standing. He was gone.

"Get that, Thomas: dark complexion, gray beard, long, gray hair.

"I saw—but who could he be?"

In November, Edison filed a caveat of his own on an "acoustic telegraph." It was capable of transmitting three tones over a wire simultaneously. The tones were produced by vibrating reeds.

The prototype, presented by John Kruesi, was tested at the Western Union Office in downtown New York City. It also failed. Orton was delighted.

Edison pleaded for more money and promised to extricate Western Union from any liability.

When he was gone, Orton said softly to himself, "He trades promises for dollars."

On the tenth of November, Mary Edison gave birth to a son, Thomas Alva Edison Junior.

Edison had not seen his wife for more than seven of her nine months of pregnancy. Now that she had delivered his second child, he saw her even less, though he was building her a country house near his new laboratory.

On December 29, Mary Edison signed papers and a mortgage statement to the effect that she was the sole owner of the house. It had been intended as a Christmas gift to her.

He took one of his infrequent baths just to please her, then he was off the next day for New York City and the Western Union telegraphy lab.

In his place, he sent for his father to help build the new laboratory. This disconcerted Mary Edison even more than her husband's absence. She sat with her sister Alice at the breakfast table.

"He's a loathsome man," Mary stated.

"Who—Thomas, or his father?"

"Both of them. Alice, I just don't know anymore. I just don't know...."

"There, there, dearest, tell me."

"Well, at least old Samuel will be too busy to leer at me. Alice—that old lecher! I don't know what sort of family...he's seventy-something! That girl of his—she's just a girl, Alice—she's been his mistress since he was seventy-one, so help me!"

"No!"

"Yes, oh yes, Alice—there's more! So—this girl, this Mary Sharlow—she bore him a child two years ago, a daughter. They named her Marrietta, and they've been living together like a husband and wife ever since."

"No!"

"She's barely a teenager now—and she's a mother already! Oh, Alice!"

"There, there, dear...."

While Alice comforted her sister, Thomas Edison experimented in New York City, testing mouthpiece senders for acoustic telegraphs.

They suspended rubber discs between powerful magnets. They spoke to the rubber discs, shouted at the rubber discs. They tried to make rubber respond to magnets, magnets respond to rubber. The magnets did not respond and the rubber did not respond.

They experimented with a powerful vibrating electromagnet. It generated sparks from every metal fixture in the lab. Edison's nephew, Charlie, hung from a gas pipe and drew sparks from the tip of his knife. The electricity "tingled" him.

Edison was obsessed with learning who his rival, his unseen competitor, was.

On February 14, 1876, two caveats were filed with the United States Patent Office. Edison had requested such caveats from Zenas Fisk Wilbur. One of the caveats had been filed by Elisha Gray.

The other, a much shorter, simpler description, had been filed by a man named Alexander Graham Bell.

After hours at the patent office, Zenas Fisk Wilbur was nowhere to be found.

Chapter Eighteen

Bell

Edison was in a panic. He arranged to meet Batchelor at Oliver's Cafe, in Printing House Square. When Batchelor entered the dive, he found Edison seated at a table in the corner, nursing a cup of tea and puffing on an especially foul cigar. He quickly ordered an ale at the bar and asked that it be brought to his table. Then he joined Edison.

"What ho, Batchelor? Whaddya say? Anything on this Bell character yet?"

"Some. Some of it's very disconcerting, Tom."

"Yeah? What? Tell me. I think I can take anything, at this point."

"Well, try this one: this Bell character tested out a basic model of his 'acoustic telegraph' on the Western Union wires back in February of last year."

"Where was Orton all this time?"

"In on it, really. Orton knew. Bell had just taken out his basic patents. Orton knew. He just didn't want *you* to know!"

"Holy hell, Charles. Orton, the scab! So he knew all about this Bell character—and, presumably, Gray—and he kept it under wraps all this time."

"You and he weren't too friendly during that time, if you recall."

"Don't remind me."

"It apparently was quite easy to keep the truth from you. You have rivals other than Bell or Gray. In fact, in some ways they're the least of your worries."

"Whaddya mean?"

"Wilbur and Orton both kept this from you—they're not inventors."

"I see whatchya mean."

"Wilbur's loyalties have swayed somewhat, apparently. A lot has gone on with all of us in the past five years...."

"We could still get him on that one, Charles."

"Oh, certainly, we could, we could, Thomas, but where would that get us? We're the best character witness he has—and he's always relying on us whenever he gets...investigated."

"I see. So, he's our man at the patent office, like it or not, eh?"

"Whether we like it or not, Thomas. Unless you know somebody better?"

"Hell, I don't know anybody, Charles, anybody. No, Wilbur's unreliable. We knew that when we first started working with him. It's Orton's actions that have started to bother me."

"It's disconcerting...."

"I seem to remember such a test! Yes. But everybody told me it didn't work, that the guy was a crackpot or something."

"That's what they were told to tell you. By Orton. You were so busy with the quadruplex patents and building your new lab that you didn't seem to notice—at the time, old boy."

"Yeah. I see. It didn't seem important at the time, so I forgot all about it."

"See? That explains Orton's change of heart toward you, playing against Prescott and Gould, even."

"I see that clearly, now."

"He needed duplex and quadruplex systems—a backup plan, in case acoustic telegraphy failed to live up to its promise. Oh, yes, he needed patents for every conceivable system, to keep Western Union ahead. But, you see, old chap, Orton was playing you against people you were not even aware of at the time."

"Damn. Godammit."

"We knew of Wilbur's weaknesses all along, Tom. We knew where his loyalties lay—in a bottle. Not in favor of you or I. So it was natural for him to sell out to someone else."

"Who the hell *is* this Bell character, anyway?"

"I wish I knew, Thomas, I wish I knew. One thing's for certain: he got to Wilbur through family connections, not an overabundance of unwanted wealth or any such thing. The question remains: which family?"

"Get Gumshoe on it, immediately."

Gumshoe was Joseph F. "Gumshoe" McCoy—private detective and Edison's personal fact finder. He was an expert at blackmail, patent piracy, and invasion of privacy.

At McCoy's office. Edison heard the truth unravel.

Gardiner Hubbard was Alexander Graham Bell's prospective father-in-law.

"Well, Edison, as near as I can figure it," McCoy drawled, "he's a complete nobody, a schoolteacher—"

"A schoolteacher!" Edison roared. "Batchelor, didya hear that? We got beat out by a schoolteacher."

"Go on," Batchelor said.

"Yeah, a schoolteacher, alright. Teaches deaf girls. At a private conservatory. Rich girls, y'see? Anyway, so this guy Bell falls in love with one of 'em. And her father is Gardiner Hubbard—and you *know* who *he* is!"

Edison shook his head. It was all too clear.

"So, Hubbard hates Western Union, but he's got a friendly acquaintance with Bill Orton, and he knew Wilbur, our friend, Mister Wilbur, through George Harrington and Postmaster General Creswell.

"So, Hubbard says 'Not so fast!' to this guy, and makes development of acoustic telegraphy part of the condition of marriage. After all, what do you do for a dowry when y'want t'marry a rich girl? Ha ha! Anyway, so Bell says he doesn't know anything about science, he doesn't even know math or anything—"

"No math!" Edison roared. "I knew it!"

"So," Gumshoe shot Edison a cold glance, "so this guy Bell doesn't know any science, nothing about electricity, but Hubbard says, 'Leave it t'me!' and tells Alexander that he can take care of the whole thing.

"Well, he does. He sets Bell up with a workshop and a lab assistant, some guy named Tom Watson, one of Moses Farmer's former assistants, so this Bell guy got expert help from the get-go.

"They pirated Gray's patents through Wilbur, got friendly enough with Orton to get permission for a test, patented the test instrument, and you were kept busy with quadruplex, so they kept you out of it deliberately and effectively, I'd say."

Edison glared at the detective.

"Don't lose your touch, Thomas," Gumshoe McCoy said. "You know what I mean, too."

"Don't give me that, Gumshoe. Why'd Orton get friendly with Hubbard and Harrington?"

"He needed to know just exactly what quadruplex telegraphy was going to be competing against. So, when they came callin' for permission to use their lines, Orton said yes, provided he view the demonstration. So, it was a sure thing. Orton needed to know what Bell had so he could figure out what Gray had, so he agreed to the deal. No mystery. Just mutual advantage."

"I see," Edison said. His face grew dour.

"That's how it goes in this business," Batchelor said.

CHAPTER NINETEEN

Light

The harsh winter of 1877 had an auspicious beginning for Edison.

It was the winter the Jew came to visit, on the first clear, cold night after the last big storm of the season. Mary had banished him from the bedroom for his refusal to bathe—it meant removing his clothes, which he hated—and late that night he looked up from his book when someone pounded at the front door.

Not certain because of his hearing, he let a few minutes go by, then got up when he heard it again.

At the door was a Jew.

Edison studied the face for what he called the "Semitic proboscis." He knew the man was a Jew, despite lack of evidence. Edison prided himself on being tolerant of all fair-skinned people except the Jews, so when he saw the man and felt immediate mistrust, he knew him to be a Jew.

His face was brown, craggy, gaunt. His features were sharp and pointed. His skin was raw with sores, boils, infections. His clothes were brown rags, tattered and smelly. His feet were bandaged; he wore no shoes. He stated his case quite simply: he was going from door to door looking for any morphine or opium, whichever he could find. He saw the light on and decided to inquire.

Edison's first impulse was to throw him out. Then an idea came to him: it had been a long time since he had experimented on anybody. He invited the gentleman inside.

Edison "just happened to have" a sizable quantity of morphine sulfate on hand. He poured twice a lethal dose on the polished tabletop, then prepared the injection. He warned the man that his laboratory was not "a hotel for suicides."

The man grinned eagerly, then politely suggested that such a small amount might not do anything to cure his "many ailments." After the injection, the man seemed unchanged.

Edison studied the man. "Head of abnormal size; face intelligent; emaciated, signs of starvation, malnutrition, dehydration...." The man wanted more morphine.

Edison spilled out many times a lethal dose and the injection was prepared but the injection seemed to have no effect.

"More?"

"You want—more?"

"Oh, yes! Please—may I?" At least he was very polite about it.

"I'll be right back. I have something good for you in the lab."

"My, my!"

Edison returned from his private pharmacy with a vial of strychnine. A massive dose was prepared. Injected.

The man was delighted He sighed. His eyes became dreamy and excited at the same time. He grinned. His body undulated, writhed. "Do you have...any more...?"

Edison gasped. "No! That's the last."

"Well, I *do* wish you had some opium!"

Edison was confounded. He had just used up the last of the household strychnine. He decided to let him finish off the opium as well. He was getting low—down to three pounds. He let the man eat it if he consented to be on his way.

The visitor chewed off pieces of the tarry, black opium. Three pounds were soon gone.

He suddenly became normal. He stood up without trembling, shook Edison's hand, and vanished into the snowy night. Three days later, the man was found dying in a neighbor's barn.

Edison felt so sorry for the man he spent a dollar wiring the county commissioner to pick up the body.

The Gray-Bell-Farmer patent lawsuits collided in the courtrooms. Somebody named Leon Scott invented something called the "phonautograph" back in 1857. It did the same thing as "acoustic telegraphy"; the courts had to contend with that.

Wilbur finally confessed, under pressure, he didn't know who submitted the patents first, but both Gray and Bell had submitted patents the same day.

Edison and Batchelor went to work immediately on a new and improved telephone. They created a rubberized diaphragm that served as a mouthpiece transmitter. In the process, they came up with a loudspeaker that broadcast an amplified signal, converted to sound.

The first Edison telephones were nicknamed "shouting phones": the loudspeakers amplified and bellowed voices loud enough to be heard a thousand yards outside the laboratory walls.

In November 1877, *Scientific American* ran an article entitled "Graphic Phonetics" by two French scientists, Dr. Rosapelly and Professor Etienne Marey. Edison kept his eye on that development: sound recording and reproduction. He and Batchelor walked into Kruesi's shop after hours one night with sketches of what Kruesi could not make heads or tails of—a month after those French scientists tried to establish preeminence in sound recording by publishing their experiment in a scientific journal.

When a prototype was completed, Edison's assistants betted on whether the contraption would work or not. Edison bet Kruesi two hundred dollars. The assistants bet a box of cigars.

Edison shouted into the speaker as the tinfoil on the cylinder moved.

Kruesi rewound the cylinder, cranked the machine. Silence.

Edison shrugged. "Well, I guess you've won your box of cigars.

The workers were dispersing when Batchelor suggested a second listen. They were shocked—and Edison was delighted—to hear:

"Well, I guess you've won your box of cigars...."

Those words triggered frantic experimentation to find a suitable recording surface for his "sound embossing" machine.

Z. F. Wilbur's first cousin, Rutherford B. Hayes, ran for president and won, replacing scandalized, corrupt Grant and guaranteeing Wilbur's secure position at the patent office.

Edison now had two sons, Will and Tom Junior. His daughter, Marion, acquired the nickname "Dot." Mary Edison admitted that although Thomas had been an imperfect husband, he was actually a good father. He doted on his three children.

They did not complain about the smell of his overcoat. He never mistreated them. He would lift them onto his knees and tell them stories, sing songs with his

Alexander Graham Bell

coarse, gravely voice, and take mechanical wonders out of his pockets to delight them. They shouted into his deaf ears to be heard. They missed him when he went away for so long to work in his laboratory. They did not understand why their mother and father fought whenever they spent time together.

William H. Preece was the electrician at the British post office. He had established a friendship with Edison during Edison's sojourn to England. This friendship continued until May of '78, when another British electrician, David Hughes, invented the microphone.

Hughes had been a friend of Preece's. Preece was a friend of Edison's. Immediately after dispensing with the diaphragm (Batchelor's innovation) the microphone worked—and one month later, Edison and Batchelor patented an identical microphone, one that had not only dispensed with the diaphragm but was identical in every other way. Edison claimed complete credit.

Hughes claimed: "Piracy!"

Preece claimed: "Abuse of confidence!"

Preece lost two friendships. He denounced Edison throughout the British Isles. Orton died of a stroke. Conveniently. He was replaced by Hamilton McK. Twombly.

Twombly was a clever fool: he had married one of Commodore Vanderbilt's nine attractive daughters. Edison knew what an aphrodisiac large amounts of wealth could be. Twombly approached Edison with awe touched with fear. He would stand by Edison, no matter what. The inventor was God.

He invented the tasimeter, which was based on the ear horn. It consisted of a three-inch horn focused on a piece of hard rubber and mounted on a disc of carbon.

He finished the tasimeter the first of June. He departed immediately on a train to Colorado to view the eclipse on the twenty-third of that month.

The expedition reached Colorado in time to view the eclipse—and measure the heat from the sun's corona.

Edison fumbled with the device, standing in the pitch-black shadow of the moon, cast on the granite mountaintop. The hot air baked the rubber and carbon disc. The indicator dial soared.

"What's wrong, Thomas?" Professor Barker peered over Edison's shoulder.

"Uh, well, George, I don't know what t'tell you."

Professor Langley looked up at the blazing corona, silhouetting the dark side of the moon.

"Sam—George—I don't know what to say! Sam—can you account for this reading? It's ten times higher than anything I expected. That can't be it. If the sun's corona was this hot, why, we'd all be fried to a crisp where we stand!"

The scientists could not explain it.

Midnight's brief visit to the world at noon ended, and light returned to the Earth from the sky.

Even in the bright sun, the indicator needle stayed at the highest mark on the dial.

They departed for a two-week hunting and fishing trip in Rawlins, Wyoming. On the journey from Colorado to Wyoming, Edison insisted on riding on the cowcatcher of the train. For the first time in his life, Edison was overcome by awe.

The peaks of the Rocky Mountains were capped with snow and glaciers—even in summer. The trees were impossibly big. The cliffs were jagged, the peaks—pinnacles.

Edison was at home in the West: in Rawlins, he wandered the streets, peered into livery stables, saloons—he and Ed Fox even peeked inside the town jail to take a look at a horse thief and a train robber.

"Hell, Tom, you look more like a tough guy than either of them do!"

Ed Fox shared Edison's hotel room that night: they had been asleep for a few hours when the door thundered. A huge man pounded the door wide open. Edison and Fox sat up and stared, awake, terrified.

"Which wunna you guys is Thomas Edison?"

After a long pause to summon courage, Edison croaked, "I am."

"A pleasure, pardner! I'm Texas Jack, boss pistol of the West! He dropped to his knees and fired one shot out the window. A weather vane across the street spun with a loud *clang*!

"Holy Jesus!" Edison exclaimed, and stood up—already dressed.

Texas Jack laughed.

He offered Edison whiskey. Edison declined. He introduced himself to Fox. They shook hands and Fox eagerly accepted the whiskey. They swapped stories in the middle of the night. Texas Jack suddenly left. Neither Fox nor Edison could remember how many men he said he'd killed.

Upon returning to New York, Edison immersed himself his work: he was determined to conquer the problem of electric illumination.

He had patents and technical articles that predated the work of Joseph W. Swan. In 1847, British chemist Joseph Wilson Swan acquired the unfinished research of an American, J. W. Starr, and by 1860, Swan perfected an electric lamp. He had inserted carbon strands, burned to ash, inside a glass globe filled with nitrogen gas. In 1850, another Englishman, W. E. Straite, tried carbon strands, then switched to tiny iridium wires.

Edison had seen electric lighting a long time ago, in Charlie Williams' shop in Boston. Moses Farmer had been making lamps since 1859. During Edison's trip to Colorado, Professor Langley had brought up around the campfire the subject of incandescent lighting, but Edison was only faintly interested. Zenas Wilbur greeted him upon his return from the West with the news that new developments in electric lighting had been proposed by William Sawyer. Edison responded by saying he'd seen electric lighting in Virginia City. He had been invited to inspect a gold mine. He'd gone eighteen hundred feet under the earth, guided by electric lights all the way.

Wilbur was undeterred. "You don't see any evidence of that out here."

"I don't see what you mean."

"Where are these lights? They aren't here. Not in New York City, just gaslight. And carbon-arc lights. They're both smoky and smelly."

"Carbon-arc is worse, Zenas. It's just brighter."

"You better look into this soon, Thomas. Sawyer just filed another patent. We don't know how damned good it is, but that's irrelevant: what's relevant is that he's been marketing his lamps for a while, but nobody out here knows who he is. So, the market's wide open, for a while at least."

"I see."

William Sawyer was a gifted electrician. He was also an ill-tempered drunk. Edison thought maybe it was best the public didn't know who William Sawyer was. That conversation had taken place the night before the birth of Will Edison, on October 26.

By the fifteenth of November, the Edison Electric Light Company was formed. All that was missing was the invention of the Edison lamp.

Sawyer had begun to denounce Edison loudly to the press: his fears were genuine, but his quotes were distorted to sound like jealousy.

The day Mary Edison gave birth to Will, William Sawyer and his New York attorney, Albon Man, visited Western Union patent lawyer Grosvener P. Lowrey. Sawyer presented his "platinum light." It had been patented the year before. Now, he was about to produce a superior lamp-carbon, in a globe filled with nitrogen gas. Edison immediately contacted Francis Upton.

Upton held an M.A. from Princeton. He had been a protégé of Ludwig Helmholtz, and was already wealthy at twenty-six. Edison summoned Upton to his office to discuss incandescent illumination.

"Dig out all patents, descriptions, ideas, and articles. In fact, summarize the history of lighting for me!"

Immediately after the formation of the Edison Electric Light Company, another company was formed—the United States Electric Light Company. Hiram S. Maxim had been hired to produce lamps based on his own patents, which he had been unable to market for years. That had been in 1878.

Edison denounced his competitors, accusing them of "hoaxing their investors." He had three hundred thousand dollars in capital. He had the attention of the Vanderbilts, Western Union—even John Pierpont Morgan.

Morgan contacted Edison: that was the way Edison wanted it. Was he interested in investing money? Interested enough to come to the lab?

Early in the month of December, in a "claptrap, clapboard building in a muddy field," protected from the winter by shuddering walls of pressed wood teased by snow flurries, John Pierpont Morgan and his partner Anthony Drexel negotiated with Thomas Alva Edison for the rights to electric illumination. They were promised that Edison had perfected it, and that it worked.

Morgan wanted all European rights. Edison wanted money. They managed to get something written down on paper and signed by all. The race was on.

Baron Rothschild wrote to Morgan's New York representative, August Belmont, stating enthusiastic interest in anything Edison might develop.

Belmont visited the Menlo Park laboratory the first Saturday in December. Edison promised to light all of Menlo Park with two thousand lights on telephone poles. This would cost a mere 100,000 to 150,000 dollars—a pittance, by Morgan's standards.

Scientists found Edison's claims to be absurd. Physicists argued that electric illumination was impossible in principle. Despite success marketing viable light globes in mining camps and western cow-towns, Sawyer and Maxim faced bankruptcy as financiers questioned whether their lamps really worked at all.

Edison was playing both sides against the middle-and he knew it. He could delay another meeting with Mr. Morgan no longer. He had been terrified of a second meeting.

He showed the Morgan men an old Jablochkoff light globe. He showed them a coil. They were impressed. He showed them, but did not demonstrate, a lamp with a wire of nonfusable metal-no one knew just what. They were all very impressed, including Mr. Morgan.

Someone brought up the matter of "impossibility."

Edison proclaimed, "The intensity of the light increases to the square of the current. On this, they figure an enormous loss in the subdivision, but fortunately there is another law which is not known to these scientific gentlemen, if certain conditions are brought about compensates for the loss. These conditions are exceedingly difficult to obtain."

He was, of course, lying. Edison had acquired only rudimentary math skills. He refused to learn Ohm's law.

"I do not depend on figures at all. I try an experiment and reason out the result, somehow, by methods I could not explain."

Batchelor's skills at math were no better than Edison's. In their blind rush toward success, they had nowhere to go. They experimented blindly, fusing materials, electrifying other materials, starting small accidental fires and hastily putting them out....

While he struggled to produce a viable electric lamp, Edison's Phonograph Company perished.

He announced to his employer that he had searched American and European patent files and came up with nothing comparable to the Edison light globe. He was wrong. He failed to mention that a German named Siegfried Marcus had just patented another light globe.

Marcus had invented a "motor car" two years before. It had been banned in Vienna due to "harrowing accidents and toxic fumes."

Three thousand dollars was spent on an experimental steam lamp that failed. By January, Edison came down with bronchitis.

Sawyer had struck financial barriers: the more skeptical the press became of Edison, the faster investors withdrew their funds from his company.

The *New York Graphic* charged: "As day after day, week after week, month after month passes, and Mr. Edison does not illuminate Menlo Park as he has so often promised to do, doubts as to the practicality and value of his widely advertised and much—lauded invention begin to be entertained in the public mind." *Puck* contributed to the foray: "Edison is *not* a humbug. He is the type of man common enough in this country—a smart, persevering, sanguine, ignorant, show-off American. He can do a great deal and he thinks he can do everything." Frank

Pope, Edison's first partner, added his comments to the ammunition fired by the press: "I know of no one here who has any confidence in the practical success of Edison's scheme. The way the world stands agape, waiting for the Edisonian mountain to bring forth its mouse is really absurd."

J. P. Morgan and his associates gathered in New York City to discuss the future of the Light Company. Grosvenor Lowrey overheard a "joking" remark to a fellow executive, who had been asked by an Edison representative if he knew anybody "gullible enough on whom we could unload Light Company stock onto." Lowrey took the joke seriously and reported it to Edison.

"You may feel that it would be prejudicial to let us see how great the difficulties are, but I would like to have a talk with you right down to the bottom of everything, and I would like to have Mr. Morgan join in it."

Edison was stunned. Could he hide his failures and blind experiments from Morgan? Francis Upton had been a cinch. The kid only knew science. Morgan knew *people*.

Edison responded to this ultimatum by coming down with serious illnesses the next day.

Early 1879 was a harsh winter: blizzards, prolonged cold, poor lab ventilation, and nearly constant inhalations of toxic fumes caused everybody else to get sick as well. Mary Edison had suffered a collapse into depression after the birth of Will. Edison sent her, her sister Alice, Tommy Junior, plus his father and Jim Symington on a wild party in Florida.

His financial empire deteriorated. His experiments proved futile. He slept at night under the dog coop. He spent his days furiously attacking the keyboard of his steam organ, despite not knowing how to play the organ.

Upton and Batchelor stayed away from the house while Edison savagely pumped out bellowing discords.

On March 22, 1879, Edison proudly announced he was prepared to give a demonstration. Lowrey and the other Light Company executives arrived at the rickety Menlo Park station and strode the distance to the library. There, they were offered cigars and told to wait. Edison was greatly relieved that J. P. Morgan was not among them.

They were led from the library to the two-story machine shop, adjacent to the laboratory. With the flourish of a carnival barker, Edison commanded the gas lights to be turned off. Darkness followed.

Sixteen lamps on a work table started to glow as the current was applied. First dark red, then orange, then yellow they burned. At twenty-two candlepower, the bulbs flickered and sparks flew. Two lamps went off together. The flashing increased.

One bulb increased in brilliance. It blinded the bankers and the technicians. Upton his behind a workbench. Batchelor slipped out of the room. Edison flapped his arms excitedly.

The single brilliant light exploded. Shards of shattered glass flew around the room. Miraculously, no one was impaled.

Batchelor swiftly returned with a resistance coil. He shoved it in place, bypassing the burned-out lamp. Another lamp brightened and burst, then another....

Edison blamed the fireworks on the generator.

William Sawyer had run out of Albon Man's money, While his bulbs were practical, he lacked the funds to make them airtight. They leaked gradually and burned out within days.

Another laboratory had been built in record time, still unpaid for. Edison moved out of Menlo Park. His experiments had been the most expensive in the history of science.

The *New York Herald* let Edison off the hook: they ran a story entitled "The Triumph of the Electric Light." The story was a hoax.

Edison had accomplished two of his three goals: he had created a new company and run his competitors out of business, but he still had not controlled incandescence. He constantly tried not to think about J. P. Morgan.

Edison realized—with a shock—that he feared the Morgan nose. His nose had been scarred by boils.

Morgan was a big man. Edison was short, stoop-shouldered, almost squat. Morgan was well over six feet tall and two hundred pounds. He never laughed. He never smiled.

Edison shivered, remembering his few meetings with Morgan. Edison had used up fifty thousand dollars of Morgan's money the month before; he was paying off debts with promises.

Bell was suing Edison over a pirated telephone receiver.

Charlie Edison showed up at the lab one morning with a workable chalk receiver.

By February 27, Edison sent Charlie, with Sam as chaperone, to England to negotiate rights for the chalk receiver and start production of a telephone system.

Charlie took over the telephone system and on May 10, 1879, successfully demonstrated his perfected telephone before the British Royal Society. Jim Adams, Edison's old telegraphy pal, had been sent to England the year before to manage the development of the phone systems there. He suddenly died on a trip to Paris.

Charlie rushed to Paris to comfort Jim's widow. He fought Gouraud over the visit, so soon after the demonstration. When he returned, four days later, he found himself fired and barred from the company.

He wrote to his famous uncle, attacking Gouraud: "He is a domineering, overbearing, self-conceited Lardy duck, a swell, parts his hair in the middle and doesn't know a telephone from a Dutch clock."

Edison cabled: "Return home immediately."

Charlie departed for Calais.

In exactly the middle of May, a London telephone company was formed. Edison received twenty-five thousand dollars. Immediately, he loaned Gouraud twenty-five hundred, paid Batchelor an equal sum, sent Mary a thousand dollars, and ordered five hundred books for himself.

He vainly tried to recruit a London manager.

Charlie's chalk receivers disintegrated after two days of use.

Edison announced on July 7 that he was ready to demonstrate electric illumination.

"I'm either gonna create light or prove it's impossible!" The result was fiery pyrotechnics lighting the New Jersey countryside.

Upton was due to be married by late August: he read a paper before the American Association for the Advancement of Science entitled "On the Phenomenon of Heating Metals in Vacuo by Means of an Electrical Current." He generously attributed his lecture to Thomas Edison.

While Upton was wed in Manhattan, Charlie had abandoned his wife, Nelly Edison, for a fellow photographer he had met in Paris, a man named D. Murray. The meeting had been love at first sight.

Charlie had just gotten a job from Cornelius Herz, to build the first Paris-Brussels telephone line. He met a fellow American, a fellow photographer—and moved into the apartment next door to his. They opened the doors between the apartments, set up a darkroom and a lab, and, as Murray put it, "We not only lived and pleasured together, but we also worked together." The news ignited explosive emotions in port Huron and Menlo Park.

Edison wrote to Nelly: "William is not acting right. I advise that you come to get him home." Charlie refused to leave Paris.

D. Murray taught Charlie about exotic combinations of pleasure and pain. Murray said of Charlie: "I have never known such intimacy before."

Gumshoe McCoy exploited his European connections and piped the information directly to the infuriated Edison.

Early Wednesday morning, on the eighth of October as Charlie and Murray were returning to their apartment, Charlie complained about a pain. Murray dismissed it. By nightfall, Murray prepared poultices and administered laudanum while Charlie hallucinated in agony.

A doctor was summoned. He applied a dozen leeches. This did not help.

He injected morphine. That helped.

The doctor diagnosed him: "Peritonitis. Inflammation of the bowels. Maybe a cold of the bowels." Prognosis: "Death."

Charlie lived for five days, hallucinating in pain and screaming against the horrors in his mind.

The doctor bathed him in Epsom salts—repeatedly. Charlie became so weak he was taken off morphine, and he got far worse immediately. The doctor realized he had not had a bowel movement in five days, so he administered a powerful emetic. Charlie vomited endlessly for hours. He died at 6 A.M. Saturday, October 18.

William Pitt, his father, and his wife Nelly were devastated. The family was carefully shielded from public scandal.

By Sunday night, the Edison men were back on the job.

On Tuesday, October 21, Batchelor and Francis Jehl, the glassblower who also operated the vacuum pump, carbonized a thread 1/30,000 of an inch thick and attached it without breaking it to two platinum wires.

On Wednesday morning at nine, the loop of thread was inserted into a glass globe. The air in the globe was carefully evacuated by Jehl. Current was applied. The loop incandesced.

It sustained half a candlepower for several seconds. The resistance was 113 webers. Edison announced that all "burners" were to be called "filaments." Edison tested everything that could be carbonized to find a filament better than thread for incandescence. He carbonized fishing line, cotton, paper, tar, paper, and cardboard. He tested celluloid, coconut fibers, cork, wood shaving, even playing cards.

Tuesday, October 28, Batchelor spent the usual several hours preparing a globe for testing when Ludwig Bohm evacuated the air and the glass cracked. Batchelor was furious. "Shit! Busted by Bohm!"

A furious fight ensued.

Batchelor screamed: "Incompetence!" Bohm accused Batchelor of arrogance.

That had been the same day Edison applied for a patent: "The object of this invention is to produce carbon conductors of high resistance to produce Electric Light by incandescence." The rest of the description was purely hypothetical. Even after he had filed the patent, Edison and Batchelor were still experimenting to make it work.

On the afternoon of Wednesday, November 12, Edison and Batchelor constructed a light globe that burned on and off for a total of sixteen hours before burning out the following Monday.

On November 22, Upton announced, "During the past week, Mr. Edison has succeeded in obtaining the first lamp that answers to the purpose we have wished for."

Three days later, on November 23, Edison signed the British patent application for rights to incandescent lighting. He announced: "My light is perfect!"

When he burst into his house on the eve of Wednesday, the third of December, announcing that a group of businessmen were due to arrive momentarily, Mary nearly panicked. Upton, Jehl, and Batchelor arrived and set up a small wooden display platform on which was mounted a series of light bulbs. As the sun set, Edison turned on the current with a telegraph key. The bulbs blazed—then they burst. Sparks showered the curtains and rugs of the parlor.

Alice hurled blankets onto the fire. Edison turned off the current immediately. Then the businessmen showed up.

Mary met them at the door and explained that she was "remodeling." The businessmen went away.

While Edison signed papers to get more money, his experimenters tested everything from hemp fibers to spiderwebs ("they gave off a pink and green glow"), as well as palmetto, Southern tree moss, manila fiber dipped in rock candy syrup, and beard hairs. The men placed bets on which beard hairs would incandesce the best. On the afternoon of Friday, July 9, 1881, Francis Jehl plucked a strand from a bamboo fan and instructed his assistant to carbonize it. The loop was placed inside one of Jehl's glass globes. When electrified, the loop seemed to incandesce indefinitely.

Edison sent teams of explorers to gather bamboo samples from all over the world for purposes of experimentation. He wrote to consuls in Panama and Puerto Rico, Jamaica and Paraguay, requesting samples of native bamboos. He sent a man to Japan, two men to the Amazon, and tried to talk Joseph Murray into going to India. He sent the famous explorer John Segredor to Florida. He reported back, "What makes this job so interesting is the strong possibility of getting bitten by a snake." A month late, Edison ordered him to go to Cuba, where, on October 27, he died of yellow fever.

Batchelor and Edison fought their worst—and last—battle. Their friendship came to an end.

Edison reminded Batchelor of his triumphs and successes. Batchelor reminded Edison of those who had broken ground before him. This was more than Edison could take. He ordered Batchelor out of his office. He paused at the door to quip, "Learn some science, Edison."

Batchelor took his family to Europe a month later. When he returned in the fall, he was met by a cold-hearted, impersonal employer. Their relationship was to be purely one of business from then on.

Batchelor returned to Europe to explore business opportunities there.

Ludwig Bohm had been persecuted out of a job at the Edison lab. He had never fit in with the rest of the men. He played zither and yodeled. Edison called him "sensitive" and "egotistical." In his spare time, Bohm made glass toys, including tiny glass swans that squirted water when he blew into their tails. The men were hard on him. They threw rocks against the window of his room in Sarah Jordan's boarding house. They put a remote-controlled tapping device on his window. When he was hard at work in his shed, they riled him up with a "corpse reviver"—a huge ratchet that gave off angry rasping sounds when run against the corrugated metal walls of the shed.

By October, he burst into the Edison office with tears in his eyes, blubbering about "a kind of treatment which no man with any honor can bear." Edison demanded to know what he could do about it. Bohm left, still blubbering.

The next morning at breakfast, one of his fellow workmen drew a pistol and waved it in his face.

"Pass the butter, Bohm."

Bohm resigned and found employment at the United States Electric Light Company. His employer, Hiram S. Maxim, patented light globes in October of

1878 and December 1879. Although American, he lived in England and operated his business from there.

William Sawyer's men had wanted Maxim to take over production of the Sawyer lamp after financier Albon Man went bankrupt.

Sarah Burnhardt visited Edison at his lab in Menlo Park. She was met by Upton, Jehl, and Edison. He showered her with "Edisonian charm." She compared him to Napoleon and told the press he was "the giver of light." When she returned to Paris, she painted two landscapes and shipped them to him as soon as the paint had dried.

Morgan had not been so easily gulled: Edison had finally been cornered into demonstrating his incandescent bulbs. The demonstration at the Morgan mansion in New York City illuminated the parlor brightly—with exploding sparks and flames.

While Sawyer, and finally Maxim, drowned in financial obscurity, John Pierpont Morgan and Anthony Drexel usurped the Edison Electric Light Company.

Chapter Twenty

Persephone

"Dear Mary, I picked you up a treasure in town today."

"Oh, Alice, how thoughtful! Let me see it!"

She unwrapped the shiny linen from the tiny statue and held it up to the parlor window to examine it in the late afternoon sunlight.

"I got it because it looks so much like you."

"Yes, it does! It's a Greek figurine, isn't it? I wonder who it's supposed to be."

"Persephone, I think. Yes, it says so on the bottom of the statue: Persephone. The Greek goddess."

"Who was she the goddess of?"

Alice suddenly realized Persephone might not have been such a good choice of mythological figures to have purchased. Reluctantly, she said, "I think she was married to Hades...."

Mary peered into her sister's face. "Alice—what's wrong? Why are you looking at me like that?"

"Oh, never mind, Mary...."

"That won't do, Alice. What is the matter? I can tell—"

"Oh, Mary, I know it's silly...but how are you and Thomas getting along?"

"Is that it? Me and Thomas?"

"That's...partly it."

"Oh, Alice, that man's impossible!"

"I thought so. It troubles me so much, Mary."

"Alice, I was so young when we got married! You're lucky. I was so young...."

"You didn't know. How could you?"

"It isn't just Thomas, Alice. It's his whole family. His father is worse than he is. That harlot he's taken up with—that Mary Sharlow—she's born that old man three children and they aren't even married.

"And that nephew of his—Charley—how horribly he died! I tell you, Alice, it's the whole family, the whole Edison family!

"Did Charley care about his wife's feelings? Did he care about anything? Oh, how could a man hurt a woman so much and so deeply? I saw how she suffered. I saw what she went through, Alice, and maybe it's better this way. Maybe it's better...he died."

Mary broke down and cried. Alice comforted her.

She gathered her strength.

"Then—there were those *men*, Alice, those evil *men* at the laboratory. Did you see how they ran that nice man, Mr. Bohm, away? It was Thomas' own brother-in-law, Neil, who pulled the gun on him at the breakfast table. He was the only one of them who had any manners, except that nice Mr. Upton and Mr. Batchelor. But Thomas even drove Mr. Batchelor away! Can you imagine that? Now he's in Paris, still working for Thomas, but they aren't on speaking terms. Oh, no. Now, it's strictly money, and Charles makes a lot of it, working for Thomas."

"Well, Mary, be grateful he has such a gift for making money!"

"Oh, please, Alice, I don't mean to sound ungrateful...but...." She burst into tears again and spilled them on her sister's shoulder. Outside, the three children played in the yard. Marion—"Dot"—was bossy. She was shouting commands to Will and Tom Junior.

Mary faced a secret fear, which she dared tell no one—not even her sister. They were almost out of money.

The house, the bank account in her name, the gifts—these had been her only source of comfort. Plus the fact that he spent so much time away from the house, in the laboratory or his office. He had been agreeable when she forbade him from sleeping, fully clothed and reeking of chemical stench, in the same bed with her. She felt chills of horror to know that he slept under his desk, under the cellar stairwell, or in the battery room of the machine shop. Everything she knew about him frightened her.

Mary trembled. Something was happening. Something evil.... She gathered her strength and slipped out of her sister's embrace. She moved to the sofa, picked up the statue of Persephone, and held it, contemplating the little image so much like herself, especially her face. She held it to her bosom. "Thank you, Alice. Thank you dearly."

Alice Stilwell married William Holzer on the second day of December, 1881. There had been no romance, no forewarning, and now Mary suddenly felt completely alone.

Staggering financial problems forced Edison out of Menlo Park. He leased the four-story "Bishop's Mansion" at 65 5th Avenue, north of Washington Square. Over the front door, a gold-lettered sign proclaimed: The Edison Electric Light Co. He then purchased the Roach Iron Works factory, on Goerck Street, also in New York City.

He forced the directors of the Electric Light Company to grant permission for an Edison Lamp Company exclusive on the right to manufacture electric lamps. The Edison Lamp Company was a nightmare. The working conditions were so humanly unbearable that the only poor creatures who could be hired were orphaned children off the streets of poverty-riddled New York.

Zenas Fisk Wilbur had been investigated for corruption at the patent office for the last time. Immediately after his cousin, Rutherford B. Hayes, left the office of the presidency, Wilbur was found guilty of so many counts of graft and corruption, his career with the government came to an end. He went to work immediately as Edison's patent solicitor.

Mary slept with the .38 Smith and Wesson Edison had bought for her during his Colorado expedition. She kept it under her pillow. Once, when Edison returned to the lab late at night without a key to the front door, he climbed the porch roof to the bedroom window—and nearly received a bullet in his brain.

Mary became sick again. She had never fully recovered from Will's birth, back in '78. He was four years old now, and developing problems.

So was Mary. She had put on weight—two hundred pounds—drank volumes of port, and gave many, many parties. Her husband never attended them, although the elite of society did. Now he wanted to sell her house in Menlo Park. It had been his Christmas present to her.

Edison I.O.U.s were so common throughout Menlo Park that they were used as a form of surrogate currency.

Edison had fallen into disfavor with Lucy Seyfert, William Seyfert's wife. She had loaned him a considerable sum—neither remembered how much—and ten years of delays on Edison's part had resulted in legal action: she was forcing him to sell his assets in Menlo Park.

In addition to Lucy Seyfert's loan, he had borrowed forty-three thousand dollars from the United States Electric Light Company, Maxim's firm, owned by Drexel and Morgan. Morgan wanted the loan accounted for. He wanted it *paid.*

Edison feared him. He did not fear Lucy Seyfert, but he did have more than a little respect for the sheriff—and he was wanted in New Jersey, banished, exiled to New York City.

With heavy-handed cunning, he exhorted Mary to sell the country cottage so he could pay off Lucy Seyfert and move back to New Jersey. She was too weak to respond with fury. She was propped up in bed, leaning against a pile of pillows. Involuntarily, she uttered, "…I…want…a…divorce."

A shocked silence followed. At last, he responded. "A divorce, huh? I shoulda known. Damn. Damn you, Mary. They'll look at you as a fallen woman, Mary. All of society will look down on you. You'll see. You know that, too. And you—being the woman who wouldn't stand by Thomas Edison! Whaddya say t'that, Mary?"

She burst into tears.

Edison roared with rage. He snatched a tiny white object off the chest of drawers and hurled it against the wall. It shattered. It had been Alice's gift to her, the statue of Persephone.

She sobbed even harder now. Finally, he turned abruptly and left the room.

A foreclosure notice had been posted on the entrance to the Menlo Park properties. The date of the sheriff's auction was July 22. After promising more money to Lucy Seyfert, Edison managed to get the sale postponed until August 12.

Edison absconded with his very reluctant wife on a trip to Florida. They were accompanied by his father and Jim Symington, ostensibly for her recovery.

Mary Edison languished in Florida from February throughout March. Edison left her almost entirely alone. She started to recover.

They returned to Menlo Park, in defiance of the law. Mary learned that her father was dying. Upon hearing the news, she suffered a nightmare while wide awake at the dinner table.

Edison sent an immediate telegram to Sam Insull:

> "SEND TRAINED MAN NURSE WHO IS NOT AFRAID OF PERSON OUT OF HER MIND. SEND AS SOON AS POSSIBLE."

Edison fled to New York to be as far from his estranged wife as possible.

Four days after her return from Florida, Mary's father died. Mary returned to New York. By the end of April, she was suffering delusions again. Edison announced his diagnosis: "A brain tumor. I am certain she is suffering from a brain tumor."

Dr. Ward questioned him. "How can you be so certain?"

"The intensity of the hallucinations, doctor."

"Hmmm. I see. Mind if I—"

"No need to examine her, doctor! I already have. And an Edison diagnosis is as good as from any medical doctor."

"I see...."

"Don't be taken aback, doctor! I've taken the liberty of prescribing a medicine of my own concoction."

"Do you mind telling me what's in it?"

"I certainly *do* mind! It includes some native herbs that must be mixed in such delicate precision that if some fool tries to duplicate the formula, they could poison a patient with such a tumor. Understand?"

"Uh, well, I...."

"Very good, doctor. Now, I'll see you tomorrow. Let's hope her condition improves, shall we?" He escorted the doctor to the door and bade him farewell.

For Mary, there was no sleep, no awakening, just the endless nightmares, the vicious hallucinations. She suffered headaches. Her skin was cold to the touch. Edison gave her stronger and stronger doses of his self-prescribed medicine, and her symptoms worsened gravely.

On May 13, the sheriff of Middlesex County in New Jersey visited the Edison Menlo Park lab to take inventory for the sheriff sale in August. Sheriff Andrew Disbrow even made note on the inventory of "a lot of manure."

Edison pleaded with Mary for her to sign the cottage over to him. She swore that everything in Menlo Park belonged to her. Then she lapsed back into incoherent ravings. She never recovered from her madness.

At two o'clock Sunday morning, on the ninth day of August, 1884, with Dr. Ward and Thomas Edison present, Mary Edison stopped clinging to the suffering of her body and her broken heart.

She had lived only twenty-nine years.

Years later, Edison explained to his daughter Dot, "Your mommy died of typhoid."

CHAPTER TWENTY-ONE

Foreigner

The sheriff's auction was again postponed until the tenth of November.

Batchelor made a special trip from Paris to attend the auction, and bought the entire property for a mere 2,750 dollars. Batchelor knew Lucy Seyfert was entitled to more than twice that amount, according to the judgment of the court, but he hesitated for so long to turn the deed over to her that he lost it by the time he was scheduled to return to Paris.

Francis Upton had worked for Edison for five years without pay, although he had officially been placed on salary. Edison promised him two hundred dollars per week at first, then three hundred. Knowing Upton was rich, Edison frequently borrowed money from him and never paid it back. Upton had really been paying to work for Edison.

Soon after Batchelor returned to Paris, he started sending enigmatic letters and telegrams to Edison about a "great man," a "genius" who had appeared seemingly out of nowhere and taken a job at the Paris office of the Edison Company. This man, this "gifted foreigner," had single-handedly revolutionized their overseas operation.

"Very good, Batchelor," Edison said, throwing down the latest letter in utter disgust. "Batchelor—when he gets worked up over something, no tellin' what it'll be."

Word had reached Edison that J. P. Morgan was about to take complete control of Edison General Electric—and that he planned to unseat Thomas Edison as president of the company.

Edison fought the takeover any way he could, but his unpaid debt to Morgan, a sum of forty-three thousand dollars, was just what Morgan needed to gain leverage for the takeover.

Gumshoe McCoy informed Edison that Morgan intended to rectify Edison's failure to make a viable light bulb; although the filaments burned for a time, the inside of the glass lamps turned black with carbon fumes within days. Morgan was considering turning the operation over to Hiram S. Maxim and William Sawyer.

Edison couldn't be bothered with the dealings of any "small-brained capitalist." He was attempting the greatest accomplishment of his entire career—his only truly original invention—the Magnetic Ore Separator.

Batchelor continued to rave in his letters about a mysterious gentleman scientist who appeared out of eastern Europe—of all places!—and performed miracles of redesign at the Paris installation. The man had a funny name that Edison couldn't remember.

He was obsessed by his Magnetic Ore Separator, his electric railway experiments—and he was trying not to think of the hostile takeover of Edison General Electric by John Pierpont Morgan.

That year, 1884, was a year of financial panic as well as the year that the French government gave the people of the United States a great statue, depicting the spirit of liberty as a woman holding a great torch.

During the summer of 1884, in the heat of a frantic day after the shipping manager for the *S. S. Oregon* gave Edison an insulting phone call about the unrepaired dynamos delaying the departure of the ship, Edison lied and said an engineer had already been dispatched to make the repairs. No one had been sent. A messenger boy burst in, gasping for breath, announcing trouble with a junction box at the corner of Ann and Nassau Streets.

Edison gave orders to a foreman, then sat down at his desk again to chew a cigar and ponder a newspaper article. He looked up suddenly, aware of a figure towering over him. He sat upright, startled. "Help you, Mister?"

The man said his name. Edison couldn't hear it. He raised his ear horn to his ear and offered a handshake.

The man stared at Edison's hand, then looked into Edison's eyes.

Edison withdrew his hand uneasily.

The tall man had blue eyes. Edison had blue eyes and considered them to be a sign of mental superiority. John Pierpont Morgan had blue eyes.

This man's eyes were metallic blue, electric blue, with silvery flecks.

"I have a letter from Mr. Batchelor, sir."

"From who? Speak louder."

"I have this letter, from Mr. Batchelor."

Edison didn't like this man. He felt something was wrong. "Batchelor? Something wrong in Paris?"

"As far as I know, sir, there is nothing wrong in Paris!"

"Nonsense. There's always *something* wrong in Paris!" Edison laughed raucously. The tall young man winced. His long face gazed down at Edison as he drew an envelope out of the pocket of his lapel.

Edison opened it casually. He unfolded it, studied it, frowned. It read:

> I KNOW TWO GREAT MEN, AND YOU ARE ONE OF THEM.
> THE OTHER IS THIS YOUNG MAN.
>
>   SINCERELY,
>   CHARLES BATCHELOR

So that was it. Batchelor, like Mary, like Charlie Edison, had probably gone insane. Edison threw the letter down.

"Can you fix a ship's dynamo?"

"Of course!" The stranger brightened, stood at attention.

"Good. Go down to this address. Here's a work order. Give this to the captain. Give this to the general manager. D'ya think you can do that?"

"Yes, of course, sir!"

"Good. Now get outa here!"

The tall man vanished. Edison shivered. He did not know why, on such a hot day.

He'd hired foreigners before, to pick their brains. Batchelor was English—a foreigner. Jehl was a foreigner, Kruesi was a foreigner. Bohm had been a foreigner...Edison hated foreigners.

This guy was a foreigner.

PART THREE

Titans

CHAPTER TWENTY-TWO

Americans

A young man wearing the colorful attire of a Montenegrin shepherd glanced down and spied a ten-dollar bill in the gutter. He paused to bend down and pick it up, then laughed and raised his arms. He announced, "My first day in America—and why should I work?"

Nikola Tesla watched the incident—part comedy and part drama—from the sidewalk in front of the Castle Garden Immigration Office. He looked out upon the streets of Manhattan. It was June, 1884.

Tesla fingered the coins in the bottom of his pocket: four cents. He was destitute. He had heard you could not be destitute in America.

He stepped into the swarm of pedestrians and worked his way to where the Montenegrin fellow had seen the ten-dollar bill, but it was gone. A bit of good fortune had been passed over by a foreigner—but snatched up by a native.

Tesla heard an outburst of profanity nearby. A man was swearing and kicking a big wooden platform supporting a generator.

"Pardon me," Tesla stepped up to the man.

"This gol-durned machine won't work! It just—*stopped!* That's all—it just *stopped!* Gol-dammit!"

"Perhaps I should take a look."

"You know about these machines?"

"Yes. It's a direct current generator."

"Durn right—it lights my store. We got those Eddy-son light globes—hey, if you kin fix it, you gotcherself twenny dollars."

Tesla's eyes widened. "Certainly. It should be repaired by the end of the day."

"You repair it by sunset'n'you gotta job!"

Tesla snatched a wrench from the toolbox, matched it to a half-inch nut, and twisted. He unscrewed the nuts and bolts that held the casing together and lifted it apart, assisted by a young man from the shop. Together they opened the casing and exposed the armature in less than half an hour.

"That is the problem," Tesla said, pointing to a sliver of copper that had come loose from the coil and fallen between the armature and the casing. "Let me remove it. There. The metal hasn't been badly scored, let me fix the wire coil and we can put it back together in ten minutes."

The owner of the shop was amazed. The generator roared back to life, the lights went on in his shop, and evening was still a few business hours away.

"Hey! Here's that twenny dollars! An'—Mister—you need a job? Cause I sure could use a guy like you around here!"

"Employment awaits me, sir! I thank you anyway, for the opportunity." Tesla departed, amazed and refreshed. Something exciting was happening here.

He heard people laughing, crying, cussing, arguing, and saying things he could not comprehend.

He saw a policeman waving his nightstick at a small dog. He yelled profanity at the pitiful animal.

"Officer—may I have a moment of your time?"

The man faced Tesla—then blasted him with a barrage of gibberish Tesla assumed was also profanity. At the end of the onslaught: "Well?"

"Uh, sir, I need to find Fifth Avenue. Can you direct me?"

The policeman stiffened. He eyed Nikola suspiciously. Then he shouted: "Six blocks down, then to the left!"

He secured himself lodging at a boardinghouse not far from 65 Fifth Avenue— office of the Edison Electric Light Company. He reported to the office of Thomas Edison the next day.

Explosions of shouts and curses filled the office Tesla had been guided to. A messenger boy standing before a huge desk clutched a telegram while several men stood grim and expressionless and a gray-haired, squat little man erupted with rage: "Get a work gang—if you can find any *men*—cut the current and *fix* that leak!" The gentlemen departed. The messenger boy fled. The square-jawed man sat back down, picked up a newspaper, and chewed his cigar.

Tesla stepped through the doorway, had his brief exchange with Edison in which he brought out his letter from Batchelor, and received his first work order. He hurried out of the office, out of the Light Company building. Edison impressed him for the same reason America impressed him: coarse, loud vigor. He glimpsed in that small, square-jawed, square-bodied gray-haired man the concentrated essence of the spirit he felt out on the streets.

He wondered if he had been cast onto a land colonized by barbarians. He sensed he was in a world one hundred years behind Europe. Yet, there was promise here: it was the promise of a fresh start. This was the land of Mark Twain.

Tesla and a crew of workmen boarded the *S. S. Oregon* and commenced making the repairs on the ship's lighting plant. They worked through the night and finished, weary, before dawn. The captain, first mate, and the shipping manager were greatly impressed.

Tesla returned to Fifth Avenue and encountered Edison and Batchelor ducking into a diner for breakfast, before getting an early start on the job.

"Well, here is our Parisian, running around at night!"

Tesla glanced up at the rising dawn. He answered nonchalantly, "Less than an hour ago I fixed the second of the two generators."

Edison cocked an eye, chewed his cigar, then said, "No kidding around...."

"I am serious, Mr. Edison."

"Yeah...I can see you are."

Batchelor leaned close to Edison's ear and said, "If he says he finished the repairs, sir, I think he means—he finished the repairs."

Edison looked up at Batchelor and winced. "Yeah? Is that what you think?"

"Let's go inside, sir." Batchelor pulled Edison by the elbow, off the sidewalk and into the diner.

Tesla looked into Edison's hostile stare—even as he vanished through the door. He was puzzled by Edison's attitude. Just as the door closed, he heard Edison remark, "Batchelor, that is a damned good man."

Tesla stood, silently pondering the final remark.

Perhaps, despite the glare of defiance, he had won Edison's approval. Strange, these Americans. They always seemed to be putting up a fight.

Tesla spent the rest of the day working hard on the job, then he ate dinner and retired.

On the brink of sleep, his mind served up wondrous visions.

The next day, he contemplated how to present his polyphase induction system to Mr. Edison.

For several days, he observed Edison as much as he could—which was infrequently, since Mr. Edison stayed in his office or took sudden trips to the Machine Works on Goerck Street.

Tesla was sent frequently to the generating station, 255–257 Pearl Street. The generator served all of Wall Street and most of downtown New York City, and the business district was completely reliant on that single station for power—for its telegraph offices. After his first few weeks of service, Tesla seized a chance to arrange such a demonstration.

Edison had called him to his office immediately after arriving at work one morning at the Electric Light Company.

"You wished to see me, sir?"

"Yeah, Tesla, sit down."

Tesla sat, crossed his knees, and folded his hands in his lap.

"You worked in Paris under Batchelor, right?"

Tesla was puzzled: Edison already knew that. "Yes, I did, sir."

Edison looked down at some papers he shuffled nervously on his desk. "Yeah, yeah, yeah, he knows you." He looked up suddenly. "What was Batchelor's title?"

"Why, manager of the works, sir."

Edison scrutinized Tesla. "Why, so I seem to recall...."

"Sir?"

"Tell me—who was the foreman at the mechanics department?"

"Why, a man named Cunningham, sir."

"This guy Cunningham ever get in any business deals with you, Tesla?"

"Why, yes, he did. Almost. Once."

"Yeah? What was the deal?"

"It had to do with...alternating current."

"Tesla, stay out of alternating current."

"But—sir—if you could imagine the advantages—"

"The States and all of Europe are set for power by direct current, Tesla. Do you know what conversion would cost?"

"I know that, sir, and I have entire systems already planned—"

"Yeah?" Edison leaned forward, over the desk. "What do you have planned?"

"Entire systems—"

"What kind of systems?"

"Why, Mr. Edison, I have charts and diagrams, a working prototype has already been built—"

"Working prototype? For what?"

"For my alternating current motor and generator."

"Great. That's all we need. A *new* alternating current model. Well, show me sometime. Just—get it over with."

When the time arrived, Tesla spread out schematics and diagrams with a flourish on the conference table. Edison and Batchelor were both present. Tesla glanced around—he did not know the other men present, and introductions had been withheld. When Edison looked up from the diagrams, he said, "Fine. Now— explain it all to me."

Tesla held up the diagram of the induction motor and explained the idea of the rotating magnetic field. He showed Edison drawings of generators, utilizing the same principle, converting mechanical motion and a rotating magnetic field into alternating current.

"And we can therefore dispense with secondary generating stations and the bulk of direct current wiring. Efficiently. Easily."

"Not so," Edison interrupted. He waved his cigar, stood up, paced. "I've seen it all before, Tesla. Not efficient cost-wise to convert. Let me tell you: this country, Canada, and all of Europe are already hooked up to direct current, y'hear? What's gonna happen when we—they, the civilized world—convert over? Who foots the bill on all this, huh? You do? Ha! My, you must be rich! What do we do with all the generators already in service? Scrap 'em? The batteries—I guess you know all this, they taught you this in school, did they?—these batteries, why, almost all the current generated is by batteries! You gonna make them obsolete, too, Tesla? Ha! They'll never build a battery that produces alternating current, Tesla, and the two systems will never be compatible. Not running through the same wire at the same time."

Tesla was silent for a long time.

"That's how it stands, Tesla. Sorry. Can't help you. Got that?"

Tesla gathered the drawings.

"There's one thing you can do for me," Edison said as Tesla reached the doorway.

"Yes?" Tesla's eyes lit up with renewed interest.

"C'mere."

"Sir?"

"There's fifty thousand dollars in it for you, if you take me up on this."

"Sir? Fifty thousand dollars?"

"Yes, Tesla, if you can face the task. It's this: these dynamos we've been making are obsolete. Archaic. We're capable of much better engineering than when we first made them. Well, I haven't got time to redesign our generators and systems, Tesla, so if you could take on that task for me.... Or I could let somebody else have a try. Whaddya say?"

"Fifty thousand dollars—sir, I'll take the assignment. Yes. I can design a better generator and system to go with it. You will see."

With that, the meeting adjourned. Tesla set about immediately to accomplish the task ahead of him. For fifty thousand dollars.

Edison waited a few moments after Tesla departed, then summoned a messenger and sent a personal letter to Gumshoe McCoy for a private conference. He showed up an hour later.

Edison lectured to him about tightening security measures at the Edison offices, laboratory, and Machine Works. Edison brought up company spying.

Gumshoe asked a few questions, chewed his cigar, grumbled. Edison repeated words McCoy had heard many times before: "Everybody steals in commerce and industry. I've stolen a lot, myself. But I know *how* to steal! They *don't* know *how* to *steal!*"

A long silence followed those words. They were almost the same words that had detonated that final argument with Batchelor.

Gumshoe McCoy nodded gravely. "Understood, sir."

Tesla labored at redesigning the dynamos and transmission system. Edison watched the young Serb with a mixture of suspicion and indignation. He made disparaging remarks about Tesla in his absence.

Even Batchelor, just before his return to Paris, was lured into Edison's derision and sarcasm. Summoned to Edison's office, Batchelor was introduced to a man sitting in a padded chair across from Edison's desk. His name was Thomas Commerford Martin. Batchelor stood in the doorway momentarily, then closed the door and sat down.

"We were just trying to find Croatia on a map," Edison said.

Thomas Commerford Martin chuckled. "We've been having a bit of difficulty locating it."

Edison handed Batchelor a map of Europe. "You find the place."

Batchelor took the map slowly but did not look at it. "To tell you the truth, I don't know where it is!"

Edison laughed. "That's what I thought."

Thomas Commerford Martin laughed loudly—a snide laugh, with a curl at the end of it.

"I wonder if there are cannibals there," Edison suggested.

Thomas Commerford Martin yowled. "I wonder if he *is* a cannibal!"

"Nikola Tesla—a cannibal! That's a thought. Whaddya think, Charles? Tesla a cannibal or not?"

"Come on, Edison. If he had any lack of talent, why did you choose him to redesign your outmoded generators?"

Edison shot Batchelor a sharp glance, then replied, "I'll tell you why, Batchelor! I have other projects to work on, and you know that. And you know what they are."

"If you mean your Magnetic Ore Separator, Mr. Edison, you are no closer to success with that than when you started. May I remind you, also, that you haven't progressed much on your electric rail system, either."

"What are you saying, Batchelor?"

"Well, you always did have a certain propensity for relying on the talents of other people, sir."

Thomas Commerford Martin laughed as the argument heated up.

Edison turned to Thomas Commerford Martin and said, "I think I'll ask our Nikola if he's ever eaten human flesh."

Batchelor: "Don't do that!"

"Why not?" Edison laughed. "The woods of Serbia must be filled with lunatics like him."

Suddenly, Batchelor chuckled—and exploded into laughter. Thomas Commerford Martin roared. Edison grinned. Victory.

Batchelor struggled to regain his composure. "You know...he *is* a bit eccentric. A bit *too* eccentric, I have to admit!"

"Eccentric!" Edison roared. "He's a madman, if you ask me! Charles, I have to give you this much: you sure found a prize-winner when you sent me Nikola Tesla!"

"Summon him," Thomas Commerford Martin said. "Get 'im in here!"

"You aren't going to do it," Batchelor gasped. He was appalled—yet he still laughed. "You aren't going to ask him? Not *that!*"

Edison lowered his voice. "Get that young Serb or Cro-ate or whatever he is, in here."

Batchelor abruptly stopped laughing.

"Good idea," Thomas Commerford Martin said. "Let's not laugh when he gets here."

Tesla appeared moments later. The men were silent. All eyes were upon him. He was slightly bewildered.

"Is anything wrong, Mr. Edison?"

"Oh, no, no, no! Hell, no, Nikola. It's just—" he shot a guarded glance at Batchelor. "Well, we were just wonderin', Nikola—" Edison gestured with a finger, drawing Tesla up close.

"Yes?"

"Well, Tesla, y'see…we just wanted t'know…have y'ever eaten human flesh?"

Tesla was shocked. He stiffened and stared down at Edison, aghast.

Thomas Commerford Martin and Thomas Alva Edison exploded into seizures of laughter. Charles Batchelor turned white with horror, red with embarrassment, then involuntarily exploded with laughter too.

Tesla, mortified and indignant, slammed the door behind him. He labored furiously the rest of the day.

He toiled hard every day on the task of redesigning the dynamos. He arrived for work two hours ahead of schedule and stayed long after the assistants had gone, completing tasks in their absence.

As if in atonement, Edison took him aside one day and commented, "I have many hardworking assistants, but you take the cake!"

Tesla was grateful.

After nearly a year of intense development, the new generators were ready for mass production. Tesla had designed a series of twenty-four different generators. He eliminated Edison's long-core magnets. He designed short-core magnets and made them of uniform size. He replaced the old control switches with fully automatic controls. The prototypes were successfully demonstrated, and Edison was impressed. "We go to full production on these immediately. Kruesi! Let's git on this!"

Edison hurried away abruptly.

Confidently, Tesla confronted Edison in his office. Uncautiously, he asked, "When can I expect it, sir?"

"Uh? Expect what, Tesla?"

"Payment, sir."

"Well, at the end of every pay period, damn it!"

"No—you don't understand—remember when you first mentioned this task to me? Do you remember now?"

"Yeah, I said our dynamos were obsolete, and you were given the *opportunity* to design a better generator for me! Was there anything *else* on your mind?"

"Yes! You promised me payment of fifty thousand dollars upon completion!"

Edison laughed crudely. "Nikola, you just don't understand our American sense of humor!"

"I see," he said, his voice cold. "If that was a joke, then I'm afraid I don't get it. I resign, sir."

"Aw, don't quit, Tesla. Where else're you going to find a job? How much're you gettin'? Eighteen dollars a week? I'll raise you ten—*you* find me an electrician in this city who makes twenty—eight dollars a week!"

Tesla was gone. Edison sat down, indignant.

He mumbled, "Damned Cro-ates! Half-mad Serbs!" He slammed his hands hard on the desktop, stood, and roared: "Where *else* is that half-mad Turk or Serb or whatever he is—where *else* is *he* gonna get another *job?*"

CHAPTER TWENTY-THREE

Toil

"Good morning, gentlemen," Tesla said. "What can I do for you?"

"You are Nikola Tesla?"

"Yes."

"My name is Carmen. James D. Carmen. This is my associate, Mr. Joseph Hoadley. We have come to discuss a business proposition, Mr. Tesla. Wonderful morning, isn't it?"

"Yes. It is. Come this way."

He led them up a brief flight of stairs to his room.

A modest interior led to a spacious balcony area, where the three men sat in the warmth of the early spring.

"Mr. Tesla," James Carmen gestured enthusiastically, "it has come to our attention that you are the man responsible for redesigning the Edison Company dynamos, is that correct?"

"Yes, it is."

"Very good. You have considerable education in electrical engineering, do you not?"

"I completed two years at the Polytechnic Institute in Gratz, and another two years at the University of Prague."

"You worked for the Edison Company here and in Paris, is that correct?"

"Yes."

"Before then, you worked for the Central Telegraph in Budapest, is that right?"

"I did work for the Central Telegraph Office of the Hungarian Government, that is true. Now, what is it that you wish to propose, gentlemen?"

"You have quite an impressive series of accomplishments, it seems to us. You've improved the telephone speaker-repeater systems and rebuilt the Edison dynamos. Tell me—have you received compensation for any of these...innovations?"

"Mr. Edison gave me a spoken promise of fifty thousand dollars upon completion of the task of redesigning his 'archaic, obsolete' generators, as he called them himself. But you are obviously aware of the circumstances that forced me to leave his employ."

"Yes, we are, Mr. Tesla, and we are sorry. You see, Mr. Edison has somewhat of a...reputation, if you catch my meaning."

"I was not aware of that—though I began to suspect as much, after working for the man for a while."

"Well, your suspicions were correct, Mr. Tesla. He is not one to be trusted."

"What about all his other achievements?"

"Hell, he never came up with a thing! Not that we're aware of. You see, Mr. Tesla, business in this country is competitive, tough. That's the way it is and I bemoan that fact. We've been keeping our eye on you because we think you could be the next great electrical talent. Soon, the world will start to wake up to the fact that there isn't much more than borrowed talent behind the name of Edison."

"Stolen talent seems more appropriate," Tesla said.

"It would seem so," Carmen replied. "Think about it, Mr. Tesla—you need investors, not another high-paying job."

Magic words rang in Tesla's ears. Before morning melted into afternoon, a contract had been drawn up between Tesla, Hoadley, and Carmen.

In the business meetings that followed, Tesla found that his investors wanted nothing to do with alternating current; they wanted to produce an improved arc lamp. Tesla busied himself with the task at hand.

The headquarters of the Tesla Electric Light Company were located in Rahway, New Jersey. Tesla worked in the branch office in New York City.

While Tesla toiled frantically to create the perfect arc light, the United States struggled to recover from the financial collapse of 1883 and the terrible economic relapse of 1884. That had been the year of his arrival, and so much had happened since then.

By 1885, Grover Cleveland occupied the White House. He would be unable to repair America's financial wounds alone.

That year, Nikola Tesla worked to produce a new arc light in a country that faced an uncertain economic future. When he presented his light to investors, he was given a beautifully engraved stock certificate with no redeemable value. He had been denied business influence in his own company.

In the spring of 1886, he suddenly had no company. He was penniless.

The rent was due on his room in the boarding house and he was unable to pay.

He sought for a flophouse, answered Help Wanted ads in the local papers—anything. Anything to stay alive.

He secured a bunk in an abandoned gymnasium that now served as a shelter for the homeless. He dug ditches with a dull shovel for a work crew in the heat of the day. The twelve-hour work days dragged by endlessly....

He arose every morning at five whether he had slept or not. By five thirty, he was given a work order by a foreman and sent off to the site of some excavation.

Pure survival seemed like less and less of a reason to live. The summer of 1886 would never end.

CHAPTER TWENTY-FOUR

Mina

Love came to Thomas Edison in the form of Mina Miller. At first, he found love to be terrifying.

This was not the same emotion he had felt toward Mary Stilwell. He thought he loved her—but his feelings toward her had been so much easier to control. Easier than the strange, exciting torment he felt in the presence of Mina. He had pursued romance, thought it to be safe, thought himself to be immune. Now, emotions surged with a vengeance. Edison tried to control the daring impulses his heart was urging him to take.

He met her at a party. He had never seen a woman gaze at him like that before. She was dark-haired, just a bit plump, attractive. He liked women with firm bodies, like Reubens painted. In a corset, she looked slender.

He tried to steal away from the party, but she cornered him on the balcony and tried to lure him into small talk; his reluctance and sudden, obvious shyness aroused her sympathy. Now was not the time to meet—and get to know—Thomas Edison.

Edison had been to New Orleans that year, until late May. While there, he met Lewis Miller, who had just invented a new type of grain mower. Edison was attending the World Industrial and Cotton Centennial Exposition in New Orleans with Ezra and Lillian Gilliland.

During his months in New Orleans, he came to know Lewis Miller and his wife, Mary Valinda. He also met Mina Miller, their daughter.

Mina sensed that Edison found her to be threatening. She waited to see him again; that was inevitable.

The inevitable took place in the elegant dining hall of the hotel Edison and the Gillilands were staying in. Lillian Gilliland was last to sit down. She made certain all the guests knew each other.

"Thomas? Have you met Lewis and Mary?"

"Why, yes I did, just the other night."

"That was a wonderful party," Mary said.

"And, Thomas, have you met John and Theodore?"

"Glad t'meetchya. Both o'ya."

"We met at the party," John said.

Theodore was shy. He looked up from his empty dinner plate.

"Have you met my daughters, Emily and Mina, Mr. Edison?" Mary asked.

"We've met," Mina said.

Lewis was suddenly interested. He raised an eyebrow. "Oh?"

"At the party, Father. Mr. Edison and I had a brief chat on the balcony, as I recall. Didn't we, Mr. Edison?"

"Why, uh, yes, uh, we did, as I recall...."

"I haven't met you yet," Mina's youngest sister called out.

"Uh, hello, I'm Thomas Edison."

"I know. I know all about you. They taught us about you in school."

"Oh, my," Mary exclaimed, blushing.

"Well, I'm Emily Mary, Mr. Edison. Pleased to meet you."

He kissed the girl's hand from across the table.

"My, that was gallant," Lillian said.

"You have—seven daughters, is that correct?" Edison fumbled for conversation.

"That is correct. Mina is my eldest. Daughter, that is."

Edison glanced at Mina fleetingly. She smiled.

She had dark hair and dark eyes—Edison had always been attracted to dark-haired women. She flirted with him silently, teasingly, with her eyes. His heart pounded. He pretended not to notice—or care.

"Lewis is responsible for another great invention," Mary said. "Aren't you, Lewis?"

Edison looked blankly at Lewis, seated across the table. Lewis smiled proudly.

"Uh, what else did you invent...besides the mower?"

"Sunday school," Lewis announced.

"You see," Mary said brightly, "I don't know if you know this or not, but we are Methodists, Mr. Edison."

"I invented Sunday school," Lewis continued. "I took the idea up with the pastor of our church, and he thought it was a good idea, so he instituted it, and it's been a standard program of the Methodist Church ever since."

"Not just the Methodists, dear, but the Lutherans now have Sunday school, and the Baptists have it—"

"So, Lewis came up with a great American institution, didn't you, Lewis?"

Edison let the conversation drift around him. At least they didn't ask him *his* view of religion.

In Boston, Edison saw the intriguing Mina once again.

Edison and Gilliland were working to overthrow the Bell telephone empire. From August 21 to 24, in 1885, Edison, the Gillilands, and the Miller family formed a party to visit a resort at the top of Mount Washington, the highest peak in the eastern mountains. They ascended the slopes by an old cog railroad, chugging laboriously up the steep tracks over the mighty trestles.

Edison taught Mina Morse code during that sojourn. He tapped, "You look lovely, my dear" on her knee. She tapped out her answer: "How romantic."

After she returned to her home in Akron, Ohio, Edison petitioned Lewis for permission to marry his daughter: "I trust you will not accuse me of egotism when I say my life and history are so well known as to call no statement concerning myself. My reputation is so far made that I recognize I must be judged for it, good or ill." The Edison letter shocked the people of Akron: he was almost twice Mina's age. Mary was unsure about atheism and had no illusions about Edison's religious views.

Lewis consented to the marriage of his daughter to Thomas Edison by the end of September, and Edison bought property near Fort Meyers, Florida, and attempted to buy a mansion in West Orange, New Jersey, which had been built by a tycoon named Henry C. Pedder. Pedder named it Glenmont.

If Edison had bought the mansion, he would not have been able to live in it. He was wanted throughout the state of New Jersey. Twice he had failed to show up in court over his debt to Lucy Seyfert—and he had two citations for contempt of court as well. He would be arrested upon crossing the state line.

February 24, 1886, fell on a Wednesday. Edison and Mina Miller were married in the afternoon, standing under an arch of red roses in the Miller Mansion. After the ceremony and dinner, Edison and his bride rushed to catch the 6:18 train for Cincinnati.

Their first night in Fort Meyers had been the first real night of their honeymoon. Mina insisted Thomas that he take a bath.

In the luxury of the grand bathroom in their hotel suite, Mina demonstrated to Thomas what a bath, for a married couple, should be.

Servants poured kettles of hot water, then bath oils were added, then the maids and servants departed. Edison took off his black coat, silk shirt, undergarments—and stepped slowly into the almost-too-hot water.

She called to him from the next room, "Are you ready?"

He was shocked. He had not expected this.

She must have presumed he was "ready," because she stepped from her boudoir into the bathroom, clothed only in her natural loveliness.

His mouth fell open. She was beautiful.

She was the daughter of religious parents, but she was approaching his bath-tub—naked! And she seemed to *enjoy* her nakedness!

The morning after the first real night of their honeymoon, Edison emerged a changed man.

Chapter Twenty-Five

Hate

Edison was glad that Serbian fool was gone. He was a clever electrician, yes; he had done a good job of creating new dynamos to replace the obsolete long-waisted Mary Anns. But he was a fool. A despicable fool. How had Batchelor's letter read? "I have known two great men. You are one and this guy is another." Something like that. Confound that Batchelor!

Batchelor tried to reprimand Edison for bullying people, but he would hear none of that. He waved Batchelor away.

"No wonder you don't keep friends long," Batchelor said coldly. "To you, we're all expendable."

Edison glared at him. "I like you better in Europe."

"That's only a few days away," Batchelor said nonchalantly. "To tell you the truth, Thomas, I like you better when I'm in Paris. Especially if you're in the States."

"Very funny, Batchelor."

"I'll admit that letter I sent with Mr. Tesla was a bit embellished—in it, I had to resort to calling you a 'great man' just to flatter your rather exalted ego. 'Everybody steals,' isn't that what you said? 'But I know *how* to steal.' Isn't that what you said, Thomas?"

"That's enough, Batchelor!"

"Mr. Tesla has resigned, Edison. That's a pity. You had another chance to steal. From another, um, rival."

"Is that why you sent him to me? Because of his ideas?"

Batchelor leaned forward. "Yes. Why do you think, Thomas?"

"His ideas are utterly impractical, Batchelor."

"He has the answer to alternating current—unpatented!—and you think his ideas are *impractical?* You must be mad—or blind!"

"Batchelor, I don't want to see the country converted to alternating current!"

"Why not, Thomas?"

"It's too dangerous."

"Nonsense, Edison. You can't even stand next to an electric street lamp in a rainstorm without nearly getting electrocuted!"

"The problem would be worse with alternating current!"

Batchelor laughed. "No, it wouldn't! Do you know why you are so afraid of alternating current, Thomas?"

"It's dangerous, impractical, and that's all there is to it!"

"It's because it's complicated, Thomas. You do best at simple things. That's why you are staggered by mathematics and you don't care to learn Ohm's law. You would need to learn a little about physics, Thomas, and I think that thought frightens you."

"That's a lie!"

Batchelor nodded. "Zenas Fisk Wilbur gave you your education in physics, as I recall. Didn't he, Thomas? The two of you in the patent office, after hours, getting him drunk on red wine or whiskey, whatever you could bribe him with, and the two of you would study science, alright, the science of plagiarizing other people's patents!"

"One more word—"

"And what? You'll fire me?"

"I might."

"Well, then, I won't be in Paris to help you make more money than you deserve!"

"Damn you!"

"Perhaps I would get to retire, after all."

"Get out of my office!"

"Certainly. Just tell me if I've been fired or not."

"I'll think about it."

"If you have to think about it, I'll consider myself retired." Batchelor paused on the way to the door and turned around slowly.

"Let's smooth this over, Batchelor."

"Perhaps."

"I need you in Paris."

"You need that?"

"Yes, I do!"

"How much?"

"Batchelor, don't do this. We still need to keep together. It's a good partnership. I trust you."

"Yes, that's it, isn't it? You've surrounded yourself with people you don't trust."

"Batchelor, I don't trust that…Mr. Morgan."

Batchelor laughed. "Now is a fine time to discover you don't trust J. P. Morgan!"

"He owns General Electric, now. He took it over."

"You owed him money. Wouldn't pay it back. What else could he do?"

"He's a capitalist. A goddamned capitalist."

"So are you, Thomas."

Days later, Batchelor departed again for Paris. Edison was relieved.

He was even more relieved when he learned Tesla was bankrupt.

During May of 1886, while Tesla labored as a ditch digger, Edison summoned Batchelor back from Paris to deal with a strike.

The skilled mechanics at the Goerck Street Machine Works were complaining of hazardous working conditions, poor pay, canceled paychecks, forced overtime, and often having to take the brunt of Edison's cruel temper—or his evil sense of humor. The strike ended in a lockout.

Edison and Batchelor bought the McQueen Locomotive Works. Those workers were not affiliated with any union.

Skilled mechanics were paid a dollar seventy-five to two twenty-five per day. Edison saw no reason to pay a skilled mechanic any more than a dollar a day. The lockout and takeover were successful. After seeing their jobs taken over, the mechanics acceded to Edison's demands. The railroad workers went back to work at the McQueen Locomotive Works, and Edison and Batchelor purchased an abandoned factory in Schenectady to convert into another laboratory.

Edison had begged Batchelor to remain with him in the States, but Batchelor's reply was immediate and unequivocal: *"No!"*

Batchelor returned to Paris.

CHAPTER TWENTY-SIX

Joy

Thomas Alva Edison had not been the only one. In fact, Edison had to vie for her hand in marriage. Mina sighed. There *had* been George Vincent, the Reverend John Vincent's son. Mina's mother had liked him. He was so nice looking, so cultured and sophisticated. Very dapper. But just not *right*.

Mina was glad she had married Thomas Edison.

Edison was crude, sometimes boorish. He despised baths (though his attitude was softening) and he often stayed out all night, not always remaining in the lab. The Reverend Vincent had become a personal friend of Edison's, through Mina's father.

That was what she admired about Thomas: he was bold. He got what he wanted. Even while courting a woman deeply loved by a man, he sought out that man's father for friendship—and financial gain. Edison was so persuasive, Reverend Vincent put up some of the money for development of the phonograph. That impressed Mina. He had been such a rascal.... Now, she was discovering what her choice entailed.

He was a sullen, angry man. He treated other people with bitter contempt. He had been an insensitive lover, at first, but she taught him how to touch. From their first bath together, he had become her pupil.

But his temper and his cynicism disturbed her. He frightened her, the way he railed on and on against his former employee, Mr. Tesla.

"Serves 'im right!"

He reveled in the triumph of his competitor's failed business enterprise.

She pursed her lips. "Now, Thomas, don't start in on that poor man again—"

"He's not natural, Billie."

"I wish you wouldn't call be that," she told him sternly. "I don't know what made you think of that awful nickname for me."

"Aw, don't git all riled up, Billie. Everybody's gotta have an affectionate name for their loved ones. I like the name. It fits you."

"Well, I don't like it."

"Ha ha! Well, it fits you. Billie! I like it!"

She frowned and shook her head.

Edison raved against Tesla: he wasn't natural, he wasn't married, he came from a cannibal country somewhere in the Slavic wilderness. Edison feared "that Tesla." If she managed to say something to divert him from "that Tesla," he only condemned someone else....

She played piano well, or so Edison thought. He knew nothing about music, aside from having learned how to strum a few guitar chords, years ago. Mina played loudly, and Edison liked that. Until she started singing.

She inspired the best in him. She stood by his side when he crushed the strike at the Goerck Street Machine Works. He appreciated that.

There were drawbacks, like her singing.... But a man cannot go unmarried for long and retain any credibility, not in this world. Edison counted his blessings, which were many, thanks to Mina.

She loved music. She sang Italian operas. He hated opera.

Tonight, she would be taking him to an opera. Not an opera, exactly. A concert. A symphony. A chorale symphony.

It was by Beethoven.

Beethoven was one of Edison's favorites: he had heard the Fifth Symphony, poured through his ear horn at his private booth in the concert house. He was very impressed. He attended a performance of the Seventh, and found himself overwhelmed, especially by the Second Movement. Edison admired Beethoven: he, too, had been deaf.

Edison bathed and wore a freshly laundered suit.

He climbed into the carriage with Mina. He took her arm, folded it in his own, and together they rode through the streets of New York City to the concert hall. When they arrived, there were so many people to meet, to shake hands with. They saw Colonel John Jacob Astor. On the balcony stood Dr. Leslie Ward. Edison caught sight of the young actresses Lillian Russel and Maxine Elliott standing with Lewis Cass Ledyard and Chauncey Depew, talking to John Pierpont Morgan. Edison shuddered at the sight of Morgan.

Mina quietly guided her husband to their seats. The music was about to begin.

"Freude, eine Gottelfunken,

"Tochter aus Elysium—"

Edison felt more uplifted than he had ever felt before. He was hearing Beethoven's *Ode to Joy.*

CHAPTER TWENTY-SEVEN

Westinghouse

He was sore. His body ached. He was impossibly tired. He had not slept in many nights.

The handle of the shovel inflicted sores and calluses on his hands. His gloves wore down to holes in just weeks. His hands ached most of all....

He was different from the rest of the workers. He knew it and they knew it.

While he toiled under the summer sun, while he labored in the winter snows, he tried not to think of Daniel. Daniel, the shining star of the Tesla family, would not have had to endure this grim toil. Daniel was different. He was a living, human godsend. Such people are spared the degrading agonies that other humans are forced to endure.

Where had Nikola gone wrong? Was it pride? Tesla struggled to survive. Regrets were futile and he knew it. He had been exiled, banished, probably defeated. His visions were lost. He was buried by the winter, by the very muck he was digging in, every day.

Spring was emerging. The sun was down. He had eaten. The other men were either playing poker or lying in their bunks, trying to go to sleep.

The foreman entered the bunkhouse. "Where's Mister Tesla?"

Nikola sat upright. Chills shook his spine. He felt dizzy. He did not know why. "I am here."

"Ah, Mr. Tesla. Would you come with me?"

He was still dressed: he was too tired to undress. He followed the foreman out of the bunkhouse and to his office overlooking the excavation site.

A man with a round face stood at attention, as if waiting to greet Nikola. He extended a hand. Tesla bowed formally.

"Mister Brown, I'd likeya t'meet Mr. Tesla."

"Thank you," Mr. Brown said.

The foreman departed quietly.

"I hear you are sitting on a discovery, sir."

"What do you mean?" Tesla felt his heart pound, his temples throb.

"I am interested in alternating current, Mr. Tesla. I have been for years. I am manager of the Western Union Telegraph Company."

Tesla hastily looked around for a chair. He sat down and drew a deep breath.

"You look exhausted, man!"

Tesla could not reply. Tears stung his eyes.

"Let me explain. I have generated a certain amount of consideration among investors regarding the practical advantages of alternating current over direct, which is in use right now. I have one friend who has put quite a bit of time and money into the problem, but hasn't had any success at it yet. Anyway, he is willing to invest both time and money in developing the idea, if someone else could make the useful breakthrough."

"Who might this person be, Mr. Brown?"

"George Westinghouse. Ever hear of him?"

"Yes! He invented the air brake!"

"Yes. So, you see, he is no idle tinkerer himself."

"When may I meet Mr. Westinghouse?"

"I can arrange a meeting at your earliest possible convenience, Mr. Tesla."

"I see...." The excitement was almost intolerable. He was racing forward toward something vast, inexplicable; something he could not comprehend. Within days, he was on his way to Pittsburgh to meet Mr. Westinghouse.

Tesla met him in his office. They exchanged cordial greetings.

Tesla explained his system to Westinghouse. The fellow inventor saw immediately the simplicity of the design, and they drew up a contract on the spot. By the end of the afternoon, Tesla was working with the chief engineer, William Stanley, on implementing the new technology.

Half a million dollars were provided automatically for capitalization of the Tesla company. Another million was placed in a development fund. The work had begun.

Tesla felt new life flood his mind and body. His senses were cleansed. His intellect was clear. His spirit was reborn. Nothing could prepare him for the battle that waited just ahead.

CHAPTER TWENTY-EIGHT

Power

The Tesla Electric Company opened in early April 1887. The address was 33 to 35 South Fifth Street. It was just blocks from the headquarters of the Edison Electric Light Company, at 65 Fifth Avenue.

When Edison heard the news, he was furious. He predicted disaster:

"That Westinghouse might be pretty good with air brakes, but he doesn't know anything about electricity!"

Alexander Graham Bell was attempting to take credit for the phonograph. He had filed a caveat on something called the "graphophone," which he said pre-dated the Edison phonograph by months, although he couldn't prove it. Edison approached one of the French scientists whose "sound embosser" had predated his phonograph. Etienne Marey was asked to assist him in the development of motion pictures.

Marey, immediately suspicious of Edison, soon found him to be likable and friendly. Both men marveled at how "the same idea can strike several minds at once." Marey agreed to assist Edison with his motion picture device.

William Kennedy Laurie Dickson reminded Edison of "that Tesla." He had first written to Edison about a job in 1879. He exploited his family connections and in the summer of 1885 he got his wish.

Neither Edison nor his men were inclined to take him seriously. He was twenty-nine years old, and somewhat effeminate, a trait Edison hated. He was a photographer. He wore hats—never took them off, except while dining.

Dickson was assigned to solve the problems Edison was having with his magnetic ore separator. The problems were insurmountable.

Dickson seemed oblivious to the reactions of the men around him. He was immune to the derision his presence aroused. He strode nonchalantly through the laboratory, ignoring hoots and catcalls.

Even Edison got the idea that Dickson was the wrong man for the ore separator, so he assigned the photographer to a new task: that of perfecting the kinetoscope. Dickson was delighted. From that time on, motion pictures were all he could think about.

Charles Tainter invested a huge sum of money in recording equipment: his confidence in Edison was strained to the breaking point. Every innovation brought lawsuits for patent infringement—and Edison still had not produced a reliable phonograph *or* a graphophone. Amid storms of controversy, Edison launched an attack against Westinghouse, Tesla, and alternating current.

George Westinghouse had been buying up all the patents in the developing field of alternating current from the late '70s, when Elihu Thomson built the first alternating current generator

to power lights at the Thomson-Houstin factory at Lynn, Massachusetts, to the distributor system patented by the French-English team of Goulard and Gibbs. However, an alternating current motor did not exist—that he knew about—nor an efficient means of generating the new current. Then he heard about Nikola Tesla. Rumors had reached him about a brilliant and eccentric genius who had worked for Edison. Westinghouse disliked Edison from the start, and it seemed like a matter of principle someone should go up against that patent-thief, that pirate. Westinghouse fancied himself to be that man. Now, he had his chance to defy—and beat—Edison.

Westinghouse knew that Edison was siphoning a stream of Morgan's money: he also knew that Morgan barely tolerated Edison. Edison was only an inconvenience Morgan put up with to control the Edison patent block. The Edison patent stranglehold needed very much to be broken.

Edison turned the full force of his attack on Westinghouse and Tesla. He fired off a letter to Edward Johnson:

"Just as certain death Westinghouse will kill a customer within six months after he puts in a system of any size. He has got a new thing and it will require a great deal of experimenting to get working practically. It will never be free from danger." Edison also warned Johnson that even though "none of his plans worry me in the least; the only thing that disturbs me is that W. is a great man for flooding the country with agents and travelers. He is ubiquitous...."

The next day, pamphlets and leaflets hit the streets of New York. Most bore the heading, Warning! The contents were nothing but lurid descriptions of being electrocuted by alternating current. This was referred to as being "Westinghoused."

William Kennedy Laurie Dickson refused to give up on motion pictures. He established a small motion picture studio and photography lab in his house, unbeknownst to Edison.

Tesla moved to Pittsburgh. There, he worked as a consultant to George Westinghouse for a salary of two thousand dollars per month. Living in a relatively modest style was easy for Tesla; he buried himself in the laboratory and performed countless experiments to perfect his system.

One day, Westinghouse called him into his office for a brief and private consultation.

"Yes, sir?"

"Have a seat, Mr. Tesla. You are aware, are you not, that your former employer, Mr. Edison, has launched an all-out attack on our system of alternating current?"

"'I am vaguely aware of that, sir."

"He has flooded New York City with leaflets of a defamatory nature."

"I see."

"It has come to our attention that he resorted to similar tactics against the gas companies during his campaign to implement direct current for use in lighting in place of gas."

"I understand this. I did not know these things when I worked for him."

"How could you? You were living in Europe at the time."

"I am glad to be informed of these things now."

"Tell me—what was your impression of the man?"

"I was impressed—at first. But then…."

"Then?"

"Well, I began to…I became disillusioned, sir."

"How so?"

"He remains…a somewhat unoriginal thinker, in my opinion."

"I see."

"He is a tinkerer, a buffoon! A bumbler in the laboratory. I have never seen so many people waste their time on utterly foolish experiments. He knows nothing of mathematics and relatively little of science. He refuses to learn Ohm's law, says it would 'impede the process of experimentation,' of all things! If he knew what he was doing, he could do away with a lot of useless experiments."

"Well, Nikola, you have certainly made our current systems and transformers efficient ahead of schedule."

"I see things, sir, with my mind."

"Eh?"

"I picture things clearly. I envision all the parts. Then I go to work."

"I see."

"This motor came to me in a flash! A *real* flash, mind you, while I was taking a walk with my friend in the park in Budapest. My friend—Anital—and I were walking when suddenly I remembered lines from *Faust* and I saw this machine, clearly, as if it was real."

"That's an amazing story, Nikola. What else do you have—" Westinghouse pointed to Nikola's head, "up there?"

"I have ideas that are clear to me, now, Mr. Westinghouse. For one thing, it has been my boyhood dream to tap the power of Niagara Falls."

"I see."

Tesla smiled—a rare event, Westinghouse noted.

"It is also my boyhood dream," Tesla went on, "to meet Mark Twain."

Westinghouse laughed. "I hope you satisfy both dreams, Nikola."

"If you can help me fulfill the former, I will be satisfied."

"What—tap Niagara? If anyone can do it, I believe you can, Nikola."

CHAPTER TWENTY-NINE

Animals

While Tesla worked diligently in Pittsburgh, Edison's campaign against Westinghouse and alternating current took a gruesome turn. He was paying boys in West Orange, New Jersey, twenty-five cents for every dog or cat they could catch. Soon, the strays had vanished and family pets were in danger. The animals were being "Westing-housed" in a crude booth set up on the public sidewalk outside the laboratory.

Soon, throngs of people gathered to watch members of the local animal population dropped by Thomas Edison onto metal plates electrified by alternating current. Horrified spectators watched a famous inventor fatally shock helpless felines and canines with "Westinghouse current."

Edison lectured about the dangers of this new current: "What are the lives of but a few dumb animals compared with the very lives of your wives and children?"

People left the "demonstrations" shaken and horrified. The sight of murdered house pets would not easily be forgotten.

Tesla's plan to establish a generating plant at Niagara Falls sparked another round of fury from Edison. He stepped up his propaganda assault in all the big cities. He nearly ran out of animals in the state of New Jersey to electrocute. And he had no plans to develop alternating current on his own. He was battling to keep a few basic patent rights on telephone equipment, make a workable phonograph, and build his magnetic ore separator.

On October 12, 1887, Tesla's patent attorneys, Duncan, Curtis, and Page, filed the application for his patent on the polyphase motor and related systems.

Edison was frantic. His temper was more explosive than ever, around the lab and at home. He hated Westinghouse. He *hated* Tesla.

Every Saturday, Edison held special press conferences on the laboratory grounds. These were called "educational seminars." Newspaper reporters were invited to watch dogs and cats "get Westinghoused."

Reluctantly, George Westinghouse responded. He issued fact reports that were unfortunately more technical and less entertaining than the lurid shock accounts. Thomas Edison, Samuel Insull, and a former carnival barker named Harold P. Brown formed a traveling entourage, a road show, in the grand tradition of the snake-oil medicine show...only this caravan featured the electrocution of large dogs and half-grown calves.

Harold P. Brown introduced himself as "Professor Brown," although he was not a professor at all; he had no college training in his background. His "credentials" came from traveling with Thomas Edison.

Throughout the midwestern states and on the outskirts of every major city, the Edison road show condemned Great Danes, German shepherds, and young cows and bulls to death in front of crowds of incredulous spectators. The agony of the beasts intensified the Edison message: this new current was lethal, dangerous, uncontrollable. The spectacle of the carnage proved it.

CHAPTER THIRTY

Magic

The crowd roared with applause.

Professor William Anthony of Cornell University insisted that Tesla lecture; he agreed to, and delivered a fabulous speech before the American Institute of Electrical Engineers on May 16, 1888. The result was overwhelming. The name Tesla had been a vague rumor to most of them, but now he was embedded in their memories.

The scientists and engineers craved answers, and Tesla delivered them. He lectured eloquently about the advantages and benefits of this new current. To those whose jobs were to send the current through lines, dispensing with the secondary stations to boost the current over long distances, word of high voltage, low amperage conduction was important. To men who worked to overcome the dangerous tendency of electric streetlights to arc and shock pedestrians in the rain, solutions to problems of safety were of absolute importance. To the electricians, an efficient motor driven by alternating current was the greatest breakthrough of the century. Professor Anthony witnessed the first American demonstration of the polyphase motor. Impressed, he wrote articles for various trade publications, reviewing the system favorably.

The eminent Dr. B. A. Behrend attended the lecture, then called a special conference of his own. He told the press:

"Not since the appearance of Faraday's 'Experimental Researches in Electricity' has a great experimental truth been voiced so simply or clearly.

"He left nothing to be done by those who followed him. His paper contained the skeleton of even the mathematical theory."

Such praise resounded through the company of engineers, electricians, telegraphers, inventors, physicists, and mathematicians. Michael Pupin, a fellow Serbian engineer, also recognized the superiority of alternating current over direct, and hailed it as a breakthrough. He had earned degrees from both Columbia and Cambridge Universities, and was recognized as a physicist as well as an electrical engineer. With such praise from scientific circles, Tesla emerged into a strange limelight no one else had ever shared.

He had been given sixty thousand dollars from the Westinghouse company. Six thousand of this was in cash, plus 150 shares of stock. He had been promised royalties oftwo dollars, fifty cents per horsepower of electricity sold. He frequently commuted with George Westinghouse between New York and Pittsburgh whenever their trips could be combined.

Westinghouse owned his own railcar—a small but grandiose palace on wheels decorated in wine colors, with Persian rugs and Oriental tapestries. Tesla reclined in a padded sofa while the rails raced behind them.

"That was quite some speech you gave at the AIEE, from what I managed to hear."

"Thank you. I meant to talk to you about that. Has it been of any benefit financially? From what Albert Brown told me, the Edison campaign has intensified and could still be doing us damage."

"I get telegrams every day, Nikola. They should be piled on my desk when we get back. Most of them are from technicians, electricians—should I say more?"

"I sincerely pray the response from scientists and engineers will continue."

"It won't abate. Edison's scare tactics seem pretty shallow in the face of scientific inquiry."

"Let's hope so."

Westinghouse chuckled. "From what I've heard, things aren't so peaceful in the Edison camp. He sent Batchelor off to Canada on business, as soon as he returned from Paris this time. They aren't getting along at all. Edison has become more intolerable than ever."

Tesla laughed. "Is there anything more I should know about, George?"

"Yes, there are things, Nikola."

"I was wondering about the infringement suits...."

"There have been two more. In addition to the Bailey suit, somebody named

Deprez and somebody else named Bradley have filed claims. Frankly, I don't think anything will happen. The cases will go into litigation and probably stay there forever."

"What about General Electric? Surely, Edison has taken something out on alternating current by now."

"He commissioned Steinmetz to make some kind of transformer. He's filed a caveat—I don't know any specifics—but he came out last week and said it was only a transformer, and that your polyphase system has nothing to do with a transformer. So Edison didn't like that."

"I can well imagine."

"Have you heard anything about the Niagara Falls Commission?"

Westinghouse shrugged. "Not promising. They are still considering the possibility of installing a dynamo, but the members of the Commission are very stodgy, to say the least."

"You can't tell me they will still choose in favor of direct current!"

"It is a possibility, Nikola. They might still. Who knows?"

"Who is on the Commission?"

"That is the problem, Nikola: Lord Kelvin was recently appointed to be head, and he's a staunch advocate of direct current."

"Good God—why?"

"Don't ask me. He's an old man. Direct is all he knows. Simpler engineering problems—*he* thinks. Who knows? One of us should ask him."

"I've heard something about money—"

"Oh, yes. Some contest—three thousand dollars in cash for whoever submits the most feasible plan to construct a generating station at the Falls. So far, Thomson-Houston and General Electric have not submitted any plans. The Commission says they've received a lot of entries, anyway."

"What are your plans, George?"

He shrugged. "Three thousand dollars isn't much money just to build a direct current generator that will be obsolete in a few years."

Tesla laughed. "Don't do it, George."

"I have no plans to, Nikola. Let 'em try. We'll be there when they fail."

CHAPTER THIRTY-ONE

Chair

"We need a demonstration!"

Batchelor and Insull stared gravely out of the darkness. It was a hot night in the office. Insull's eyelids and mustache drooped. His cheeks were hollow. Batchelor had turned gray. His lean and handsome face was weary. He looked haggard and old.

Edison was just back from the Paris Exposition. The tour had been a succession of banquets and parties, exhibitions and lectures.

Back in New York City, he was faced with growing excitement in scientific circles over alternating current. And constant mention of the name Nikola Tesla.

"We need a demonstration!"

"Yes, Thomas," Batchelor agreed. He intended his monotone to convey boredom. He had heard it all before. "What should this great demonstration be?"

"Something that will leave the public so scared, so terrified, they will never trust a company that uses alternating current. Ever."

Insull raised his shaggy eyebrows. "That's a tall order, Thomas."

Batchelor leaned over and said dryly: "Al thinks he can do anything and the public'll eat it up. Don't you, Al?"

"Batchelor, they don't care about facts and figures. They just care about their tiny little lives. And if they're scared—"

"You tell 'em, Edison. What are you working on, now? You've been struggling with that 'ore separator' for years now, and how far have you gotten with it? You had Dickson working on it for a while, now he's still trying to make the phonograph work, which no one has quite been able to do yet."

"Are you quite through, Batchelor?"

"I think you've spread yourself too thin, as they say, Thomas."

"T'hell with you, Batchelor."

Batchelor laughed. Insull shot him a hot glance, then returned his gaze to Edison.

"Have you anything to say, Sam?"

"I'm with you," Insull said. "I agree—we need a demonstration. A show of power that'll make them think. Shake 'em up, real good."

"Batchelor, I think you should depart now." Edison gestured toward the door.

Batchelor nodded, stood, and departed.

"Sam, I no longer wish to include Mr. Batchelor in any of our plans in the future."

"We see eye to eye on that, Al."

"Good. He's a loose cannon on the deck, as they say."

"Y'got any plans, Al?"

"Yes. Professor Brown has secured three alternating current patents through a fictitious name for a New York company. They don't even suspect yet."

"What can we do with them?"

"Brown's got ideas, but nothing concrete, nothing viable—yet."

"He's a bit of a showman. He should be left out of the demonstration—whatever it is."

"I agree. It should be something that will strike fear into the domes of the intellectuals as well as the common men."

"Not a sideshow."

"Oh, I agree!"

"Talk to Brown. Talk to McCoy. Gumshoe knows people. He has connections we all envy."

Three nights later, after Brown returned from one of his famous road shows, Edison met with him secretly at the Menlo Park lab. Joe Gumshoe McCoy was also present, as was Samuel Insull.

"Well, boys, what we've come up with so far is this—the Professor here knows a coupla the boys at Sing Sing. Got that?"

Gumshoe grinned. *He* got that.

Insull blinked, shrugged.

Brown folded his arms and tilted his head back smugly.

"Well, if you need me t'spell it out for you, I will: Sing Sing, the prison system in general, is looking for a new method of execution. Got that?"

Insull leaned forward, gasped, then settled back in his chair slowly. A faraway look drifted over his face. Bliss.

"So, what we do is send Professor Brown here to New York, to arrange a proposal to the prison people based on these...experiments. Then—let's hope they take the bait."

Gumshoe McCoy nodded slowly. "Clever, Edison. Very clever."

"I thought you'd appreciate that, Joseph. Now—what I want to do is case out Sing Sing. Find out if the officials there have any little secrets, any vices they are not very public about. See if they can be tempted."

"That's a start," Gumshoe said.

"Brown, I want you to go back to Sing Sing. I'll have Upton write you up some kind of report—he's very good at that, and he takes everything so damned seriously."

Insull laughed. His voice was hollow.

"Sam, I want you to stay here and help me design an electric chair."

Insull nodded and smiled.

The plan had been proposed and implemented. Gumshoe McCoy did his job and found the prison officials to be corruptible—cavorting with prostitutes, drinking, and accepting of sexual favors and political gratuities. Government jobs *were* political jobs.

While Francis Upton wrote a report on the deaths of hundreds of animals, Insull and Edison designed what was intended as a device of execution.

A commission had been established by the State of New York to investigate the possibility of using electricity to kill murderers. A man named A. P. Southwick was contacted, and he and Brown discussed details. When the plan was given clear approval, Edison, Brown, and Menlo Park laboratory manager Arthur Kennelly conducted experiments on human beings.

Gripping two electrodes and standing barefoot on a metal plate, the workers took turns letting low-amperage current flow through their bodies while Edison measured their resistance capacities.

The electrical resistance of human beings varied from 6,100 to 9,900 Ohms.

Edison ordered a horse to be led into the dynamo room of the lab. The horse weighed 1,230 pounds.

Killed—in half a minute.

The deal was finalized: on August 6, 1890, one William Kemmler was to die by electrocution at Sing Sing Prison in New York. Edison elected to be present.

He recommended low voltage—"One hundred and fifty volts of alternating current will do damage comparable to five or six thousand volts, continuous." The executioner set the voltage at one hundred and fifty, threw the switch—and Kemmler screamed. His agonized wails were grotesque to hear. Torture inflicted amazing distortions on the human voice.

Edison giggled. No one noticed. He remembered the day he burned down the barn, when he was a boy....

The switch was cut, and Kemmler's screams melted into eerie, quavering moans. Edison clenched his teeth and fists. He was struggling against laughter.

"I need to raise the voltage!"

Edison caught his breath. He called out, "That should've done it!"

"But—it didn't, sir!"

"Then take it up to one eighty five. That'll do it."

"There! Now!"

Kemmler screamed louder than before. Edison burst out laughing.

Now all eyes were upon Thomas Edison. He froze—for an instant—then giggled hysterically.

Kemmler continued to scream frightening, shrieking, high-pitched, unearthly wails. Edison laughed uncontrollably, now. He didn't care. He was clearly without restraint, completely in abandon. He was having a wonderful time. The current was shut off.

The warden ordered, "Take it to two hundred."

"Yes, sir."

Two hundred volts: more screaming. Weaker, due to exhaustion.... The current went off.

"Three hundred."

Kemmler was still partly conscious. Edison was escorted from the room. He shook as hard as Kemmler had, and his own laughter acquired an eerie tone similar to Kemmler's unearthly cries.

After the debacle, George Westinghouse was asked to comment. He met with reporters, speaking from the balcony of his railcar the next day.

"They could have done it better with an ax."

CHAPTER THIRTY-TWO

Institute

"There is no subject more captivating, more worthy of study, than nature. To understand this great mechanism, to discover the forces which are active, and the laws which govern them, is the highest aim of the intellect of man...." He paused, gazing out at the ocean of eager faces crowded before him. Every chair was occupied—and people crowded the back and stood in the aisles.

"Nature has stored up in the universe infinite energy. The eternal recipient and transmitter of this energy is the ether. The recognition of the existence of ether, and of the functions it performs, is one of the most important results of scientific research. The mere abandoning of the idea of action at a distance, the assumption of a medium pervading all space and connecting all gross matter has freed the minds of thinkers of an ever-present doubt and, by opening a new horizon—new and unforeseen possibilities—has given fresh interest to phenomena with which we are familiar of old...."

He stood behind a podium beside a wide table, displaying an assortment of machines. One was his polyphase motor. One looked like a wheel, a thin disc, mounted vertically. One looked like a cone, coiled with copper wire, standing upright, supporting a silver ball.

"We still admire these beautiful phenomena, these strange forces, but we are helpless no longer; we can in a certain measure explain them, account for them, and we are hopeful of finally succeeding in unraveling the mystery which surrounds them.

"In how far we can understand the world around us is the ultimate thought of every student of nature...."

He expounded upon knowledge, philosophy, and "natural philosophy." His words explored relationships between matter and energy; he was exactly the way Edison described him: "the poet of science."

"The old theory of Franklin, although falling short in some respects, is, from a certain point of view, after all, the most plausible one...."

He reminded them of the role of science: "But a theory which explains the fact is not necessarily true. Ingenious minds will invent new theories to suit observation and almost every independent thinker has his own views on the subject.

"It is not with the object of advancing an opinion, but with the desire of acquainting you better with some of the results...."

As he spoke, he walked to the table and demonstrated one of the machines— a vertical wheel mounted on a brief armature, brushed at the top by copper wires. Tesla started the wheel by hand; it rotated and a current arced between electrodes at the base of the machine.

"It would be uselessly lengthening the description were I to dwell more on the details of the construction of these machines. Besides, they have been described somewhat more elaborately in the pages of *The Electrical Engineer*, of March 18, 1891."

The lights dimmed. The loud electrical spark continued snapping.

"In operating an induction coil with very rapidly alternating currents, among the first luminous phenomena noticed are naturally those presented by the high-tension discharge."

A cylindrical machine had begun to hum. Beside it, arcs of blue light flashed from two small boxes at its base. Above the droning cylinder, a shaft, wound with a tight coil of thin copper wires, started throwing off brilliant filaments of light. Electricity snapped and buzzed, leaping and writhing out of the ball atop the shaft.

"The paradox exists, that, while with a given current through the primary the shock might be fatal, with many times that current it might be perfectly harmless, even if the frequency is the same."

He raised his hand beside the slim shaft—and his fingertips intercepted the blue-purple sparks.

"To avoid misunderstanding in regard to the physiological effect of alternating currents of very high frequency, I think it is necessary to state that, while it is an undeniable fact that they are incomparably less dangerous than currents of low frequencies, it should not be thought that they are altogether harmless."

He stepped up the voltage; the discharges got brighter, longer, louder.

"The streaming discharge of a high tension induction coil differs in many respects from that of a powerful static machine...."

He raised a glass tube near the blazing discharge: it flashed three times, then blazed with white light.

"At this point, the luminous stream is principally due to the air molecules coming bodily in contact with the point; they are attracted and repelled, charged and discharged, and, their atomic charges being thus disturbed, vibrate and emit light waves."

He demonstrated several different types of induction coils.

He spoke with a high-pitched voice with only a trace of an accent; every word he enunciated was pronounced with perfect clarity.

Added to his six feet and two inches of height was the thickness of the cork platforms on the soles of his shoes. Behind him stood a metal Faraday cage, intercepting the dancing lightning bolts. He waved the blinding glass rods like magic wands—he called them his "carbon-button lamps." They received the power cast off by the towering coil without wires. Tesla lit his tallest high-energy induction coil.

The audience drew back, awed. Lightning bolts like fiery pythons streamed from the four-foot shaft, supporting a blazing coppery ball.

Without a word of warning, Tesla put both hands on the discharging ball. The audience was horrified as Tesla was consumed in blazing arcs of lightning. When showers of sparks from his head subsided, his hair was standing on end and blazing streamers of current were arcing from his hair to the Faraday cage behind him. He was laughing ecstatically.

Chapter Thirty-Three

Lectures

"Nikola! Over here. I need to talk to you."

"Ah, George! I am glad you could make it."

"Brilliant demonstration, Nikola. Are you busy?"

"No, not at all, Mr. Westinghouse."

"Call me George at all times, Nikola. Listen—that was a dramatic demonstration! No one could have pulled it off as brilliantly as you."

"Nikola! Nikola!"

Tesla turned around. He had been spotted. A tall, thin man and a short man approached.

"Professor Anthony," Tesla called, waving. "Have you met Mr. Westinghouse?"

"No, sir, I haven't. I am William Anthony, and this is my friend, Michael Pupin. I represent Cornell University, Professor Pupin is from Columbia."

"Mr. Tesla," Professor Anthony beamed. "Brilliant lecture. Brilliant."

Professor Pupin extended his hand. Tesla looked at it, then bowed. Professor Pupin was sightless taken aback. He managed to say, "Most convincing, Mr. Tesla. Tell me—how many volts did you have running through your body?"

"Between one thousand two hundred and one thousand six hundred."

"Amazing. But—" Pupin shook his head. "You mean to say you were in no danger at all?"

"None, gentlemen. I stand before you unharmed."

Professor Anthony nodded. "This might solve all of our present electrical engineering problems."

"It makes possible many things," Tesla said. "What you have seen before you goes a long way toward transmission of both power and messages over global distances without wires."

Professors Anthony and Pupin stared at each other, then at Tesla.

"You mean," Pupin stated flatly, "you think you will be able to transmit signals—messages—without wires?"

"Yes, Professor Pupin."

Westinghouse nodded. "You never told me that, Nikola."

"George, I have many things in my mind that I have never told you about."

"Why not?"

"I never speak of things, George, unless I have nearly completed a design for making it go directly into operation."

Professor Anthony was wide-eyed. "You mean…you think you are almost ready to put into operation…a way of transmitting signals without wires?"

"Not just signals, Professor Anthony, but messages. As complex as you want to send. Voices, maybe even pictures. Yes, I have solved the engineering problems for both voices and pictures."

"Excuse me, Nikola. May I speak with you privately?"

"Certainly, George. Excuse us, gentlemen. Business."

Tesla followed Westinghouse into a corridor. They found an open window admitting the fresh breeze of the night. Far from where other ears could reach, Westinghouse said, "I saw our legendary Professor Brown tonight."

"Oh, really? Well, it *was* open to the public…."

"Yes, and I'm glad. He nearly fled the building when you placed your hands on the ball of that induction coil."

Tesla laughed. "I thought I glimpsed someone running for the door at that moment."

Westinghouse chuckled. "That was him."

"He is probably informing Mr. Edison right this very moment about the festivities of the evening."

Westinghouse laughed. "Serves 'em right. If *they* want to give the public a scare, let 'em. But it took you and your Tesla coil to scare them *right!*"

That had been the night of May 20, 1891.

Early in 1892, Tesla crossed the ocean to lecture before the electrical engineers of Great Britain. His London lecture at the Institute of Electrical Engineers was hailed as "a major scientific event."

Tall, slender, debonair, he was the instant toast of British society. Charming yet eccentric, he caught the attention of both the academic community and the sphere of wealth and aristocracy.

After the lecture, British physicists and engineers attempted to persuade him to repeat his lecture before the Royal Society, but he declined.

He explained, "I never repeat the same lecture."

Sir James Dewar invited him to his office for a private drink. Tesla excused himself and followed the elderly scientist down the darkened hall to a spacious and ornate room furnished with a vast mahogany desk and several padded chairs.

"As you know," Sir James Dewar spoke, his voice thick and resonant, "Michael Faraday occupied this office before me."

"I am aware of that, sir. I feel honored that I can occupy the same space as Faraday on this evening."

"That was a Faraday cage grounding out those sparks sent by your induction coils, is that right?"

"We are all well aware of Faraday's contributions to science, Sir Dewar."

"That is true, Nikola. His discoveries have changed the world. As will yours, I know."

"Thank you, sir."

"You mentioned sharing the same space as Faraday. Mr. Tesla—how do you like that chair?"

"Well, sir, it's a comfortable chair. A *very* comfortable chair!"

"Is it, sir? I'm glad you think so. You see, that was Faraday's favorite chair." Tesla suddenly looked down at the thick velvet upholstery, the elegant burgundy fabric with ornate gold trim.

"May I offer you a drink?"

"Certainly!"

He opened a cabinet behind the desk. He drew down an unopened bottle of fine Scottish whiskey. He poured two goblets of the drink, kept one, and handed the other to Tesla.

"That bottle of Scotch is more than thirty years old, Nikola. Unopened."

Tesla tilted his head back and closed his eyes. "It *is* very good. Very good, sir."

"Faraday's favorite whiskey. Yes, Nikola, it is good. Very good, in fact."

Nikola looked at the glass, tilted it, studied it. "I appreciate this honor, sir...."

"Tell me—if the occasion is great enough, do you break your own rules?"

"What do you mean, sir?"

"I was saving that whiskey for a special occasion," Lord Dewar said. "I can't think of anything more fitting."

Tesla lowered his head reverently.

"I'm sure you appreciate this moment, sir," James Dewar said. "Give it some consideration."

"Very persuasive," Tesla said.

"Oh, I *do* mean to tempt you! Oh, yes, I am being unabashed about that. Yes, I want you to lecture before the Royal Society of Great Britain. Let me be clear about that! But—do as you will, Mr. Tesla."

Tesla savored the whiskey. Sir James Dewar poured him another glass.

"It is more than just tempting. To be bestowed this honor, Faraday's chair, his favorite whiskey...it is like being with him, while I savor his whiskey. Yes, I think I will do it, Sir Dewar. Yes, I will."

The lecture of February 3 was repeated within the week. It was received with praise and enthusiasm by the scientists and technicians present, then he departed for France to deliver a lecture accompanied by a demonstration before the Society of Electrical Engineers of France.

The veritable show was the source of immediate excitement on the part of the scientific community. The awesome sparks, the high voltage electrical discharges, and the illumination of the Faraday cage by writhing arms of lightning—airborne current—were displayed on the stage before them.

The peak moment came when Tesla demonstrated the safety of alternating current by grabbing the ball atop the high-energy induction coil with his bare hands. Streams of electricity rocketed through his hair into the bars of the Faraday cage behind him. After the lecture was a reception, after which Tesla found himself on the streets of Paris conversing enthusiastically with a fellow scientist on the patio of the Cafe de la Paix.

A woman departing from a theater party passed nearby. She glanced over her shoulder coyly as she passed Tesla's table. As she walked down the sidewalk, her lace handkerchief fluttered onto the hedge by Tesla's elbow.

He did not pause to finish his sentence. He swept the handkerchief off the hedge and swiftly handed it back to the young woman before she could walk away.

He glimpsed her face. She was beautiful. And familiar. He sat down and finished his statement. The young lady gasped with such rudeness. Abruptly, struck with a hurt look in her eyes, she walked away.

"Do you know who that was?"

"No. Should I?"

"Good God, man—that was Sarah Bernhardt!"

Tesla shrugged. "I do seem to recall some old tradition of dropping a hankie to denote romantic interest."

"Yes, that's exactly the point!"

"Really, sir, if I had been interested, so to speak, I would have reciprocated. But, because I have no romantic interest, I chose not to respond."

The French scientist stared at Tesla as though he had gone insane. He would not let the subject go. "The Divine Sarah Bernhardt was given to notice you, sir, and you have no interest in pursuing—pardon me—romantic possibilities with our favorite Lady of the Stage?"

"I prefer to live a celibate life, sir. Now—where were we? Oh, yes. I will be lecturing before the French Society of Physicists within the week, and I'm thinking of preparing some new demonstrations...."

CHAPTER THIRTY-FOUR

Amnesia

He awoke suddenly. He sat up.

He was in a bed, but he did not know where he was. He did not know *who* he was. He looked around the room. Faint blue light trickled through the windows. The walls were high and made of gray stone. The furniture was old. He saw an old wooden desk. An old table. Some old wooden chairs.

An old man sat in one of the chairs. He wore a black suit. He had a long black-and-gray beard. The old man said, "Nikola?"

"Yes? Hello?"

"Nikola, are you alright?"

"I—I don't know…who am I? Who are you?"

"I am your uncle Petar. Petar Mandic. Surely, you remember…?"

Tesla closed his eyes and shook his head. He was shocked by the flash of a recent memory: he was in an elegant room, discussing something with an older man with a white mustache. They were discussing spiritualism. Then the memory faded.

Tesla blinked his eyes, bewildered. "You are—my Uncle Petar, is that correct?"

"Yes, Nikola. You have known me all your life."

"Uncle Petar, do I also know someone named Sir William Crookes?"

"You might. That sounds like the name of one of those scientists you have been meeting. Probably an Englishman."

"Yes, I would think so. I seem to remember him. And—a hotel in Paris, the Hotel de la Paix. A street. A cafe. Tables on the sidewalk."

"Good. Good."

"What am I doing here?"

"You gave some lectures in England and France and you had some kind of a breakdown. Nikola, your mother is not well."

"Where am I, Uncle Petar?"

"In the monastery of Gomirji, near Ogulin, in Croatia."

"I think I remember...I once lived in Croatia. Is that true?"

"Very good. You were born in Serbia. You lived most of your life in Croatia."

"What else do you know about me, Uncle Petar?"

"You are a great scientist, Nikola. You are a very famous inventor."

"I remember only details, nothing whole."

"Give it time, Nikola, give it time."

Days passed. Weak, exhausted, Tesla forced himself to concentrate on every detail he could remember—about anything. Anything at all.

He remembered flowing arcs of electricity. He remembered seeing a young boy thrown off the back of a horse.

He remembered many, many faces, seated in rows of chairs, looking at him, watching him—then clapping, applauding....

He passed swiftly in and out of sleep.

Sometimes his Uncle Petar was there when he woke up, sometimes he was not.

"Who are you?"

"I am your Uncle Petar. Don't you remember me?"

"I don't...remember you. Who am I? What is my name?"

"You are Nikola Tesla."

That conversation was repeated many times.

He recalled glimpses of the sidewalk cafe outside of the Hotel de la Paix. He remembered discussing spiritualism with someone named William Crookes in a room somewhere in England.

"Who are these people? Why do I know them?"

"You are a famous scientist, Nikola, and you have given some very important lectures to the people of the world."

"I see...."

He remembered learning that the man named Crookes attended seances to discover whether or not there was life after death. Sir Crookes was convinced that the soul survived after the body was dead. The man who was beginning to know himself as Nikola Tesla had argued the opposite point, that human beings were nothing more than meat machines.

He remembered seeing a fantastic engine, a quiet motor, humming on a hillside in a park somewhere.

"Szigety! I can see my motor! Do you see it? Do you hear it—?"

Then he was lying in bed, trying to concentrate, trying to stay awake.

He remembered receiving a telegram at his room in the Hotel de la Paix in Paris, informing him that his mother was dying. He saw himself on a crowded train, daylight, mountains—

He remembered waking up in bed and asking the man seated next to him what his name was...

"Your mother is ill, Nikola," the man said. "Are you well enough to see her? Do you think you can travel now?"

"Yes, I think so...you are my uncle, Petar Mandic, and I am Nikola Tesla, your nephew."

"That is correct."

"My mother is Djouka Tesla."

"That is also correct. How do you feel?"

"I feel...confused still. I feel dazed, minute by minute."

"But you still remember who you are?"

"Yes, I think so...."

"Who are you?"

"Nikola Tesla."

"Who are you?"

"An inventor. A scientist."

"Very good. You can travel. You have recovered considerably since you have been here."

Nikola laughed. "I remember Ohm's law!"

Petar laughed. "That's very good!"

"That is strange: I could always remember things scientific. But I couldn't remember anything about myself!"

"That is strange, Nikola."

"What does it mean?"

"It doesn't matter. You will be departing, then?"

"I think I must."

He boarded a coach and headed for Gospic. It departed later than scheduled, and Tesla stayed awake until the carriage reached the Gospic station.

Exhausted, knowing he was too tired to walk to his childhood home, he sought a room in an inn near the station. The innkeeper led Tesla to a room upstairs. As soon as the innkeeper departed, Tesla undressed and was suddenly overcome by exhaustion. He fell onto the bed.

His mind turned to white light—

The room spun—

For an instant, he could see the bed from above, as if he was looking down at himself from the ceiling. Then he saw the sky. He saw clouds. Vast, billowing clouds.

He saw, as he later described, "angelic figures of marvelous beauty.... One of whom gazed upon me lovingly and gradually assumed the features of my mother.... The appearance slowly floated away and vanished....

"I was awakened by an incredibly sweet song of voices [and felt] a certitude, which no words can express that my mother had just died. And that was true."

CHAPTER THIRTY-FIVE

Contracts

After his mother's death—and the vision that accompanied it—Tesla departed for Belgrade to recover more fully. His arrival sparked celebration and festivities: he stayed for several weeks, then departed for Zagreb and Budapest. On August 31, 1892, Nikola Tesla arrived in New York.

During his absence, George Westinghouse faced financial ruin. The Thomson-Houston Company had run aground some months before, victim of a hostile Morgan buyout. Morgan executive Charles Coffin took control. Coffin waged a price war against all other electric companies—the chief competitor being General Electric, which still survived on Edison money.

When the effects of price competition injured Westinghouse, Coffin offered to come to his aid: at a meeting in Pittsburgh, Coffin told Westinghouse how he and J. P. Morgan took control of Thomson-Houston—then he offered financial assistance to Westinghouse.

Enraged, Westinghouse shouted, "You sit there telling me how you ran your own stock down, how you deprived both Thomson and Houston of the benefits of their increased stock issue, then you tell me you used the decline in stock *which you forced* to renegotiate your agreement with them? At which point they lost control of their own company? Then you tell me that you and Mr. Morgan can extend to me financial assistance without obligation?

"You *tell* me how you treated Thomson and Houston; why should I trust you?"

The meeting ended abruptly.

Tesla had just departed for Europe. It was February.

In the months that followed, Edison General Electric was forced to merge with the shattered remains of Thomson-Houston, and the name Edison was dropped from the company.

Charles A. Coffin became president of the firm. The price of electricity continued to drop.

Westinghouse poured his fortune into the development of alternating current—and the Westinghouse Company declined. Dynamos were being mass-produced and either sold at a loss to insure their sale at all cost, or simply left to block warehouse space.

Upon returning, Tesla confronted a desperate Mr. Westinghouse. Night pressed against the office windows. Yellow electric lights fought off the shadows.

"How can I help you?"

"It's Coffin. He's been cutting prices fearfully, I'm afraid, and he makes it clear he's trying to knock out other electrical firms."

"I'm dreadfully sorry to hear that! What can be done?"

"I'll get to the point, Nikola, though it makes me sad to even approach the subject with you...."

"Tell me! I'll do anything—tell me what to do!"

"I knew you'd respond this way. You're a good man, Nikola, maybe too good. Yes, I think that's it; you're too good, Nikola, for your own good, if that makes any sense to you."

"I find it perplexing, sir."

"I thought you would. Listen, Nikola, we need to hurry to get our system city to city, using trolley services and railway systems. Then lighting. But first—transportation. That's vital. After that, let 'em go wherever they want for service—they won't be able to compete with the system that's already there. And it needs to be ours, Nikola. It needs to be alternating current."

"I'll do whatever I can to assist you in this, George. Please go on."

"Coffin talks about 'boodle.' Payoffs to politicians, the competitors he's bought, the aldermen, and so on. He wants to raise the prices of our streetlights from two dollars to six so we won't have to lose any profits and he still gets to pay his boodle, if you understand."

"I see, yes, I understand."

"Good. So I see no advantage in this! Then came those rumors, those stories on Wall Street, that I'd mismanaged my own companies, that there was illegal collusion with General Electric for profit-sharing, that that was how I got the money to develop alternating current. They were all stories and lies, but our stocks went down, Lord, they *fell!* That was just during the past few months, Nikola. So I'm afraid I can't hold onto your patents anymore...." Tesla pondered the events in silence.

Westinghouse spoke again, "My investment banker advised me to get rid of my royalty contract with you! It's been in effect for four years, and you haven't claimed any of your royalties, Nikola. Either I have to sell out to you, which would bankrupt me in the middle of this operation, or I would have to yield the patents to you entirely, in which case I still lose. So, you see the terrible situation I am in."

Tesla stood. He waved a hand above his head. "Mr. Westinghouse, you have been my friend. You have believed in me when others had no faith. You supported me when even your own engineers lacked the vision to see things ahead that you and I saw. You have stood by me as a friend.

"You will save your company so you can develop my inventions."

"What are you proposing?"

"Let me ask you—suppose I refuse to give up my contract, what would happen to you then?"

"In that event, you would have to deal with the bankers, because I would no longer have any power in the situation."

"And if I give up my contract, you will save your company and retain control? You will proceed with your plans to give my polyphase system to the world?" Westinghouse cleared his throat and looked directly into Tesla's eyes. "I believe your polyphase system is the greatest discovery in the field of electricity. It was my efforts to make it available to the world that brought on this present difficulty. But I intend to continue, no matter what happens, with my original plan to put the country on an alternating current basis."

"Then, I see no other alternative: here is your contract, and here is my contract, and I will tear them both to pieces."

"Nikola!"

"Now you will no longer have any trouble with my royalties. Is that sufficient?"

Westinghouse gasped and stared as pieces of the contracts fluttered to the desk and the floor.

When Westinghouse returned to Pittsburgh, where the proposed mergers were being held, he confronted the Morgan forces and emerged unscathed.

CHAPTER THIRTY-SIX

Niagara

Tesla found something he had not experienced in years—leisure time. He accepted invitations to banquets, dinners, and parties, where he met high society. When he dined or mixed with company, his phobias and compulsions manifested fully.

Women were told in advance to remove their pearls or any other round adornments they might be wearing. The waiters were instructed to serve the inventor from only oval bowls and plates.

Tesla briefly measured the area and volume of the tableware, computed the volume of the food he ate. He would measure individual pieces of braised duck or roasted mutton, working out his calculations on a note pad, handling his pencil with equal dexterity in either his right or left hand. He usually sat by himself when he dined.

After dinner at one of New York's more fashionable restaurants, Tesla elected to pursue an invitation to visit the Fortune 400 Club in Manhattan. A dance band played. The sweeping dance floor was uncrowded. Thomas Fortune Ryan greeted him.

"Nikola! How good of you to show up! Permit me, I have some friends I would like you to meet."

Tesla followed Ryan to a table occupied by several elegantly dressed men and women. One of the faces was familiar.

Thomas Fortune Ryan gestured over their heads with a flourish. "Ladies and gentlemen, may I present the Man of the Hour, who is favoring us with his attention, that is, in place of the rather prodigious task of creating the modern future!"

All eyes swept to the tall, slender man with the sharp nose and chin, the high, wide forehead. He smiled faintly.

"Mister Nikola Tesla!"

Men reached for a handshake. Women extended their wrists. Tesla bowed courteously.

"Mr. Tesla does not care to shake hands, gentlemen. He refrains from such gestures."

The hands were withdrawn.

"May I introduce the party?" Ryan faced Tesla. "This is Julian Hawthorne, son of Nathaniel Hawthorne, and quite a writer in his own right. This is Mr. Andrew Carnegie—"

"We've met," Carnegie put in.

"Yes. In Pittsburgh."

"Very good!"

"That is right. I had no idea it was you at the time."

"Yeah!" Carnegie laughed. "You met me as Andy. No pretense, no high-falootin' expectations. I like to keep it that way."

"I appreciate and respect that, sir."

"Mr. Tesla, may I present the Johnsons? Robert and Katherine? She's the lovely one of the two."

Everyone laughed.

Robert Johnson said, "Thomas, you can be so charming."

"So can you, Robert. Always." To Tesla: "Two more names for you to remember, though that shouldn't be any trouble for you at all."

"Thank you, Mr. Ryan."

"May I introduce Chauncey Depew? And the lady across the table from him is the celebrated actress Maxine Elliott."

"Good evening, Mr. Tesla," Depew said.

"I'm delighted to meet you, Mr. Tesla," Maxine Elliott said.

Tesla caught himself gazing at her, then turned away nonchalantly.

"I am in the process of developing wireless telegraphy," he said.

"Tell us about it," Robert Johnson said.

"While in England, I discussed the feasibility of wireless signal and image transmission with Sir William Crookes, inventor of the Crookes tube, for generating invisible radiation. We believe that radiation to be the future of communication, maybe even transmission of power without wires. Ultimately, both power and signal transmissions will be carried at the same time, over many different transmitted invisible wavelengths.

"Sir William has worked out the rudiments of a mathematical theory; I don't have the details, so I cannot compare it with mine. I have a letter from him outlining the basis of his theory; he intends to publish his work in journals in the spring.

"I have a lecture scheduled this spring for the Franklin Institute on this very subject—as well as some disclosures of my own, which I care not to disclose as yet."

"My, how exciting!" Katherine's eyes gleamed. "Isn't it, Robert? Very exciting!"

"Yes, it certainly is. Tell me, Mr. Tesla, you speak of 'wireless telegraphy'—how is this possible?"

"I plan to transmit through a distribution transformer connected by a spark gap and a bank of Leyden jars to an antenna.

"I plan to receive through a similar antenna and coil, with another bank of Leyden jars, but without the spark gap. Instead, I will install a Geissler tube. It should light up when power is transmitted to it through the air."

"My goodness!" Katherine exclaimed. "That all sounds so mysterious."

"I'm not certain I understand all of that," Maxine Elliott said. "What is a Geissler tube? What are Leyden jars?"

"They are the devices by which we are learning to study these invisible forms of energy."

"Can you explain to us what these energies are?" Robert Johnson asked.

"They are like colors of light that we normally cannot see."

"Like sounds too high-pitched to hear?"

"Exactly," Tesla said.

"Hey! Tesla! When you have a minute, give me an ear!"

Tesla turned and faced the white-bearded industrialist.

"You have my attention, sir."

"Good. Now, Mr. Tesla, how was George the last time you saw him?"

"George Westinghouse, sir?"

"Yes. George. He took quite a beating at the hands of Coffin and the Morgan crew."

"Yes, that is true, but he held his own at the merger meetings, or so he informed me."

"Very good. He's a good man, George Westinghouse."

"I heartily agree, Mr. Carnegie."

"Call me Andrew."

"Certainly…Andrew." Tesla was clearly not comfortable with the name.

"Well—call me whatever you like!"

"Mr. Carnegie would be suitable, sir."

"Very well. George Westinghouse is a damned good man. He's an engineer, like yourself—a machine engineer, to be sure, mechanics as opposed to electrical work, but he's a master mechanic and an engineer with the best of 'em."

"I appreciate your appraisal, sir."

"Converting the country to alternating current was hard on him financially, I understand that. But I would rather deal with Westinghouse any day than that Morgan chap.

"Oh, don't get me wrong! J. P. Morgan is a close friend of mine. I've known him and we've stayed on good terms for years—although he tends to have an unflattering opinion of me, personally, that I find to be rather amusing.

"But don't let anyone fool you. Don't go up against J. P. Morgan unless you've got guts and integrity—or you just plain *want* to lose....

"I'll tell you a little about Pierpont, if you don't mind! You might have to go up against him yourself, Tesla, and he's a good judge of character. He can see right into you; that's how he beat Gould and Fisk back in '69.

"Jay Gould had a heart like a wharf rat—pardon me, but that's the truth. In confidence, of course. But it's the truth.

"Pierpont will only go one step farther than you in any business deals. You go ten steps to protect what you've got, he goes eleven. Never one step farther. That's because Pierpont hates competition. I get the feeling that's all he does it for—railroad reorganization. Hell, he gathers companies because he fancies himself the great controller, the man who balances by buying, if you ask me.

"You've got to know these things, Tesla, because you're going to meet up with him sooner or later, and I'll tell you why.

"Because he wants control of both alternating current *and* direct. That's why. That's why he went after Westinghouse. Hell, he squashed Edison like a bug!"

"I heard a debt of over forty thousand dollars was also at stake," Fortune Ryan remarked.

"Do tell!" Tesla leaned forward.

"Oh, he's a bastard!" Carnegie ex-claimed. "I met him several times at Morgan's house. Terrible little man. Pierpont says he's been nothing but trouble, too! Too bad Bill Swayer died. He beat Edison to the punch with electric lighting, or so I hear."

"Edison has done nothing original that I know of," Tesla said.

"That's what everybody says when they've worked with him awhile."

"I'm relieved to hear someone else shares that opinion."

"My goodness!" Katherine Johnson said.

"I always thought Mr. Edison was one of our great inventors," Maxine Elliot said.

"That depends on who you ask," Carnegie said.

"How would you like to submit an article to *Century?*" Robert Johnson announced. "I am associate editor of that magazine, and we would favor any words you would care to write us about your amazing visions of the future."

"Certainly, Mr. Johnson. I welcome an opportunity to write for you."

Tesla went back to his room at the Waldorf-Astoria Hotel.

He delivered two highly successful lectures in March of 1893. The first was given before the Franklin Institute in Philadelphia. The other was given before the national Electric Light Association in St. Louis. He demonstrated the fundamental principles of wireless telegraphy. His fellow engineers were amazed.

Weeks later, he met with George Westinghouse to design the lighting and the science pavilion for the Chicago World's Fair, also publicized as the Columbian Exhibition.

The fair opened on a cold, wet day in Chicago, the first of May. Despite the weather, throngs of people crowded the fairgrounds.

G. W. Ferris built the world's first Ferris wheel. It was 260 feet in diameter and seated sixty people to a car. The faint-hearted were discouraged from riding to such a spectacular height; men with cameras often stood at the peak of the ascent to take pictures.

"Little Egypt," the renowned belly dancer, performed on a stage surrounded by live cobras. A life-sized Venus de Milo had been sculpted out of pure chocolate and displayed in the arcade.

Tesla built a huge hall, commemorating the geniuses of electrical history. Edison was omitted, although Tesla had seen fit to include a Serbian poet, Zmaj Jovan. The illumination was powered by wireless—from a high—energy magnifying transmitter twenty-two miles away.

Tesla's displays also included "teleautomatic" submarines, controlled by wireless signals, in a vast tank of water. Propeller-driven flying contraptions took off and hovered over the multitudes. Gaseous tubes, emitting light, flared their brilliance against the night sky.

Twenty-five million people—one third of the population of the United States—turned out to see the "event of the century." The wireless transmission of power to the fair enhanced Tesla's fame around the world.

On August 25, 1893, he lectured before the Electrical Congress of Chicago. Again, he demonstrated wireless transmission of signals and power, as well as experiments with invisible radiation, including X-ray images on a fluorescent screen. The lecture ended with a gala reception.

Thomas Commerford Martin offered an apology for having been "involved" in the incident, years before, when Edison asked Tesla if he had ever eaten human flesh.

"It was Edison," Thomas Commerford Martin explained. "He's uncultured, has no sense of the world. He doesn't travel. Oh, two trips to Europe—but he hates traveling. He told me so himself. So, it was natural for him to ask you that. I've never known anyone to pride himself on ignorance more than Thomas Edison."

"I see."

"So, tell me, Mr. Tesla, what grand designs do you have for the future of electricity?"

"At this time, I am trying to find a way to implement my greatest of all ideas— I wish to build a power-generating station underneath Niagara Falls."

Thomas Commerford Martin gasped. "That's impressive, Mr. Tesla!"

"Oh, yes, it should be that!"

"Mr. Tesla! Mr. Tesla!"

The two men looked around. They were approached by a small, familiar man and an elderly gentleman unfamiliar to Tesla.

"Mr. Martin, do you know Mr. Pupin?"

"No, I can't say I've ever met…either of these two gentlemen."

"I am Professor Michael Pupin and this is my distinguished colleague, Professor Hermann Helmholtz."

"Thank you, gentlemen. I am Thomas Commerford Martin."

"I have heard of you," Pupin said. "You are a science writer, are you not?"

"Yes—and an editor, too, I might point out."

"Freelance?"

"Sometimes. I'm also on the staff of *Century* magazine."

Two other figures called out to Tesla: two men, one older, one younger.

"May I present Mr. H. P. Broughton and his son, William, who was my assistant during tonight's lecture…."

Introductions were exchanged again, and the conversation resumed. Tesla elaborated his plans to harness the dynamic power of Niagara Falls. The subject came up again and again.

Upon arriving in New York, Tesla met again with the Johnsons, this time to meet with the novelist Rudyard Kipling and the naturalist John Muir. He reassured John Muir that one of his primary goals in building the Niagara Falls station would be to leave the natural scenic beauty of the falls unspoiled.

"I seek not to interrupt the awesome spectacle of nature," Tesla explained. "It can be done without being visible from above, which is why I insist upon my plan being implemented. I know of no one else who would take the beauty of the Falls into consideration."

"Amazing!" Rudyard Kipling said.

John Muir said little, studying Nikola Tesla for the rest of the evening.

In October of 1893, Tesla received a late-evening phone call from George Westinghouse.

"Nikola! What are you doing?"

"I've just returned from the laboratory, George."

"Have you got a minute?"

"Yes. Why?"

"This might be important. You see, those lectures, those demonstrations you've been giving, they might have paid off. Apparently, Sir William Thompson—Lord Kelvin himself—has given you quite a close ear over the past two years. Your discoveries have not escaped his attention. And the Edison propaganda has been spread pretty thin over scientific circles.

"Anyway, Lord Kelvin has taken all things into consideration in issuing a license to construct two generators at Niagara. He has elected to issue the license to my company, with you as special consultant on the project." Tesla was amazed. He stared at the telephone, stunned. "Did I really hear you correctly?"

"If you heard me say that the Niagara Commission has chosen you and me to install generators under Niagara Falls, then you heard me correctly."

"I was just talking to Rudyard Kipling and John Muir about that very project."

"Really? I know how this has been your life's dream, Nikola."

"Thank you, George. Yes, it truly has been."

"So—you met John Muir?"

"Yes. Mr. Muir was concerned about our endeavor disturbing the natural beauty of the site. Of course, I told him the dynamos would not be visible from the rim of the falls."

"Good. Because, ideally, they shouldn't have to be visible. Get on the next train and get to Pittsburgh. I'm going to need to move quickly on this. From here, we'll go to Michigan and get started."

"Very good, sir."

"See you when you get up here. Good-bye."

"Good-bye, sir."

CHAPTER THIRTY-SEVEN

Movies

During the years Edison worked on his magnetic ore separator, William Kennedy Laurie Dickson worked secretly to build a moving picture camera and synchronized projector.

Edison filed for numerous caveats covering his kinetoscope. It was a crude device for animating twirling pictures seen through a peephole.

Edison had already established a personal income exploiting the device: with Eadweard Muybridge he photographed nude women and sold the resulting "peephole shows" to such subscribers as Cornelius Vanderbilt, Anthony Drexel, and John Pierpont Morgan.

In October and November of 1892, the patent office rejected several of Edison's claims for motion picture and stereoscopic viewing devices.

Dickson continued to experiment with his own devices in secret.

Edison's temper became more violent as Tesla's fame spread. The fact that Tesla chose not to represent him in an exhibit at the Science Pavilion stung Edison more deeply.

Machinist John Ott designed a nickel-in-the-slot compartment for the kinetoscope, and it was featured at the Chicago World's Fair.

Fred Ott assisted Dickson at the ore mining project, and neither got anywhere. Huge quantities of ore were crushed between immense rollers—which shook so violently that they frequently had to be replaced. The rock was broken into finer and finer fragments until it was reduced to a fine powder. Conveyor belts sifted it through beds of immense electrified magnets. The entire process required immense amounts of power. Edison, to prove a point, utilized only direct current.

The breakup of equipment, short circuits, generator overloads, and the inevitable destruction of the rollers reduced the project to an endless succession of problems. Weary, Dickson and Ott put in long, hard hours—only to report to Edison that they were making no headway.

A room made of tar paper on boards, mounted on a track, appeared on the grounds of the Edison laboratory in Menlo Park: it was the first motion picture studio. Edison named it the Black Maria.

This was where Edison's picture shows—primarily of naked women—were filmed. Alfred O. Tate had worked with Dickson on developing the "projecto-scope," and they planned to present it to Edison for a percentage of the royal-ties—and shared credit, of course.

Two investors, Frank E. Maguire and Joseph Baucus, approached Edison for the rights to start a chain of kinetoscope parlors. Edison agreed, and soon there were kinetoscope parlors all over the United States, as well as in London, Liverpool, Paris, and Copenhagen. Another group of investors, Virginians Otway, Enoch Rector, Grey Latham, and Samuel Tilden, Jr., approached Edison for the right to display films of boxing matches. He eagerly agreed.

The Kinetoscope Exhibition Company was formed. Dickson approached Otway and Latham with his own plans. They agreed to circumvent Edison, if need be: Dickson informed them that he had been taken off the kinetoscope and assigned to the ore mill venture, but he had been developing something of his own.

Edison sent a message to William Brady, manager of the greatest boxing cham-pion of all time, "Gentleman Jim" Corbett. Originally a bank teller, Corbett's career started on a bet—and climaxed when he claimed the boxing title away from fight-er John L. Sullivan.

Corbett, with unlimited talent, had risen from bank teller to prizefighter and was now staring in a musical, *Naval Cadet.*

Corbett agreed to the ersatz match—but no one could be found who would go up against him.

Brady suggested to Edison, "We'll have to get a man he can knock out on the first round, with one blow as soon as they give the signal."

This was agreed—just as it was also agreed that the man shouldn't necessarily know who he was going confront in the ring.

Later, Brady told Corbett: "We found a candidate for the fight, a guy from up in Newark, name of Pete Courtney. He's a fighter, and he's as big as you are, but he's not very good."

Corbett laughed. "Sounds like a sure thing."

At ten in the morning, September 7, 1894, the Black Maria was prepared for the filming. The day was hot—even for September. The black tarpaper walls absorbed the heat and trapped it inside. The film and cameras were recalcitrant; mechanical difficulties taunted the crew. For hours, the two fighters were prevented from seeing each other.

Finally, at four in the afternoon, the filming was ready to begin. Dickson chalked a wide "X" on the floor and told Corbett, "Be sure when you hit him, you stand on this chalk mark. Otherwise, you won't be in focus."

Meanwhile, Brady switched Courtney's gloves from eight ounce to five ounce.

Edison stood in the back of the room, snickering. The signal was given.

Courtney was terrified. He faced Gentleman Jim Corbett over a twenty-five dollar bet.

Corbett connected with a right uppercut. Courtney staggered back toward the ropes.

"You're out of focus! You're out of focus!"

Someone pushed Courtney back into the ring—and Corbett struck him in the face. He went down.

Later, after the match, Courtney met Corbett. They shook hands and Courtney said, "Say, Corbett, you're pretty good. But I don't think you could do it again!"

In December of 1894, Latham, Eugene Lauste, and W. K. L. Dickson secretly formed the LAMBDA Company to develop the synchronized camera and projector. On April 2, 1895, the LAMBDA group presented their finished projector to Thomas Edison.

Edison responded by firing Dickson on the spot and confiscating the machine. Edison was determined to control the motion picture industry. He had been the first to film nude women. He established a network of "ethics committees" that had a tendency to censor everything that failed to support family values—a vague standard that hurt independent producers while Edison films were immune to censorship.

Gumshoe McCoy hired gangsters to pose as extras in crowd scenes in films by the "independent" (non-Edison) producers. As soon as the cameras were rolling, the thugs would break into a riot, beating up cast and crew and destroying equipment. By the end of the decade, the independent film producers fled as far from Menlo Park as they could.

When dawn shone upon the film industry in 1900, the majority of independent producers had settled in a sleepy little town in southern California called Hollywoodland.

CHAPTER THIRTY-EIGHT

Combustion

The Niagara Falls powerhouse was completed and put into operation in 1895 by George Westinghouse and Nikola Tesla. It generated fifteen thousand horsepower of electricity. The celebration and honors were ongoing.

Tesla enjoyed the festivities, but his real love was for constant experimentation. He felt most alive in his laboratory.

Social obligations mounted. Robert and Katherine Johnson sent him many invitations to their famous parties. The sun had gone down. Tesla was finishing up with his assistant, Kolman Czito, when he impatiently decided to depart, as the workers had done an hour ago. He employed no fewer than three hundred workers at his South Fifth Avenue laboratory.

Unlike the Edison lab, which bustled with busy workers during the day and remained dark and vacant all night, the Tesla lab lit the streets every night with weird flashes of light that shot down from the windows. People who passed by feared what the Tesla laboratory might contain, to roar with the dragon fire of electricity.

"We haven't heard from Mr. Edison in quite a while," Czito said.

"That is quite agreeable, as far as I'm concerned," Tesla said. "He is trying to take pictures with continuous-film cameras. Let Edison fade with the rest of the past."

"I appreciate your feelings, sir."

"I shall say goodnight, Mr. Czito."

"Where are you off to, so early this evening, sir?"

"Delmonico's, after dinner. I promised to meet the Johnson's there."

Tesla went to his room at the Waldorf-Astoria, bathed, ate dinner in the Palm Room, and strode onto the streets in his black Prince Albert jacket, top hat, and gray-gloved hands. He entered Delmonico's and was immediately approached by tall, stately young Anne Morgan. She was unabashedly infatuated with Tesla.

"Nikola!" she called to him.

"Good evening, Miss Morgan," he said, keeping a respectful distance from her.

"Oh, I am delighted to see you, Nikola! Tell me—are you here to see someone?"

"The Johnsons."

"Oh, tell them 'hello' for me, please. Nikola, how have you been? I haven't seen you for so long!"

"It has been a while, hasn't it? I have been well. Very busy with my work, as you doubtless imagine."

"Oh, yes, you must be the busiest man on Earth."

"At times, I feel like it, Miss Morgan."

"Nikola—you need a woman. You really do—"

"Let's not hear of it, Miss Morgan. My life is far too demanding to allow for romantic attachments."

"Oh, Nikola, you're just…procrastinating."

They laughed over her remark. Then he said gently, "If I were ever to decide to reconsider about romance, for one reason or another, I think you would make a wonderful choice, Miss Morgan."

"Oh, thank you, Nikola!"

"You're welcome, Miss Morgan." He was looking past her, to see the table reserved by the Johnsons. She was insistent.

"I congratulate you on your latest accomplishment, Nikola; harnessing the power of Niagara Falls. Imagine…."

"Thank you, Miss Morgan. Have you seen the Johnsons in there?"

"My father wishes to congratulate you, too, on the achievement. He tells me he is interested in investing in your company, Nikola."

"Tell him I wish to preserve my independence, Miss Morgan."

"Oh, don't misunderstand Father! He truly means you well."

"I am glad to hear that, Miss Morgan. I wish you and your father well, too."

"Wonderful. I will tell him that. He *does* wish to meet you."

"Perhaps that can be arranged, Miss Morgan."

"Perhaps. Oh, I *do* hope so!"

"Please excuse me—"

"Oh, of course. Nikola—you must be with the Johnsons!"

He made his way past the tables, between the vast Oriental vases and towering potted palms, along the serpentine table occupying the middle of the room, to one of the smaller tables at the side where he hoped he would see them. The electric chandelier, suspended from the ceiling blazed with a shower of crystalline light. Waiters in neat tight uniforms skipped between customers, balancing trays of drinks.

Tesla caught sight of Katherine, waving to him from across the room. He hurried to the spot.

Katherine and Robert smiled at him. Robert looked very debonair. Thomas Commerford Martin—that bore—was seated across the table from Marguerite Merington.

Lovely Margeurite, who plays the piano so delightfully....

He took Marguerite's hand—for an instant, in his own gloved hand—and then bowed respectfully to the others present. He sat down opposite of Robert, beside Miss Merington.

"Nikola, we're so glad you could come!" Katherine exclaimed.

"Yes, dear chap," Robert said dryly. "You simply haven't been showing enough of yourself! Not at all."

"Sorry, Robert. I have been busy, as you can well imagine."

"Of course, Nikola. I'm just amazed—and delighted—that you made time for Katherine and me, all things considered."

"I was just telling them about the time," Thomas Commerford Martin said, "when I introduced you to the Underwoods here."

Tesla scrutinized him. "I don't think so, sir."

"Huh? How so? It was over at the Fortune 500 Club, wasn't it?"

"It was just over two years ago at the Fortune 500, but it was Thomas Fortune Ryan who actually made the introductions. You were present, as I recall."

"Oh, yes, it must have been something like that…are you sure?"

"I have eidetic memory, sir."

"I see."

"Mr. Tesla envisions things in his mind that are so real—" Katherine gazed upward, in awe.

"So I've heard," Thomas Commerford Martin said.

"Tell me, Marguerite," Tesla said, "do you hear music without your piano?"

Margeurite's eyes fluttered. "Oh, yes, of course! I sometimes hear grand compositions—they are the source of the themes I've written!"

"I can well imagine, Miss Merington. Just as you sometimes hear grand symphonies, I see visions of machines that have yet to be built."

"This is all most amazing," Katherine said.

"Would you favor us with another article or two for *Century*, Nikola? The readers love everything you write."

"I promise I will send something off the moment I am no longer impossibly busy."

"Oh, Robert, do think of someone other than your readers," Katherine chided.

Nikola watched them, his eyes half closed as he folded his napkin. He wondered: were they getting along well? One couldn't be quite certain, knowing that couple….

"Robert is so devoted to *Century*," Katherine explained to Thomas Commerford Martin.

Lewis Cass Ledyard passed by their table. He called out his congratulations to Tesla for the Niagara Falls powerhouse.

"Another trusted Morgan man," Robert Johnson said quietly.

"Speaking of Morgan," Katherine said, leaning over the table toward Marguerite, "that Anne Morgan has been *flinging* herself at Nikola these days—shamelessly!"

"Oh, goodness!" Marguerite turned to Tesla. "Have you taken notice of such…adoration, Nikola?"

He tilted his head casually. "I live above such things, Miss Merington. But— yes—I have noticed a certain…affection…on her part."

Marguerite glanced away, indifferently. "I see."

"Have no worry, Miss Merington, for neither she nor any other woman will keep me to herself."

Marguerite shrugged. "Perhaps. Perhaps not, Nikola."

"What do you mean, Marguerite?"

"Well, Nikola, it seems obvious to me…you are already married to your work."

"So it seems," Robert said quickly. His right hand slipped across the table and gripped his wife's left wrist.

Katherine glanced over her shoulder at Robert—her look was cold and angry— for an instant. Then she looked down and turned away from him.

"What do you have against marriage, Nikola?" Thomas Commerford Martin asked, pronouncing each word slowly, deliberately.

Tesla looked at him and his face hardened slightly. "I have nothing against marriage, Mr. Martin. I recommend it."

"Indeed?"

"Of course. Absolutely. Just—not for scientists. Not for inventors. Not for those who are as committed to personal pursuit of knowledge as I am. This takes an intensity of concentration that would be diminished by the diversion that marriage would necessarily entail. Do you see?"

"No, I don't," Thomas Commerford Martin said coldly.

"Now, oh dear—" Katherine turned to him, "don't start—"

"It seems odd that you should feel that way, Mr. Tesla."

"Not at all, sir. I think marriage is a fitting relationship for a poet, an artist, a musician, even a composer…although Beethoven never married. But then, neither was da Vinci, who wrote, 'Intellectual passion drives out sensuality.'"

"Da Vinci was not just a great painter," Robert said. "He was an inventor, as well."

"Newton never married, sir, and neither did Galileo. The greatest men of science seldom, if ever, are married."

"I see...." Martin's listless eyes were focused on Tesla.

"So, you see—"

"I've heard da Vinci was a homosexual," Thomas Commerford Martin said.

"Oh, no," Marguerite chimed in. "He was actually in love with Mona Lisa Gionconda, but she loved her husband, and the painting he commissioned of his wife was the only thing Leonardo had of her, so he never parted with it. It's sad: I wonder if he would have lived longer, had their love been consummated."

"We'll never know," Martin commented.

Marguerite gazed demurely at Tesla. She said, "Nikola, why do you think science must become...such a preoccupation?"

"Could we talk about something else?" Martin scowled, then stood up. "Never mind. I think I see Tom Ryan. Good evening, all."

In his absence the conversation started back up slowly.

Robert: "Well, I'm glad that's over!"

Katherine: "How can you work with him?"

"It's...trying at times."

Marguerite: "It must be! He was so...coarse."

Tesla was nonchalant. "Let us hope, Robert, I finally get time to send off a few words to *Century*."

"Do you want a drink, Nikola?" Robert looked over his shoulder for a waiter.

"Not tonight. I'm very tired, actually."

"Ohhh—" Marguerite protested. "It's still early—"

"Sorry, but I must attend to matters of importance tomorrow. It is time I caught up with my other projects, especially my wireless experiments, now that the Niagara station has been completed."

"I see." Marguerite was disappointed. "I wanted you to come with us to the Johnson's and hear me play, Nikola."

"I wish I could, Marguerite. You're right, it is early. Perhaps if we left right now...oh, but I can't. I have to be at my office before hours, to help with some paperwork."

"Oh, Nikola, I'm sorry. How frustrating."

Tesla stood, gave his salutations, and departed.

He took a coach to the Waldorf-Astoria, then checked into his room. He went to bed immediately.

He waited for the visions, but none came. He knew he faced a sleepless night. Outside the Waldorf-Astoria, the night stretched with silent tension.

On South Fifth Avenue, a night watchman took his last sip of coffee at his desk. He yawned—and leaned forward. He rested his head against his arm.

In the alleyway behind 33 to 35 South Fifth Avenue, a figure carrying a large cardboard box slipped from shadow to shadow. The figure stopped at a door underneath a fire escape. He put the box down beside the door.

He applied something to the door handle that jingled quietly. After a few seconds a *clack* nipped the silence and the door swung open. The figure slipped inside, and the door swung closed quietly.

A yellow flame flickered inside the vast, dark room.

In the light of the match, the figure carried the cardboard box to the far corner of the room and placed it under a row of shelves containing bottles of chemicals. The box was filled with newspapers and rags soaked in fuel oil. A candle was placed atop the rage and papers. The candle was lit and the figure hurried out of the room.

The candle burned for an hour. It dripped wax onto the oily combustibles. It burned low.

The flame touched the newspapers and spread to the fuel oil at exactly 2:30 in the morning, March 13, 1895.

The sudden yellow fire billowed with clouds of thick, black smoke. Flammable smoke. The fire reached the wooden shelves on which the chemicals were stored. The bottles cracked, and the contents exploded. Fire swept against the wall, spilled onto the floor—

The smoke exploded.

Fire raced through the first floor of the laboratory. The windows shattered. Air swept in and whipped the flames with fresh oxygen. Blazing, magnificent flames ate away everything. The cement of the walls and floors crumbled. Then the massive generator on the fourth floor crashed through, and the interior of the building collapsed.

Fire danced on the ruins of the Tesla laboratory, defying the roaring hoses of the firefighters until dawn.

CHAPTER THIRTY-NINE

Devastation

The old world had been destroyed.

The new world consisted of four gutted, charred, black walls. The laboratory and the machines were gone. He stood before the half-molten remains of the generator, illuminated by a shaft of light streaming down from where the collapsed upper floors had been.

Firemen far behind him pushed back a noisy crowd; their voices faded away as Tesla stared at the smoldering remains of his laboratory. He suddenly departed.

"Mr. Tesla! Mr. Tesla!" The fire chief waved papers in his face.

Tesla ignored the papers and pushed past the man. The police chief intercepted him. "It's important, sir—"

Tesla scowled. Officials and onlookers stepped out of his way.

He wandered through the sidewalks of South Fifth Avenue. The shops and offices and apartment buildings dissolved from his senses. He saw only a sea of floating faces, parting before him like balloons, not quite real....

He crossed streets and strode sharply around corners. People hastily stepped out of his way. If anyone knew who he was, no one announced it; they saw only a scowl of intense pain on the face of a very tall man.

He walked until the sun was at its zenith in the sky. He strode aimlessly all over New York, and everywhere he walked people backed away from him. Late in the afternoon Tesla found himself sitting on a park bench staring into space. Nearby, children fed pigeons with crumbled bread crusts flung onto the sidewalk. Tesla stared at the birds, unblinking.

He was fascinated. He had no thoughts. His attention was filled with the iridescence of the wings of the pigeons.

Sie rukt und weicht, der Tag ist uberlebt,

Dort eilt sie him und fordert nueus Leben,

Oh, das kien Flugel mich vom Boden hebt

Ihr nach und immer nach zu streben!

The words repeated themselves, over and over in his mind. Goethe's *Faust*. He had recited that poem, that Teutonic melody, once before—so long ago, in the city park in Budapest the day he clearly envisioned his polyphase motor.

The glow retreats, done is the day of toil,

It yonder hastes, new fields of life exploring;

Ah, that no wing can lift me from the soil

Upon its track to follow, follow soaring!

His mind continued:

Ein schoner Traum indessen sie entweicht,

Ach, zu des Geistes Flugeln wird so leicht

Kein korperelichter Flugel sich gesellen!

His mind settled on that phrase, repeating it endlessly.

A glorious dream! though now the glories fade.

Alas! the wings that lift the mind no aid

Of wings to lift the body can bequeath me.

Nearby, the pigeons strutted majestically. Tesla glimpsed a depth of painful emotion he had never known before. Life was pain. Death was pain. Life subsisted upon death: carnivores, predators, herbivores killing plants…endlessly. Endlessly….

A pigeon took off from the sidewalk and flew past Tesla: the fluttering wings radiated purple iridescence in the sunlight.

Alas! the wings that lift the mind no aid

Of wings that lift the body…."

He had felt this misery once before. When his brother Daniel reached forward, sitting up in bed—

"How could you…?"

Just before he died.

Memory was pain. He must sleep. Sleep. Sleep….

He jerked himself to his feet and walked blankly away just as the sun dipped behind a building.

He wandered to his room at the Waldorf-Astoria. He did not eat. He sat on the edge of his bed for a long time, then undressed and reclined. He watched the room darken. He existed in limbo through the night. He listened to his heartbeat and experienced, with fascination, this pain. Memories crystallized and melted, blurring together then coming into focus, forever, into the night.

He was vaguely aware of the dawn, the morning, pulling himself out of bed, dressing, walking downstairs....

Once again he found himself seated on a park bench, watching children feed the pigeons. The morning blended into afternoon.

"Mr. Tesla! Mr. Tesla!"

His introspection was shattered. He looked up, startled. A tall, stocky man in a gray suit hurried toward him, waving, crossing the street.

"Mr. Tesla, I'm deeply sorry about the tragedy you suffered yesterday. My condolences, please...."

He reached out to shake Tesla's hand, waited, then withdrew.

"I'm deeply sorry, sir."

Tesla said nothing.

"Allow me, please, to introduce myself. I am Edward Dean Adams, of the Cataract Construction Company. We have been in communication since the Niagara Falls project. I am pleased to finally meet you, Mr. Tesla."

Tesla's eyes flickered to life. "Y-yes...?"

"Well, as you must know, sir, I am also one of the organizers of the International Niagara Commission. It was I who sponsored the development of your polyphase system, which was chosen to be utilized by the Cataract Construction Company, sir."

"Yes, sir."

"Well, Mr. Tesla, I have an offer for you."

PART FOUR

Morgan

CHAPTER FORTY

Fortune

John Pierpont Morgan had been bred for the throne.

He was one of two sons born to Juliet Pierpont and Junius Morgan. Following the revolutions between 1776 and 1789, the merchant class of Europe and the United States, although outwardly democratic, secretly dreamed of creating its own aristocracy. Appropriately, this emergence occurred in America.

The Emperor of Capitalism was named John Pierpont, of the House of Morgan.

The wealth of the Pierpont family had been established before the American Revolution, based on a shipping empire that existed between the colonies and Mother England.

In 1835, a dry-goods merchant named George Peabody fled to London to escape the Great Panic. While banks collapsed and railroad companies perished, George Peabody thrived.

He was a tall, dour man with cold blue eyes and muttonchops that whitened with age. He lived alone, seldom spoke, and spent almost no money at all. He seldom smiled.

Junius Morgan shared the street corner with him as he waited for the late coach. They seldom spoke to each other. Junius finally forced an introduction out of Peabody while they stood, waiting for their respective carriages, in the rain.

"Junius Morgan, sir."

The younger man extended a hand.

"Eh? Oh, I see...Mr. Morgan."

"And—you are?"

"Sir? I beg your pardon!"

"Just being friendly, sir."

Peabody scrutinized Junius Morgan mistrustfully. "Well, you're an American, like myself...." Peabody spoke slowly. "You look like a decent chap...my name's Peabody. George Peabody." He did not offer a handshake.

"Thank you, Mr. Peabody. Imagine—two Americans sharing a street corner in London. What brings you to London, Mr. Peabody?"

"Business." His voice was colder than the rain.

"I see...."

The year before, Junius had been living in the States, taking care of a wife and boy. Shortly after John Pierpont's birth, Junius Morgan moved to London. John Pierpont remained in school in Boston.

Nine years after John Pierpont "Pip" Morgan was born, Junius Spencer Morgan Junior was born. He was a sickly child.

Neither child saw much of either parent.

Junius lived in London. Juliet preferred living in the States.

Junius met Peabody again on the same street corner, in the rain, cold and sick.

"Mister Peabody! With that cold you ought not to stand here!"

Peabody was silent.

"Here, Mister Peabody, take my coat and umbrella. You're suffering, so take the earlier horsecar home."

This offer must have touched George Peabody, for he agreed reluctantly.

Morgan returned from the Royal Exchange half an hour later. Peabody was still standing in the rain.

"Mister Peabody! I thought you were going home!"

"Well, I am, Morgan! But there's only a two-penny carriage come along as yet. I am waiting for a penny carriage."

Thomas Perman, Peabody's assistant, sometimes sought out Junius and filled his ears with lurid accounts of Peabody's niggardly and cruel nature. Peabody's office manager, Charles C. Gooch, a haggard, sad-eyed man, reluctantly became Peabody's junior partner. Gout, rheumatism, and frequent colds forced Peabody to spend more and more time away from work.

Confronted with the inevitability of his death, Peabody espoused Biblical Christianity and doled out thousands of pounds to charities, mostly orphanages.

In May of 1853, Junius Morgan brought his family to England, where young

John Pierpont was exposed to—and ensnared by—British culture.

He found George Peabody to be a queer old man, but also fascinating and likable.

In 1854, Junius Morgan received an unexpected proposition from old Peabody at the end of a business discussion in the late afternoon in Morgan's office.

"You know, I shall not go on much longer…but if you will come along as a partner for ten years, I shall retire at the end of them, and at that time I will be willing to leave you my name. And if you have not accumulated a reasonable amount of capital during this time, some of my money also, then you can go ahead as the head of it."

Morgan considered the proposal for a moment, then quietly answered, "Mister Peabody, that sounds like a very good offer, but there are some things to be considered. I could not think of giving a final answer until I have looked over the books of the firm and have some idea of the business and the methods by which it is done."

Morgan's answer impressed Peabody.

He moved his family to London by the summer of 1854 and became Peabody's full partner by October.

In 1858, Junius Spencer Morgan, Jr., died. John Pierpont was devastated by his brother's death.

Pierpont had been a quiet boy who had spent much of his childhood infatuated with Napoleon. The boy was now a man: John Pierpont Morgan was twenty-one years old.

His father called him into his office several months after the death of his brother and bade him be seated.

"Yes, sir?"

"John, you are now a man, legally, morally, responsibly. I must talk with you, my son; you are about to go out and face the world and I need to share some of my thoughts with you, and you must share your thoughts with me as well."

"Yes, sir."

"John, your teachers say you have a lot of promise, You have been educated at the finest schools in England and the States, and your marks, especially in mathematics, have been exemplary. You have gone beyond my expectations, John, and I congratulate you."

"Thank you, father."

"Keep a level head on your shoulders, John! Always be practical. If you can translate that head full of numbers into dollars and cents, pounds and francs, so much the better."

"I will try, Father."

"Now—do you know what will make the difference between the survival of the American economy and its collapse in times of financial panic?"

"Let me think, Father."

"Take your time—but you'd better come up with the answer. If you can't, I'll tell you."

"I think—a good banking system, Father."

"Very good! They've been instructing you well. Can you explain to me the reason?"

"Banking finances are the backbone of a strong economy, sir."

"That's correct, John."

"Cooperation among bankers discourages ruinous competition, sir."

Junius Morgan's eyes lit up with surprise and delight. "'Ruinous competition'! I like that phrase. Where did you hear it, John?"

"I thought of it myself, Father. Ruinous competition—the railroads are a prime example, Father."

"So they are."

"Cooperation between bankers has stabilized the American economy. In the past, it's been the only security the Treasury ever had."

"That's true, John. Let me tell you something: to many serious bankers, an American lack of culture is a strong disadvantage. For centuries, the world has looked to Europe for their standard of civilization. For it is civilization, John Pierpont, that separates men from the beasts and places us closer to God."

"I understand that, Father."

"Tell me, John, do you believe in the Bible?"

"Yes, Father, every word."

Junius Morgan solemnly studied his son. He was tall and slender, with a long face mottled with acne. His eyes were alert. He seemed receptive to his father's words.

Junius Morgan cleared his throat and resumed. "The House of Pierpont and the House of Morgan have combined, John, and you shall be executor of the combined estates."

"Yes, Father."

"I hope you understand the immensity of this opportunity, John: a young banker's introduction to the marketplace is seldom, if ever, Wall Street."

"I understand that fully, Father."

"Good, Then you may go, John. Good-bye. We will discuss this further tomorrow evening."

"Adieu, Father."

"Adieu."

CHAPTER FORTY-ONE

War

The United States was rushing toward catastrophe when twenty-one-year-old John Pierpont Morgan made his debut on Wall Street as a sales representative for Peabody and Company.

Throughout his life, John Pierpont's only connection to his father was lengthy sermons about business. He was not spoiled by his family's wealth, nor his inherited prominence. His days as a college dandy at Gottingen were behind him. He had emerged somber and mature. He knew the banking business well.

James Buchanan was President. War seemed inevitable.

John Pierpont wondered which side the House of Morgan would support.

No one was more conscious of the interdependence of the Northern textile mills and the Southern cotton plantations than the dry-goods merchants—including Junius Morgan and George Peabody.

While James Buchanan condemned African slave trade, Morgan took advantage of his job and departed for the Southern states to look for business opportunities, on consignment with the firm Duncan, Sherman and Company, close allies with George Peabody and Company.

Abraham Lincoln became President in 1861—the same year Pierpont and his cousin, James Goodwin, formed J. P. Morgan and Company, with an office at 54 Exchange Place, New York City.

The year before, South Carolina had seceded from the union on December 20, with the words, "The union now subsisting between South Carolina and other

States is hereby dissolved." February 4, 1861, seven other state representatives met in Montgomery, Alabama, and formed the Confederacy.

Lincoln, the new abolitionist President, stepped into office just in time to see the Union disintegrate—or at least rip violently in half. When dawn brushed the sky over Fort Sumter, April 12, Confederate soldiers opened fire on what they believed was a cache of arms and ammunition. Lincoln called for seventy-five thousand volunteers. He blockaded the South.

He gave a speech:

"Bread, not bullets, went to Sumter. ...I will say that I am not, nor ever have been in favor of bringing about in any way the social and political equality of the white and black races—that I am not nor ever have been in favor of making voters or jurors out of Negroes, nor of qualifying them for office, nor to intermarry with white people.

"And inasmuch as they cannot so live, while they do remain together there must be the position of superior and inferior, and I as much as any other man am in favor of the superior position assigned to the white race." He ended with the words, "Right makes might!"

Morgan followed the Lincoln-Douglas debates intently.

There were now two presidents—Abraham Lincoln and Jefferson Davis—and young Morgan, whose primary loyalty was to England, viewed as restrictive any loyalty to either North or South.

In May, after the outbreak of the war, he was approached by Simon Stevens and his partner, Arthur M. Eastman of Manchester, New Hampshire, who had a scheme to sell defective guns to Fremont. After Morgan and his cohorts successfully sued for the money that was owed them, the Union courts were immediately filled with "dead horse" claims in which other speculators, buying and reselling defective, obsolete military equipment and ammunition, lined up to receive settlements under the words of the Morgan decision: "A contract is a contract."

Chapter Forty-Two

Amelia

Love came to John Pierpont Morgan in the form of Amelia Sturges. He was twenty-five years old. Tall and moderately handsome, he spoke softly but with confidence about his plans for the future.

She listened quietly and patiently while he spoke impatiently about how he was going to build the biggest banking empire the world had ever seen.

He visited her at her father's house. One day, his visit ended with a proposal of marriage.

Calmly, she responded, "No, John, I am not ready."

Quietly, he said, "I see." Silently, his heart broke.

She fell ill with a cold early in the year, and he persisted with his intentions even though she did not recover. Shortly after he concluded his dealings with Stevens and Eastman, they eloped.

They were married in the afternoon and by evening were sailing for England aboard the steamship *Persia*. The lovers were saddled with problems. Amelia was still sick, and the cold foggy air of Liverpool was making her worse. They fled to Algiers by steamship and railroad. The climate was an improvement, but still Amelia suffered.

"What can I do?" he pleaded with her, night and day.

"Oh, John, I don't know...what can be done...."

They left Algiers for Nice, boarding a train that wound its way down a convoluted track over mountain passes. She continued to succumb.

In Nice, John Pierpont Morgan did everything he could to keep his young bride alive. He nursed her, paid doctors to examine her and offer their prescriptions. He knelt by her bedside, held her hand, worshipped, and grieved for her. She continued to weaken.

Her coughing spells worsened—she coughed blood. Leeches were applied. The doctors said there was no hope. Their medications and the leeches failed.

After barely four months of marriage, Amelia Morgan died.

Young Pierpont's heart broke again. He returned to the States, reluctantly, ashamed. He begged his father to be taken back into his company, to continue representing Peabody and Company in New York City. There was a war going on. Profits to be made.

"If you're the man to make them," Junius responded. "*If* you can accept the responsibility, that is."

He trudged out of his father's office, utterly defeated. He knew of two kinds of defeat: being vanquished at the hands of an enemy, and self-defeat. The first kind is heroic; the second kind is unbearable. The lesson he learned in 1861 remained prominently in his memory the rest of his life.

Amelia
Sturges

Chapter Forty-Three

States

The North was losing the Civil War.

President Lincoln's eleven-year-old son Willie died in 1862. Mary Todd Lincoln fell into a deep depression and could only be rescued by seances; spiritualists and trance mediums tried incessantly to contact the dead boy in the Red Room of the White House. Because of the seances and Mary's Southern kinfolk, many Northerners believed she was a Confederate spy.

Secretary of War Edwin M. Stanton made it clear from his first day in office he thought Lincoln had been utterly incompetent from *his* first day in office.

On July 4, 1863, General Robert E. Lee was pushed back by Union forces to the banks of the flooded Potomac. Lincoln cabled Meade to "exterminate the Confederate soldiers." Surrender was not acceptable.

The inundation subsided, and Lee's troops escaped.

On the eve of Lincoln's consecration of the graveyard at Gettysburg with a ten-sentence speech that was ridiculed by the popular press, General Ulysses S. Grant delivered death to Confederate forces at Chattanooga, evicting Lee's troops from Tennessee entirely. By March 12, Grant was named general-in-chief of the Union Army, replacing Meade.

In an area called "the Wilderness," the North suffered sixty thousand deaths while hailing bullets upon Confederate troops. Grant prevented Lee from going back home and, though his own casualties were high, the South was defeated in the continuous ten-month Battle of Petersburg.

These events were witnessed by the growing ubiquity of John Pierpont Morgan. Morgan's intelligence system rivaled Union intelligence networks for both promptness and reliability; U. S. military intelligence secretly opened an office down the hall from the Morgan office on Wall Street for the purpose of monitoring his news wire. Despite "top secrecy," Morgan knew in advance the Secret Service agents were posing as bankers—he dropped by in the morning of their first day of business, informed them who he was, informed them he knew who they were, and offered to sell them a daily subscription to his intelligence reports and bulletins. Stunned by this unexpected introduction, they had no choice but to agree to his proposal.

By June 8, Lincoln was elected to a second term in office.

A year later, in early April of 1865, Lincoln had a strange dream: he recalled the next morning he had intruded upon a cluster of people around a catafalque in the East Room of the White House. He had stepped up to a military guard, standing nearby.

"Who is dead?"

"Lincoln. Killed by assassin."

The president woke up suddenly.

On Good Friday 1865, conspirators Lewin Pain, George Atzerod, David Herald, and John Wilkes Booth nearly botched the assassination plot that resulted in the murder of Abraham Lincoln.

In 1865, John Pierpont Morgan fell in love again and married Frances Louisa Tracy. He affectionately called her "Fannie" and doted over her. Her vitality, practicality, and cultural interests guaranteed young Pierpont that theirs would be a lasting marriage. The marriage did last, but the romance did not.

Lincoln was replaced by Andrew Johnson. Nicknamed "Old Lush Andy" or "Andy the Lush," the new president displayed a tendency to slur his words during speeches. Hecklers found him easy to provoke into fits of profanity and invective.

The "Radical Republicans" staged a coup to overthrow the president.

The impeachment trials lasted three months.

John Pierpont thought the eleven "Articles of Impeachment" were ridiculous. He did not even know what the first nine articles were. The tenth was condemnation for having "degraded and disgraced" both the congress and the presidency by "having made some of his speeches in a loud voice." Hell, Pierpont thought, he was half-drunk all the time….

Secretary of the Navy, Gideon Welles, proclaimed, "A mountain of words but not a mouse of impeachment material!" "Old Lush Andy" was not convicted of any impeachable offense. He finished his term in office, far from sober but still president.

Young Pierpont resented the fact that, again, the United States was the laughingstock of European society.

Pierpont's obligation—and challenge—was not just to become America's premier banker, but to prove to the eyes of the European banking community that at least *some* Americans were capable of acquiring culture and becoming civilized.

Grant unleashed fury upon the Radical Republicans shortly after entering office. He dismantled Congress and fired scores of appointees. The first of the infamous Grant scandals came almost immediately.

The scandal that caught Morgan's attention was when speculators Jim Fisk and Jay Gould entertained Grant aboard their yacht to ask him to stay out of the gold market, which they were trying to corner. Their plan was to buy up cheap gold sources, hoard it, drive up the price of gold, then sell reserves at exorbitant prices. This would, in turn, they predicted, drive up the price of wheat. Of course, the government could foil the plot by selling its own reserves....

Convinced that Grant was their ally, they courted his brother-in-law, Abel Corbin, and General Daniel Butterfield of the Subtreasury in New York. Corbin begged the Treasury not to sell its gold reserves.

When the scandal broke, the public was outraged. Grant was forced to sell U. S. gold to stabilize prices on the commodities market.

John Pierpont Morgan journeyed west to attend the driving of the "golden spike" at Ogden Utah, where the west coast and the east coast were symbolically united. He had became interested in the railroad business.

In railroads, Morgan saw business opportunities of the present, and in telegraphy he saw opportunities for the future.

CHAPTER FORTY-FOUR

Railroads

Samuel Hand was getting desperate.

He had dismissed himself from the meeting at the Delavan House. His employer, J. P. Morgan, and his father-in-law, Charles Tracy, had met to discuss the impending takeover of Joseph Ramsey's Albany-Susquehanna Railroad by that infernal weasel Jay Gould and his fat, ugly, wire-haired, obnoxious, and corrupt henchman Jim Fisk. Fisk was the darling of a gang of criminals who called themselves the Bowery Boys. They were the enforcers and extortionists employed by Boss Tweed, who controlled New York's nucleus of political power, Tammany Hall.

Ramsey's company, the Albany-Susquehanna, was at stake.

Hand excused himself from the meeting to say good-bye to a friend who was departing on a night steamer. While in the friend's cabin, excitedly explaining the situation, the gentle rocking of the boat fooled him: he discovered that the boat had pulled away from the dock while he was still aboard.

He helplessly described his predicament to the ship's officers, who were sympathetic but unable to get him back to shore. No one seemed willing—or able—to help him.

Hand's presence at the meeting was crucial. The future of Ramsey's Albany-Susquehanna hung in the balance; it joined the Erie Railroad, which was owned by Gould as the result of another heavy-handed takeover.

The company office was in Albany, New York, where Gould-Fisk forces converged for the purpose of taking Ramsey's company away from him. Gould's dummy corporations had bought up a huge percentage of Albany-Susquehanna stock. Judges Cardoza and Barnard were puppets of Boss Tweed and Tammany Hall: they declared a ceiling on the stocks issued and posted a bankruptcy notice, appointing Fisk to be receiver of the railroad and barring Ramsey from participating in the 1869 annual election of the Board of Directors. The Sheriff of Albany seized the property and declared it off-limits to its owners. One of Ramsey's own directors locked him out of his office; the doors were kicked in and now they could not be locked at all.

William L. M. Phelps, the secretary-treasurer, had also been locked out and the books forcibly removed from his office. All this in August, just after Morgan's return from Ogden, Utah.

A tunnel on the way to Binghamton from Albany became the vortex of the conflict: Bowery gangsters and railroad workers converged at opposite ends of the tunnel and prepared for war. Governor Hoffman summoned the militia—and six thousand men wreaked havoc in the greatest riot in the history of the railroads.

Governor Hoffman appointed General Robert L. Banks to be executive agent for the railroad, excluding Ramsey from management completely.

Gould and Fisk were unconcerned with Ramsey. Their goal was to destroy the railroad empire built by Commodore Cornelius Vanderbilt—and own all of the railroad lines throughout North America.

Samuel Sloan, creator of the Hudson River Railroad, had been Ramsey's close friend for years. Upon hearing of Ramsey's plight, Sloan told him, "Why don't you see Ed Morgan's cousin Pierpont?"

The shocked railroad executives listened, spellbound.

Casually, Sloan went on, "He has brains and, from what Ed tells me, plenty of spunk."

Albany-Susquehanna executives converged the next day at 55 Exchange Place and hurried up the first flight of stairs to the office of Dabney, Morgan and Company.

Morgan received the men and came to the point:

"Give me a statement of your exact condition. Let me know just exactly what Gould and Fisk have done. Put it on paper. Come back day after tomorrow. I will give you my opinion."

The next conference with Morgan was more reassuring. He stated flatly, "You gentlemen will have to fight those fellows in the courts. I think you can win. Do you want me to go ahead?"

The vote was unanimous: John Pierpont Morgan would become champion executive of the Albany-Susquehanna Railroad.

Charles Tracy was retained on the executive staff. So was attorney Samuel Hand. Papers were drawn up to be submitted to Supreme Court Justice Rufus W. Peckham, requesting a restraining order preventing Gould and Fisk from interfering with the annual stockholder's meeting and the election of the Board of Directors.

Hand had excused himself from the meeting to say good-bye to his friend just as the papers were being finalized.

He explained to an indifferent captain the importance of the meeting.

"I will pay one hundred dollars for that lifeboat," he cried.

"I cannot do that—unless you have that much money in cash, Mister Hand."

"Yes! I have it! Here. I can pay you. Now lower it into the water! I have to get back to work at all cost."

The captain counted the bills while the lifeboat was lowered into the water.

Hand rowed ceaselessly. The water was choppy, and a strong wind blew away from the shore. Hours passed.

Hand reached the rocky shore in the blackness. He climbed to the top of an embankment and discovered he was just a few hundred yards from a railroad station on the outskirts of the village of Hudson. A train was due to arrive.

Hand waited behind the water tower. When the train stopped, he climbed inconspicuously aboard the rear platform of the caboose. He started to open the door of the caboose, then froze.

At a table sat a short, fat, ugly man talking loudly to a gang of ugly, vicious-looking men.

Hand realized as long as he remained outside, in darkness, they could not see him. He sat against the railing as the train started pulling away. He leaned against the corner of a window to listen to what Jim Fisk was saying:

"...Then we turn the town upside-down. Yeah, fellahs, we can smash Albany into a thousand pieces. The law won't resist us. Judge Barnard is on our side!"

"Yeah! Break 'em. Smash 'em! Give 'em hell!"

"Yeah! I like that! Give 'em hell!"

Fisk yelled, "Sack the town! I don't give a God-damn about the law. There's only one law those bums understand. And we know what it is!"

The men seated around the table laughed, then they got down to business: they planned to seal all roads to Albany and blockade the railroad tracks. Then— invade the town and wreak havoc, inflict devastation, beat every man, woman, or child who had not evacuated themselves in advance of the scheduled meeting. The train stopped again—in Albany. Hand slipped off the rear platform. He burst into the Delavan House long after midnight. He excitedly recounted his adventure—and the plans he had overheard on the rear of the caboose.

"This sounds like a battle that will not be carried out in the courtroom," Morgan said decisively. "It will be a battle pitched on the streets themselves."

"What can we do?" Charled Tracy cried.

"Send your most trusted workers out by sunrise. They will act as scouts. We will locate Fisk's forces. In the meantime, gentlemen, I have a plan...."

They listened intently to their mentor. Morgan proposed a bold and daring maneuver.

The next morning, the meeting started on time—and the streets were flooded with rock-hurling, torch-bearing rioters. Jim Fisk boldly strode up the stairs to the office of the stockholders, flanked by his bodyguards.

Ramsey lost his temper at the top of the stairs and hurled Fisk back down.

Fisk ran up the stairs, his hands grabbing for Ramsey's throat. Ramsey ducked inside the office. Fisk burst in behind him, and the office exploded into chaos.

Chairs were flung, filing cabinets overturned. Desks were smashed. Jim Fisk screamed, waving his arms wildly. John Pierpont Morgan smiled at him from across the room, quietly puffing a cigar.

The door burst open again, and the rioting executives froze. A huge policeman burst in. He strode to Jim Fisk, put his hand on his shoulder, and proclaimed, "You are under arrest, Mister Feesk. Come with me."

Blurting incoherent gibberish, "Jubilee Jim" Fisk was dragged out of the office and across the street, where his sudden appearance, apprehended and marched into custody, dampened the riot immediately.

The policeman pushed Fisk into the police station, past a man standing in the corner wearing only underwear, and into a jail cell. The door clanged shut and locked behind him.

"Hey! Hey! What're the charges?"

The policeman and the man wearing only his underwear stepped inside an adjoining office and closed the door. The town sheriff looked up from his desk and smiled.

"What're the charges? What'm I in here for?"

The door to the police chief's office opened again, and the man who had been standing in his underwear was now wearing a policeman's uniform and the "policeman" was now wearing the gray suit of a banker.

"Hey! Hey! Lemme outa here! You can't do that! Hey—this is illegal! You can't keep me here! You can't keep me here!"

The sheriff smiled and nodded.

Order had returned suddenly to the stockholder's meeting. Morgan surveyed the broken furniture, the broken faces.

His arms were folded across his chest, his chin was raised, and his gaze was steady, even, and unblinking. Men stared up at him, blank, dazed, and slack—jawed. John Pierpont Morgan spoke. "At this moment Misters Tracy and Hand are arranging with Judge Peckham to have an injunction drawn up restraining the very kind of interference we have already seen here, and, if this meeting proceeds as planned, the gentlemen who are to be served will be easy to locate by the court—appointed marshal, who shall be here shortly.

"Meanwhile, while we are awaiting his arrival, we shall take care of business. I have power of attorney over the matter of financing the overlarge debt that Mister Gould's acquisition of Albany—Susquehanna stock has incurred. I am prepared to back surplus common stock sold on the market to cover the Gould acquisitions with my own funds and funds accessible to me. For this, I do not request direct representation in the company. I do this only to stabilize what has already been established by Mr. Ramsey. What I require in return is of no consequence: I ask

Jim Fisk

Jay Gould

only that proceedings go on from this time without disorder, for what I have seen before me is an utter disgrace to the principle of civilized business.

"I am obliged to point out that a nation's economy is a direct reflection on its business practices, and this very year we have already weathered another crucial financial panic and the U. S. economy still looks unstable, to say the least.

"As long as American bankers still depend on European gold, just as the railroad industry itself is still financed by Dutch gold, it is the obligation of every American businessman to contribute to a stable economy or this nation will fall into a depression that will benefit no one.

"Just as one hairy and crude man is probably swearing in a jail cell at this very moment, the eyes of Europe are upon you. For, you see, gentlemen, the eyes of European banking interests fell upon this meeting precisely when this railroad's troubles caught my attention.

"With that said, let this meeting proceed. A call to order is hereby submitted, and I would like the meeting to be given over to Mr. Ramsey. You may have the floor, Mr. Ramsey."

"Thank you." Ramsey's voice was calm, steady, self—assured.

A tentative Board of Directors was chosen and the injunction was served. The meeting was adjourned, and Morgan returned to the Delavan House. Greater havoc was unleashed the next day by Gould—Fisk forces.

The Bowery Boys converged on Binghamton. There, they rolled down the rails in flat cars to overturn boxcars, destroy the train station, and seize every piece of rolling—stock they could find along the way.

They confronted gangs of Ramsey workmen—and the riot exploded. Windows were smashed. Rails ripped up. Rifles were fired: no one was killed, but the destruction did not cease.

During the weeks that followed, twenty-two injunctions were drawn up and fired from Gould to Morgan and from Morgan to Gould. Judges Peckham and Barnard worked frantically to referee the feud. A railroad collision just outside the Binghamton tunnel sparked war. Newspapers reported daily on "the Battle of the Susquehanna." Governor Hoffman threatened to call out the militia.

Morgan coerced Gould and Fisk to sign a joint note submitted by the governor, requesting the appointment of a state official to run the railroad. The governor appointed A. Bleeker Banks, an Albany businessman and councilman.

Morgan immediately made an unannounced visit to Ramsey's office and within a few hours a special stockholder's meeting was called.

The executives were spellbound while Morgan produced the missing books and ledgers that had been stolen from the office of the company treasury.

After Fisk's men had locked secretary-treasurer Phelps out of his office and had stolen the books, the records were hidden in a tomb in Albany, then secreted in the attic of a house in Pittsfield, Massachusetts, heavily guarded by Bowery henchmen. Morgan produced the books at the meeting, no questions asked.

The stockholders responded by electing a Morgan-Ramsey Board of Directors. Morgan was empowered to lease the railroad at once. He transferred the lease, as prearranged, to LeGrand B. Cannon, president of the Delaware and Hudson Canal Company. The new lease was signed and ratified immediately. Morgan received five thousand shares of Albany-Susquehanna stock as his commission for having saved the railroad from the hands of Jay Gould.

The stock gained suddenly on the New York Exchange, from 18 to 120 points.

"Jubilee Jim" Fisk never failed to swear vehemently at the mention of the name Morgan. He died soon after by the gun of a jealous husband.

Morgan returned to Wall Street. He was thirty-two years old. He commanded new respect from the bankers and financiers. He walked with grace and dignity— and on the heads of his opposition.

Chapter Forty-Five

Morgan

He was a physically imposing man. He was well over six feet tall. His hair was dark, long, and straight, parted to the side and combed straight back. His eyes were dark blue.

He had grown a handlebar mustache when he was twenty-four, and he kept it for the rest of his life. He let it grow much, much longer when he was in his fifties, so that it flowed to his jowls and the ends curled up his cheeks. His mustache grayed when he was sixty, and his hair turned white when he was sixty-three.

His immense nose had become inflamed with acne. It never healed. The scars he bore on his nose shocked those who were not prepared.

When he was a boy, he fell ill with rheumatic fever. One of his legs became temporarily paralyzed; it remained shorter than his other leg, forcing him to walk with a slight limp thereafter.

He was scarred by the memory of his meeting with Dwight Morrow's little girl. Morrow was a friend of Ann Lindberg's, and it was she who had warned the child not to make any remarks about "the old man's nose."

The girl walked stiffly toward Morgan, carrying a tea tray with a teapot and two delicate teacups, and asked in a trembling voice, "H-h-how m-many lumps do you want in your nose?"

The terrible pain of humiliation still remained.

His marriage to Frances had not fulfilled his expectations. She was a fine woman and a good mother to their children: Louisa, John Junior, Juliet, and Annie Tracey. Perhaps Annie was his favorite....

He was forced to spend long periods away from his family, but spent as much time with them as he could, often taking them along on his travels. Once, in Egypt, he had arranged a fireworks display for his children over the Nile, at Karnak.

Morgan shuddered: his visit inside the Temple of Karnak had left him badly shaken. He never told anyone what happened in those catacombs. He was drawn back to Egypt repeatedly, and spent much time in Cairo, at Karnak, and on steamers, gliding down the Nile.

Morgan was deeply religious. He experienced epiphanies whenever he saw the altar in St. George's Cathedral, or any of the ancient cathedrals in Europe. He frequently told people, "I would rather lose my fortune overnight and die a pauper than come to learn that even one word of the Bible is not literally true."

He had told those very words many times to his pastor, the Reverend William Rainsford.

Frances Louisa Tracy

His grandfather, John Pierpont, had attended seances. He had often told young Pierpont, "People could communicate with the dead, if it weren't for unbelief." He remembered those words years later when he learned that Thomas Edison was also attending seances.

Morgan thought Edison was a preposterous fraud. Edison had befriended Madame Helena Blavatsky. He espoused a theory of reincarnation—that the soul was like a swarm of bees that leave the body at death and search for a body to inhabit, just after conception. Morgan thought Edison was a heretic.

Edison was clever—he had been devilishly clever that day, many winters ago, in that shabby wooden shed in Menlo Park, where they first met. He promised to deliver to the world a new kind of light. The lighting globes he demonstrated in Morgan's own home burst into sparks and caught the rug and draperies afire. The small, dingy, smelly man offered excuses, then hastily departed.

Edison made lofty pronouncements for two years about having "perfected" electric lighting while spending Morgan's money freely. Morgan expelled Mr. Edison from Edison General Electric and hired the two American pioneers in illumination, Mr. Sawyer and Mr. Maxim. Sawyer was a bit of a drinker.

Railroads and telegraphy went hand-in-hand. Telegraph lines followed railroad lines. This was so the lines could be accessible to repairmen; two electricians in a hand-car could follow the tracks out to remote regions of the West, hauling tools without horses.

Morgan hated telephones. He sent messengers, telegrams, agents—or had people answer for him—anything to keep from speaking into the damned things. The way telephones distorted the human voice almost terrified him. Then there was that foreigner, that inventor from eastern Europe.... He was a madman and a genius. A very mysterious man.

Viewing Edison's career, which consisted of touring in a sideshow with a phony professor and electrocuting animals, Morgan decided to gain control of the Edison empire and turn his attention to that new gentleman, Mr. Tesla.

He did not know what to make of the man, but told himself that geniuses are frequently eccentric. He also told himself that whoever controls the railroads will control communications, and whoever controls the patent block on electrical communication must be a source of stability among men.

Too much innovation overnight saturates the marketplace, creates rising prices—then prices fall, workers are laid off, and the economy is struck down by a depression. That was why the buying of patent blocks by financiers was necessary: to introduce new products to the marketplace slowly, developing them when it was economically feasible, not merely expedient. Cost of development must not exceed a company's reserves: first profits are seldom as great as hopeful entrepreneurs expect—or require.

A banker had once told him during a financial panic, "I am very disturbed. I am below my legal reserve!"

Morgan snapped, "You ought to be ashamed of yourself! What is your reserve for at a time like this—except to use?"

He supported Grover Cleveland—a democrat, in spite of Morgan's republican leanings—because they had been "smoking buddies" and because he had always known Grover to be an honest man. Grover had stood up to Tammany Hall and lost.

The president of the United States had been defeated by Boss Tweed. In 1889, Cleveland was victorious at the polls by a hundred thousand votes. He had promised to rid national politics of the corrupt influence of Tammany Hall, but immediately after the election, the electoral votes vanished on the way to being counted—at Tammany Hall.

The popular vote was not considered an indicator of who had won the election; the decision went to Congress, and the benefit of the doubt was given to that coward Benjamin Harrison.

Morgan scowled. Harrison was a worm whose only redeeming value was that he didn't tarnish the presidency too badly.

Cleveland returned to politics after four years of impatience with Harrison's mediocrity. He ran for president again, and won.

He stepped back into the presidency just in time to face the Great Panic of 1893. That motley crew "Coxey's Army" was rioting and demonstrating throughout the midwest. They were mostly homeless farmers and unemployed workers seeking compensation privileges. Sixteen thousand people set out to march on Washington D.C., but by the time they reached the Capitol, fewer than nine hundred stragglers remained and they were either shot to death or beaten up and arrested by police.

When confronted with scandal, Grover always said, "Tell the truth!"

The first time he ran for president, the public was treated to lurid newspaper stories revealing Grover's mistress and child, even though he was a married man. "Tell the truth!" His policy was rewarded: he won the election in spite of the scandal.

Ten days before he stepped into office the second time, the great Philadelphia and Reading Railroad went bankrupt. Upon returning to the presidency, Cleveland witnessed the collapse of the American economy. Fifteen thousand houses fell, among them some of the wealthiest American families.

Cleveland called for the repeal of the Silver-Purchase Act and a complete return to the gold standard. The Silver-Purchase Act was repealed on October 30, 1893. Disaster was postponed—but not prevented.

August Belmont and Company were the American representatives for the House of Rothschild at the time. William E. Curtis was Secretary of the Treasury under Cleveland, and his assistant and Treasury liaison man was John G. Carlisle. By January 29, Secretary Carlisle's chief assistant William E. Curtis visited August Belmont at Belmont's home in New York City. They had conferred secretly five days before to assess whether or not the government could float a loan in Europe. They came to no conclusion.

President Cleveland had sent Congress a very distressed message to the effect that the entire United States economy was sinking into oblivion.

Cleveland proposed that American gold be converted to bonds and sold in Europe. When January 29 arrived, the official meeting of Curtis and Belmont could wait no longer. No conclusion was reached: the American economy no longer held any credibility in the eyes of European bankers, and they, due to debts incurred, owned the United States Treasury lock, stock, and barrel. That same day, William E. Curtis demanded a meeting at the United States Subtreasury in New York.

The Rothschilds were so appalled by the thought of financial catastrophe—and what the loss of their American holdings would mean—that they were easily persuaded to modify their insistence upon "gold only" payment of bonds. The morning of January 30 brought a bold visit by August Belmont himself. He strode into J. P. Morgan's office, alarmed by a cable he had just received from London stating that U. S. gold was already being seized from the United States Treasury.

Morgan had anticipated Belmont's "surprise" visit. He greeted the fellow banker with a proposal he had already drawn up. They finalized their agreement in extreme haste and drew up a memorandum outlining the details of a syndicate proposal. Then they strode arm-in-arm down Wall Street, their faces surly, their eyes intense. Morgan's nostrils flared as he puffed hot steam on that bitterly cold morning. They walked all the way to the office of William Curtis. They announced that they would save the United States economy—for a price.

Curtis frowned.

Morgan announced, "I don't know if we can get enough gold, here or abroad. But we are willing to try. In our opinion, no popular loan is possible. Here is a memorandum of our terms. You can take it to Washington and let the president and Mr. Carlisle look it over, then tell us what they think of it."

He showed the government no mercy.

Morgan and Belmont agreed to take a 34 percent bond at equivalent 104 percent. This caused the government to face a great loss: U. S. bonds were getting 111 points only.

A four-million-dollar gold shipment, already boxed and loaded aboard freighters, waiting to be shipped, was suddenly returned to the Subtreasury...due to a rumor that the president and Secretary Carlisle liked the agreement. They were in no position to dislike it.

The United States economy remained in a state of tense limbo until February 5, the next year.

That morning, Cleveland received an urgent visit from J. P. Morgan and August Belmont regarding the future of their private loan.

Morgan had been unsympathetically told, "Thank you, Mr. Morgan, but I have decided to rely upon Congress. The government does not desire a private loan." The meeting ended abruptly.

The Springer Bill, authorizing bonds payable in gold, was buried by the House, 167 to 120. Only a miracle could prevent the suspension of the U. S. Treasury in less than twenty-four hours.

Morgan received word of the defeat of the Springer Bill at three o'clock in the afternoon. He snatched up his hat and satchel, burst from his office, and bowled over a gaggle of newspaper reporters crowded around the door of his office. He hailed a horse cab and rode to the Cortlandt Street Ferry, bound for Washington. His departure had been announced by wire. He had no way to prevent that.

When he arrived in Washington, he received a message from Secretary Lamont, asking for a delay in his meeting with Cleveland. Morgan was furious. He demanded a statement from Cleveland, but the president was silent. Morgan was told on the steps of the White House, "Grover will not see you. The president refuses."

"Very well! Then I will get back on my train and let the country go bankrupt!"

He went to Arlington, where he met with his partner Bob Bacon. They attempted to hold a private meeting at their hotel suite but were interrupted by a stream of panic-stricken visitors. Bacon went to bed at midnight. Morgan played solitaire until dawn.

At nine the next morning, Bacon and Morgan resumed their discussion over breakfast.

"Suppose, Pierpont, Grover still refuses to see you."

"Then I will have no choice but to let the worst happen, let the depression run its course."

"But we can't let that happen...."

"Well Mr. Bacon, there might be a way out. I hope they have time to think this over, because if they're receptive to me at all, I think I might have a way."

"How in heaven's name can you do that?"

"Well, there is a law on the books, unless it has been repealed, that gives the Secretary of the Treasury power to purchase gold whenever he needs it, at the best price he can make, and to pay for it in any authorized obligations of the United States. I think this section is number four thousand and something of the Revised Statutes. It was passed, I think, in 1862 during a Civil War emergency. I remember Mr. Lincoln's sending Secretary Chase to New York, where he worked out the legislation with some of the bankers. I know the government got gold because my family furnished some of it."

Morgan and Bacon strode directly to the White House, Morgan carrying an unlit cigar in his jaws all the way. Frightened, hostile Grover Cleveland met them on the front steps of the White House. August Belmont had not arrived; he had been detained by the snowstorm.

They pushed past the president and strode into his study. Officials—including Secretary of the Treasury Carlisle and Attorney General Olney—had conveniently gathered in anticipation of the Morgan visit. Morgan and Bacon quickly sat down, waiting for August Belmont. Cleveland burst into the room, angry and adamant. He swore he would resist "the bond issue."

Someone handed Secretary Carlisle a yellow slip of paper that evoked a startled response: "Mr. President! It seems only nine million dollars worth of gold remains in the New York Subtreasury!"

His opportunity had arrived. Morgan stood up and forcefully announced, "Mr. President, the Secretary of the Treasury knows of one check that is outstanding for twelve million dollars. If this check is presented today, then it is all over for the United States economy."

Cleveland broke. He pleaded, "Have you anything to suggest, Mr. Morgan?" Morgan spoke quietly about "Section four thousand and something," and of the circumstances surrounding the passage of the statute.

Cleveland checked into the matter. Olney identified the statute as number 3,700, passed on March 17, 1862. Olney read it aloud at the meeting:

"The Secretary of the United States Treasury may purchase coin with any of the bonds or notes of the United States authorized by law and upon such terms as he may deem most advantageous to the public interest."

Cleveland silently read the act to himself. Finally, he said, "Gentlemen, I think our problem is solved. This Act seems to empower us to negotiate a bond sale at our own discretion. Though Congress, of course, must and shall be informed of our intentions."

While the terms were being drawn up, Cleveland suddenly became pensive and asked, "How about this drain of gold abroad? Suppose the government *does* purchase gold from the bankers and it is immediately withdrawn from the Treasury and sent abroad? Mr. Morgan, can you guarantee that such a thing will not happen?"

Morgan instantly replied, "Mr. President, I will so guarantee."

A long pause elapsed. Cleveland broke it. "All right. It is now two o'clock and you gentlemen had better go out and get some lunch while I formulate the terms of the plan for transmission in a message to Congress so as to send it up to the Capitol without delay."

Morgan heaved a sigh of relief—then looked down at his lap in amazement. He had been so agitated waiting for Cleveland to make up his mind that he had shredded his cigar. He stood up and brown tatters fell from his pants as laughter resounded through the study.

Cleveland announced: "It is time we all had a smoke. Mr. Morgan, will you remain while I dictate a message to Congress?"

A contract was drawn up with the Morgan-Belmont banking syndicate. The government would receive for six months the gold equivalent to 65,116,244 dollars and to issue in payment 62,315,400 dollars in bonds. The contract provided:

"At least one half of all coin deliverable hereunder shall be obtained in and shipped from Europe."

Also:

"...The parties of the second part and their associates hereunder...as far as lies in their power, will exert all financial influence and will make all legitimate efforts to protect the Treasury of the United States against withdrawal of gold, pending the complete performance of this contract."

These provisions established a precedent between government and private purchasers. The Silverites howled in protest. Morgan pondered how long the security derived from this agreement would last.

Cleveland had been replaced by William McKinley. War with Spain looked inevitable. The national economy had failed to prosper.

Morgan was preparing for a meeting. Fannie was in the water closet; he could hear her down the hall. He would be going to the Palm Room of the Waldorf-

Astoria tonight, and if all went well he would be meeting that man Mr. Tesla.

He thought back on another longtime friendship he frequently relied on for support, confidence, and advice. He fondly remembered William Rainsford, who had been a revivalist from Toronto. Morgan had been impressed with his style of preaching when they met back in 1882.

By 1884, Morgan used his influence to secure Rainsford the position of head of the vestry at St. George's Cathedral. Immediately, Rainsford declared the vestry democratic—which provoked Morgan's resignation.

"I cannot accept this," Rainsford said, shoving the letter back into Pierpont's lapel pocket.

Morgan was incensed—but Rainsford would hear nothing of it. He stated flatly, "You knew I was a radical when we met. You've known I was a radical all along! I cannot accept this letter of resignation, Pierpont, because your contract is as binding with me as mine is to this church."

"I cannot go along with the democratization—"

Rainsford shut the door to his office. They were alone.

Morgan began: "Mr. Rainsford, it is my opinion that the democratization of the church is taking the principle of democracy too far. You cannot democratize the vestry when the structure of the church is determined by the hierarchy of the Kingdom of God—and that is *not* democratic!"

"Do you really believe that, sir?"

"Yes. Of course I do."

"Then what do you think of petitionary prayer?"

"Absolute heresy, sir!"

"Nonsense, Pierpont! What is *any* prayer if not petitionary?"

Morgan did not know what to say. He crumpled the letter of resignation, and Rainsford retained his democratic vestry. That had been so long ago.

Now he was considering financing that inventor, Nikola Tesla, whose laboratory had burned down.

PART FIVE

Tesla

Chapter Forty-Six

Pierpont

"Father!"

"Well, hello, Annie! What a surprise to see you so early."

"I hope I didn't disturb you, Father. I know you are preparing to depart soon."

"No, not at all. Come in, come on in."

"I saw him again last night, Father."

"Who?"

"Nikola. He was at Delmonico's."

She doesn't know, Morgan thought. She has not yet been informed…. He ruffled his newspaper. His legs sprawled under the table and his feet rested on the chair opposite him. His teacup was by his elbow. He puffed on his cigar. Poor girl, he reflected sadly. She doesn't know.

The telephone had rung just over an hour ago—that infernal machine!—and a blur of a voice on the other end said something about Tesla. Said his lab caught fire. Burned to the ground. Damned bad, Morgan thought.

Anne sat down beside him. "What do you think, Father?"

"About what?"

"About—Mr. Tesla?"

"Of course. Well, he certainly seems to be the man of the times, Annie."

"Yes, he is, Father. Do you think he…might come to…find me…attractive…?"

John Pierpont Morgan smiled. "From what I've heard, our Mr. Tesla isn't the marrying type."

"Well, perhaps he hasn't found the right woman, Father."

Morgan drew in a deep breath. He remembered Amelia—Mimi, as he had called her—and sadness stung him, reminding him of how much he had loved her. He opened his eyes. He did not realize he'd closed them.

"You seem lost in thought, Father. Perhaps I should leave you. It's this voyage, isn't it? You always get so distant when you are about to travel."

He chuckled. "Is that it?"

"Oh, Daddy, you are impossible!" She laughed. "Well, that's not quite true, but it's true enough. It's the country, isn't it? You feel the Treasury is still in trouble and that Grover didn't do enough about it, is that what you're thinking?"

"Oh, nothing is troubling me...."

"It's that evil little man, Harriman, and the railroads again, is that it?"

"Part of this excursion will be to meet Mr. Hill, that is true."

"Do you think you will go into partnership with him?"

"I don't see why not. He's a respected railroad businessman. I've studied his record; it's very impressive."

"Well, I'm sure you'll reach an understanding, then. Is mother about? I want to speak to her, too. In fact, I have something to show her; perhaps you'd like to see it, too."

"Oh?"

"Aunt Sarah gave me a gift yesterday." She opened her handbag and drew out a small object wrapped in a white Oriental linen. She unwrapped a tiny white figurine and handed it to her father. "Aunt Sarah says she came upon this in her attic. She said it looks just like me. Do you think so, Father?"

"Why...why, yes, it does.... It—she—looks just like you."

"Why, thank you, Daddy. She's very beautiful. Aunt Sarah says this is a statuette of Athena, Goddess of Wisdom."

"So she is."

Anne laughed. "If this is Athena—and she looks just like me—then you must be Zeus, Father!"

Morgan scowled. He did *not* want to be compared to the King of Olympus. "Zeus—indeed!"

"Oh, don't be offended, Daddy!"

Morgan winced. He recalled the words of one Wall Street wag: "That Morgan! He's a real Jupiter!" He grumbled, chewed his cigar. "Show your mother. It's a lovely little statue. But don't tell her I'm another Zeus!"

Anne stood and departed.

Pierpont smoked his cigar for a few more minutes, then stood and walked inside.

Anthony Drexel, Morgan's former partner, died two years ago in 1893. Five years before, his father, Junius, died in a railroad accident. Morgan was quite alone on his pedestal of power.

The carriage pulled up to his office—J. P. Morgan and Company—at 23 Wall Street. Morgan paid the driver and stepped inside the building. He ordered his secretary to summon Mr. James and Mr. Baker immediately.

D. Willis James and George F. Baker had worked for the Morgan firm for many years; both had been longtime friends of the Morgan family. After a brief deliberation, Morgan requested that Francis Lynde Stetson also be called in.

When the three men arrived, Morgan closed the door and gestured toward the chairs at his vast conference table. "Gentlemen, I suppose you have heard the news. Which one of you telephoned me about it this morning?"

"I did," Mr. Stetson said.

"Good. I can't hear your voice very well over that Goddamned telephone. Well, Mr. Stetson, what can you tell us about the fire?"

"In the Tesla Company laboratory, sir? Only that it happened, and the fire chief is investigating it, that's all."

"Any idea how it started?"

"Nothing official."

"How about unofficial?"

"We've managed to gather no information, sir."

"I see."

"He had enemies, sir." Mr. James spoke up.

"Sir?"

"Yes, Mr. Morgan. He acquired one principle enemy, as I'm sure you know."

"You mean Tom Edison, don't you?"

"Yes, sir, I do."

"I thought so. Yes, this Mr. Edison is a rascal—yes, I know what kind of a man we're dealing with. Mr. Edison is as unscrupulous as Harriman."

Mr. Stetson continued, "The fire started sometime after midnight. The guard was asleep—which might mean somebody slipped him something. Tesla and Westinghouse had a number of enemies, the most visible and outspoken of whom is Thomas Edison, of course.

"The fire started near the rear entrance to a storage room, a door that provided easy access to anyone who can jimmy a latch. It started on or near a shelf containing chemicals. Just what chemicals, we may never know. There were electrical wires near that shelf, so we cannot rule out the possibility of an electrical fire, especially if corrosive chemicals were on that shelf."

"So arson is only a possibility?"

"Yes, Mr. Morgan."

"Do any of you have anything to add?"

"No…" said Mr. Baker. "Except…."

"Yes, George?"

"Well, Mr. Morgan, I think it might have been Edison."

"What makes you think that?"

"We know how bitter he is about the success of Tesla's system and the Niagara Falls station, how he's upstaged Edison in every conceivable way. Well, sir, some of the men who worked the Niagara project were also former Edison men—and they thought Mr. Edison might try something like this, even back when the station was being built. Of course, no one can prove anything. There is no word…."

"Anything on the streets? How about that scoundrel detective Edison employs?"

"Joseph McCoy, sir?"

"Yes, has he made mention to any of our boys, working with Edison, about any plans for…retaliation for injustices real or imagined?"

"Not that I know of. If this is Edison's doing, then it's being kept really quiet."

"As, no doubt, it would be." Morgan leaned forward. "This incident could be used to our advantage."

"How so, sir?"

"I've been wanting to get Mr. Tesla to sign with us for a long time. If he has to start over again, he might have to."

Mr. Stetson smiled. "It would be nice to have exclusive rights to the Tesla patents."

"Very nice, indeed," Mr. James said dryly. "Who knows what this inventor will come up with next."

"That is not entirely why I want that, Mr. James."

James eyed Morgan, curiously. "Why, then?"

"To keep a closer eye on Mr. Tesla."

"Why, sir?" George Baker spoke up.

"Why? Why, indeed?" Morgan puffed on his cigar and folded his hands across his chest. "Well, sir, our country and now Europe have both been transformed drastically by a new kind of electrical current, given to us by a most unusual man."

"Yes...?"

"Don't you see the implications of that?"

"Well, it does seem quite—how should I say it?—quite...remarkable, to say the least...."

"To say the very least, Mr. Baker! Think about that: who *is* this man, Nikola Tesla, anyway?"

"We seem to know very little about him, sir," Stetson said.

"So, we have a man who is relatively young," Morgan mused, "who comes from some little foreign country in the region of many other little countries.

"He has vast ideas, ideas about electricity, new ideas, and one of these ideas has already changed the world. Overnight. But why? And by whom?"

"That's what we'd all like to know, Mr. Morgan," Mr. Stetson put in.

"Yes, that's true, Mr. Stetson. We'd all like to know. Baker—" he pointed at the man he had often called his "Secretary of the Treasury" and lowered his cigar at him—"can you move a man in by tomorrow morning? I don't think anyone's going to approach Tesla by then, but we need to make our move before the shock of this setback wears off."

"I'll find somebody, sir—"

"He must owe somebody on that big laboratory of his. Find out who."

"I know who," Stetson announced. "A man by the name of A. K. Brown."

"Very good, Francis. Word has it that Tesla isn't doing very well on his alternating current royalties."

"He tore up the contract with Westinghouse so that George could keep his company."

"Yes, Francis, I know that. And a lot of good it did them, isn't that right?"

"Yes, sir."

"This fellow Tesla also displays a disturbing lack of understanding of human nature."

"He is astonishingly...trusting, sir," Mr. Stetson said.

"That is an understatement, Francis. A dramatic understatement."

"It was intended to be, sir."

"Then it should be a simple matter to entice him to sign with us," George Baker said brightly.

"Perhaps," Morgan said. "However, we've approached him in the past—and he hasn't been too trusting."

"It's true," Stetson added. "He has told our representatives that he prefers his independence."

"I see," Mr. James frowned. "Tell me—what does all this point to?"

"So far," Morgan leaned over the table, "the only way I have of keeping my eye on this man is through my daughter, Anne. She knows him socially, and they have become quite good friends, or so she tells me. The only drawback is this: she has no mechanical or scientific inclinations. She's infatuated with the man, but she doesn't understand a thing he tells her. Oh, he announces everything he intends to build or invent—but his explanations are wasted on her.

"We need someone who will keep an eye on him, someone who understands his designs, how his inventions work, someone who will report to us what is going on in his laboratory."

"Who?" Mr. James called out.

"Stetson, Baker, who do we have in the field who can we move out on short notice? Someone who could influence Mr. Tesla?"

Francis Lynde Stetson, Morgan's personal "Attorney General," responded enthusiastically: "Our man at the Cataract Construction Company did a lot of business with Tesla by wire during the construction of the Niagara Falls dynamo. He's in a perfect position to approach Mr. Tesla. If we could cable him and send him instructions—"

"Has he ever met Tesla?"

"Not to my knowledge, no, I don't think so."

"Arrange for Cataract Construction Company to make their move. Who is in charge?"

"Edward Dean Adams."

"Good. Call up Mr. Adams and get him to move on this. Immediately. I want an exclusive on the Tesla patents, as well as regular reports as to what he's doing, what his plans are."

"Yes, sir."

"Oh—and Stetson...."

"Yes, sir?"

"This could be the biggest venture we ever undertake. And I want it understood, gentlemen, that this entire discussion is to be kept in absolute confidence."

"Yes, sir."

"Yes, of course, sir."

"Yes, sir."

"Very good, gentlemen. Then this meeting is hereby adjourned."

CHAPTER FORTY-SEVEN

Phoenix

Katherine Johnson responded to the news of the burning of the Tesla laboratory by writing him an impassioned letter, offering to "console" him for his irreparable loss. She wrote, "It seemed as if you too must have vanished into thin air.... Do let me see you again in the flesh that this awful thought may vanish...."

He read her fancy handwriting: "Today with the deepening realization of the meaning of this disaster and consequently with increasing anxiety for you, my dear friend, I am poorer except in tears, and they cannot be sent in letters. Will you not come to us now—perhaps we might help you, we have so much to give in sympathy...."

As usual, he ignored her letters. He lived cloistered in his room at the Waldorf-Astoria to recover from his tragic losses. He had secluded himself to consider the offer extended by Mr. Edward Dean Adams. He would be meeting with Adams shortly.

He had already accepted an unconditional advance of forty thousand dollars from the Cataract Construction Company—and he feared that might have been a mistake. Someone knocked at the door.

"Mr. Adams is here to see you, sir."

"Send him in, please."

"Well, Mr. Tesla," Adams said brightly, "have you considered the Cataract Company's offer?"

"Yes, Mr. Adams."

"And, have you reached any conclusion?"

"Yes, I have. Tell your associate Mr. Morgan I have the highest respect for him."

"Is that all?"

"Tell him I have great respect for him and for the companies he has chosen to represent. Especially his own company, which I regard with esteem. And tell him I have utmost respect for his daughter, Anne, who is an acquaintance of mine."

"Yes, Mr. Tesla—"

"I guess you know what I am leading to, Mr. Adams."

"Please tell me, Mr. Tesla."

"I am grateful for the forty-thousand-dollar advance; I shall endeavor to make good use of the money."

"And—?"

"And, about the greater offer, I have decided to decline it."

"What? You can't be serious—"

"Of course I am serious, Mr. Adams."

"But, Mr. Tesla, forty thousand dollars won't go far in rebuilding what you've lost, much less the development of your future plans."

"I realize that. However, just what those future plans are must remain to be seen!"

"What? I don't understand."

"As an inventor, I must remain independent. That is the only way I will be able to concentrate my mind on the tasks at hand, problems that businessmen cannot, by training or profession, understand. Do not be offended! It is not your specialty. You cannot be expected to—"

"Is that your final word on the offer?"

"Yes, it is, Mr. Adams."

"Then I guess this discussion is finished."

"Yes, it seems to be...concluded."

Edward Dean Adams stood. "Then, I guess I have no further business here."

"It seems not."

He strode to the door. "Good-bye, Mr. Tesla!"

"Good-bye, sir."

Tesla remained seated as Adams hastily departed. He was determined to overcome his losses. *And* stay independent.

He had a dream. A vision, a theory. It was grand, perhaps grandiose, but it was feasible, and it would mean converting the entire planet— Could he share such a dream with J. P. Morgan? He doubted that he could.

Tesla envisioned the transmission of free global power and all signals carried by the power flow and received by every family, every human being in the world. Could a man like John Pierpont Morgan comprehend this sublime vision?

For dinner, Tesla dined at a sidewalk cafe on a street corner. Some of the clientele tried not to stare at him while he measured the volume of his soup bowl and carefully computed the area of his dining plate.

The next day, he resumed his efforts to build his laboratory.

By the end of the week, he located a building at 46 East Houston Street. He set up an office immediately.

Edison had not spoken of Tesla since the Chicago Exposition in 1893, when his name had been left out of the pavilion. The Edison works were kept busy by what Edison called his greatest achievement—the magnetic ore separator.

In 1894, Sir Oliver Lodge duplicated Tesla's experiments in wireless transmission. He sent the letter "S" in Morse code 150 yards.

That was also the year Edison's competitor, Hiram Maxim, flew a fantastic new machine called an "aeroplane." Propelled by a steam engine and lifted with twelve wings—carrying three men, a water tank, and a boiler—the fantastic device flew until a gust of wind pushed it into the cables mounted on towering poles that were intended to guide it. That had been on the last day of July in that year.

Edison corresponded with Michael Pupin, of Columbia University. Professor Pupin had met Tesla twice—and acquired a distinctly bad impression of him. Edison cultivated Pupin's low opinion of Tesla. He wrote letters to Pupin, emphasizing that Tesla obstinately refused to commit to marriage. He hinted there was something "unspeakable" about him.

Tesla launched a barrage of letters to prospective investors. Newspapers were still describing the fire as "a tragedy of the highest order" and "a calamity of the highest magnitude." He suddenly became more accessible to the public and New York's social elite. His appearances in cafes and at Delmonico's or the Fortune 400 Club continued to arouse much talk. Although he always arrived alone, he was soon joined by his entourage, a bevy of young ladies often including Marguerite Merington or Anne Morgan.

The company of adoring young women included Katherine Johnson as well. Katherine was obviously in love with Nikola; this fact did not escape her husband's attention.

She wrote letters to the inventor and occasionally left them open on her bureau or makeup table, as if for Robert to read....

When he found them, he did just that; perusing them indifferently, noticing her openly flirtatious phrases and—sometimes—her desperate, pleading style. He never mentioned the contents of those letters to her. She might have left them open accidentally—she sometimes drank, occasionally to excess, and they did quarrel a lot....

Katherine thought her husband had grown indifferent toward her.

Robert Johnson was not jealous of his wife's infatuation with Tesla; of all the men he knew, he trusted Tesla most with women. He suspected that Tesla, like himself, was not entirely heterosexual. Yet as long as Tesla continued to be seen in the company of young and glamorous women, there was no cause for scandal.

Tesla was rebuilding. He was preparing to conduct experiments on invisible radiation. He had begun to measure invisible rays from natural sources, concentrations of minerals and radiation from space. He was making discoveries—again.

CHAPTER FORTY-EIGHT

Society

Everyone was at Delmonico's.

Tesla manifested—he did not just arrive. A waiter escorted him to his favorite table, reserved for him by "the Filipovs"—his nickname for Robert and Katherine. Luka Filipov had been a Serbian hero. "Luka" became Robert's nickname. Katherine became "Madame Filipov." In his notes and letters to her, he always maintained a sense of distance. She sent him communiqués by messenger several times a day, at times. Occasionally, he allowed her to tempt him into joining the night life at Delmonico's or the Player's Club, but even then he usually departed early to continue his experiments until late into the night.

They were waiting for him at his table, and they had several guests seated with them. A handsome young man with brown hair smiled. An elderly gentleman looked up. Marguerite was present, as was Anne Morgan.

"Luka!" Tesla called out to Robert Johnson.

"There he is! Our friend Nikola, the Great Inventor!"

"Nikola!" Katherine waved.

Robert said, "We have some friends we would like you to meet."

"Certainly, Luka."

"Nikola, this is Joseph Jefferson, the famous actor, and this is none other than our longtime friend Mark Twain."

"Dear God!" Tesla's eyes widened.

"What's wrong?" Katherine was concerned.

"Oh, nothing's wrong, Katherine! Mr. Twain—I am indebted to you beyond the measure of words to express!"

Twain was surprised. "Really? How can that be?"

"Mr. Twain, when I was young, just a boy, I lay deathly ill in bed for weeks with my mother at my side, desperately trying to nurse me back to health. When all else seemed to fail, my mother went to the library in Gospic and brought some books back for me to read. Well, Mr. Twain, the book on top of the stack was one of your first novels. When I read it, I sent my mother back to find anything else there by you. She returned again with a collection of your stories, and I read them all in one day. That is what saved me."

Mark Twain was stunned. His eyes filled with great tears. He said, "Why, Mr. Tesla…I don't quite know how to respond!"

"Accept my debt of gratitude that my very life, my will to live, was rescued from oblivion by your books, most notably *Huckleberry Finn* and *Tom Sawyer.* That is true, sir."

Silence befell the small party at the table. Finally, Mark Twain spoke. "This is the most joyous news of my life, sir! To think— those books I wrote influenced such a towering figure of a man. I am humbled, Mr. Tesla, truly humbled."

"As I am humbled before you, sir."

Katherine lifted her voice: "Nikola, why don't you tell us something of your latest experiments?"

"Thank you, Katherine, but Mr. Twain and I have much to talk about. Tell me about yourself, Mr. Twain."

"Call me Mark!"

"Certainly! I am honored! Call me Nikola, please. This is a great moment in my life— in certain ways, the greatest. Speak to me of yourself. Tell me about Mark Twain."

"I don't know where to begin!"

"Mark tends to be a very modest man, Nikola," Robert put in.

"No, I don't!"

"You've had so many adventures," Katherine said.

"Oh, yes," Twain said. "I've been known to spin a yarn or two.... One time, when I was editor of the Virginia City *Star*, I come upon a Chinaman sitting on a hillside, flying a kite in a storm. Only, t'wasn't really a kite—it was a wood door, strung on a cable, with a chain for a tail! Of course, he had the cable wrapped 'round and 'round the trunk of a fairly stout juniper tree, but there he was, sittin' on a rocky hillside, flying a kite in the wind of one of our fierce desert storms out there...."

"That's amazing! The wind velocity must have been not less than one hundred miles per hour!"

"At least that, Nikola! I've seen storms that brought down barns. Storms that would amaze you. Hell, out in the desert, a storm can come up in ten minutes. Ten minutes, mind you! The wind out there can blow down a tamarisk tree or a desert pine."

"My goodness!" Katherine exclaimed.

"Mr. Twain," Anne Morgan spoke up, "when were you the editor of the Virginia City newspaper?"

"Not long after the Civil War, my dear. It was in those days that they discovered gold in Caly-fornya, as you may well reckon. Saw wonders out there, too."

"Tell me about them!" Anne Morgan's eyes gleamed.

"They've got this big lake out there, Mono Lake—after an Indian word—and it's all lined with salt towers, taller'n'statues, like giant castles, all made of mineral salts.

"And these peculiar flies line up on the shores every summer, in a big ring, and completely encircle the lake.

"Then there's a valley called Yosemite, Nikola, that will take your breath away! It's big and vast and deep, and completely surrounded by mountains. Snow on the summits, even in summer."

"It sounds beautiful," Anne sighed.

"I want to see California again, sometime," Robert said. "It's been a long time. I never made it to Yosemite Valley. I didn't make it to many parts of California."

"This is exciting," Joseph Jefferson said, leaning over next to Robert, "the meeting of Nikola Tesla and Mark Twain."

Marguerite nodded. "Tell us more, Mr. Twain."

"Tell us about the savages," Joseph Jefferson said.

"They aren't savages," Twain said. "It's true, their ideas of civilization differ from our own, but I've known many honorable redskins in my time, and I've come to respect them as a people, something durned few cavarly officers do!"

"That is terribly tragic," Tesla said.

Marguerite turned to Joseph Jefferson and said softly: "This was a meeting that was destined to happen."

Jefferson nodded.

"Seems inevitable," Robert commented.

Seated at a nearby table was William Vanderbilt. He decided to make his presence known. "Good evening, Mr. Tesla! Is that Mark Twain seated with you?"

"None other," Robert called back.

"Modesty forbids me from announcing myself," Twain said. Everyone laughed.

A waiter served white wine, sparkling in long-stemmed glasses. Tesla accepted a glass with a gloved hand.

"Nikola," Vanderbilt resumed, "I expected to see you at the opera last weekend. You should have come! I keep a reservation open for you—and a guest—at my box in the theater."

"I am grateful for that," Tesla replied courteously. "I am indebted to you for that. However, my experiments preoccupied me that night."

"Have you any miracles to tell us of?" Katherine asked.

"Mr. Vanderbilt, perhaps you should bring your chair over here for a moment."

"Oh? Certainly, Nikola."

Vanderbilt spun his chair around, sat in it with his arms folded across the back, leaned forward facing Tesla.

Tesla dipped into the pocket of his lapel and drew out a tiny rosewood box. He held it in his gloved hand for a moment, eyeing it intently. "I have been experimenting with a new phenomenon. Lightning has the ability to form itself into globes. Little balls of fire that do not diffuse or dissipate if contained properly for periods of time." He opened the box. Gloved fingertips plucked out a tiny fireball: gleaming white, silent, and flickering red and blue.

The dinner party hushed in amazement. Eyes were fastened to the electricity.

"It is a globe of lightning. When the ether is in a state of equilibrium, it can contain itself by magnetic attraction for an indefinite amount of time. I've had this little spark in my pocket for ten days now."

Marguerite gasped. Katherine put her fingers to her lips. Anne Morgan could not look away. Mark Twain stared in awe.

"I've never seen anything like it," Anne Morgan said at last.

"It's...very beautiful." Marguerite said.

"Very peculiar," Mark Twain said, still unable to look away.

Vanderbilt said, "Very impressive, Nikola. Very impressive."

"He is the true 'Wizard of the West,' as we've come to call him in journalism," Mark Twain said.

"The Wizard of the West," Katherine repeated. "Yes, that certainly applies to you, Nikola!"

"And we don't mean Edison!" Robert said.

They laughed.

Joseph Jefferson offered a toast to Nikola Tesla.

"See you at the opera," Vanderbilt said, and went back to his table.

Tesla slipped the ball of lightning back into the box and pocketed it.

"That was marvelous," Robert said. "We never know what to expect from you."

"Come to our house again," Katherine said. "Agnes would so dearly love to see you!"

"Come over for an evening," Robert said. "Have dinner with us sometime."

"I fear I must depart," Tesla said. "The hour is precisely ten."

"Oh, I'm so disappointed," Anne said. "I was looking forward to spending a little more time."

"Ten o'clock is still early!" Robert Johnson stood, raising his arms expansively. "You can't end our evening with you on such short notice!"

"Not at all," Tesla said. "You're right—the evening is still young. Why don't you meet me at the laboratory at midnight? The evening will still be young then, too." There was laughter, and the rendezvous was agreed upon.

Tesla departed and returned to his laboratory. He was alone in the great building—except for his machines, his fabulous machines. He wandered from the work tables to the dynamos, to the vast arena where he had built his oscillators and oscillating platform. He charged up his giant Tesla coil.

The entire chamber flashed and roared with twisting, snapping arms of light. Ozone clotted the air with a coppery smell. Tesla stepped toward the fiery pillar of the coil. Sparks flew toward him. He reached forward and electricity twisted around his arms. His skin tingled as the current flowed through him. Electricity was his rapture, his ecstasy, his bliss.

When the appointed hour arrived, Tesla found himself hunched over a desk, pouring equations onto a piece of paper and solving them just as fast. A loud knock snapped him back to attention.

"Please—come in, come in!"

Chauncey McGovern, the esteemed British journalist, led the party inside.

"Mr. McGovern! So glad you could come!"

All were present except for Anne Morgan. Marguerite linked herself to Tesla. Although she did not dare hold his hand, she stood as close to him as she could.

"Behold, my latest exploration!" Tesla announced as he threw a light switch and electric illumination flung back the oily shadows.

In the center of the room was a wide low platform supported on blocks of compressed rubber, surrounded by girders and a railing, The ceiling was hidden by catwalks. Arc lights hung over the platform, glaring down cones of light.

Mark Twain and Joseph Jefferson stepped forward. Their eyes were wide with wonder.

"Well, the moment is all yours, Mr. Tesla," McGovern said. "What do you propose to do with this...marvel?"

"With this, my friends, I shall demonstrate the wonders of oscillation. Vast forces of energy can be generated by a device no larger than a hatbox." Tesla hastened to the far wall on the other side of the platform and threw a switch. A droning hum swelled inside the laboratory.

"Very interesting," Mark Twain said. "But what does it *do?*"

Everyone laughed.

"Let's watch," Robert Johnson said.

"A most impressive sound," Marguerite said breathlessly.

"Yes, it is very impressive, that sound." Twain frowned. "But you know what I always say, don't you, Robert?"

"Uh, you say many things, Mark...what is it this time?"

Twain looked directly at Tesla and his eyes crinkled with amusement. "What I always say, Mr. Johnson—and Mr. Tesla—and, mind you, they'll be quoting me into the hereafter—is that the thunder is impressive and very *good*...but it is the *lightning* that does all the work!"

Everyone laughed gaily.

"So tell me—" Joseph Jefferson asked cautiously. "What does that little machine and that big platform *do*...other than make noise?"

"Now that the oscillator has been running a while, step onto the platform!"

The ladies declined to participate in this adventure, as did Robert Johnson, but Jefferson, McGovern, and Twain stepped eagerly onto the vibrating platform.

"Woah!" Mark Twain whooped as his balance temporarily faltered. He grabbed the metal railing.

McGovern steadied himself, clinging to a vertical girder. Joseph Jefferson danced to the middle of the platform, laughing hysterically.

McGovern clung to the pillar, terrified. "Are you sure it's safe?"

Tesla laughed. "It is, if you do not stay on too long!"

The floor continued to vibrate wildly.

"Come on, Chauncey!" Mark Twain hooted. "Step toward the middle! Quit clinging to the side! Enjoy this!"

Jefferson laughed. "Hey—hey—this *is* rather fun! Exciting! Exciting!" Twain and Jefferson hooted and shrieked, shimmying in circles around the platform, arms flailing. Suddenly, Jefferson said, "I think I'm going to get off!"

Twain continued to taunt McGovern, who continued to clutch the beam beside of the platform.

Suddenly, Twain called out, "Where is it? Where is it?"

"What do you mean?" McGovern cried out in concern.

"Where is it, Tesla? Where is it?"

Tesla leaped onto the platform and helped the elderly writer down. He hurriedly escorted Twain to the washroom. Rejoining his guests, he explained, "The oscillator connected to this platform has what I call a 'laxative effect' after a while...."

The guests howled with laughter.

Tesla turned off the oscillator. The pulsing hum faded into silence.

"That was a dirty trick, Tesla," Twain said when he returned.

The guests laughed again.

"Come over here, then." He led the guests to another part of the vast room. Coils lined the walls and a Faraday cage surrounded the central pillar of a giant Tesla coil.

"Watch this." Tesla threw a switch and the laboratory went dark. "And—now!"

He threw another switch. The Tesla coil erupted with roots, branches, limbs of electrical fire. Tesla walked toward the blinding energies, unafraid.

"Nikola!" Twain cried.

Tesla stood before the blazing coil. Tentacles of lightning embraced his body.

"No—no—he knows what he's doing." Johnson restrained Twain from attempting to rescue Tesla from electrocution. "Just watch!"

Tesla walked closer to his machine. Tendrils and ropes of fire enveloped him.

"Oh—Nikola!" Marguerite was fearful.

"He has done this before," Robert Johnson said. "I have witnessed this many times."

Tesla was no longer visible at the center of blinding, glaring light. The Tesla coil roared, snapped, thundered. The guests—including Robert Johnson—were terrified.

Slowly, Tesla emerged from the chrysalis of fire. He walked quietly to the wall and threw a switch. The machine snapped off. The room was dark and silent. The guests were awed.

Nonchalantly, Tesla admitted he was starting to feel fatigued.

Very few words were uttered while the guests solemnly dismissed themselves.

Even Twain entertained the notion that there was something...not quite human about Nikola Tesla.

CHAPTER FORTY-NINE

Zeus

"Good afternoon, Mr. Stetson."

"Good afternoon, Mr. Morgan."

"Good afternoon, Mr. Baker."

"Good afternoon, sir."

"Have a seat, gentlemen—and close the door."

The walls of Morgan's office were hung with paintings. He sat behind his wide black mahogany desk, puffing a cigar indifferently. "Cigars, gentlemen?"

"Thank you."

"Thank you, sir."

"Very well. As you know, gentlemen, Mr. Hill has worked into a viable partnership with us, and the restructuring of the Northern Pacific and the Great Northern Pacific is proceeding smoothly."

"You and Hill spent much time together at the Triennial Convention, as I was informed," Stetson said.

"Mr. Hill is a fellow Episcopalian. I find that reassuring. We discussed matters of the spirit as well as business. Personally, I like the man. He represents all that is good about American character."

"That Harriman—he's a nervous little person, and he makes *me* nervous! He's audacious and he has no conscience."

Stetson chuckled. "I remember what he once told Otto Kahn: 'Let me be but one of fifteen men around any table, and I will have my way.'"

Morgan grumbled. "Those words would be true—except for me!"

Baker nodded. "That's history. Why bring it up?"

"Because I see disturbing alliances forming, outside our influence."

"Such as?"

"George, it has come to my attention that there is a dangerous alliance forming between that rascal Carnegie and John David Rockefeller."

Baker and Stetson exchanged glances.

"That's why I bring up this 'history,' as you call it: it seems to me we might have wasted a certain amount of time and concern over the attention we have given Harriman and the Supreme Court attempting to prevent the merger. The result is that we now control rail traffic throughout the Pacific Northwest, and we can set rail fares significantly lower than the standard of 'all the market will bear' that has been set by such men as Rockefeller and Carnegie."

"In other words," Stetson said, "the result of unbridled competition."

"Exactly," Morgan said, lowering his eyebrows critically. "Competition. Ruinous competition."

Stetson knew his employer well. "What else concerns you?"

"Gentlemen, competition is the greatest peril in the marketplace. It does not preclude that sharpers will not prevail! It's no longer supply and demand setting the prices.

"So, while these two men stand to make a great deal of money, they, and the rest of us, stand to lose a great deal more when the market collapses."

"That is true," Baker said. "But what can be done about it?"

"Well, that remains to be seen." Morgan frowned, grumbled. "Another case in point I wish to draw your attention to, gentlemen, is the case against Edison and Westinghouse. You know, no doubt, that it was Westinghouse who bankrolled that new current we now use in place of the standard Edison current."

"Yes," Stephen said slowly. "Go on...."

"And Westinghouse went bankrupt because of it," Morgan said. "He took on too much and perished."

Baker and Stetson nodded.

"Westinghouse was a good and noble man! Of that I am certain. In the long run, his company perished and we acquired his assets along the way. This stabilized the economy, for a time."

"This new current was the brainchild of Mr. Tesla, was it not?" Mr. Baker asked eagerly. "Tell me, sir, what do you think of him?"

"I will tell you tomorrow morning, gentlemen, because I have an engagement to meet him after dinner tonight at Delmonico's."

"I see," Stetson frowned.

"That is why you called us here," Baker said.

"And that is why I caught you both up on our latest business! That is why I brought up our history and our principles to you. Because I do not want you to forget what we represent. You asked me what I think of him. He's a strange man, Mr. Baker, a very strange man. And I'll tell you this much: he guards his privacy and practices abstinence."

Baker: "Abstinence, sir?"

"Apparently, from all matters of the flesh. At least, he has gone far to give that impression."

"I see."

Stetson: "What do you make of that, sir?"

"Well, it's not natural! But is it bad? Good? The Bible says that when Our Lord was here among us, in the flesh, he abstained from pleasures of the flesh. But a natural man? A carnal man? I don't know."

Baker and Stetson exchanged puzzled glances.

"I have nothing against earthly indulgences, myself!" Morgan said. "No one takes abstinence seriously anymore—except the Catholics, maybe. But that's not my point.

"My point is this: this man Tesla seems to be, well, different from the rest of us in certain ways I find disturbing. For example, he cannot walk around a corner unless he circles the block three times first. Now, I've discussed that with Mr. Rainsford and he seems to think it might be...an indication of witchcraft, among other things."

"You must be joking!" Baker was appalled.

"Oh, now, George, I don't really believe in such things, but who knows what this man Tesla believes? Rainsford only pointed out that witches and all kinds of Satanists draw a circle three times to cast a spell. We're living in apocalyptic times! Even Mr. Edison has been attending seances lately, and our informants have even told me he is not-so-secretly studying Theosophy! Hell, he even knows that 'Madame Blavatsky' or whatever her name is. An occultist! And he's been espousing some fool theory of reincarnation, to boot! Now, that's Edison—the unbeliever!"

"So, what you're saying," Baker was trying to reconstruct Morgan's train of thought, "is that this Mr. Tesla might be...involved with some kind of Satanic or occult society?"

"Something occult, very likely."

"Well," Stetson said, "this certainly complicates things."

"Yes, you see, it does, gentlemen. I, for one, don't approve of the values some of these newfangled notions in science seem to represent. That heretic Darwin, for instance. Not too long ago, Edison was an atheist, if you'll recall. Although I don't know what you'd call him now, now that he attends seances and occult meetings and such...."

"A heretic," Stetson said. "But how about Tesla? Surely, he doesn't practice the occult. Scientists—except Edison—frown on such beliefs, I thought."

"Perhaps most. Most scientists tend to be atheists, unbelievers, that is true." Morgan frowned. "Abstinence is not natural, but it can be an attribute of a saint. And a saint is not a natural man."

"Are you saying Mr. Tesla might be a saint?" Stetson asked, incredulously.

"Not a saint, but perhaps saintly. Yes. On the other hand, he might be a sinner, a great sinner, in disguise."

Stetson: "Do you really think, sir, that Mr. Tesla might be influenced by occult forces?"

"I cannot say, Francis. Rainsford assures me that such forces are real."

"So," Baker spoke up, "what do you think Mr. Tesla's reasons—his good reason and his real reason—are?"

"Well, I've been trying for some time to discern that, but I can't make too much sense of what I see. He accepted Mr. Adam's offer of a forty-thousand-dollar advance on the rebuilding of his laboratory but then he rejected our offer of a financial alliance. He said he wanted his independence."

"Who is financing him now?"

"He's currently accepting funds from his friend Colonel Astor."

"But John's money won't last forever. I know John Jacob: he wants returns on his investments, and Mr. Tesla had better come up with something spectacular pretty damned soon or his funding might be suddenly cut off."

"That is true," Baker agreed.

"I'll tell you this much," Morgan resumed, "his achievements might be the most advanced in electrical science, which leads me to this point: if the market is flooded with newfangled inventions, prices will be kept low and competition will be undercut because no one else will have the wherewithall to introduce competitive products.

"That might be all well and good, if we manage to secure an exclusive on these patented items and release them on the market a bit at a time, so we don't flood our prospective consumers—but if the market is flooded, it will stagnate. Then where will the economy be? Do you see what I'm getting at, gentlemen?"

Baker and Stetson nodded in unison.

"So far, the process of acquiring and reorganizing companies has not included forcible control, as our detractors have accused us of so frequently. No. Ours is a difficult and specialized task: we must see to it that everybody is satisfied.

"All we ask at the outcome is representation, not control."

"Of course," Stetson agreed. "That much is fair."

"We do not seek to dominate, and we are in no danger of losing money! That is why I gave up reorganizing the Union Pacific—I just gave it to Jacob Schiff."

"That turned out to be a mistake," Stetson said.

"Thanks to Harriman! That's why I endlessly reiterate, gentlemen, that a man has those two reasons—a good one, and a real one."

"What do you think of Mr. Tesla's two reasons?" Stetson asked.

"Well," Morgan said slowly, "his first reason, his good one, is that he wants to make a lot of money. Lots of it. I don't blame him. Wherever he's getting his ideas from, he deserves to be rewarded for producing them.

"But his real reason? Well, I hope to find that out this evening—if I find out anything at all." Morgan abruptly stood. "This meeting is adjourned."

Stetson and Baker stood.

Morgan strode to the door. "I have to get ready, gentlemen, for tonight I have an appointment that might influence the course of history." He dismissed his two closest associates, then he departed from his office and took a carriage to his home.

He dined with his wife and his daughter Anne. She had apparently overcome her infatuation with this mysterious gentleman who had first charmed her then failed to respond to her charms.

That was all well and good, Morgan mused. He had not been pleased with the prospect of having an inventor for a son-in-law.

Anne sat across the table, chatting with her mother. Morgan noticed one subject had been entirely absent from his daughter's conversations lately: men. Morgan suspected that the pain his daughter felt at Tesla's rejection of her was much greater and deeper than she had let on.

Anne suddenly exclaimed, "Father, aren't you excited?"

"About what, Anne?"

"About meeting Nikola tonight! Obviously."

Morgan had been avoiding the subject of Nikola Tesla.

"Oh, yes, yes, of course...."

"Well—?"

"Well, I am...'interested' would be a better word than 'excited.'"

Anne Morgan laughed. "He's the most wonderful man—"

"You and Mr. Tesla have become good friends, I see."

"Oh, yes...I had once wished for something more, but he's too passionately committed to his work. I just had to face that: Nikola's greatest passion, his true love, is science."

"You don't say."

"Yes! That's the way it has to be, Father, if he is to accomplish the great things he envisions."

"I see."

"I have been to his laboratory at night, Father, and I know the things he is capable of. Wonders. Miracles. I've seen his laboratory light up with sparks of fire—lightning, just like in a storm—and I'm at a loss for words to describe it."

"My! That's some recommendation!"

"You will see, tonight."

"I look forward to it." He remembered his words from earlier in the evening: *I have an appointment that might influence the course of history....* He sensed his words were true. "Let us hope Mr. Tesla lives up to his reputation."

With that, the subject of Tesla vanished from the conversation. Anne excused herself after dinner; she had a mysterious appointment to keep.

Frances had gone to the bedroom. He could hear her quietly hurrying to get ready.

What would this Mr. Tesla be like? What did he think of the Bible?

Mark Twain might be there. Morgan had met Twain before, and disliked him. He was so...irreverent. He had no respect for the rich, this Mr. Twain—but he had so *many* rich friends!

Fannie had gone from the bedroom to her toilette, then walked briskly down the hallway. She announced, "I am ready to depart, Pierpont."

Morgan stood. "Very well. We shall depart."

They boarded the carriage waiting for them in the drive.

"Well, I am certainly eager to meet this mysterious Mr. Tesla...."

His wife did not respond.

The carriage hurried roughly over the cobblestones. Morgan had come to expect only silence from his wife during the little time they spent together anymore. Even the silence they shared required many compromises.

The carriage slowed to a halt before the steps at Delmonico's, and the crowd on the sidewalk parted for the arrival of John Pierpont Morgan. He and his wife were escorted up the white marble steps and were intercepted by Colonel John Jacob Astor.

"Mr. Morgan!"

"Colonel Astor."

"Right this way, please."

Astor led Morgan and Frances to a cluster of tables between two towering potted palms. The people at the tables were beautiful—dark-haired, perfect ladies and handsome young gentlemen. Except that Twain fellow. The writer.

Mark Twain sat on the far side of the last table, leaning back in his chair. He eyed Morgan as he approached.

"Pierpont, Frances, I would like you to meet the Johnsons, Katherine and Robert, Miss Marguerite Merington. I think you know Mr. Twain, of course, and our guest of honor—Nikola Tesla!"

"It is a pleasure to meet you at last, sir," Tesla said, rising, bowing slightly, then returning swiftly to his seat.

Morgan noticed that he avoided a handshake. He met Tesla's gaze and said, "At last. You are preceded by legend, Mr. Tesla."

Tesla nodded respectfully. "As are you, Mr. Morgan."

Morgan sat across from the inventor. "I hope you will not be too influenced by adverse publicity."

"Not in the slightest, sir. In fact, I looked forward to this meeting to see first-hand what kind of a man you are."

"I came for precisely the same reason, Mr. Tesla. It is not but once in a lifetime that one gets to sit before a creative genius of your caliber."

"Thank you, sir."

"Anne tells me you have some wonderful new experiments going on at your laboratory. Is that true?"

"Oh, yes, tell us, Nikola!" Katherine was eager to hear her mentor's latest words on the subject of scientific miracles.

"Nikola has a new device called 'diathermy,'" Robert Johnson said. "Would you favor us with a word about it, Nikola?"

"Certainly, Luka. I have been experimenting with high-energy rays and the internal heating of muscle tissues. The therapeutic effects are superb; experiments have proven that the healing quality imparted by such high-energy magnetic rays can repair damaged tissues of the muscles and internal organs in far less time than if left alone."

"Why is that?" Morgan asked.

"It provides a small, artificial fever, sir. The increased temperature induces increased blood flow, providing greater accessibility to oxygen and nutrients to the body part affected by the damage."

"How is that superior to, let us say, ordinary heat sources?"

"Because the skin is not heated, sir. The distribution of heat is equal, not from the surface to the inside, which heats the body unevenly and causes the skin to burn."

"I see."

"Nikola just hired a new assistant," Katherine said.

"Yes. His name is George Scherff. Brilliant man. Excellent mathematician."

"Good fortune," Morgan said.

"You now have two assistants, don't you?" Robert asked cautiously.

"Yes. Kolman Czito and George Scherff. I need at least two men capable of understanding the experimental nature of my work."

Morgan leaned forward slightly. "I've heard tell you compute the amount of food you eat before you consume it."

Silence fell around the table. All eyes were upon Morgan.

"That is true, sir."

"Why is that, Mr. Tesla?"

"Because if I don't, the food somehow tastes bland to me. I cannot explain that, sir. I can only assure you it is true."

My God, Morgan thought, this man is incapable of telling anything but the truth! He is, to say the least, unselfconsciously *honest* about himself, even his eccentricities. Uncanny.

"Tell us of you researches...on the invisible rays from the sun." Morgan sensed Katherine was hiding something. She was not quite certain how to address Nikola Tesla. She was probably in love with him. She's lost her attraction to her husband, Morgan observed. They keep a respectful distance from each other, typical of couples who are no longer intimate. He knew that such a distance separated himself from Frances.

"I speak of wonders," Tesla said, "but these are not wonders incomprehensible to ordinary minds. No. What I do is science, not sorcery. The principles of electricity are simple: every current generates a magnetic field, and every field, when moved across a wire, generates a current."

"Really?" Katherine said. "It sounds like the current and the—is it a 'magnetic' field? Is that it?"

"That's it, precisely."

"Well, it sounds like the two are like two sides of the same thing!"

"The field we call the 'ether' is an interaction between electrical and magnetic forces, to be sure."

"This is fascinating!" Marguerite exclaimed.

"Very interesting, Nikola," Colonel Astor said. "What are your plans for the future?"

"I have many plans for the future, which I'm sure Mr. Morgan will be interested in, especially since he was one of the principle investors in the Niagara Falls project."

"That is true, and I owe you a debt of gratitude, Mr. Tesla." Morgan looked into Tesla's blue eyes. Then, slowly and respectfully, he added, "You have given the world a great gift, Mr. Tesla. Perhaps not just by this new current you have discovered, but by the harnessing of Niagara Falls itself. The world owes you a great debt."

"Thank you, sir."

"Tell me—where do you get your inspiration? What gives you ideas?"

"I see things internally, sir. I can visualize an image almost as distinctly as if it were really there."

"Amazing. Have you always had this gift?"

"Ever since I was a child, sir."

"So you see things clearly before you build them?"

"Precisely."

Twain was smiling impetuously at Morgan, who ignored him.

"What is your ultimate goal, Mr. Tesla? What do you *see* for this world?"

"Well, Mr. Morgan, I have thought about that very much. You see, after my first company failed, sir, I was forced to spend a year doing very hard labor. I was exclusively in the company of those you might call 'common men.' This was very hard, laborious work that nearly broke my spirit. You must know the rest, sir, because it was your funding that helped, in a large part, to elevate me from that difficult state.

"But what you might not know, sir, is that during that year I reflected much on the fate of those common people, and I felt that the human spirit deserves much more than toil. Political reforms won't help us. Until society is transformed by machines, we will still need the manpower.

"But imagine what it could be like if men no longer needed to struggle for what they get, if men no longer lived in poverty. For one thing, if everyone had enough, no one would resort to crime."

"That is true," Morgan agreed.

"I believe it will be feasible, over the next ten to twenty years, to replace human labor with much more efficient and less costly machine labor, all based on my patents for alternating current and motors."

"Well, it certainly sounds...sounds..." For the first time in his life, Morgan was at a loss for words.

"How do you feel about our fellow, Mr. Tesla, now?" Mark Twain called out.

Tesla continued. "Neither politics nor economic reform will liberate the common workingman. Only science holds this promise. And when it happens, sir, everyone will be better off."

"Oh, yes!" Twain announced. "With enough prosperity all around, the poor won't hate the rich anymore."

"I dare say," Morgan said quietly, "that the workingmen on the Northern Pacific have far less to complain about now than they had working for Jay Gould."

"Perhaps so, sir," Twain said.

That damned Twain! Morgan thought. Ever the socialist sympathizer. Morgan noticed that Tesla said something quietly to Marguerite Merington; she giggled slightly, blushed, and gazed adoringly at Tesla.

He flatters these women, Morgan observed. Most strange. He is allegedly celibate, yet he casts plenty of charm upon these women, especially Katherine, who more than admires him. But then he becomes aloof....

Edison had said—and put in print—innuendo to the effect that Tesla was "unnatural," perhaps homosexual. Morgan studied what he saw, and came to the conclusion that Edison was wrong.

There is something else going on here at this table, Morgan thought. He might be celibate and ascetic, but he is not homosexual. He is alternately flirtatious and indifferent, almost uncaring. I must find out why.

"I've heard you oppose marriage, Mr. Tesla. Can you tell me why?"

"That is not true, Mr. Morgan! I favor marriage. You are a married man; you must know its benefits." Frances Morgan pursed her lips and eyed her husband.

"Then why don't you acquire a wife, Mr. Tesla?"

"That is a fair question, sir. If you'll permit me, I will explain. In my profession, one must focus every bit of one's energy and attention on the problems at hand. I must concentrate my will on the task of perfectly visualizing the machines that will transform our future. To accomplish this feat, I must apply my total self, my entire will, to this task. Otherwise, my goals will remain eternally elusive."

"And you think that marriage would interfere with this process?"

"I know with certainty it would, sir."

"I see." Well, Morgan thought, he minced a lot of words—but what did he *say?* That was a memorized speech—emotionless. That was all. What was this damned man *hiding?*

"If you will notice, sir, the very greatest men in science were unmarried."

"Is that true?" Morgan looked at Tesla, then Astor, then Robert Johnson.

"He's the expert," Robert Johnson said.

Tesla spoke automatically. "Let me say that marriage might complete the life of a poet or an artist. And it is a good institution for the common people, to be sure.

But to a man of science, it is a reckless investment, demanding more time and attention than true devotion to the pursuit of knowledge can allow."

"So you do not oppose marriage. You simply do not require it, right?"

"Truly, sir. I am quite self-sufficient."

"That's reassuring!" Robert Johnson laughed.

"Nikola, tell Mr. Morgan about that immense tower you plan to build."

"In the near future, Mr. Morgan, I shall seek a new location so I can conduct experiments in the transmission of power safely, without causing harm to people or buildings."

"That location certainly cannot be New York City!"

Everyone laughed at Robert's comment.

"Go out west," Twain said. "Lots more room out west. And from what you've told me, Nikola, you want to study lightning storms, is that right?"

"Yes, among other things...."

"Well, then you *should* go west, young man!"

Laughter resounded again.

"Yes, Nikola! There are mountains out there that would astonish you—Colorado, Utah, Montana. Wide-open spaces, too. And, if you want lightning storms, well, you'll get them by the bushel!"

"That sounds promising, Mark."

So, Tesla and Twain are close friends, Morgan noted. Twain's socialistic propensities don't put Tesla off. Interesting. I can see, too, that Tesla's not interested in politics—reassuring, since he lives a cloistered life. Probably knows he's out of his element when it comes to politics. So is that damned Mark Twain—but he doesn't *know* that! Writers never do. And they're all socialists.

"I've heard your experiments in wireless telegraphy have been performed by others," Morgan said. "What do you think about that?"

"Sir Oliver Lodge sent a signal at Oxford some years ago," Tesla said. "He is a good man. He has given me full credit for perfecting the principles on which all wireless telegraphy and telephonics might be based."

"Telephones? Wireless telephones?"

"Pierpont hates telephones," Frances stated flatly.

"Why is that?" Tesla asked innocently.

Morgan turned red. "Oh, well, Mr. Tesla, let's just say it's one of my own little aversions."

"Oh! Then you can understand my aversion to certain things, as well."

Morgan pondered this for a moment, then said, "Comparing such aversions to my own hatred of those dastardly voice-contraptions, yes, I can."

Tesla nodded. "Perhaps we all have our...aversions."

"It would seem so," Morgan said, slightly nervously.

"I'm not too friendly with snakes," Mark Twain said, still eyeing Morgan.

"Neither am I," Robert Johnson said, almost inaudibly.

Morgan leaned forward and looked Tesla directly in the eye.

"Tell me, Mr. Tesla—what do you think of the Bible?"

"It is an interesting book. I have read it. My father was a minister...."

"Really?" Morgan's eyes widened.

"Yes. Of the Serbian Orthodox Church. My uncle Petar Mandic was the high priest of the Serbian Orthodox Church of Bosnia."

"I had no idea!" Morgan nodded with approval.

"I didn't know that, either," Mark Twain said.

"You don't do any...occult practices, do you? I mean—Tom Edison's been attending seances lately.... Then there's Theosophy...."

"I have no interest in the occult, sir."

"Really? That's a relief. I mean—there's so much superstition in society these days. You'd think we were back in the Middle Ages!"

"I know people are attending seances," Tesla said. "They are even reading fortune-telling cards and studying horoscopes these days. This I cannot help. My domain, Mr. Morgan, is science, not religion or spiritualism."

Frances Morgan spoke up. "What do you think of Mr. Edison's theory that the soul is made up of particles, and that when a person dies, these particles fly like a swarm of bees to find an unborn body to inhabit?"

Tesla frowned. "Thomas Edison is not one of our most gifted thinkers."

"That sounds a lot like reincarnation," Morgan said. "That's a belief that comes out of the heathen countries."

"Most certainly, sir," Tesla said. "But then, Theosophy is the theory Madame Blavatsky was taught on a trip to the Orient, if I am not mistaken."

"So it is," Morgan said.

"There might be something to it," Frances said. "I know quite a few people who believe in it."

"Ha! Women and dunces! Our friend Mr. Tesla isn't too impressed with Mr. Edison, I've noticed. Well, Tom is a good tinkerer, but he isn't the most honest man I've ever dealt with.

"I'll concur with Mr. Tesla's opinion—that Edison's expertise was not so much at creating new things, but borrowing money!" Morgan laughed at his own joke; he had wanted to say those words to someone for a long time.

"Borrowing money—and stealing ideas...." Tesla spoke quietly, but Morgan heard him distinctly. He said quietly, "I see...."

Tesla nodded.

Morgan leaned forward. "Tesla, let's talk about wireless. How does it work?"

"Very simple, really. As I proved in my demonstration some years ago, the transmission and reception of electrical energy, from signals to power itself, requires the application of some very simple principles.

"First you need an antenna to collect the magnetic energy. Then you need a ground connection of some sort. You also need an aerial-ground circuit for induction capacity. You need an adjustable induction and capacity circuit to tune your signal, and you must finally utilize electronic tube detectors in your transmission and reception devices, and these must be tuned in resonance with each other to carry the signal."

Morgan nodded. "What's the potential to send and receive signals?"

"With the proper equipment, unlimited."

"How about those dratted telephones? You can send those messages without wires, too?"

"Of course, sir. Actually, the human voice might be easier to modulate than a telegraph signal."

"Why might that be?"

"Because speech is continuous. A telegraph signal in Morse code is not. It is on-off, on-off-staccato. When it is off, the circuit is broken. Another pulse of electricity, to overcome resistance in the air, is required to send the next bit of signal."

"How many years do you give it?"

"If I can start work on my large-scale experiments, perhaps only a few years."

Morgan nodded thoughtfully. "Mr. Tesla, I have been considering extending to you my financial assistance. Your ideas interest me. Of course, there would be a matter of representation—"

"An inventor must be free, sir, if you'll pardon me, free to explore the laws of nature and their various applications to humanity. It is death to the mind, to the imagination, to be pressed under the obligations of another's interests."

"I see. Is that your final word on the subject?"

"It has to be. I have no other choice."

Morgan glanced at Colonel Astor—who had been silent all this time—then at Tesla, then at Twain, whose huge mustache hid a mischievous smile. Morgan said, "I can appreciate the advantages of unfettered freedom, especially in a field as…innovative…as yours…but might it not be prudent of you to insure that freedom you need with a certain amount of financial security?"

"That would be an empirical ideal, sir."

"What exactly do you mean by that?"

"Tangible benefits," Robert Johnson said quickly.

"Oh. I see. Think of those 'tangible benefits,' Mr. Tesla."

"It is a generous offer, sir. One which I will consider."

"You don't need to give me an answer tonight. Think about it. Give it some time. You can contact me through Anne." Morgan drew his gold pocket watch out of his breast pocket. He flipped it open with his thumb, glanced at it, then snapped it closed and pocketed it. "Frances, it's getting to be late, don't you think?"

"I thought it was still early, Pierpont."

"Yes, Mr. Morgan," Mark Twain said. "Surely you aren't going to depart at this early hour!"

"I have much business to attend to."

Frances agreed. "Pierpont's mornings always begin early."

"That's the way it has to be, Frances. I have much to attend to, including a meeting with William Rainsford over the matter of the vestry."

In the carriage, on the way back to his estate, Morgan thought about the events of the evening.

Morgan's suspicion had been confirmed: *He doesn't understand people! We're foreign to him!*

That's why the poor bastard's celibate, Morgan thought. He's attracted to women, alright—he flirts with them, flatters them, leads them on. But he's afraid of women because he's afraid of people. He doesn't understand people. He's too trusting, too naive. You can't be naive in this world. Naivete is just another word for ignorance.

Why is he so damned ignorant of people?

Everyone has two reasons for the things they do: a good reason and a real reason. Tesla had a good reason—and a better reason. But what were his *real reasons?*

The problem with people, Morgan reasoned, is that they don't always know themselves what their real motives are.

CHAPTER FIFTY

Scherff

George Scherff worked for Tesla for two years before the inventor prepared to leave for the American West to further his experiments. During that time, Scherff witnessed many bizarre and spectacular events and came to know—but not understand—the man he considered to be the greatest of living geniuses. Scherff saw Tesla as a strange, complex, and mysterious man. Knowing him was a chance to view a living human mystery.

Scherff recalled Tesla's experiments with oscillators. He remembered one in particular that Tesla called dangerous: Two workmen bolted a small mechanical contrivance directly to the concrete foundation of the laboratory. Tesla measured the exact middle of a steel bar two feet long and two inches thick. He clamped the bar at the mid-point to the machine, then ordered his workmen back, all the way to the rear of the laboratory.

The tiny machine began to hum. The hum pulsed. The pulsations grew louder. Minutes crept by. The steel bar exploded.

The ends flew in opposite directions and clanged against the walls of the laboratory.

Silence.

Anxious mutterings began stirring through the crowd of workers.

Tesla, in his black suit and gloves, stood like a stage magician. "That box you saw was an oscillator—a tiny electromechanical oscillator. It sent a fusillade of taps, tiny beats of motion, not one of which, by itself, could have harmed a baby, but together resonated in unison along that two-foot bar of steel until the energy yield was sufficient for one tiny final shock to break the bar."

The workmen came forward and eyed the tiny box with awe.

That had been the first of the experiments, Scherff reflected. Tesla even claimed he could build a machine that could destroy the Earth in less than two months. Scherff had seen demonstrations that led him to believe that. He remembered the afternoon Tesla came to him in his office unusually enthusiastic.

"As I was walking at noon, George, I passed a skyscraper, the steel frame of a skyscraper being built. I happened to notice that the workmen had just climbed down for lunch. This suited me: no one noticed me as I took the device I was carrying—this device here—" he extended the oscillator, which was the size of a shoe box, "—and I strapped it to the central beam of the skyscraper.

"All tall buildings, George, are supported by a vertical central beam, set very deep in the foundation of that structure."

"I am familiar with that, Nikola."

"So, I wrapped the metal bands around the shaft, which was approximately two feet in diameter, and I connected it to the battery and turned it on. Within a minute, the structure was vibrating. It hummed and hummed, getting louder and louder, then the girders began to shake. Boards from the scaffolding fell all around me, then I decided to shut it off."

Scherff was shocked.

"Naturally, the press was very concerned about the incident, so I consented to an interview this very afternoon. That is where I have been all this while."

Sure enough, Scherff read about the incident in the papers. He found it disconcerting that his employer nonchalantly stated he could collapse the Brooklyn Bridge in just a few moments. The building he had shaken was a ten-story skyscraper on Wall Street.

The account read:

"In a few minutes, I could feel the beam trembling. Gradually the trembling increased in intensity and spread throughout the whole great mass of steel. Finally, the structure began to creak and weave and the steelworkers came to the ground panic-stricken, believing that there had been an earthquake. Rumors spread that the building was about to fall, and the police reserves were called out. Before anything serious could happen, I took off the vibrator, put it in my pocket, and went away. But if I had kept it on ten minutes more, I could have laid that building flat in the street. With the same vibrator, I could drop Brooklyn Bridge in less than an hour."

There had been a day when tremors shook the city.

The ground throughout Manhattan, Brooklyn, and the Bronx shook violently. Fearing an earthquake, the residents panicked. Shelves collapsed in stores, and plumbing burst in private homes and apartment buildings. The telephone lines to all city offices were flooded with calls—until the lines themselves started to snap. The tremors continued—and increased in intensity.

The police suspected the Tesla lab was the source of the earthquake. They converged on the laboratory just as Tesla lifted a sledgehammer and struck a small metal box strapped to the central supporting beam of his building.

An air compressor had powered the oscillator: if he had just turned it off, the residual air pressure would have continued to run the oscillator for almost another devastating minute. Most of Manhattan would have been destroyed. Later that day, Scherff discussed the principle of oscillation with Tesla.

"We have been working with powerful and subtle principles, George. I have been experimenting with forces that could destroy the entire earth, if unleashed without control…."

"If today's test was any indication of such power, I believe you!"

"Yes, George, yes, it was. I had no idea the oscillations would travel so far. Apparently, the shock waves increase in intensity farther away from the epicenter. That has been known about earthquakes for quite some time."

"But how can you harness such energy?"

Tesla shrugged. "It would make demolition of buildings much easier."

Scherff laughed, but knew Tesla's comment had been utterly serious.

"George, the earth has a vibration of its own, like all things. Countless earthquakes—most of them infinitesimal—ripple through the crust of the Earth at every moment. This gives the Earth a vibrational periodicity, according to my calculations, of about one hour and forty-nine minutes, give or take a few seconds.

"Imagine this, George—if I sink a shaft into the Earth a hundred miles or more, and explode a ton of dynamite at the bottom of that shaft, every hour and forty-nine minutes, over and over again, I would be adding an equal amount of energy to the expansion I have created, the expansion wave of the earth itself.

"Eventually—probably in less than two months—the earth would split in half like an apple."

"My God!" Scherff exclaimed.

"It is true, George. The force of mechanical resonance is powerful enough to do just that."

"Nikola, have you thought about the dangers of such research?"

"Frequently. And very, very deeply. I have considered the dangers of all the work that I do."

Scherff contemplated those words.

He remembered the year before, in 1898, when the United States was "forced" to attack Spain and the Philippines and Cuba to protect the Monroe Doctrine. Teddy Roosevelt and the Rough Riders fought the Spanish from Cuba to Guam, implying that even the islands of the South Pacific qualified as part of the Americas. Reporter Frederick Remington had been stationed for weeks in Havana. His well-publicized cable to Hearst read, "Everything is quiet. There is no trouble here. There will be no war. I wish to return."

Hearst cabled his famous reply, "Please remain. You furnish the pictures, and I'll furnish the war."

The next day, the battleship *Maine* exploded and sank in Havana harbor. War. It had been such a corrupt war, Scherff thought. Obviously so. All wars were. People can be so gullible, so easily misled—they were inevitably misled.

Scherff feared for Tesla; if his awesome devices were ever applied to war, the world would be doomed.

Tesla opposed war, in principle. Scherff was reassured. Tesla, cloistered and secretive, was also vulnerable to persuasion because he was too trusting, too easily misled. Scherff felt protective of him.

Wm. Randolph Hearst

Tesla mystified Scherff. He wondered why Tesla felt compelled to circle a block three times every time he turned a corner. Why he measured the exact volume of the food he ate. He wondered why Tesla felt such horror at the sight of round objects. He was convinced Tesla was a genius. He was also convinced of Tesla's innocence.

Tesla announced, early in 1899, that he had accepted funds from J. P. Morgan to build a laboratory out west. Scherff prepared to move to Pittsburgh, to continue business there, while Tesla and Kolman Czito arranged to establish a laboratory in Colorado. Tesla's patent attorney, Leonard Curtis, was also a partner in the Colorado Springs Electric Company.

He wrote, "All things considered, land will be free. You will live at the Alta Vista Hotel. I have interest in the City Power Plant so electricity will be free to you."

Tesla and Kolman Czito departed by train from New York on May 11. They stopped briefly in Chicago to demonstrate his radio-controlled submarine boat, and arrived in Colorado Springs on May 18.

The train pulled into the station late at night. Tesla didn't trust the elevator in the Alta Vista Hotel, so trudged wearily up the stairs. He chose Room 207.

He could not inhabit a hotel room unless the room number was divisible by three.

CHAPTER FIFTY-ONE

Czito

Lightning silhouetted the mountaintops.

"Quick! Get the electrical recorder!"

Czito emerged from the workshop carrying the recording equipment. He and Tesla hurriedly set it up at the window in the second-story office.

"These lightning bolts are discharging at regular intervals," Tesla said. "They vary a bit, from seventy to ninety seconds apart."

"Amazing. What do you make of it?"

"The electrical recorder indicates a growing level of static electricity as the storm increases. The waves peak and subside. The peaks coincide with the lightning flashes."

"It would seem we are moving through a field of magnetism as the storm moves over us."

"Yes, Kolman, it indicates layers of magnetism surrounding the storm like invisible shells, with the storm itself in the center."

"Fascinating, Nikola. Fascinating."

Another flash lit the western peaks. Thunder rumbled briefly, echoed, and subsided. Dawn was less than an hour away.

"This is truly a momentous event, Czito. We are witnessing the invisible aspect of a phenomenon of nature."

"It is amazing, Nikola."

The storm loomed overhead. Swift winds hurled it across the plain. Black clouds engulfed the morning sky.

"Interesting. The indicator shows that the static charge of the air has dropped with the rainfall."

"Amazing," Czito echoed.

The wind carried the rain to the east. The sunrise gleamed coppery through the black clouds. Lightning split and shattered the darkness.

"This is amazing, Kolman. Again, we have the same periodicity in the discharges and we have the same peaks. in the static charge."

"Layers of magnetic electricity."

"Exactly. This proves what I have suspected for many years, Czito."

"What is that, sir?"

"It proves the existence of stationary waves. Waves of magnetism that do not spread from a source, like ripples, but are frozen in space relative to a point of origin."

"You are right, Nikola, this is a great discovery."

"Make note of this date! On the third of July, in 1899, I have measured the stationary waves in relation to a natural storm accompanied by electrical discharges."

This note was duly entered in Tesla's Colorado Springs logbook.

Kolman reflected on a long list of miracles and astonishing discoveries he had witnessed during his employment with Mr. Tesla.

Tesla took the first X ray photographs on the second of January, 1896, just two weeks after Roentgen, from Germany, announced *his* discovery of X rays. He remembered laughing with Tesla over the publication of the "Edison Memo" by the newspapers: "Batchelor: get me everything you can on these 'rotgon' rays! We could do a lot before others get their second wind."

Roentgen was offended by Edison's refusal to spell or pronounce his name correctly, as well as the implication that Edison intended to preempt his claim. Edison had become the laughingstock of the popular press.

In May of 1898, Chauncey McGovern published an article in *Pearson's Magazine*: "Fancy yourself in a large, well-lighted room, with mountains of curious-looking machinery on all sides. A tall, thin young man walks up to you, and by merely snapping his fingers creates instantaneously a ball of leaping red flame, and holds it calmly in his hands. He lets it fall upon his clothing, in his hair, into your lap, and finally, he puts the ball of flame into a wooden box. You are amazed to see that nowhere does the flame leave the slightest trace, and you rub your eyes to make sure you are not asleep."

After the alternating-current debacle, as Edison lost credibility in the eyes of the

press, Tesla had grown in prominence to almost epic proportions in the public eye. He was a sorcerer of electricity.

Often, when electrical storms loomed over New York City, Tesla would turn off the lights in his office and talk to himself. He would say things no one could understand—rapid, disjointed phrases about electrical resonance, harmonics, and magnetic fields.

Shortly after he announced the results of his X ray photography, he built a strange device that he placed against his head. He used it to recharge his brain every time he felt tired, and wrote of its effects, "A tendency to sleep and the time seems to pass away quickly. There is a general soothing effect and I have a sensation of warmth in the upper part of the head. An assistant independently confirmed the tendency to sleep and a quick lapse of time."

That assistant had been Kolman Czito.

He remembered the experiment: he sat in Tesla's favorite chair as the device, a modified cathode tube, was lowered against his temple. Tesla turned the machine on, and soon Kolman felt drowsy and dizzy.

He woke up with a start. He blinked and glanced around. He was still in Tesla's office. The lights were low.

"Fifteen minutes have elapsed," Tesla said.

"That was just a moment!"

"Fifteen minutes and almost forty seconds," Tesla told him.

Czito felt refreshed. He worked with Tesla almost until dawn, without need for rest. He had, indeed, seen miracles. All the same, he found Tesla to be slightly frightening.

He was glad to see George Scherff join the personnel at the Tesla lab; he appreciated Scherff's protectiveness over Tesla, a feeling he shared but could do little to express. He is not of this world, Czito thought many times. He was born here—he is human in form—but he is not one of us.

Sometimes his concerns over ordinary things, simple matters, become obsessions. His passion for neatness, for absolute cleanliness, often offended people who did not know how different he was. He would expound on lofty principles of electrical physics to people who barely knew how to converse with him.

The Colorado Springs laboratory, for which Tesla submitted detailed plans and exact specifications, was built in just weeks. The building was like a huge barn with a section of the roof cut away. Rising out of the aperture was a tower, Tesla's latest wonder to be tested. His high-energy magnifying transmitter stood over two hundred feet tall.

The huge sign on the door to the laboratory read: Keep Out—Great Danger! Below that, in a workman's bold, ironic scrawl: Abandon all hope, ye who enter here!

Their nearest neighbor on the windswept plains was a school for deaf and blind children.

Tesla announced his intention to send a wireless message from Pike's Peak, directly to the west, to Paris in time for the Paris Exhibition. The new century would open with a radio message beamed from one continent to another.

Inside the laboratory was a primary coil, fifty-two feet in diameter, consisting of a copper coil wound around a circular superstructure supporting it from five feet off the floor to a height of nine feet. This coil could boost a charge from six thousand to over a million volts.

The current was carried to a secondary coil, which was wound around a tower eighty feet tall and aimed toward the sky through the open section of the roof. The tower supported a platform from which jutted a shaft of metal crowned with a copper ball three feet in diameter.

Tesla hoped to boost the voltage to over ten million volts and transmit it from the tower. The transmitter was more than two hundred feet tall and dominated the landscape for miles. At six thousand feet above sea level, the land was arid, dry, swept with wind, and charged with static. Sagebrush studded the gray badlands from the mountains in the west to the flat eastern horizon.

The sunset had been fiery, darkening from red to purple. Night consumed the afterglow as Tesla and Czito tested the circuits, connections, transformers, and coils. Everything checked out to Tesla's satisfaction.

"Czito! I want you to go to the top of the stairs and man the switch. I will stand just outside the doorway. I must observe the primary coil and watch the effects of the tower."

"Yes, sir."

Czito ran up the stairs to the station overlooking the coil. His hand wrapped around the handle of a great switch.

Tesla walked through the wide double door onto the sweeping plain, to a point twenty yards from the laboratory. He could see Czito manning the platform, holding the switch, and he could see the ball atop the tower high overhead.

A dozen workmen mulled about in the dark corners in the building. Tesla raised his right hand, then swung it down. "Now!"

Czito threw the switch and the transformers hummed. The coil snapped and flickered with sparks. The secondary coil glowed purple. Then, veins and arteries of liquid light erupted with a roar from the tower.

Tesla reveled in ecstasy. His magnifying transmitter was alive.

Floods of radiant electricity shot from the copper ball. Purple, blue, and white arcs sizzled into the night. Flaming branches hundreds of feet long flew into the black starless sky. The air was shattered by a crackling roar. Sparks tingled against Tesla's skin. He walked backward, between the clumps of sagebrush, staring up at the tower. Electricity crackled under his shoes, static prickled his skin and hair, and the coppery stench of ozone thickened the air.

The entire sky flashed with power.

Tesla raised his arms and sparks flew from his fingertips as the air crackled, roared, and heated up. His feet merged with the ground, and his mind flew into space; he glimpsed the stars and saw them as atoms....

Suddenly, the lightning stopped. Tesla was jolted back to the ordinary world.

The air was silent and the sky was dark as he ran back to the laboratory.

"Czito! Czito! Why did you do that?"

Kolman Czito stood silent.

"I did not tell you to touch the switch. Close it again, quickly!"

"I did not touch it, Mr. Tesla!"

The workmen had abandoned the building; Tesla and Czito were alone.

"I must call the company and find out what happened." Tesla rushed to the telephone in his office and called the Colorado Springs Electric Company.

"Tesla! Damn it, you blew out our dynamo! Your damned—*experiment!*—caused an overload and the damned thing's on fire!"

Colorado Springs had plunged into darkness. When the fire in the main dynamo was extinguished, the emergency generator was put on line—but Tesla was denied access to power.

By noon the next day, Tesla had negotiated for continued electrical service: he and a team of workmen would repair the generator at Tesla's expense, and Tesla would go back on line to continue his experiments. By the end of the week, the repairs were completed. Tesla even modified the generator to take the load.

Czito prepared himself for wonders undreamed of....

CHAPTER FIFTY-TWO

Colorado

"I have installed a safety spring on the main switch, Czito. Now, when you close the switch, the spring snaps it shut."

"I didn't know the switch presented any problems, sir."

"I cannot afford to have the switch accidentally open during an experiment, Czito. Now—I must ask you to go downtown for me to pick up some supplies. Here's a list. When you return, later this afternoon, we will begin experimenting."

Czito departed. Tesla was alone.

The workers had taken a day off, and Tesla used the time to catch up on some electrical calculations for future experiments, make final adjustments in instruments yet to be tested, and walk outside under the cloud-streaked sky to appreciate the hot dry wind and the Rocky Mountains, far to the west.

He tried not to think of Scherff's recent communiqués: "Mr. L. has been coming to the shop intoxicated and has made many errors in drilling...." "Mr. Meyers fears your eight-foot weather balloons will not rise to the desired altitude...." "The New York Herald continues to boom Marconi...." Apparently, some upstart was attempting to take credit for the advent of wireless transmission.

Tesla walked back to the laboratory, ducked under the primary coil, and started examining the power couplings behind the coil.

High overhead, on the wall beside the platform, the spring on the main switch pulled—and clamped—the switch shut. Sparks crackled and leaped as the central coil blazed with blue light. Explosions of electricity threw Tesla to the floor. He looked up and saw brilliant arcs of blue-white light twisting, writhing, and convulsing over his head. The stench of ozone burned his nostrils and eyes, and the air was seared with heat.

He flattened himself to the floor. The powerful arcs struck everywhere.

A sour smell clotted the air—nitrous acid. The overpowering discharges were oxidizing the nitrogen in the air, and the mist that was forming stung his face and blinded him. He rolled onto his belly and squirmed on the floor in the direction of the platform and the main switch. He could barely see.

He crawled under the coil while fingers of lightning stung him and the nitrous acid ate into his clothes. Paralyzing jolts of electricity struck him with spasms. Furious globes of ball lightning bounced and shot around him—splattering into wild sparks and striking the walls and superstructure of the primary coil. The heat of the discharge was unbearable.

He pushed himself against the wall. He had made it that far—all that remained were the stairs to the top of the platform.... Lightning bolts struck near him, but he pushed his way to the top of the stairs, gripped the switch—

The current magnetized the metal shut. Tesla struggled, summoning his strength and straining with both arms until the switch snapped open and the pyrotechnics ceased.

He fell to the floor of the platform, wiped his eyes with his acid-drenched sleeve, blinked—

He saw fire. He leaped for the fire extinguisher and sprayed a multitude of small, dancing fires with billowing clouds of foam.

Obviously, not all of Tesla's inventions worked.

However, the experiments continued through the summer of 1899. Energy was transmitted to wire antennas suspended from weather balloons half-filled with hydrogen. Power was beamed to fluorescent lights mounted on a distant hillside. Their shine was distinctly visible from the laboratory.

As the Paris Exhibition of 1900 approached, Tesla became preoccupied with the creation of something vast and new—and secret.

Czito sensed this and remained silent.

Tesla worked long after the other men had left; he was experimenting with directional antennas tuned to very fine wavelengths, aimed at the stars. He was adjusting the frequency of his high-powered sensitive radio receiver late one night as Mr. Dozier, the carpenter, was finishing repairs on a work table—when the signals came.

"Do you hear that?"

The old man looked up.

The radio receiver was emitting distinct oscillations punctuated by rapid, staccato beeps. The rapid beeps clarified into signals, and Tesla started scribbling notes on a pad. Mr. Dozier stood at the top of the stairs, astonished.

"Do you hear this?" Tesla looked up from the notepad.

"What can it be, sir?"

"Signals, Mr. Dozier, signals! We are listening to signals from outer space!"

Mr. Dozier trembled. "That cannot be, sir! Signals? From outer space? How can that be?"

"There can only be one answer: somebody—or some*thing*—is sending them!"

"Oh, my God!"

"The directional antenna is aimed at the planet Mars."

"My God, sir! Signals from the planet Mars?"

"Apparently so, Mr. Dozier."

The elderly carpenter stared at the equipment.

The signals resembled Morse code, but they were not. They consisted of clusters of high-pitched beeps over a background of eerie, whining oscillations. Tesla stared out through the opening in the roof, past the transmitter tower, and at the stars beyond. He trembled with excitement as the signals grew louder and more distinct.

He now had proof of the greatest question he had ever pondered: there *was* intelligent life elsewhere, capable of creating machines. Capable of transmitting signals. Tesla could not help thinking the signals had been *meant* for him…and if they were capable of transmitting such signals, they could receive them as well.

CHAPTER FIFTY-THREE

Marguerite

As the Paris Exhibition of 1900 approached, Tesla ordered his Colorado Springs laboratory to be dismantled. French expectations to receive a wireless broadcast went unanswered.

When Scherff returned from Pittsburgh, Tesla could not wait to discuss the discovery of signals from Mars with him. He cornered Scherff in the office of his New York laboratory.

"The experiments, George, not only prove we can transmit power as well as signals without wires through atmospheric conduction, but I have proven that there is electrical resonance in the earth itself."

"Amazing! What does this mean in terms of application, Nikola?"

"Power and signals can be transmitted through the ground as well as the air. Instead of drawing current from the air and grounding it into the earth, we can put current into the ground and tap into that current anywhere—in any city in any home—and utilize that current and send it back into the air."

"So you can put power into the earth and draw on it someplace else?"

"Not only power, George, but signals! Signals!"

"Can you modulate the frequencies so efficiently, Nikola?"

"Absolutely. That is what I have proven. I sent current into the earth at the rate of 150 oscillations per second and drew it out at various distances from the source. Each pulsation apparently had a wavelength of approximately six thousand feet apart. I can now calculate distances and energy requirements needed to supply the field of resonance that is already there with a power input modified harmonically to encode a signal content, as well, to anyone who taps into it—theoretically, anywhere."

"So, what is the outcome of these experiments? Do you think you can make this plan practical?"

"Yes. Of course. It is already practical. I can make it real."

"I hope so. Colonel Astor might want his money back!"

"He will get it! I plan to meet with him tonight."

"Really?"

"Yes. I have even heard that Mr. Morgan might show up as well."

"Good luck, Nikola."

"There's something else, George."

"What is that?"

"While I was in Colorado, I received signals from space."

"Are you sure?"

"I am certain. Absolutely certain."

Scherff sank deep into the padded chair. "Tell me about the circumstances of this...reception."

"I was in the laboratory late one night, scanning the sky with a directional antenna...just...seeking distant radio sources, which is to say I was listening for such sounds, such encoded signals. I was using my high-frequency receiver, since I believe those frequencies, like high notes in music, might carry farther."

"I understand."

"I thought I was alone for a while, so intense was my concentration."

"You weren't alone?"

"No. Fortunately, Mr. Dozier, the carpenter, also had to work late, and he was my witness."

"Where was Kolman?"

"This was very late. He had taken off hours ago."

"I see. So, it was only you and Mr. Dozier.... It would have been better to have some kind of confirmation. An independent observation."

"That is true, but my mind was preoccupied with the larger task of...listening." Tesla stared at the ceiling.

"What do you plan to do with the news of this discovery?"

"I do not know what to do with this observation just yet."

"Permit me, sir, but I think you should be cautious about mentioning anything about this to, let's say, Colonel Astor...or Mr. Morgan."

"I understand, George. Perhaps I should be cautious...."

"I want to talk to you about the Marconi patents, but that can wait until tomorrow, I guess. It's getting late; you should go, too, if you have a dinner engagement."

"I have nothing to fear from Mr. Marconi, George; my preeminence in wireless has already been established."

"I sincerely hope it's been established well enough, sir."

"Of course. I must depart, George. And I thank you for your advice."

"About the signals?"

"Yes. They were pulses—sounds, like Morse code, little groups of pulses. I wrote down some numbers, but they make no sense to me. No mathematical patterns, nothing I could recognize."

"I wonder what they could have been."

"I intend to find out, George. I must see if I can transmit a message and get an answer—but we must keep that confidential, for now."

"Of course."

Tesla departed from the laboratory to his room at the Waldorf-Astoria, bathed, dressed himself in a black suit and gray gloves, and strolled the streets of Manhattan to the dining hall of the Fortune 400 Club. He was escorted to his seat by Thomas Fortune Ryan.

The Johnsons were there, and they had brought Marguerite. Tesla smiled and bowed to her.

Her eyes fluttered when she saw him, and her cheeks flushed. She thought, There is so much love in this mysterious man.... He claimed to be celibate, but could he be saving himself for—dare she think it? The right woman.

There. The thought was frozen in her mind. She could deny it no longer. He sat next to her, as he usually did. But not too close. Not close at all.... He preferred sitting slightly apart from others, and she respected that.

Colonel Astor said, "How good to see you, Nikola. How was Colorado?"

"Oh, it was wonderful, Mr. Astor. Very refreshing. I got much good work done."

"What did you accomplish?"

"I proved and measured the electrical resonance of the earth."

"Meaning...?"

"The free transmission of power and even signals, Mr. Astor, through the earth without wires."

"Let me see—you sent power through the ground without wires?"

"Exactly."

A waiter materialized beside Tesla and slipped him a note: MEET ME IN THE LOUNGE—MARK

"Excuse me, Colonel Astor. I must exchange a few words with an old friend." Tesla stood and abruptly departed. Mark Twain was seated at a table in a corner, nursing a stein of dark beer.

"Nikola! I heard you were back in town—knew you were going t'be here, too, I daresay! How did you enjoy your stay out West?"

"It was everything you said it would be, Mark."

"I knew it. If there ever was a feller more suited t'see the West, it'd be you! Yes, a fellah has got t'go out there to see it fer himself. Tell me—what miracles did you bring back?"

"Many, Mark. Many miracles."

"Tell me!"

"Electrical resonance; the earth vibrates with electricity. We measured the oscillations. I even used the ground to conduct my own oscillating current."

"Amazing!"

"It can be modulated to any frequency. In the future, the earth itself will be a free medium of conduction!"

"Imagine that!"

"And imagine, if you will, Mark, a landscape uninterrupted by wires."

Twain laughed. "I can appreciate that!"

"In order to conduct current to the big Western cities, we will either have to spoil the countryside with wires and poles, or use ground conduction, which would be wireless and invisible."

"One thing the West still has," Twain said, his eyes sparkling, "is telegraph poles!"

"Yes!" Tesla laughed. "But they are not nearly so unsightly. They are actually a symbol of progress. They embroider the horizon. Sadly, they too will be vanishing from the landscape if my new researches are fruitful."

"What else have you accomplished?"

"Signals through the ground."

"So even telegraph signals can be conducted through the earth, too, eh?"

"Yes. And telephone messages—every impulse we need to transmit can be sent through the earth most efficiently."

"Good Lord, Tesla, you're amazing. Well, here's to the future!" Twain lifted his glass.

"There is more news: please keep this confidential. I received signals from outer space, Mark."

"That's astonishing, sir! Where could they be from?"

"Mars, most probably."

"You don't say!"

"I aimed a directional antenna at the planet Mars and sat in the laboratory one night, just listening, tuned to the higher frequencies on a highly sensitive receiver. I heard a clear arrangement of signals!"

"What does this mean? There is a civilization on Mars?"

"There must be."

"This is the greatest news of the century!" Twain melted into his chair, stunned by the revelation.

"Mark, it is the greatest news of all time. But please—keep that news under your hat! I must return to my party now."

Marguerite watched him approach. He sat beside her again. "How was your friend?" she asked politely.

"Oh, Mr. Twain? He had to remind me of how beautiful he knew I would find the West to be."

"It must have been magnificent! Tell me about it, Nikola!"

"It is wild and it is very, very wonderful. It stretches as far as the eye can see. The sagebrush smells so fragrant in the summer air. The sunsets and dawns were spectacular. And the lightning storms defied description."

"Tell me of your discoveries, tell me what you invented while you were there!"

"Yes!" Colonel Astor announced his enthusiasm. "Tell us all!"

"I measured the stationary waves that surrounded such a lightning storm."

"Stationary waves?" Robert Johnson was curious.

"I found that the center of electrical discharges, such as storms, emanates standing waves, like invisible shells, stationary relative to the source of the discharges. We can utilize these waves in wireless transmissions."

"Good God! That's amazing! Are you certain?"

"Yes, Colonel Astor. I am completely satisfied with the results of my experiments."

"Perhaps I should tell you something. Mr. Pierpont Morgan has requested permission to attend this dinner tonight. Would you have any objection to that?"

"No! In fact, I was under the distinct impression he would be here."

Morgan arrived within the hour. He strode between the tables, towering above the guests—both seated *and* standing. He was a tall and very imposing man. His daughter Anne walked beside him.

"Where is Frances?" Colonel Astor quickly asked.

"She couldn't make it tonight," Morgan said. "She was busy. I asked Anne if she would accompany me, since she is a friend of Mr. Tesla's."

"You have a wonderful daughter, Mr. Morgan. She is one of my closest friends."

"Did you hear that, Anne?"

"Oh, yes, Father. Nikola knows I am very fond of him."

"As I am fond of you, Miss Morgan."

Pierpont noted the sincerity of Tesla's politeness.

Marguerite announced, "Nikola was just telling us of his accomplishments in Colorado, Mr. Morgan. Please continue, Nikola."

"Yes!" Morgan exclaimed. "Tell me about your work there!"

"I arrived in May, as you know, and set up my laboratory immediately upon arrival. My first experiments were on the study of certain electrical phenomena, whereby I used my magnifying transmitter to produce tiny, controllable spheres of lightning."

Colonel Astor spoke up. "How did your experiments go with the—you call it your 'magnifying transmitter,' is that it?"

"Yes, that's it, exactly. The experiments were very remarkable. Very successful." Marguerite was lost in Tesla's voice. His precise explanations for things she did not understand were mystical poetry to her. His language was the poetry of science, a tongue she did not speak but which still held beauty for her. He explained electrostatic resonance, harmonic principles that reminded her of music: harmonics, resonance....

"One evening my assistant Kolman Czito and I were experimenting, trying to generate a low-energy high-frequency oscillating field. Suddenly, all around the laboratory condensed a thick fog! You can imagine how excited we were. If these energies can be experimented with further, think of the relief we could bring to areas affected by drought, if we can use electricity to cause precipitation.

"These are no longer theoretical possibilities, gentlemen. They can become true—tomorrow." Marguerite was transported to a world of wonder. She loved him. If only she could *have* him....

Mr. Morgan brought up religion again. Apparently, he was having doubts about Nikola's convictions.

"As you may remember, Mr. Morgan, I mentioned that my father was a minister."

"Yes, I do recall."

"Well, my opinion is that Christianity and Buddhism will merge to become the religion of the future."

"Eh? Christianity—and Buddhism?"

"Yes. Let me explain. I have read the Bible, as my father instructed me to do, and I studied the teachings of Christ, most notably the Sermon on the Mount, and found these teachings to be exceptionally in line with what is ultimately my materialist point of view."

"Eh?"

"Essentially, Mr. Morgan, I see no evidence to suggest that even Jesus had anything other than a view of things I would call in keeping with a scientific understanding."

"Yes, but Buddhism? How does that fit in with Christianity?"

"Because Buddha was, essentially, a scientific thinker. Buddhists, for example, do not believe in an afterlife."

"They don't?"

"No."

"How about that reincarnation idea?"

"From what I have read, sir," Tesla stated, "that is primarily a Hindu notion."

"That is true," Colonel Astor said. "I have spent some time in the Orient. I know what Mr. Tesla is saying is true. Buddhists, as a rule, don't believe in reincarnation."

"Oh?" Morgan raised an eyebrow. "How can they live with that? Not believing in an afterlife?"

"Apparently, quite easily, sir." Astor shrugged. "They seem most comfortable accepting death as a mystery."

"My God—how can they?" Morgan scowled and shook his head.

"In my view," Tesla resumed, "human beings, quite properly, are meat machines, much like electrical machines. Instead of circuits and wires, we have nerves and muscles. Instead of oil, we have blood. But the principle is the same: we are nothing more nor less than what nature made us."

"I see," Morgan said cautiously.

"Buddhism is quite popular among the intellectuals, Father," Anne Morgan said. Her voice was almost a monotone.

Pierpont shot his daughter a silent, cold glance, then his face softened as he looked back at Tesla. Marguerite sensed apprehension and decided to change the subject.

"Mr. Morgan," Marguerite chimed, "you are an expert in art. What do you think of this new style of painting that is so popular? 'Impressionism,' as it is called?"

"Hmph! Crude! Hardly respectable art! Those painters can't paint. Their canvases show no discipline. There is no texture, no attention to detail. Study the Classical masters, Miss Merington. There is no comparison between them and the crude painters of today."

"Is there not one good painter today?" Katherine asked, taken aback.

"There hasn't been a good painter in over a hundred years," Morgan said. "America is uncultured. We have acquired a modicum of knowledge, I'll grant you—but culture? This nation has yet to truly acquire the benefits of culture—present company excepted, of course."

"I'm glad you added that," said Colonel Astor.

"Robert is one of our greatest poets," Tesla commented.

"Is that so?"

"Well, *Century Magazine* published an article on the subject of the famous Serbian poets a couple of years ago. I would say I share with him an appreciation of poetry."

The rest of the dinner conversation went well, Marguerite observed. She also noticed that Anne Morgan said little throughout the evening.

Champagne was served and the mood became euphoric and exhilarating. After Pierpont Morgan and his daughter departed, after John Jacob Astor said farewell, after the Johnsons invited Tesla and Marguerite to their home for a nightcap—which Tesla declined—Marguerite asked him if he would accept her companionship on the walk back to the Waldorf-Astoria.

"That is perfectly acceptable," he said.

Marguerite was pleased.

They stepped into the night air and walked along the streets of Manhattan.

"It is lovely," Marguerite said. "Imagine what this city had been like without all these lights, this illumination."

"It must have been dreary!"

"Oh, yes it was! The gas lamps were dark and yellow by comparison."

"I don't know how people could live without lights for so long," Tesla commented. "Personally, I enjoy the darkness—but you are right, the lights *are* beautiful."

They walked for a time in silence. The chilly autumn air froze the vapor they exhaled, lit in clouds of silver by the electric lamps overhead.

"I enjoy the new music," Marguerite said. "I don't care what Mr. Morgan thinks."

"He has very...reserved tastes."

"Is it called 'Dixieland'? Yes, that's it. I like the new chords the piano players are using. More dissonant than Mozart or Chopin."

"Interesting. So, you think there is dissonance in this new music?"

"Not unpleasantly!"

"Perhaps it imparts a livelier sound to the music itself."

"Oh, yes, it does! I love the rich sound of it—it is wonderful for dancing."

"That is not my specialty, Miss Merington."

"Oh, I understand, Nikola." She felt a twinge of sadness in her heart. Try as she could to avoid the realization, she had to confront it: her dream, to dance a dance with Tesla, would probably never come true. They walked together in silence. Suddenly, the air came alive with the rustle of wings.

"Those pigeons are my friends," Tesla said. "I have developed a certain affinity for the birds."

"I see...." Marguerite felt another chill of fear but she did not know why.

Tesla shrugged. "Just another peculiar affinity, I suppose."

"Nikola, have you ever been in love?"

"Why do you ask, Miss Merington?"

"Oh, Nikola, you are such a handsome man! You are so kind, even the birds love you. It seems...such a shame if you have never known the joy of love."

"That, for me, is the joy of work, Miss Merington. For me, work is passion, it is...everything." His tone was final, absolute.

"Oh, I know...you have told me."

"I can see how love might benefit a musician, Miss Merington. But the pursuit of science—"

"Oh, Nikola, let's not talk about that now."

They continued, again, in silence.

"Nikola, would you mind if I saw your room? Just a peek? Would you mind?"

"Why—no, not at all, Miss Merington."

She could tell by the uncertainty in his voice that he regretted the words after he spoke them. Marguerite held a deep breath. She committed herself to the suggestion. They had both committed themselves to it.

He led her up the stairs to his room. It was a grand suite, furnished in the late Victorian style, with red curtains and a royal, red Persian carpet. Everything was immaculate.

Marguerite was filled with a breathless, dizzy surge of emotion. Her legs swayed and her head spun. She stumbled against the doorway and closed the door behind her. She felt suddenly lightheaded—

"Nikola! I think it is the champagne!" She sighed, stepped toward him, reached for him, and cried, "Please—hold me!"

"Miss Merington!"

She fell against him and clutched him. Tesla toppled over backward. They plunged onto the sofa together.

"Miss Merington!" Tesla nearly screamed.

Her heart broke. She burst into tears and clutched him even harder.

When her hair touched his cheek, he screamed. He scrambled off the sofa, scurried onto the floor, and pressed his back to the wall. He was breathing heavily. His eyes glared wide with terror.

Marguerite saw the look on his face and burst into tears. She drew herself into a huddle at the far end of the couch, then burst free from the weight of shame and humiliation on her shoulders and stood, backing toward the door. "Oh—oh—oh, I'm s-sorry, Nikola! Oh, dear…I feel so dreadful…." She had brought it on herself. At the mercy of self-inflicted blame, she opened the door.

"Miss…Merington?"

"Y-yes…?" She forced herself to look at him, look into his eyes. Again, she felt the urge to cry.

"Miss Merington, let us not speak of this…shall we?"

"N-no. No. Of course not."

She fled from the room silently.

CHAPTER FIFTY-FOUR

Reasons

He was alone when he entered the Cathedral of St. George. His hands trembled violently. His hands always trembled.

The altar was at the far end of the long room. It was a monument jeweled with candlelight. The Virgin Mary presided over her sacred infant. Angels presided over her.

He was relieved that the great cathedral was empty.

Some great force hurled him to his knees before the holy icon. He wept. Uncontrollably. He squeezed his eyelids shut, and the tears stung, burned, and flowed. Sparks of light tingled across his vision. He wept with a passion that liberated his heart. Horrible, horrible grief—the suffering of all humanity was nothing compared with the suffering of our Lord and savior. His eyes were flooded with blurry, purple light. He saw shapes of color, clouds of light...blue light, pink light. He heard the singing of angels.

His mind faded into white light and the singing faded away. He found himself seated in a pew, still looking at the altar. He was dreaming, daydreaming, remembering...and the memories were blissful. He remembered William Rainsford, the man he had come to see. He liked the man, he loved the man—God damn it! A man should love his preacher, especially if a man loves God.

Morgan enjoyed the clear state of mind that always followed these epiphanies, as Rainsford called them.

Rainsford had won Morgan's trust many years ago. It had been the obvious sincerity of Rainsford's convictions that had convinced Morgan anyone who adhered to principles as steadfastly as Rainsford must be an honest man. He was Morgan's most intimate confidant.

Morgan lit and puffed on a cigar. His senses were clearing. His memories overwhelmed his senses. A conversation out of the past filled his mind: "Pierpont, keep in mind what I am about to tell you, and keep it entirely confidential."

"Yes, sir."

"I trust you, Pierpont. In fact, you're the person I trust most."

"What do you wish to tell me?"

"Just this—you sometimes miss your real connection to God."

"I say!"

"Hear me out, Pierpont! What do you think it is?"

"Through—the church! The Bible! Through—the sacrament!"

"No, John. Not in your case. In your case, it is something special."

"Surely, not my wealth!"

"That's part of it. It is a holy destiny; you have been chosen to be custodian of your father's riches. You guard money—power—and singularly keep it out of the hands of evil forces! Your wealth enlarges your influence in both society and the church.

"Centuries ago, Pierpont, the world looked to kings and priests to represent the Divine. But too many centuries passed, and the guardians of the faith became corrupt. You are a Protestant. Do you understand?"

Morgan looked up. "That borders on heresy!"

"Not at all, Pierpont. We can't go back to that old system. It has changed. The changes gave your father the wealth that you are now custodian of! Pierpont, an old order fell. Like it or not, you and I have benefited from those changes."

John Pierpont Morgan looked into William Rainsford's eyes for a long time.

Then the memory faded.

He was again seated alone on a pew in the Cathedral of St. George.

He remembered his own words, spoken dozens of times. *I would rather lose all my wealth and die a pauper than discover that even one word of the Bible is not literally true.*

Something stirred in the corridor just outside the chapel.

Rainsford was looking at Morgan from a doorway on the far side of the altar. He was smiling gently, peacefully. Rainsford and Morgan were silent for a very long time.

"I was praying," Morgan said.

"I could see that." A nervous, anxious pause elapsed. Finally: "Well, what did you receive?"

Another long pause passed. "Well, you, I guess!"

The two men laughed.

"That's a start, Pierpont."

Morgan lapsed into deep thought.

"Confession is a good place to start, Pierpont. Do you want to talk to me about something? Perhaps in my office?"

Morgan stood uneasily. The two men walked from the chapel down a hallway to Rainsford's office.

"I've been thinking, Reverend, about...an unusual gentleman."

"That sounds like you have been having weighty thoughts. And who might this unusual gentleman be?"

"It's—our Mr. Tesla, William."

"So, I see. He's an unusual man. A bit of a godsend, in this day and age, I would say."

"I hope so. But some of his ideas on religion disturb me."

"Exactly what does he say?"

"Well, he didn't exactly say that God doesn't exist—he just said...he thought Christianity should mix with Buddhism. He said other things that were most peculiar—for instance, he thought human beings were...just...meat machines."

"Oh, I see!" Rainsford sat down. "It's these scientists. They're worse than heathen, in their own way...what can be done? In the end, the truth will out...."

"I hope you put him to rest about his views, Pierpont."

"No, not at all, William. In fact, it makes me feel...less secure."

"Oh? What do you mean?"

"The man's not natural, William! Oh, he's a likable chap, alright, a downright cultured gentleman. That's abundantly clear. But—" Morgan shuddered.

"Pierpont? Tell me about him."

"He's from Serbia, one of those little eastern European nations. He's the epitome of a gentleman. In many, many ways. Actually, I like him very much. I just have to do what's good for the country on this matter. That's my first priority, my greatest duty."

"Of course."

"I would really like to figure him out before I invest any more money in his enterprises."

"I see...."

"He was the brain behind the Niagara Falls project. I guess you know that."

"I'm not surprised."

"And he's one fine electrician."

"But his religious views bother you?"

"Yes—and *he* bothers me! He's not married. He must be forty, at least—he's very young-looking, really, but I know about how old he is. No matter...."

"He says he is too busy to get married. His work demands his complete attention. He has a whole list of fears and aversions. Strange compulsions—he measures the exact amount of food he eats, says it tastes bland if he doesn't do this, strange habits like that...."

"Pierpont, sometimes the very, very brilliant among us suffer from...eccentricities."

"It would seem so. He knows many languages and has studied mathematics and literature and art. Poetry. He enjoys poetry."

"Poetry is good for the soul. *If* it is inspired verse, that is..."

"That is true, William."

"What other things have you heard about him?"

"Well, in spite of the fact that he surrounds himself with women, yet refuses to marry, aside from his countless fears and compulsions, William, he proposes to do more than just implement new forms of current and send wireless messages. He proposes to do things that could affect us all, William. Everyone. The whole world."

"I understand, Pierpont. So yours is a great responsibility."

"Yes. The greatest. William, I have never dealt with a man I could not trust—unless it was to buy him out. And I have never invested in a man I did not consider to be honest—although that Mr. Edison turned out to be a bit of a disappointment on that point, I do consider.

"But at least I *understood* Edison! He was in it for the glory. Adulation. Fame in the eyes of the masses. I can understand that, though I don't think it's noble or good.

"But to put money toward a venture—one that, I admit, I don't understand, and not to know, to really trust the man making the proposal—well, William, I grow cautious about that."

"What does Mr. Tesla propose, Pierpont?"

"Well, in part, to electrify the earth."

"To what end?"

"Well, that's the elusive part, William. He says to supply free power to all parts of the world. He says he can transmit signals, telegraph and telephone messages, telephone voices, everything—through the earth."

"Well, that's impressive."

"Not that I don't think it's feasible! I can't say, but for the life of me, it might be...that's not the point! My daughter believes in him. She believes in all those confounded liberal causes. That's not what's troubling me. It's that this Mr. Tesla...he's just...not...one of *us!*"

Rainsford gasped, looking up with a jolt.

"He circles the block three times every time he turns a corner! He measures his food before he eats it! He's terrified of pearls, any round object he sees, and they tell me he won't touch a woman!"

"Is he...do you think he's...he's...?"

"Tom Edison thinks so, but I think he's wrong. I've seen him with women, and it's clear he prefers their company over that of men. But he...he...."

"You think he isn't a loyal American?"

"Somehow, I don't think that's the problem. Oh, he's as human as you or I—in the flesh. But that's as far as it goes."

"What do you mean?"

"He doesn't *think* like one of us, William."

"His fears and compulsions?"

"Even more than that. Do you know what I've heard him say? I've heard him say that he sees his machines in visions, William."

"Really? That might be a good sign, Pierpont. Perhaps the Divine imparts visions of future machinery through the spiritual eyes of an unbeliever. After all, he *did* include Christianity in his ideas about the future of religion, did he not?"

"Well, yes, I guess...."

"Sometimes the Lord works in mysterious ways, Pierpont."

"That might be true, William. Some of the saints practiced abstinence from the pleasures of the flesh, did they not?"

"Absolutely. Perhaps this Mr. Tesla has a saintly side that he doesn't know about."

"Perhaps."

"I can tell that's not what's troubling you, John."

"I'll come to the point, Rainsford. I can't know what his real motive is for this...electrification of the earth."

"Well, to transmit power and signals—"

"You know what I mean, William. I've always said a man has two reasons for everything he does. You've heard me say that.

"Well, I don't want to extend any funds to this man until I find out what his real motives are."

"Well, why don't you just find out?"

"How?"

"Send some money his way. See what he does with it."

Morgan smiled. His dark blue eyes gleamed. "Brilliant, Rainsford. If he won't tell me his real reason, I can probably get him to show me."

Rainsford opened the door. Morgan slipped through it, then out. He left the altar and the stained glass windows behind.

Clouds hung low in the sky and cold breezes swirled the air. Leaves stirred and rustled in the gutter.

John Pierpont Morgan was sixty-four years old. He had lived a long time. He had seen many things, known many people—

"Pierpontifex Maximus!"

Morgan turned around. Some noisy boys across the street had spotted him.

"There he is!" one of them shouted. "It's Morgan! Pierpont Morgan!"

Rude adolescents! Morgan shouted at them. "Here, here! Here here!"

"That nose! Look at that nose!"

Morgan felt a stab of sadness and rage. He raised his cane and shouted at them. One of the rascals taunted, "Pierpontifex Maximus! Pierpontifex Maximus!" Morgan flew into a rage. The words had been an insult uttered by some vaudeville comic—and the name had been repeated in an editorial in a New York City newspaper.

"Pierpontifex Maximus! Ha ha!"

"Look at the old man's nose! Ha—ha—ha!"

Morgan hurried away into the gray streets, under the stony sky, into the cold of the late afternoon.

Chapter Fifty-Five

Murder

In March of 1901, John Pierpont Morgan gave to Nikola Tesla a hundred and fifty thousand dollars for the building of a high-energy magnifying transmitter on a vast level field on Long Island. Tesla had been granted access to two hundred acres, owned by a man named James D. Warden. Tesla wrote a glowing letter to Morgan, proclaiming him to be "a great and generous man!" He went on, rambling somewhat, to Morgan's consternation: "My works shall proclaim loudly your name to the world. You will soon see that not only am I capable of appreciating deeply the nobility of your action but also of making your primary philanthropic investment worth 100 times the sum you have put at my disposal in your magnanimous, princely way...."

And so on.

Morgan soon learned that hundreds of workers had assembled on the land Tesla christened "Wardenclyffe" to build the proposed tower. It would rise from a brick building and stand 187 feet.

He was in his study one night, when painful memories fell upon him like suffocating nets. He struggled not to remember the latest insult delivered to him by the public. It was a jingle, a popular tune.

He had first heard it while sitting in a carriage, waiting for the return of the driver. The driver had dismissed himself in front of a noisy cabaret for "sanitary reasons," he explained. Then he vanished inside the loud, raucous pub.

Morgan did not know that, instead of visiting the lavatory, the driver sat at the bar, ordered an ale, and called out a request to the band. Pierpont and Frances waited for the driver outside of the vaudeville cafe, seated in silence in the coach.

A new song played, trumpeting loudly out of the loathsome dive.

The lyrics of the particularly catchy tune had caught Pierpont's attention: the singers belted out a rowdy ballad about a poor European immigrant who crossed the ocean to come to America—the land where the streets were paved with gold. Everywhere "the Pilgrim" went, according to the song, he is told to leave. The room—the street—the gutter, he is told, is "reserved for Morgan."

As the chorus of the tune was repeated, Morgan felt a boiling fury rise within him. Yet, it was impotent fury: there was no way he express his outrage and still behave like a civilized man.

The driver still had not arrived.

The lyrics, pure doggerel, Morgan judged, concluded the Weary Pilgrim's quest by having the poor man starve to death on the streets of America. But the song did not end there.

I went to the only place left for me,
So, I boarded a boat for the Brimstone Sea;
Maybe I'll be allowed to sit
On the griddled floor of the Bottomless Pit;
But a jeering imp with horns on his face
Cried out as he forked me out of the place:
'It's Morgan's! It's Morgan's!
'The Great Financial Gorgon!
'Get off that spot! We're keeping it hot!
'That seat is reserved for Morgan!'

At those words, the crowd in the tiny cabaret burst into wild applause. Morgan felt threatened by the enthusiasm of the audience. He clearly heard a voice call out, "One more time!"

Something inside of him exploded. Morgan shouted for the driver and beat the carriage door with his cane. Frances snapped at him, "Be calm! Oh, God, Pierpont—it was only a song! Only a vulgar—"

When the driver finally arrived, Morgan fiercely railed against him from inside the carriage. The haggard-looking man chuckled and reminded him he had stopped for sanitary reasons.

Morgan realized by the slight sarcasm in the man's tone of voice that the driver had instigated the incident. Morgan had been a captive audience.

It reflected a terrifying hostility that John Pierpont Morgan was forced to live with. Derision was incompatible with seriousness, and Morgan took himself very seriously.

There was a cartoon published in *Life*:

Q. Who made the world, Charles?

A. God made the world in 4004 B.C., but it was reorganized in 1901 by James J. Hill, J. Pierpont Morgan, and John D. Rockefeller.

Morgan hated the punch line of the cartoon. He had been put in the same class as Rockefeller.

Morgan was engaged in a merger with Carnegie known as the world's first "billion-dollar merger"—the United States Steel Corporation. Carnegie and Morgan had settled their differences (real to Morgan but imagined to Carnegie) over a hundred million dollars. Carnegie had new plans: he would retire, now that he could afford to....

After the merger and the creation of a vast new company, Carnegie joked with Morgan. "Pierpont, what if I had held out for another hundred million?"

"Well, then, sir, you would have got it."

Carnegie suddenly felt a surge of admiration for Pierpont. He had always liked Morgan. Now he had another reason why.

Morgan remembered the incident. He used it as a mental antidote for the pain inflicted by the memories of the song and the cartoon.

He and Carnegie had argued over the phone. Morgan hated telephones. This time, discussing the most important transaction he had ever negotiated, he lost his temper furiously. Carnegie had repeatedly refused to go to Morgan's office at 23 Wall Street to finalize the agreement. Carnegie reminded Morgan that the distance between 23 Wall Street and Carnegie's office on 51st Street was the same either way. Morgan ran out of excuses. He charged out of his office and burst into Carnegie's office, moments later.

When the papers were ceremoniously signed, Morgan announced, "Mr. Carnegie, I want to congratulate you on being the richest man in the world."

Carnegie laughed. "I made just one mistake, Pierpont, when I sold out to you."

"What was that?"

"I should have asked you for a hundred million more than I did."

"Well, you would have got it if you had...."

Sitting in his favorite chair in his study, smoking a cigar, Morgan realized that, beneath Carnegie's rough-hewn manners and coarse language—traits he shared with James Jerome Hill—Carnegie was, at heart, a gentleman.

Morgan contemplated bad news—terrible news—and drank more whiskey. There was so much he needed to face. He thought about Tesla's Wardenclyffe Tower, and the promise of electrical power. He thought about James Jerome Hill and that weasel Edward Harriman. He thought about Leon Czolgosz.

He thought about William McKinley. He thought about murder.

He thought about the anarchy, the chaos, that had swallowed up the United States—and even claimed the life of the president.

On the sixth of September, President William McKinley appeared at a public reception in the Temple of Music after a speech he gave the day before at the Pan-American Exposition. An anarchist named Leon Czolgosz shot McKinley twice.

The bullet wounds developed gangrene, and McKinley died during the early morning hours on September 14, 1901.

That's how this new century has begun! Morgan was cynical. The events of his life proved that the worst part of human nature roamed free throughout the world. Even the president could be murdered.

He was haunted by those dreadful lyrics, "... It's Morgan! It's Morgan! The Great Financial Gorgon...!" The masses were turning against the rich. The president was dead. Civilization was collapsing.... Morgan imbibed more whiskey.

He thought about one slightly troubling bit of news he'd heard that very afternoon: someone named Marconi had broadcast the letter "S" in Morse code across the Atlantic, from Cornwall to Newfoundland.

Morgan concentrated: why did that thought bother him? This Marconi fellow repeated the Tesla experiment, just as Mr. Tesla explained it one night several years ago, at Delmonico's.

He felt a touch of trepidation. A premonition, perhaps. What was that madman's reason for building that electrical tower at Wardenclyffe?

He would know soon enough.

Morgan drank more whiskey and thought, *Mark this date—the twelfth of December—as the date a man named Marconi may have forced Mr. Tesla to show his hand.*

Dealing with Mr. Tesla was like playing poker—you didn't know what hand he held.

Why, Morgan wondered, do I get the feeling Mr. Tesla was once a gambler? It's his attitude: A man has two reasons for what he does.... But a man doesn't always have to come face-to-face with his real reasons. Sometimes, Morgan knew, it's better if he doesn't.

Chapter Fifty-Six

Wardenclyffe

Tesla had taken a long walk through Manhattan with his friend, fellow engineer H. Otis Pond, on the morning of December 12, upon hearing of Marconi's announcement of a trans-Atlantic signal, sent just hours before. They spoke little of it until they came to a park.

Tesla fed the pigeons; within moments he was surrounded by the birds. The sky was gray. Clouds sagged above the buildings.

Pond finally said, "Well, Tesla, it looks like Mr. Marconi has got the jump on you."

Tesla shrugged, then nonchalantly answered, "Mr. Marconi is a good fellow. Let him continue. After all, he *is* using seventeen of my patents...."

Another heavy silence passed between them. Reluctantly, Tesla continued walking as the birds fluttered nearby.

"Wardenclyffe will change everything," Tesla said. "It will stand as something no one can deny. The world will remember Marconi—but the world will *know* Wardenclyffe."

"But Nikola, they're starting to identify Marconi with radio, not you."

"Let them. I remember when the public thought my alternating current would shock and kill a man at a distance. I persuaded the scientists and electricians that this was not true, and the changeover from direct current is nearly complete now."

"That is true, but to have your greatest accomplishment obscured so soon after the fact—it is eight years now since you introduced your principles in the lecture, and now the public thinks of Marconi in connection with wireless, not you."

"This shift of attitude seems a bit sudden, does it not?"

"No, not really, Nikola. The fact is, while you were in Colorado, Mr. Marconi was making some mighty big overtures to being the inventor of the wireless system. The Marconi Wireless Company has been in existence for some time now."

"Surely people have longer memories than just eight years!"

"Actually, far shorter memories than that, Nikola."

Tesla turned and stared at the younger man.

Some of Tesla's announcements over the past two years had undermined his credibility. He had announced the reception of signals from space. He had mentioned the signals in a letter to Julian Hawthorne, sent from Colorado as Tesla prepared to leave. Although not intended for publication, the letter was quoted on the front page of the *North American.*

Tesla's phrase "intelligent beings on a neighboring planet" immediately sparked a brushfire war among scientists and field journalists who saw Tesla as nothing more than a perpetual source of news.

Professor Edward S. Holden, of Lick Observatory in California, led the attack: "Mr. Nikola Tesla has announced that he is confident that certain disturbances of his apparatus are electrical signals received from a source beyond the earth. They do not come from the sun, he says; hence they must be of planetary origin, he thinks; probably from Mars, he guesses. It is the rule of a sound philosophizing to examine all probable causes for an unexplained phenomenon before invoking improbable ones. Every experimenter will say that it is almost certain that Mr. Tesla has made an error, and that the disturbances in question come from currents in our air or in the earth. How can anyone know that unexplained currents do not come from the sun? The physics of the sun is all but unknown as yet. At any rate, why call the currents "planetary" if one is not quite certain? Why fasten the disturbances of Mr. Tesla's instrument on Mars? Are there no comets that will serve the purpose? May not the instruments have been disturbed by the Great Bear or the Zodiacal light? There is always a possibility that great discoveries on Mars or elsewhere are at hand. The triumphs of the past century are still a striking proof, but there is always a strong probability that new phenomena are still explicable by old laws. Until Mr. Tesla has shown his apparatus to other experimenters and convinced them as well as himself, it may safely be taken for granted that his signals do not come from Mars."

That was just the beginning; other scientists were less kind.

Like a specter out of the past, Thomas Edison returned to join the fray. He was joined by Professor Michael Pupin, who launched some scathing denunciations of his own. Edison and Pupin had been corresponding for years, conspiring to bump Tesla from his position of prominence.

Wardenclyffe was being erected, girder by girder, even as the ridicule and derision persisted. Hundreds of workers assembled every morning at the construction site to build the monument to electricity. Tesla was always present when the first of his men arrived and he would still be there long after the last had departed.

Tesla buried himself in the building of Wardenclyffe; he insulated himself from the rest of society by wrapping his mind in the construction of the tower. He attended no more parties with the Johnsons.

He sometimes received visits from Anne Morgan at the construction site; they spoke about her father, the world-wireless system, the future. They spoke optimistically about the new president, Theodore Roosevelt.

"Father hates him," she said. "He says his father—Junius—used to know Teddie's grandfather, Cornelius Van Schaack Roosevelt. Father says Teddie has turned his back on the responsibilities that come with the wealth that gave him the presidency."

"What do you think, Anne?"

"I think Mr. Roosevelt has compassion for the poor. I think he cares about the people."

"What does your father think about that?"

Anne pursed her lips and shook her head. "I think Daddy is being an old curmudgeon when it comes to social issues."

Tesla chuckled. "Perhaps."

"Oh, don't get me wrong! Father has done a lot of good with his money. Like— the way he came to Grover's assistance, during the big panic ten years ago. But he doesn't understand the problems of the times! The homeless people, the way the war with Spain hurt our country. He still thinks we can work out these problems with better banking practices. He doesn't understand that we need better laws to protect the workers and the poor."

"We need to replace human labor with more efficient labor offered by machines."

He had used Morgan's money to repay Colonel Astor for his investment in the Colorado Springs experiments. He was using Morgan's money to build Wardenclyffe Tower.

"Father takes great interest in what you are doing, Nikola. He asks me about your progress every time I see him."

"I hope Mr. Morgan is doing well."

"He's preoccupied with that man Harriman over railroad concerns. He says he's sorry he can't take a more personal interest in this."

"I understand. I realize he is a busy man."

"Yes, and you are, too, Nikola. I hope I haven't distracted you too much today!"

"Of course not! You are welcome here any time, Anne. I always appreciate your presence."

Anne departed.

Tesla and George Scherff reviewed the designs for the top of the tower. They were running out of money, and had only promises to rely on for the completion of the project. Scherff had grown concerned.

Professor Pupin and Thomas Edison were not making Tesla's prospects for future funding very favorable. They were escalating their attacks, from denunciations of Tesla's bachelorhood and his reception of signals from space to his experiments, ten years before, to build a camera sensitive enough to take pictures of mental images on the retina of the eye.

Tesla had based those experiments on the research done by Hermann von Helmholtz: "Helmholtz has shown that the fundi of the eyes are themselves luminous, and he was able to see, in total darkness, the movement of his arm by the light of his own eyes."

Edison and Pupin made certain Tesla's research into retinal luminosity came back to haunt him—and it was added to the signals from space as evidence that Tesla's reputation was unfounded.

The two-story brick building had been completed. The tower's superstructure had been erected. The transformers and coil had been installed. All that remained was the completion of the transmitter tower itself.

The dome at the top of the tower had been modified several times, from a fat ring of metal to a hemisphere of copper, repeatedly scaled down in size to cut costs. George Scherff embarked on excursions throughout the United States and from Canada to Mexico, to seek funding.

Tesla moved his offices into the Metropolitan Tower so he could view Wardenclyffe, and some months later he moved his place of business entirely into the two-story brick building at the construction site.

He wrote an article for Robert Johnson, published in *Century Magazine*, entitled "The Problem of Increasing Human Energy." In those controversial pages,
Tesla discussed the unpopular issues of overpopulation, global shortages, and
increased strain on the natural environment, especially the atmosphere, due to
increasing human consumption and energy demands.

The article was greeted with the same derision that his claim of reception of signals from space had aroused.

On February 23, 1901, a reporter from the Pittsburgh *Dispatch* wrote, "The press
at large has of late been having a good deal of fun with Nikola Tesla and his prediction of what is to be done in the future by means of electricity. Some of his
sanguine conceptions, including the transmission of signals to Mars, have evoked
the opinion that it would be better for Mr. Tesla to predict less and do more in
the line of performance."

During that time, Tesla had solicited for funds from the United States Navy for
development of a wireless torpedo. He tested several, sending them in circles
around a small boat and beaching them for retrieval.

He felt uneasy about contributing his knowledge to the creation of war
weapons. He confessed to Otis Pond, "Sometimes I feel I have not the right to do
these things."

Pond agreed—and Tesla's work on military technology ceased, for a time.

By 1902, Tesla had sparked two furors in the academic world: his claim to have
received signals from space, and his prediction that population growth would lead
to global shortages.

To end this furor—or contribute his own fire to it—the British physicist Lord
Kelvin, formerly Sir William Thompson, crossed the Atlantic by steamship to argue
in Tesla's favor.

Kelvin, years earlier, had opposed development of alternating current and the
use of a polyphase system at the Niagara Falls generator. Over the years, he
reversed his arguments—and went on to become one of Tesla's most avid supporters. He joined Tesla in the dining hall of the Electrical Institute, whereupon
the two men were greeted by a handful of their fellow scientists, reporters, and
science writers—and Thomas Edison.

"Mr. Tesla!" Lord Kelvin greeted him.

Tesla bowed.

"I am so honored, Mr. Tesla. You have done so many services for all mankind!"

"I thank you, Lord Kelvin. Your own contributions are many."

"You are, perhaps, the greatest inventor alive. Your contributions outweigh all others...."

Edison snorted.

A reporter cried, "Do you have anything to say to that, Mr. Edison?"

"I say that anybody who even seriously considers to have received signals from Mars must be a lunatic."

Laughter and cheers burst—briefly—from the crowd of reporters. Tesla winced.

Lord Kelvin raised his voice. "You men cannot know what lies beyond the limits of this world. We know of other planets in this solar system—Venus and Mars, for example—that might well have scientific civilizations on them! And, if not, why not on planets circling the other stars? Are any of you going to be so presumptuous as to suggest that we human beings on Earth are the only intelligent beings in this universe?"

"I'm not saying that at all! I'm only saying...." Edison paused to carefully choose his words, "that it is very unlikely, *highly* unlikely, and I think that it is rather suspicious that...of all the people in the world, these so-called Martians have chosen to contact only one man—Mr. Tesla here! Now—isn't *that* suspicious?"

"My dear Mr. Edison," Lord Kelvin said gently, "it is not only Mr. Tesla who claims such contact. Some of my countrymen, experimenting with similar apparatus, have claimed to have intercepted similar signals."

Edison roared: "Why don't they come forward? Who are they, anyway?"

"They do not come forward, sir, because they witness the mockery this man has received."

Edison grunted. "If these so-called experimenters come forward, then we can resolve this conflict, once and for all!"

"Oh, on that, we agree! But no one is willing to come forward with similar claims, when an acknowledged leader of science has come under such harsh ridicule."

"I cannot believe this! Are you to have me believe that your 'countrymen,' as you call them, are so cowardly? Surely, if this is so, sir, then they are not men of science at all!"

The reporters hooted and jeered. Edison seemed to take a bow, as if ending a performance on a stage.

Tesla remained silent. This was a debacle. That's all it was....

"I'm afraid, gentlemen, that this has gotten out of hand...."

"Oh, not at all," Edison said. "This is only the beginning of what, shall we say, is our critical analysis of Mister Tesla's claims."

The reporters scribbled on their notepads as Edison spoke to Tesla.

"In your article about human energy consumption, Mr. Tesla, you seem to suggest that the growing population is exerting quite a strain on the rest of the world, am I not right?"

"That is a flat interpretation, sir...."

"Well, it's my impression you say we're gonna run outa fuel sometime in the future, is that correct?"

"If fuel continues to be used to generate electricity, which I have made unnecessary but which continues to be done, then, yes, I say our limited resources will run out."

"That's nonsense! Why, the Amazon jungle has enough wood fuel in it to satisfy all of industrial civilization for fifty thousand years!"

"*That's* nonsense!" Lord Kelvin exclaimed. "How did you come up with *that* calculation?"

"That's my own calculation! Take it or leave it!"

"I question it," Lord Kelvin said.

Tesla was silent again.

He was staring across the room, to the edge of the crowd of journalists and scholars. He caught sight of Professor Michael Pupin, whom he had met, years before. Now, he glimpsed him again, after Pupin's recently expressed enmity. Pupin responded to Tesla's gaze with a hostile, defiant scowl.

"Mr. Tesla?"

"Yes?" Tesla faced a young reporter.

"How do you respond to Edison's claim that there are fifty thousand years worth of fuel in the Amazon?"

"I did not know Mr. Edison had acquired sufficient knowledge of mathematics to make such an assertion."

"When I need a mathematician," Edison said, "I hire one."

Lord Kelvin asked calmly: "Oh, really? Who did you hire to reach that conclusion?"

"Hell! I forget. I do so much work, I don't even sleep."

An uproar ensued.

Tesla felt uneasy. His mind faded out of the tempest in the conference hall, and he remembered his earlier conversation with Kelvin.

"Mr. Tesla, I admit I was hard on you, those years ago when I was in charge of the Niagara Falls Commission. I thought alternating current was impractical. When Edison came out and said it was dangerous, I admit I fell for that…routine."

"Routine?"

"Yes. Like in vaudeville. He had his day, he kept us all entertained, and I, for one, believed in him, for a long time."

"He is a fool."

"Oh, he is a clever fellow, but what has he done lately? He has made pronouncements, year after year, that he is on the verge of perfecting his greatest invention, the magnetic ore separator—but he has accomplished nothing. Where is he today?

"Yours will be the world of the future, Nikola. It is yours. Everything you envision will come to pass. Much, much more will, also—and all of it will be based on the principles you have given us."

Tesla was speechless, breathless. He was filled, overwhelmed, with gratitude.

"Many of my fellow scientists and engineers, Nikola, also report to me that they have solved problems by flashes of insight rather than the process of logic. Louis Agassiz once told me that he had been trying to extract a fossil fish from a slab of rock, but the more he chipped away the matrix from the specimen, the more he feared he would damage the intricate skeleton.

"He told me he had a dream one night in which he saw the layers of rock separating like the slices of bread in a sandwich! He remembered this dream and could hardly wait to get to the laboratory the next morning, to see if he had truly envisioned a way to extract the fish. Do you know what he did? Instead of chipping away the rock around the edges of the bones, he tapped the edges of the slab. He tapped the edges slightly, and lifted off the top layer, exposing the complete fossil."

"Imagine that, Nikola! The mind solves problems even in dreams!"

"I am grateful for this discussion, Lord Kelvin, and it is I who feel deep gratitude for your mind's contributions to science. You also make me feel at ease, speaking about the mind's capacity to envision things with perfect clarity. For me, that is the ultimate task for the mind: to envision the unseen as clearly as the visible."

"Well said, Nikola."

"Sir, I have many things, pressing matters, on my mind—"

"Tell me about them!"

"As you know, I am engaged in the construction of Wardenclyffe Tower, and I hope to transmit both signals and power wirelessly—"

"Yes! Yes! I helped prove that could be done, Nikola—I published papers on atmospheric conductivity and electrical fields, as a response to your work. I have followed your work as much as I could, especially after my return to England, and your Colorado Springs experiments intrigue me, especially the work you did on electrical conductivity at low temperatures."

"We perfected a number of methods for immersing wires and other substances in canisters of liquefied air. Extremely low temperatures enhance conductivity by lowering resistance."

"Amazing. Liquefied air...."

"I designed vast refrigeration coils using helium as a coolant, so we could condense super-cooled air inside the canisters, like dew."

"You also designed cables for use underground, packed with carbon dioxide ice, is that correct?"

"Yes. Of course, the carbon dioxide ice evaporates, but it leaves compressed insulation around the cables. Compression, I have demonstrated, also helps overcome resistance."

"This might become a field to be explored! Suspension of conductors in liquefied air as a medium...."

"The future cannot be held back by the constraints of the present. My only limitation now is financial, not theoretical."

"But what can be done?"

"I do not know," Tesla said. "I do not know...."

A long silence settled around them.

Lord Kelvin said, "I have a feeling, Nikola. Let me share it with you. You are on the edge of a crowning achievement. Not your greatest, perhaps, but one that will go unequaled for many, many years."

"Thank you. I am grateful you feel—"

"May I tell you what this achievement will be?"

"Yes, please do!"

"Nikola, try to *answer* those signals! What you received, many of my less-outspoken colleagues feel were signals, deliberately transmitted by some intelligent source in the sky."

"How can we prove this?"

"Only one way, Nikola. Answer the signal. Answer the signal!"

"That, Lord Kelvin, is exactly what I intend to do."

CHAPTER FIFTY-SEVEN

Mars

John Pierpont Morgan puffed on a cigar and sat in his easy chair his study. He was waiting for Reverend William Rainsford, whom he had summoned to his estate. He avoided St. George's Cathedral because the inevitable epiphanies overwhelmed him; even the sight of the blessed Virgin Mary or crucified Jesus brought on the most intense feelings Morgan had ever known.

He expected the preacher in the hours after dinner.

He suffered deep concern, not fear. He would never allow himself to suffer fear. He had spent a lifetime building an empire that was now in danger of collapsing. He feared Mr. Roosevelt would begin enforcing the Sherman Anti-Trust Act, but that was not all he feared.

He heard a quiet tap at the door.

"Come in!"

"Reverend, the reason I summoned you is...confidential."

"I understand, sir...."

"Bear with me. We both agree the world is in a terrible state in these times, is it not?"

Rainsford nodded gravely. He feared Morgan had been drinking: he noticed an empty whiskey bottle on a shelf behind his mahogany desk.

"I've been away for a while, William, busy with Mr. Hill in our dealings with Mr. Harriman. This has occupied too much of my time. I'm getting to be an old man—it's easy for me to overextend myself in business matters...."

"Perhaps I am not the one to consult in such matters, sir."

"What I want to consult with you about, Reverend, are matters of ethics, moral questions that have been put before me which I now must act upon. Questions, Mr. Rainsford, that I did not intend to bring up."

"What sort of questions?"

Morgan stood and started pacing while he spoke. "As I see it, Rainsford, the world is no longer the safe place it used to be. Actually, it never was, but that is getting more apparent. These are times of severe moral conflict, Rainsford, and civilization as we know it is in great peril.

"This new president, this Teddy Roosevelt, is charging around Washington like a madman threatening to upset the stability of the banking system and the railroads like never before. If he invokes that dratted Sherman Act, the whole economy will be done for.

"The moral attitudes of society have fallen! Even my own daughter, Anne, has been swayed by this...liberalism of today. She has even taken up membership in that all-women social club that's so popular among the younger ladies these days. The Colony Club, as it's called. She has been seen in the company of Daisy Harriman and her rather morally suspicious friend Dorothy Whitney. Word has it that gentlemen are not allowed past the first floor of the resort!

"Furthermore, Rainsford, I've heard there are big Turkish baths upstairs, and the women, almost all of whom are single, engage in intimacies not entirely above reproach!"

Rainsford was shocked. "I see...!"

"Anne spends a great deal of time there. And she's never seen in the company of young men. Not since...."

"Are you suggesting Anne...?"

"I don't know what to think! She's changed. Changed ever since she fell in love with...."

"Fell in love?"

"A long time ago. She changed since then, William! Changed!"

"Who did she fall in love with?"

"Nikola Tesla."

"I seem to recall...."

"Well, she hasn't had a man in her life ever since. She and Mr. Tesla have enjoyed a rather long-standing friendship in spite of my daughter's unfulfilled romantic longings. No matter. What I've asked you here to talk about has nothing to do with suffrage. It has to do with Mr. Tesla."

"I see." He recalled a conversation with Pierpont on the subject of Mr. Tesla long ago. He seemed to recall it had to do with possible motives for building an immense tower for electrical transmission. They had discussed good reasons versus real reasons.

"I seem to remember that discussion, sir."

"Good! So tell me, have you kept up with our Mr. Tesla's career lately?"

"No, I can't say that I have."

"Pity! Well, Rainsford, I managed to get a good look at Mr. Tesla's reasons—both his good reason and his real reason."

"Well, I know he's designing some kind of tower on Long Island. He says it is for transmission of signals by wireless. Wasn't that done by somebody already? Someone named Marconi?"

"You're out of touch, Reverend. Yes, Mr. Tesla is designing Wardenclyffe Tower for the purpose of wireless transmissions. In fact, he recently sent me a proposal to the effect that his 'world system,' as he chooses to call it, can do everything from transmit all of our telegraph and telephone messages, to synchronize our clocks for us, even give navigational bearings to ships at sea. My informants at his laboratory tell me they've overheard him mention to some of his closest associates that he intends to transmit power, raw current, through the air without wires. So be it. Good ideas, all of them. A grand scheme—and, knowing Tesla, I have no doubt it would work.

"All in all, it's a good idea. It's his good reason. I want to talk about his real reason!"

"What might that be?"

"It's come to my attention, after a number of years now, that while he was doing his Colorado Springs work, he claimed to have received signals from another world.

"I'm ashamed to say I ignored that news at the time! Frankly, I didn't believe it when I was first informed. I was caught up in that dreadful Harriman business and I didn't have time to think about such nonsense. At least, it seemed like nonsense at the time.

"His announcement of the signals caused a sensation, but I realized after the fact it wasn't just nonsense—it was what I'd been looking for all along: his real reason!"

"I don't understand, Pierpont...."

"I had to face the obvious! Here is a man who is not like us, not like us at all. He can't even mate with human women! He's terrified of round objects—he fears even a string of pearls. He hates diamonds. Can't stand the thought of touching skin, much less hair, and can't even eat a meal without turning it into a problem in mathematics!

"He lacks human feelings to the point that he doesn't know how much to eat! He computes the amount of food he eats so he'll know when he's full!

"Such a man doesn't fit in among ordinary people, so he exploits his eccentricities to gain attention. But he's still a man, still a human being, so people just think of him as an eccentric. Nothing more.

"D'you know what I think? I think he really isn't one of us, at all!"

"You can't be serious!"

Morgan leaned forward and said, "I'm very serious, Rainsford. Deadly serious."

"Such things are impossible! The good Lord, in his wisdom—"

"The good Lord, in all his wisdom, put lions in the jungle and panthers in the forest, if I may remind you."

"I do not see your point. Are you saying Mr. Tesla is a man from another world?"

"I'm saying he *might* be!"

Rainsford stared at Morgan for a long time, then realized his friend had not gone mad.

"He sees things in his mind, Reverend, complete pictures of machines, machines like none this world has ever seen. Y'know what that sounds like to me? It sounds like those machines are already in his head! He's not seeing them in the future. He's remembering them from the past."

"That's impossible!"

Morgan ignored the protest. "*His* past—not ours! He doesn't know where these mental images come from. He isn't one of us, Rainsford! He comes from somewhere these machines already exist. His visions are not prophecies. They are memories."

"How can you be sure?"

"Look at the pattern! He fears round objects. Why? Could they look familiar, like something he's seen but doesn't remember? The world is round—the moon and all the planets are round—so even a string of pearls reminds him of a planet, high, high up. Something he remembers but doesn't want to face.

"He hates diamonds. They remind him of the stars.

"He fears skin and hair—why? Germs. Not ordinary germs, mind you! He fears *germs from outer space*. He mentioned that once, in my presence. He said that to Mark Twain. He fears germs from other planets! *Why?*"

Rainsford was pale and trembling. "But—but—what does the Bible say about such things, Pierpont? We can't lose sight of God in all of this!"

"That is why I turned to you, William. You're a man of God, perhaps you can help me see the light in all this."

"I hope so, Pierpont!"

"So—then—where were we? Oh, yes. So our friend Mr. Tesla finished up in a hurry, out in Colorado Strings, and instead of waiting around to send that signal to the Paris Exposition, he solicits for funds and starts building a second tower, a new one, right here in New York! What does that suggest to you, Rainsford?"

"My dear Lord…can it be? Would God allow such a thing…?" Rainsford mumbled an inaudible prayer.

Morgan continued, walking in tight circles.

"It's obvious—he's building Wardenclyffe so he can answer those signals!"

Rainsford went white. His hands trembled. He stared up at Morgan.

"Well, don't think what I'm saying is true—only possible! We must be prudent, we must be cautious, we must take care."

"But where could this other civilization—if that's what it is—where could it be from?"

"Who knows? Mars, maybe. Jupiter, Venus—I don't know all the names. My task is to determine whether or not any of it is true and, if it is, try to determine if our visitors will be friendly or not.

"Mars—now, that was the Roman god of war. Mr. Tesla thinks his signals might have come from Mars! Why Mars? Why a planet named after a god of war? Have we been invaded by that planet before? If that's the case, then we can safely assume they were unfriendly and the Roman army managed to fight them off.

"In any case, they must find it hard to get to our world, so they send somebody here in human form, somebody capable of building great machines, machines that will make transportation easier, and after a while, they send him a signal, something like, 'Are you ready, yet?' And he picks it up—which means he's been listening—and he builds a huge broadcasting tower so he can answer.

"But what will his answer bring? Missionaries from heaven? An army from hell? I need to know the answer to that before I can let him finish his Wardenclyffe Tower!"

"In all his wisdom, the Lord put us in the garden—"

"The Lord, in all his wisdom, put the rattlesnake and the badger in the garden, too. Remember what the Bible says? 'Beware of false prophets in the desert.' Frankly, there's a lot of evidence in the Bible that our world's been visited. Maybe we've even fought wars with invaders from other planets. Remember Sodom and Gomorrah. Remember the Tower of Babel. Could that also have been such a tower? And look what happened to the people who built it! Annihilated! Destroyed!"

"My dear Pierpont! It's so…so…incredible…!"

"Yes, I admit it sounds fantastic. But there it is, before your eyes! That tower, out on Long Island, waiting to be completed so messages can be sent—but around the world? Or somewhere else?"

"Surely, such beings, if they are so advanced, are closer to their creator—"

"What makes you think that? Mr. Tesla wants to see Christianity combined with Buddhism, of all things! He calls human beings 'meat machines' and he says he doesn't believe in the immortal soul!"

"I had no idea…."

"Yes! We discussed this once before. Remember?"

"Yes, yes, I do remember. But I had no idea his atheism was so deep."

"Yes. If ever there was an unbeliever, it's Nikola Tesla. Remember this, also, Mr. Rainsford: we live on conquered lands, ourselves. Long ago, other people occupied these lands. They had no idea there were continents on the other side of the ocean. They had no notion of gunpowder or sailing ships. They didn't even ride horses.

"Suddenly, they were invaded. They fought our ancestors, coming over from across the sea. They were killed off in the name of God and country—but what could they do? They had crude weapons. They were outnumbered. Then they were conquered. They live in squalor, now—not that they ever had much, being savages—but they've had their spirits broken, their homelands taken, their heathen tribes destroyed. By us! By our ancestors, coming over from across the sea, from lands those savages didn't even know existed.

"Do you see what I have to face? Do you see what I have to consider? I don't take any of this lightly, Reverend. None of it."

"Suppose they are friends from another world?"

"How can we know? And what would make a peaceful visit *good,* either?"

"Why, if they mean us no harm, then, maybe, they could teach us—"

"I've thought about that, too, yes, I have. But when it comes right down to it, there isn't an institution, from the churches to the government, that would bene- fit from such a blessing."

"Why do you say that?"

"Everything you see around you, from the faces in your church on Sunday morning to the faces I see every Monday morning at the stock exchange, these people need to believe in something, Reverend.

"Suppose we get peaceful visitors? What then? What will they see, Rainsford? Filth, poverty, war, pestilence—they will see us as we are, not the way we like to see ourselves. We are not an enlightened race, William. They'll see our problems, our violence, and they'll either leave us alone or they'll want to reform us, which would be as bad as conquest, for it would also deprive us of our freedom."

"So you're saying even a visit from a peaceful civilization might not be wise?"

"We don't need reformers, we don't need missionaries, we are not ready for vis- itors from another world. Too many questions are unanswered, too many reforms haven't been made. Someday, when humanity has climbed out of the mess it has made of the world, perhaps then we'll be wise enough to receive peaceful visi- tors, people like ourselves who truly have wisdom.

"Perhaps that's why I do not trust Mr. Tesla or his superior civilization—he does not possess wisdom. Great knowledge, yes; he is an undisputed genius. But to have wisdom, you must understand human beings. And it is painfully apparent Mr. Tesla does not. He has no knowledge of what makes people human."

"How can I help you in this dilemma, Pierpont?"

"At least I've been able to talk to someone about this matter, at last I've been able to voice my doubts and confusion. It's like you said two years ago, when I first brought this up: confession is a good start when it comes to finding out what's troubling a man, so he can figure out what to do about it."

"Well, if I could be of service in that way—"

"You have been! A very good service. Thank you, Reverend. Just talking to you about this problem has made me see it more clearly."

"I'm glad, Pierpont, although I still don't know what to make of it."

"Well, promise me one thing: you will keep every word of this discussion to yourself. Completely. May I have your confidence in that?"

"Yes! Of course! Nothing we talked about need ever pass through that door."

"I'm glad. I need to keep that condition with you, Rainsford."

"Then you've decided what you should do?"

"Yes. I think I will arrange to have the world forget about Mr. Tesla. I think I will encourage other investors to leave this fellow alone.

"Oh, mark my words, Rainsford, I do believe there will come a time when we will be ready to receive Mr. Tesla's visitors. And when that time arrives, we will have an invincible military, a stable world economy, no poverty, and true religion.

"And another thing, Rainsford: we will have developed all of Mr. Tesla's ideas— on our own, without handouts from faraway beings. No. We must be the ones who elevate ourselves as a society. Handouts never benefited anyone.

"Who knows? Maybe by then, whoever sent those signals will be old and weak. We will still be young and strong—and maybe we will conquer *them*!"

Morgan laughed and declared the discussion to be at an end.

Rainsford kept the dialogue secret for the rest of his life. He considered every word of it too dreadful to repeat.

Chapter Fifty-Eight

Wrath

Mr. Morgan had suddenly become elusive.

Tesla's letters to the financier had become desperate. He admonished Morgan for raising shipping rates for materials, causing the prices of valuable equipment to rise unreasonably. He wrote, "You have raised great waves in the industrial world and some have struck my little boat. Prices have gone up in consequence twice, perhaps three times higher than they were...."

Morgan refused to answer the communiqué.

Two weeks passed and Morgan received another letter: "You have extended me a noble help at a time when Edison, Marconi, Pupin, Fleming, and many others openly ridiculed my undertaking and declared its success impossible...." Tesla explained in detail his "world system" and what he hoped to accomplish with it: He would interconnect all telegraph exchanges worldwide. He could transmit government secret information without it passing into enemy hands. He promised to interconnect all telephone exchanges worldwide.

The world system would transmit news globally. Private intelligence, business communications, and the stock market could all be transmitted anywhere. Music, shows, and other entertainment could be beamed anywhere instantly. All clocks and chronometers around the world could be synchronized with astronomical precision.

The world system would allow for the simultaneous transmission of facsimile manuscripts—anywhere—including even the reproduction of handwritten signatures for checks and contracts.

The world system would facilitate perfect open-sea navigation. The world system would make possible automatic printing services anywhere in the world. The world system would make possible photographic reproduction of any image, instantly, anywhere.

Tesla carefully avoided mentioning the transmission of power through the atmosphere, to be beamed from North America across the Atlantic Ocean to Europe. The summer days lengthened.

The strange structure at Wardenclyffe stood on the edge of completion. The dome had been erected, but the electrodes had not yet been covered with copper plates. The superstructure had been built, but it had not yet been encased in walls of plywood. The power, however, had been linked to the terminals and the transmitter had already been tested. It worked.

On July third, Tesla wrote one last, desperate plea. "If I would have told you such as this before, you would have fired me out of your office.... Will you help me or let my great work—almost complete—go to pots...?"

Tesla received Morgan's reply exactly eleven days later. "I have received your letter and in reply would say that I should not feel disposed at present to make any further advances."

Tesla sat in his office staring at the far wall, waiting for the time to pass, for the workmen to leave and the night to begin.

He left the office after sunset and wandered the laboratory grounds. He avoided Scherff and Kolman Czito. He was silent.

He felt the blaze of rage and the impotent pain of despair because his dreams were slipping beyond his grasp; the world had said *no* to his gift of free power. The world rejected his attempt to answer signals from another world.

He remembered Prometheus, the Titan who had stolen the sacred fire of the gods and given it to the struggling, suffering humans of this world, only to be chained to a rock and punished by Zeus.

He would not be chained.

The afterglow of the sunset ebbed behind the New York City skyline.

He stood, staring up at his unfinished tower, the wind in his hair, slapping his face. Magnificent rage boiled within him. He remembered the words of Blake: "The Tygers of Wrath are wiser than the Horses of Instruction."

He walked to the door of the laboratory. The building was empty.

He locked the door behind him and strode up the wooden stairs to the platform at the base of the mighty transformers, and he charged the primary coil.

Static electricity bristled in the air. The machinery hummed. Spark gaps blazed with snapping discharges, white and flashing.

The crown of the tower exploded with the fire of Prometheus. Night became day.

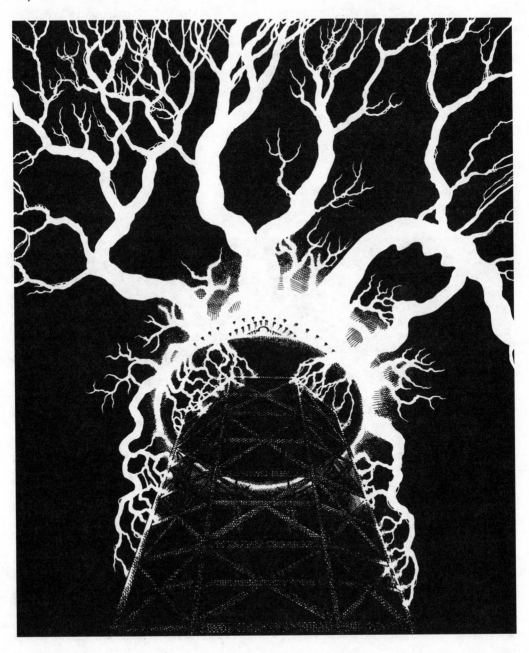

A roar burst upon New York City: the sky was on fire: the hot summer wind screamed with tortured electricity. Wardenclyffe was alive.

Like fiery snakes, lightning writhed, flashed, and twisted through the scorched night. People froze on the sidewalks and stared fearfully at the sky. The devout reminded the doubters of the end of the world. Terror struck every eye that beheld the spectacle.

The roar and the lightning continued hour after hour until the sun finally dawned over the city, only to have daylight overwhelmed by the fiery rage of Tesla. The city was powered by a grid that distributed current from a central source: to shut down the power flow to Wardenclyffe would require shutting down entire sections of the city, risking lawsuits and other legal damage. The alternative was to locate, excavate, and cut the cables.

The city officials decided not to risk lawsuits. The cables were located—after days of searching. Day and night—for three turns of the world on its axis—the display continued.

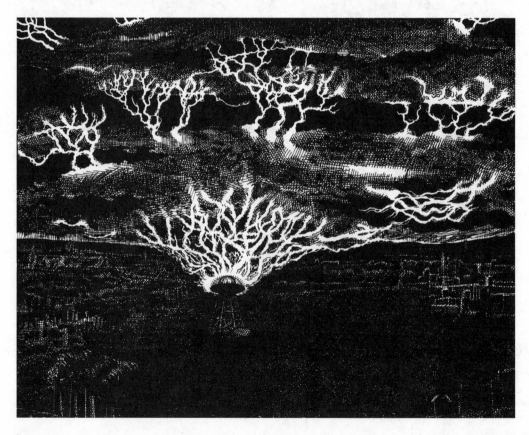

The arcs of lightning were more than one hundred miles long. Ships hundreds of miles at sea reported the aurora, which were witnessed from Maine to Georgia. Reporters flocked to Wardenclyffe.

Tesla stood at the door to his laboratory refusing to admit anyone, including his own workers, greeting reporters and consenting to interviews, while haughtily announcing his claims of genius and denouncing the name Morgan.

On July 16, after the second day of the spectacle, a journalist for the New York *Sun* wrote, "Tesla's Flashes Startling But He Won't Tell What He Is Trying For at Wardenclyffe."

Natives hereabouts…are intensely interested in the nightly electrical display shown in the tall tower where Nikola Tesla is conducting his experiments in wireless telegraphy and telephony. All sorts of lightning were flashed from the tower and poles last night. For a time, the air was filled with blinding streaks of electricity which seemed to shoot off into the darkness on some mysterious errand. When interviewed, Tesla said, "The people about there, had they been awake instead of asleep, at other times would have seen even stranger things. Some day, but not at this time, I shall make an announcement of something that I have never once dreamed of."

He had ripped the sky apart with sixty million volts of electricity.

At last, city workmen uncovered the cables the city engineers had sought. The cables were cut, the lightning bolts ceased, and the sky over New York was familiar again.

CHAPTER FIFTY-NINE

Aftermath

Everything had changed.

The world had lost a little color. Sounds were fainter, muted, and people were a little more unresponsive. Odors were peculiar. His skin was numb. He was in limbo.

He still went out at night, sometimes to the Player's Club to chat with Mark Twain, sometimes to Delmonico's or the Palm Room, sometimes to the Waldorf-Astoria, where he used to live.

He was forced to move, unable to pay his bill.

He lived in the Hotel St. Regis now. It was less lavish than the Waldorf-Astoria, but now modest accommodations were more to his taste.

He was suing Guglielmo Marconi for patent infringements. He contended that Marconi utilized equipment without rights secured nor royalties paid.

The case dragged on in a state of perpetual litigation while the Marconi Wireless Company continued to flourish throughout the United States and Europe.

Along the way, he acquired the services and friendship of a tall and lovely blond named Muriel Arbus. She assisted him in the paperwork of the litigation procedure. After a time, he hired her as his personal secretary, and they became close friends. He saw very little of Marguerite Merington anymore. She had faded from his life after that ill-fated visit to his room. He did miss her, though.

Professor Pupin testified vehemently against Tesla in court, but then he shat-

397

tered his credibility when he claimed preeminence in radio over Tesla and Marconi.

Edison was still working to perfect his magnetic ore separator.

Robert and Katherine Johnson weren't getting along well, either.

As the patent suit against Marconi dragged on and the skeletal tower that was Wardenclyffe stood desolate and deserted above the fields of Long Island, Tesla retreated into an internal world that was more real to him than the world outside of his senses.

He fed pigeons on a park bench in his idle time; he pondered their flight, their slate-gray colors, the way they strutted with their own brand of dignity.

The pigeons wore uniforms. They resembled postal carriers.

He saved crumbs for them; he sometimes fed them from his own pockets. The birds sensed his kindness and recognized him, remembered who he was. He would walk to a vendor to buy popcorn, peanuts, pretzels to break up—and the birds would surround him, encircle him, then flutter to the ground and peck furiously at the crumbs he tossed them.

Robert and Katherine departed for Europe.

Tesla experimented in his new laboratory and conducted business out of his new office at 165 Broadway.

To Muriel Arbus, Tesla was more than an eccentric human curiosity. She accepted his phobias and compulsions and stood in awe of his great scientific vision. She understood he was different, but that was what drew her to him, made her feel protective over him, allowed her to nurture a man with whom intimacy would have been completely inappropriate. She realized he was still a virgin.

She stood in awe of his choice: how many human beings have ever sacrificed their sexuality for some spark of inspiration the rest of us will never understand? How many people could spend every night of their lives alone to serve the cause of higher knowledge? Not many.

Muriel Arbus shivered. She had a date tonight….

She knew she could never have made such a sacrifice, but she felt proud and privileged to care for a man who had.

She went to work early each day because she wanted to be there standing beside the door when he came in to take his cane and coat from him, and to begin typing, filling out documents, and reviewing reports…things he shouldn't be bothered with. She arranged for Thomas Fortune Ryan and a sugar merchant, H. O. Havermeyer, to pay off his debts on Wardenclyffe.

He continued to experiment whenever he could afford to until 1905, when the power was cut off forever.

Scherff left Tesla's employ after Wardenclyffe closed. He went on to work for the Union Sulfur Company.

Kolman Czito had worked for Tesla less and less after the Colorado Springs experiments ended. His son Julius became his eager young replacement.

Tesla designed a new motor—"a powerhouse in a hat"—that delivered thirty horsepower. It was less than six inches in length and weighed under ten pounds. It actually fit inside a derby.

He and Julius Czito developed a turbine capable of twenty thousand horsepower.

In 1909, Guglielmo Marconi and Carl F. Braun shared a Nobel Prize for parallel development of radio.

Tesla went about his work. If the news affected him, he did not show it.

In 1911, Tesla interested Allis Chalmers of the Chalmers manufacturing Company of Milwaukee in his turbine. Fearing bureaucrats would redesign his turbine, he presented his designs to the president of the company directly and production began immediately.

Those who used the machines encountered an unexpected design flaw: the smaller ones worked well, but the larger ones were susceptible to "high temperatures, high pressures, high speeds, and internal vibrations." No known metals could withstand the centrifugal force exerted by such high RPMs.

Tesla hired a second secretary in 1912 named Dorothy Skerrit. She divided her time between his office at 165 Broadway, across the street from the library, or at his laboratory at 8 West 40th Street.

Miss Skerrit was a quiet woman, far less talkative than Miss Arbus.

Both women loved and protected their mysterious employer.

He was asked to share the Nobel Prize with Thomas Edison, and promptly refused.

The story, reported by the *New York Times* on November 6, 1915, surprised even Tesla. He had not been notified of such an honor.

Tesla announced to interviewers that he would never share a Nobel Prize with Thomas Edison. Edison was a "fraud," a "second-rate tinkerer," "experimenting blindly...not knowing the principles of physics...."

Two years later, he was offered the Edison medal from the American Institute of Electricians and Engineers.

The chairman of the Edison medal committee was Professor B. A. Behrend, one of Tesla's first supporters in the alternating-current battle—and, from that time on, one of Tesla's unseen champions.

Behrend knew the animosity Tesla harbored for Edison, and the hostility Edison felt for him. Still, Behrend approached Tesla with sincerity and eagerness. Stepping into Tesla's office, he greeted him respectfully, grinned expansively, and looked into the inventor's silver-blue eyes.

"Mr. Tesla, it has come to our attention that, of all those who have been bestowed with the honor of the Edison medal of the American Institute of Electricians and Engineers, none have been as deserving of that honor as you! We—many of my colleagues and I—have long thought that the foundation of modern electrical science can be traced directly to you.

"We look back on the papers published, the devices patented, and it is clear that the greater contribution has been by you. Would you permit me? The honor is from your fellow scientists who are reminded daily, by the work they do, of our collective debt of gratitude to you.

"I find it to be an outrage, Mr. Tesla, that I have seen this world transformed by the work you have done—I've witnessed electrotheraputics grow into a burgeoning new field without mention of you; I've seen radio exploited by Marconi, then Edison, without even a percentage your way—it angers me! It infuriates me! I offer you this medal for the injustices done to you."

Tesla shook his head. "Let us forget the whole matter, Mr. Behrend. I appreciate your goodwill and friendship but I desire you to return to your committee and request it to make another selection."

"But, Mr. Tesla—"

Tesla stood. "It has been thirty years since I announced my rotating magnetic field and alternating-current system before the Institute. I do not need its honors and somebody else may find it useful."

Behrend left the office but didn't plan on giving up.

Wardenclyffe Tower was destroyed in 1917. It had been blown up by the United States Navy on the Fourth of July. Rumors circulated that it sheltered German spies. World War I had caused a strange, manic fear that spread like a fever epidemic throughout the United States. People watched the skies for aerial attacks from airplanes dropping bombs.

Behrend returned to Tesla's office—unannounced—several days later to persuade him to accept the Edison medal once again.

Tesla was furious. "You propose to honor me with a medal which I could pin upon my coat and strut for a vain hour before the members and guests of your Institute! You would bestow an outward semblance of honoring me but you would decorate my body and continue to let me starve, for failure to supply recognition, my mind and its creative products which have supplied the foundation upon which the major portion of your Institute exists."

"Please, Mr. Tesla, it is not Edison we are—"

"When you go through the vacuous pantomime of honoring Tesla you would not be honoring Tesla but Edison, who has previously shared unearned glory from every recipient of this medal."

With that, he ordered Professor Behrend out of his office. Behrend departed more determined than ever. He could not erase the name of Edison from the medal, but it was the only honor he had the power to bestow on Tesla.

He returned unannounced to 165 Broadway three days later to enter his final plea.

"Mr. Tesla, never have anyone's words affected me so deeply as the words you said to me three days ago. Your name, the honor you should have been granted, the money you should have made—all these injustices and more do I feel should be atoned for. I can only do as much as I can do. Your fellow engineers and I have all steadfastly agreed that the very smallest thing we could do to honor you, the only token we have in our power to give, is this medal. Please—if we could change the name of the medal, we would. It is *not* Edison's medal. It is the medal of the American Institute of Electricians and Engineers.

"You lectured before our Institute on several occasions, the first, in 1891, when you disclosed many transformers, wonderful motors, and you first unveiled your Tesla coil. Some of the people who will attend the dinner will remember that night! Many people will wish they had been there. Your fellow scientists and inventors are eager to ask you questions. How else can they gain access to your knowledge? Would you shun the Institute when you, yourself, graced it with the presence of your inventions and your lectures? Please reconsider! Give your fellow scientists a chance to rectify the terrible mistakes and injustices of the past! This is a heartfelt plea, Mr. Tesla."

Nikola looked into the man's eyes and saw they swelled with tears. "Perhaps...I will...."

Professor Behrend was ecstatic. He trembled. He wept.

The Engineer's Club stood right across a narrow alleyway from the United

Engineering Societies Building on 39th Street. Both were across the street from Bryant Park.

Tesla accepted the honor, but appeared to be ill-at-ease. He was quiet—reticent, some observed. The members of the Institute greeted him respectfully. Questions were put to him politely, and he offered his answers cautiously.

"What do you think of that young German fellow who published those two theories last year? Einstein? Albert Einstein?"

"I disagree with him about the curvature of gravity. And what of the speed of light? Einstein, if he had experimented with light physics, as I have, would have found out that particles leave a source at nearly infinite speed, but slow down rapidly, so that even after traveling a few meters, they are far closer to one hundred and eighty six thousand miles per second than when they left the source."

"Mr. Tesla, what do you think about the Michaelson and Morley experiment as disproof of the theory of 'luminiferous ether'?"

"What Albert Michaelson and George Morley did back in 1882 does not disprove any of my observations about the ether. The interpretation and the results of their experiment are flawed."

"Mr. Tesla, what do you think about the work of those European atomic physicists, especially Max Planck and Neils Bohr?"

"I think they are relying too much on theories and equations and not enough on experimentation. They have made too much of that 'slit-screen' experiment, in my opinion."

"Mr. Tesla, what do you see ahead for the future of physics?"

"The scientists from Franklin to Morse were clear thinkers and did not produce erroneous theories. The scientists of today think deeply instead of clearly, but one can think deeply and be quite insane.

"Today's scientists have substituted mathematics for experiments and they wander through equation after equation and eventually build a structure which has no relation to reality."

"Then you disagree that a particle of light can behave like a vibration at the same time?"

"I disagree."

The banquet was dismissed and the participants were instructed to reconvene across the alley in the rented hall in the United Engineering Societies Building. En route, Tesla vanished into the night.

Gradually, the participants realized their guest of honor was mysteriously absent. Behrend was summoned.

"This is terrible!"

The headwaiter was summoned and the waiters and busboys searched hallways and restrooms for the elusive inventor.

He must have returned to his room at the Hotel St. Regis…. Behrend flew from the building to the street, peering into the night.

He started to run—without knowing which way—angry, upset, and frightened. Had the guests offended Tesla?

Behrend turned a corner, away from the Hotel St. Regis, doubling back toward Bryant Park. His intuition led him through the trees to a clearing, where beside a park bench walked a human perch covered in birds. Pigeons, cooing and fluttering, clung to the slow-moving figure.

"Tesla!"

"Sssssshhhhhh!"

"Oh—oh, Mr. Tesla, please—we didn't know where you were!"

"I was spending a little time with my friends. I will be back in a short while." Behrend waited until Tesla had finished doling out the bread crumbs he had salvaged from his dinner plate. Then he dusted the feathers off, ignored the messier aspect of being a haven for pigeons, and returned to the Societies Building via a brief visit to the men's washroom.

Behrend gave an inspired speech in Tesla's honor. "Were we to seize and eliminate from our industrial world the results of Tesla's work the wheels of industry would soon cease to turn, our electric cars and trains would stop, our mills would be dead and idle. Yes, so far-reaching is his work that it has become the warp and woof of industry.

"His name marks an epoch in the advance of electrical science. From his work has sprung a revolution. I would like to quote lines by Pope, intended for Newton but made to reflect this contemporary of ours, here.

'Nature and Nature's laws lay hid in night:
God said, let Tesla be, and all was light.'"

CHAPTER SIXTY

Pujo

He was awake but he was dreaming, and his dreams were memories. His mind shifted in and out of the past. His memories were more real to him than the soft pressure of the bedsheets and blankets, or the muffled voices in the room. He was remembering triumphs and tragedies.

He was trying to remember only the triumphs. He was trying to forget the tragedies.

The riots and strikes of 1902 had brought on the Rich Man's Panic of 1903. Teddy Roosevelt, buck-toothed and beady-eyed, invoked the "Trust-Busters" to dissolve the Northern Securities Company, incorporated just the year before, on November 12, 1901.

On Wednesday, February 19, a bill was passed that dissolved the Northern Securities Company. The day the bill was passed, Morgan burst into the White House unannounced, confronting President Roosevelt and his Attorney General, Philander C. Knox. He condemned both men scathingly.

"I could not arrange an agreement without prior warning!"

Roosevelt stared at him from behind those insidious round glasses. "That is just what we did not want you to do."

After Morgan departed, Roosevelt said to Knox, "That is a most illuminating illustration of the Wall Street point of view. Mr. Morgan could not help regarding me as a rival operator, who intended either to ruin all his interests or else could be induced to an agreement to ruin none."

Morgan hated those words, so often quoted in the popular press. From that time on, they treated him like a criminal.

Roosevelt wanted Morgan to rescue the country during the strikes and riots of 1902.

That had also been the year Morgan conferred secretly with his pastor, William Rainsford, about the mysterious Mr. Tesla. He dreaded even thinking about Tesla—the man made him nervous.

The very idea that humanity was not alone in the universe disturbed Morgan deeply: he feared hostile invaders almost as much as the prospect of somebody older and wiser seeing petty, vicious humanity for what it really is.

He thought of his daughter, Anne, who had turned against him. Not outwardly, with anger or rage, but inwardly. She marched with the suffragettes, picketed with strikers, and advocated civil rights for Negroes. She lived with two women, Dorothy Whitney and Daisy Harriman, and shunned men.

Morgan tried to forget about Anne.

He remembered true love. Amelia Sturges had been dead now, for many, many years. Now, Morgan was in love again.

He was sixty-eight years old when he met her, she had been twenty-two. She had been working in the Princeton Library. They called her "Belle of the Books." Her name was Belle da Costa Greene.

Her hair was black and shiny and her skin was dark, dark brown. Almost black. Her eyes were deep obsidian. Her lips were wide and sensuous. Her kisses were wild and passionate.

She was more intelligent than he, which he admired. He respected her more than anyone he had ever known. He appointed her to be librarian at the Morgan Library.

She appraised manuscripts he considered purchasing. She verified the authenticity of works by Thackaray and Hawthorne. He relied almost exclusively on her advice in matters of art and literature.

Amelia Sturges. Belle da Costa Greene.

He had found a little bit of love at the beginning of his life and a little at the end, and the rest had been hard, hard work.

He had saved the country in 1893. He confronted Grover Cleveland and refinanced the United States Treasury with gold from the House of Morgan and the houses of Europe.

The principle of aristocracy had not been dealt a death blow in 1789. One aristocracy had been replaced by another: an aristocracy of merchants. Honest bankers. Good businessmen.

He remembered, "It's Morgan! It's Morgan! The Great Financial Gorgon!"

He remembered Senator Mark Hanna's visit. "*Please*, Mr. Morgan! *Talk* to the union men! *Order* the strikers back to work!"

"I cannot do that. Government interference with the railroad industry is what brought it on. Therefore, it is your problem to solve. I refuse."

He remembered the Pujo Committee. They had treated him like a criminal.

After that fool Taft replaced Teddy Roosevelt, Morgan had been summoned to testify before the Pujo Committee to Investigate the Concentration and Control of Money and Credit.

He had stood before them, voluntarily, with nothing to hide, like any good American. They responded by interrogating him like a common crook, a vulgar criminal. Who *was* Senator Platt? Not just "Senator from Connecticut" or "Senator Vest from Missouri," but who *were* these men—*really?*

Senator Platt baited him with leading questions. "Why did you want to have an issue of bonds after you had commenced your negotiations?"

He answered the best he could. "Because I knew that if the call was made the public would understand that the foreign negotiation had not been abandoned."

Platt said quickly, "It was a well-known fact that you commenced a negotiation."

"I did not care about anything except to get the gold to the government! I had but one aim in the whole matter—to secure the gold that the government needed and to save the panic and widespread disaster that was sure to follow if the gold was not got."

Platt waved his hand. "Then it was understood that when you were negotiating, shipments ceased?"

"Absolutely. And they did not commence until a month afterward."

Platt nodded. His voice held a condescending, arrogant tone. "And so, your real purpose, as I understand you, in this transaction, was not the idea that you could take this bond issue and make money out of it, but that you could prevent a panic and distress in the country?"

Morgan drew in a deep breath, clutched the sides of the speaker's podium, and looked into the face of the small, dark-haired man. He said, "I will answer that question, although I do not think it is necessary in view of all that I have done. I will say that I had no object except, as I have stated, to save the disaster that would result in case that foreign gold had not been obtained."

At that point, Senator Vest, a white-haired man with a craggy face and hostile eyes, spoke up. "If that was your sole object, why did you specify in your telegraphic communication to Mr. Carlisle that your house, or you and Mr. Belmont, were to have exclusive control over the matter?"

"Because it was impossible for more than one party to negotiate—to make the same negotiation for the same amount of gold. It would only have made competition."

Vest was aggressive. "If the gold was abroad, I take for granted anybody could get hold of it who had the means to do so. If you were actuated by the desire to prevent a panic, why were you not willing that other people should do it, if they wanted to?"

Morgan cried out, "Because—*they could not do it!*"

"How did *you* know?"

"That was my opinion."

Vest laughed scornfully. "Do you believe that the government could have made any better terms with anybody else than it made with yourself and Mr. Belmont at that juncture?"

"I do not, sir."

"Do you believe that gold could be obtained from abroad on any better terms?"

"I do not! It was difficult enough to obtain, as it was."

"Was your house engaged in shipping gold abroad up to this time, or at about this time?"

"We never have shipped one dollar of gold abroad for the last three years."

That had been the truth. He had insisted on the meeting with Grover Cleveland, for the good of the country. Now, to be interrogated like a common thief—

Senator Untermeyer took his turn, ensnaring him with questions barbed for entrapment. "You think, therefore, that where you name a board of directors who remain in existence only a year and you have the power to name another board next year, that this board so named is in an independent position to deal with your banking house, as would a board named by the stockholders themselves?"

Morgan nodded. "I think it would be better...."

Untermeyer raised his hand. "You think it is a great deal better?"

"Yes, sir."

"More independent?"

Morgan replied cautiously, "Better."

"Will you tell us why?"

He told the truth. It was his moral and patriotic duty.

"Because a man I do not trust could not get any money from me on all the bonds in Christendom."

Right after the hearings, his health broke down. On January 6, 1913, John Pierpont Morgan drew up his will.

He was described by one who saw him as "a very sick man."

He arrived in Monte Carlo on January 22, and made it to Cairo on February 7. He was joined by his son-in-law Herbert Satterlee. They departed for Naples, then Rome, which they reached on March 13.

On March 27, Morgan fell into a coma.

John Pierpont Morgan turned the world of money over to the hands of other men early in the morning of March 31, 1931.

CHAPTER SIXTY-ONE

"*Beautiful!*"

They were lifting him out of his chair and putting him to bed again. He tried to tell them. Did they hear?

"It is...."

He thought he heard Mina's voice, but his body was very far away...he went back in time.

He went back to when they were all still alive, Batchelor, Kruesi...back when Francis Upton, good old "Culture," was still around...back in the days of his glory.

They had died. All of them.

His sister Marion died of cancer in 1900. The year before, John Kruesi died. He had been only fifty-six years old. That was the same year Mina's father, Lewis Miller, died. He had been ill with cholera after the Great Panic of 1893. The Miller family had gone from wealth to poverty in weeks. Lewis Miller had fought diarrhea for six years....

The year before, his son Theodore Miller had been wounded in Santiago on one of Teddy Roosevelt's crusades with the Rough Riders. After seven days of suffering blood poisoning, he died.

Frank Pope and Jim MacKenzie both died in 1895. Charles Batchelor died in 1910. Heart disease had progressed for years and culminated in a fatal heart attack.

Batchelor and Edison never resolved their "dispute."

"Everyone steals in commerce and industry! I've stolen a lot, myself. But I know *how* to steal! They *don't* know how to steal!"

A year after Batchelor died, Josiah Reiff died of pneumonia.

The Panic of 1903 had hurt him badly. He had faced a crippling strike, and hired thugs and hoodlums through the Pinkerton Detective Agency to break the strike. More than the strike was broken.

He and Mina disapproved of daughter Dot's choice of a husband. She married anyway, back in 1895, and lived happily ever after....

He remembered when his youngest son, Theodore, panicked the guests at his mother's tea party with his pet alligators.

Half-brothers Tom and Charles became drinking buddies. They frequently drank themselves into oblivion....

Mina's mother died sometime in October of 1912, after a year of serious illnesses.

He remembered how his young protégé, Henry Ford, bought the rights to C. W. Duryea's contraption, the "automobile," and, through the miracle of mass-production, turned the Model T and Model A Ford into the backbone of the American economy.

He remembered his great breakthrough in June of 1897, when the Crane Iron Works at Catasaqua yielded over 138 tons of iron per day, an increase of a third above what they had been able to produce until then.

When the new iron mill opened in 1898, it broke down by midsummer. Edison's financial backers went "berserk" over his latest financial disaster. His one true contribution to the world, his magnetic ore separator, had been a costly failure.

He remembered the first time he and Mina had attended a concert performance of Beethoven's Ninth Symphony. It became his favorite piece of music, deaf as he was. He wanted to record it. On the phonograph. *His* phonograph....

His attention shifted to the present. He could feel the bedsheets wrapping around his body as someone—a nurse—tucked him in.

He remembered seances, and attempts to contact the spirits of the dead....

He had been sitting in a chair, just moments ago, looking at a far corner of the room. A radiant light emanated from the blank corner.

He pointed to it. "It is...very beautiful...over there...."

His wife and the nurse and the doctor became very excited. They peered into his face. They tried to talk to him. He had been too weak to reply. They lifted him out of the chair and put him to bed.

He went to sleep and never woke up.

Thomas Edison merged with the radiant light he saw on Sunday, October 18, 1931, at 3:24 in the morning.

CHAPTER SIXTY-TWO

Love

Human beings did not respond well to love.

Robert and Katherine Johnson loved each other, but they quarreled, sometimes fought, and both resorted to drinking on occasion. They loved each other. Tesla was certain of that. He was glad he never married....

He tried so hard to create the utopian vision he had seen.

Somehow, over the years, many, many years after Wardenclyffe, certain things made sense that never made sense before. Those flashes of insight—pure, technical visions—how real his polyphase motor seemed to him on the slope in the city park in Budapest with his friend Anital Szigety, the confrontations with Edison, the expectations with Morgan, the building of the high-energy magnifying transmitter in Colorado Springs....

Wardenclyffe Tower. The signals had gone unanswered; he had failed. He felt hollow, empty. He had failed at a very important task. The signals had gone unanswered.

His unending poverty had grown intolerable long ago. He had designed particle beam transmitters, popularly called "death rays," but they were intended for nothing less than faster-than-light transmissions. *Not* weaponry.

His renewed quest became how to use technology to end war.

His response to the threat of airplanes dropping bombs over cities was the publication in *The Electrical Experimenter*, August, 1917, of his latest invention: radar.

He dabbled in nightmarish weaponry on the principle of inventing weapons no one would want to use—but gave this up when he realized nothing he could design would be too terrible to be a deterrent for war.

His teleautomatons—robot helicopters, submarines, and torpedoes—and his high-energy Howitzer, his electromagnetic missiles that could fly without combustible fuel, all convinced him that anything he could design on paper would result in international competition to develop and implement such armaments.

If he could repeat any part of his life, he would have had nothing to do with war. And he would have kept those signals from Mars secret.

Marriage? The attacks on him as a bachelor had been many and severe. Not just in the gossip columns or society pages of the newspapers, but the editorial pages of such publications as the *Electrical Journal* and the *American Electrician*, and the London publication, the *Electrical Review*, urged him to get married.

He felt obligated to respond. "Marriage, for an artist, yes; for a musician, yes; for a writer, yes; but for an inventor, no. The first three must gain inspiration from a woman's influence and be led by their love to finer achievement, but an inventor has so intense a nature with so much of it in wild, passionate quality, that in giving himself to a woman he might love, he would give everything, and so take everything from his chosen field. I do not think you can name many inventions that have been made by married men."

He sighed, then confessed to the young journalist, "It's a pity, too, for sometimes we feel so lonely...."

In August of 1924, he published an article he had written entitled "When Woman is Boss." *Collier's* ran it. He fanned the flames of his own controversy: he predicted a time when women would take over politics, business, and the world. Humanity would no longer strive, in competition with itself, to accomplish great things: eugenics and artificial insemination, genetics, perhaps artificial wombs would replace the agony of birth, liberating women to usurp jobs and professions formerly reserved for men. Civilization would begin to resemble the hive-societies of insects. Individuality would be lost and the human species would stagnate. Tesla sadly observed, "All too often women try to prevent men from doing great things."

He remembered the Johnsons, Robert and Katherine.

He remembered the "office scandal" that had cost Robert Underwood Johnson his job as editor of *Century* magazine. Only a few people knew the details, and Tesla had been one of them. The real tragedy had been for Katherine; she could no longer avoid facing the realization that her husband had not been faithful, and not all of his affairs had been…with women. He went to work as secretary of the American Academy of Arts and Letters. His lavish tastes could not be satisfied by his diminished salary.

Katherine Johnson died in 1925.

Robert Johnson and his daughter Agnes left for Europe with the actress who had been his mistress for several years. She was in her early teens when they departed. Robert Johnson loved the girl until his death in 1937.

Tesla remembered Marguerite. The memory of their wild embrace—and of the shock and horror it evoked—was painful. Too painful. Everything between them withered and died at that moment.

He preferred to recall the evening when she had played Mozart for him at the Johnson home, and he felt compelled to ask her, "Tell me, Miss Merington, why do you choose not to wear diamonds and jewelry like the other women do?"

She sighed. "It is not a matter of choice with me. If I had a lot of money, I could think of better ways to spend it."

"What would you do with a lot of money if you had it?"

She pondered the question for a moment, then answered, "I would purchase a home in the country—except that I would prefer not commuting from the suburbs."

"Ah, Miss Merington! When I start making my millions, I will solve that problem. I will buy a square block here in New York and build a villa for you in the center, then plant trees all around it. Then you will have your home in the country, and you will not have to leave the city!"

That was the finest moment they ever shared.

He remembered Anne Morgan. They frequently went to the movies together—Mack Sennet comedies, Charlie Chaplin, sometimes, Buster Keaton—afterward they would feed pigeons in the park and talk in the afternoon air.

She burst into his apartment at the Hotel St. Regis on a Sunday afternoon in July, 1915. The pigeons in his room rioted, then flew out an open window.

"Anna! How pleasant to see you! What a wonderful surprise."

"Please, Nikola, let us go to the park and talk. I have very bad news to tell you."

They strolled onto the streets. Anne was pensive as they made their way to a park bench nearby. Tesla sat beside Anne, who ignored the huge flock of pigeons that gathered around them.

"It's my brother Jack. He's been shot."

"How dreadful!"

"He isn't dead—it was just a debacle, not a murder. Just awful."

"I hope he will recover!"

"He took two shots from a pistol. He will be alright. A man intruded upon them just this morning, while they sat at the breakfast table. The man got past the butler. He tried to take the children as hostages, but Jack and Mr. Physick, the butler, got the better of the man. He was even carrying a stick of dynamite! Imagine that!"

"Anne, that is terrible! Just dreadful! What has become of this man?"

"Oh, the police were called. Jack was cared for by the family doctor. He wasn't hurt too badly: he is being cared for at home. There was no need to rush him to the hospital."

"That is good. But I hope this madman is rushed to jail."

"He was."

That had been so long ago.

The Waldorf-Astoria was gone now. In its place stood the Empire State Building.

Colonel John Jacob Astor was gone too, now. He had perished aboard the *Titanic.* So long ago....

He had new friends now. They were young eager visionaries who wished to share his dreams.

Hugo Gernsback edited stories in that wonderful new genre, science fiction. The visions of Jules Verne and H. G. Welles were being kept alive by such authors as Karel Copek and Olaf Stapledon. Hugo Gernsback was always eager to publish anything Tesla could write for him.

Kenneth Swezey was an intelligent young man, a science writer who gave gala birthday celebrations to Tesla. The elderly inventor enjoyed those immensely.

He was eighty years old when he announced that he continued to work on ways to send interplanetary messages. "I am expecting to put before the Institute of France an accurate description of the devices with data and calculations and claim the Pierre Guzman prize of 100,000 francs for means of communication with other worlds, feeling perfectly sure that it will be awarded to me. The money is, of course, a trifling consideration, but for the great historical honor of being the first to achieve this miracle I would almost be willing to give my life."

His new friends Kenneth Swezey, Hugo Gernsback, and the avid young John O'Neil did not cast aspersions on Tesla for his quest to answer the call he had received from another world.

Edison, in 1906, admitted to have received similar signals. Marconi, in the 1920s, intercepted mysterious signals on a receiver aboard his yacht.

"They are out there," Tesla observed.

Mystics visited Tesla. He received many such visitors and tried unsuccessfully to dissuade them from such notions as: 1) he was a Venusian emissary; 2) a reincarnated Priest of Atlantis; or 3) an ascended master of a secret occult order.

In 1927, a young Yugoslavian journalist, Dragislav Petkovic, visited Professor Michael Pupin at Pupin's apartment. Petkovic asked Pupin why he had turned against Tesla and testified against him on behalf of Marconi, when he knew that Tesla had established preeminence in radio.

Suddenly, Pupin became enraged. "How long will our people celebrate only mysterious persons, instead of what's clear to everyone to understand?"

When Petkovic called upon Tesla, he was admitted to the room at the Hotel St. Regis amid a flutter of pigeons. He asked Tesla about Pupin's betrayal of him.

"Mr. Pupin and his friends interrupted my lecture by whistling, and I had difficulty quieting down the misled audience."

When asked what he thought of Marconi, Tesla replied, "Mr. Marconi is a donkey."

Thinking about people brought on sadness. Tesla did not despise humanity. He pitied human beings. Believers were convinced Tesla was a man from another planet. John O'Neil was eager to prove his theories on telepathy. Everyone wanted to use Tesla as an example to support their mystical superstitious notions.

Tesla sought out the friendship of prizefighters, whom he regarded as noble human beings.

Once, his comrade Fritzie Zivic held a banquet in his honor in the private dining room of the Hotel New Yorker. Fritzie and his five brothers were all prizefighters. John O'Neil and William Laurence, a fellow science writer, also attended the banquet.

Tesla insisted upon ordering Fritzie a gigantic slab of beefsteak. "I am ordering you a nice thick beefsteak, two inches thick, so you will have plenty of strength for your welterweight fight tonight at Madison Square Garden—"

"No!" Fritzie protested. "I am in training and cannot eat a steak today! I must eat lightly!"

"Nonsense," Tesla argued. He claimed to know the exact amount of nutrition a fighter should consume on the eve of a grand tournament.

The argument quickly escalated. All six brothers joined in the frenzy. Soon both science writers felt their legs begin to itch.

After the argument—and the banquet—broke up, O'Neil tried to persuade Laurence that the itching had been caused by telepathic energy.

That was how humans were: to them, everything they saw was only an example of what they already believed.

He remembered the tour of the RCA Transoceanic Station in New Brunswick, New Jersey, in 1921. Two of the other guests on the tour included Charles Proteus Steinmetz and Albert Einstein.

Steinmetz had long ago abandoned Thomas Edison and supported Tesla's endeavors, from the advent of alternating current to his claim to have invented radio.

In the lunch room of the station, Tesla addressed Einstein. "Herr Einstein, I do not hesitate to disagree with your principles as espoused by your theories of General and Special Relativity."

Einstein raised an eyebrow. "Herr Tesla—you are a man of many works. With what do you disagree in regard to my theories?"

"You are wrong in General Relativity when you say space is curved. What you perceive as the curvature of space is the effect of the ether upon the flow of light."

"The ether is an old idea, Herr Tesla. It has been abandoned by most physicists."

Steinmetz sat across the table from the other two men. He was a hunchback and a dwarf, but what he lacked in physical stature he had made up for many times intellectually. He interjected, "Herr Einstein, Dr. Tesla has conducted electrical experiments with atoms."

"That is true," Tesla quickly said. "I have seen the effects of powerful electrical currents on the crystal surfaces of diamonds and sapphires. I have seen with my own eyes that atomic substances were scattered by high voltages. If anyone can say with authority that the ether exists, it is I, sir."

Einstein nodded. "What about the Michaelson and Morley experiment? What about that?"

"It proves nothing, Herr Einstein."

"So—you refute it?"

"Absolutely."

Steinmetz gave Tesla a long look. "Dr. Tesla, you have stated your opinion of General Relativity. What is your opinion of Special Relativity?"

Tesla shrugged. "I base my theories upon experiments combined with mathematical formulae, instead of experimentation alone, like Thomas Edison, or mathematics alone, which Herr Einstein seems to prefer."

Steinmetz became animated, enthusiastic. "*Doctor* Tesla—what about this talk of atomic energy? What do you think of these claims Fermi and Neils Bohr are making?"

"There is no energy in the atom," Tesla stated flatly. "Only the energy that acts on the atom."

"Even I disagree with that," Einstein said. "I have my doubts about subatomic physics, just as you do, Herr Tesla, but I have to disagree: atoms consist of special states of electricity."

"Nonsense! Atoms are inert."

"Then you disagree with the very discovery of the electron itself?" Steinmetz listened, astounded.

"There is no such thing as the electron, Herr Einstein. What you and the others call the electron is merely a unit of measurement, not a particle of electricity." Einstein shook his head.

Tesla said he would begin work on his own theory of relativity. As he got older, the flashes of technical insight came less frequently. They did come, however....

He was almost sixty years old when a car swerved toward him one night as he crossed the street. A flash inspired him: he leaped over backward, upside down, and continued to walk across the street on his hands. His feet swayed in the air.

"How old are you?" asked an astonished stranger.

"About fifty-nine," said Tesla, leaping from his hands to his feet.

"I've never even seen cats land like that! I've seen acrobats walk like that. But a man your age!"

Tesla was convinced he would live to be 125 years old. Yet, his mind was not always clear anymore. He would never admit it, but he sometimes got...confused.

He had summoned Kerrigan, a messenger boy, to his office a few days ago, on a cold brittle morning underneath an overcast sky. He gave Kerrigan an envelope addressed to:

MR. SAMUEL CLEMENS
35 SOUTH FIFTH AVENUE
NEW YORK CITY

Kerrigan, the intrepid youth, braved the bitter wind and the sporadic rains only to discover that the address was that of Tesla's first laboratory, and that Samuel Clemens—Mark Twain—had died in 1918.

Tesla's consciousness raced from past to present to past again.

He recalled what he had told Kerrigan when the lad returned to his office. "He was in my room last night and talked to me for about an hour. He is having financial difficulties and needs my help. So, don't come back until you have delivered that envelope!"

The envelope contained a blank piece of paper and twenty-five dollar bills.

He remembered something that happened much earlier, when he was living at the Hotel St. Regis.

He had fallen in love.

He feared for the life of his beloved. That was in 1921. He remembered that, now....

Sadness filled his heart. She had been gone for many years. She died in 1922. Tesla was grief-stricken.

He described his true love to John O'Neil. "I have been feeding pigeons, thousands of them, for years, thousands of them, for who can tell—

"But there was one pigeon, a beautiful bird, pure white with gray tips on its wings; that one was different. It was female. I would know that pigeon anywhere.

"No matter where I was, that pigeon would find me; when I wanted her I had only to wish and call her and she would come flying to me. She understood me and I understood her.

"I loved that pigeon...."

He was suddenly ill one day, at his 40th Street office, and refused to return to his hotel room. He never allowed a physician to treat him, and arranged, through Miss Skerritt, to have the hotel housekeeper take care of "the white pigeon with touches of gray in her wings.

When the white bird became ill, days later, Tesla remained in his apartment to nurse his true love back to health. A year later, the special bird died.

"When that pigeon died, something went out of my life. Up to that time I knew with certainty I would complete my work, no matter how ambitious my program, but when that something went out of my life I knew my life's work was finished."

In 1924, Tesla was evicted from the Hotel St. Regis and was forced to move into the Hotel New Yorker. He remained there for years, until the manager objected to the multitudes of pigeons flying in and out of the room, and the unpaid bills.

He owed Dorothy Skerritt and Muriel Arbus back pay. He owed rent. He had only one choice: to sell the Edison medal. They would not let him do it.

Weeks later, his company received a contract for X ray equipment and he was

able to pay everyone and buy more sacks of feed for his beloved pigeons.

Dorothy Skerritt left him that year. She had once described him as an "almost divine being." She had loved him. Muriel Arbus had loved him.

George Scherff had loved him. Kolman and Julius Czito had loved him. Robert and Katherine Johnson had loved him. Their daughter Agnes had loved him.

Marguerite Merington, poor Marguerite, had loved him. Perhaps too much....

Anne Morgan had loved him. He suspected he was the only man she ever loved.

He had loved them all, very much. Very deeply.

He remembered wild nights at Delmonico's or The Player's Club, loudly swapping tall stories with Mark Twain....

He remembered his brother Daniel. His heart was stung with fierce, unresolved grief.

Daniel answered him. "I am sorry, my brother. You did not push me. I know that, now. I stumbled. You reached for me. You did not push me...."

And Tesla, who did not believe in an afterlife, knew somehow his human life had been absolved.

He rested his head against his pillow and saw a background of very dark, luminous blue that broke into scattered flecks of green light. The shards of green, like splintered glass, advanced toward him....

A pattern appeared: "Two systems of parallel and closely spaced lines, at right angles to one another, in all sorts of colors with yellow-green and gold predominating.

"Immediately thereafter the lines glow brighter and the whole is thickly sprinkled with dots of twinkling light.

"This picture moves slowly across the field of vision and in about ten seconds vanishes to the left.... Leaving behind a ground of rather unpleasant and inert gray which quickly gives way to a billowing sea of clouds.... Seemingly trying to mold themselves into living shapes...."

Nikola Tesla slept for the last time on the night of January 7, 1943.

The signals from another world had gone unanswered. This world was, again, at war.

DANIEL BLAIR STEWART is a novelist and artist who resides in Northern California with his son, River. He is the author of *Akhunaton: The Extraterrestrial King* (Frog, Ltd.), an epic tale of alien contact in ancient Egypt, and *Pinnacle* (Mendocino Publishing), the saga of a band of UFO abductees lost in a labyrinth of deadly conspiracies.